RETURN

by
Marcia Aw–Agon

**Edited
by James Van Treese.
Cover Design
by Amanda Leung.**

**Northwest Publishing Inc.
5949 South 350 West
Salt Lake City, Utah 84107
801–266–5900**

Copyright © 1993
Marcia Aw-Agon

Reproductions in any manner, in whole or in part, in English or in other languages, or otherwise without written permission of the publisher is prohibited.
S M 08 20 93

This is a work of fiction.
All characters and events portrayed
in this book are fictional, and any resemblance
to real people or incidents is purely coincidental.

First Printing 1994

ISBN #1–56901–069–2

Printed in the United States of America

This book is dedicated to my dearest friend and mentor, Mrs. Helen Wong, who made dreams become reality.

Thank You.

Author's Note

I am grateful to all my relatives and friends who have shared their tears and laughter with me. Their experiences and knowledge have made it possible for me to write this book. *Return* is not history but a novel and all the characters are only figments of my imagination. I especially thank Norman Kwong and Chu Yan Yan for their encouragement. I am indebted to Daniel Wong, Nellie Yu and Allan Aw for their advice and assistance. Also I would like to thank Joyce Ng for her inspiration, Ramsay Chan for his computer expertise and last but not least, I truly appreciate my husband Dennis for his patience, understanding, tolerance, and love.

One

Life is a mystery—unaccountable astounding events surprise us. My dear friend, Joyce, once made a remark that has lodged firmly in my memory through all these years. To her, the span of a lifetime is like a long bus ride where fellow passengers are continuously coming and going. During this lengthy journey of life, the likelihood of having the same person returning to the same bus to share the adjacent seat repeatedly should be practically nil. If, by fate, such a situation should arise, would the paths of these two passengers ultimately be destined to intertwine?

I have repeatedly questioned myself—does fate control my impending future, or am I master of my own destiny? So far I have failed to provide myself with a satisfactory answer. My past devious conduct has resulted in agony and ecstasy. How often have I initiated my own laughter and tears? Whatever or whenever the situation, I was usually the initiator of my own blunders. Regrets would definitely be a squander of precious time. I would always be perceptive too and assimilate from my own mistakes. If ever I should be fortunate enough to be bestowed a second chance, I would grab it and *relish* that much *sought opportunity*....

Two

I mustn't be late for the airport.

I dried my wet hands and threw my apron on the kitchen counter, took another glance at the kitchen making certain that the food was prepared and ready to be cooked. All the minute details for the evening meal were taken care of. I dashed into the bedroom to look at myself in the mirror and checked to my satisfaction the cosmetic that I had so hurriedly applied on my face. I patted my hair and out of sheer habit applied more lipstick which was absolutely unnecessary. Then I left the house for the airport.

My small car was caught in the loathsome afternoon traffic jam. Impatiently, I tapped the steering wheel and wished that the red light would quickly change to green. I didn't want to be late. I was ever so anxious to see my friend Sui Fong Cheng—she was arriving from Hong Kong. Memories flashed before me…I could still remember when she was first introduced to me so many, many years ago. Like myself, she was small. From the first instance, I admired her black, shiny, straight hair styled fashionably. Distinctly I remembered her attractive features, gentle voice and constant smile. I have missed her terribly the last few years especially in times when I needed a faithful friend to support me.

In the arrival area of the congested airport, swarming with people waiting for their friends and relatives to arrive, I stood on my toes and strained my neck trying to see over the shoulders of the throng of people standing in front of me. Longing to see my friend, I popped up and down hoping to catch a glimpse of Sui Fong. Then she appeared at the arrival gate. Frantically waving at me, she rushed into my arms. Being the sentimental fool that I was, tears spilled on my face. Dabbing my eyes I scrutinized Sui Fong's face. Her hair was no longer straight, but long and permed. Her smiling eyes returned my gaze fondly and steadily. The few years that we were apart quickly faded away. Joyfully we struggled to put Sui Fong's heavy luggage into the boot of my car and happily we departed from the parking lot. Giggling and exchanging news I steered the car away from the Vancouver International Airport and drove toward Oak Bridge. Fidgeting with the seat belt Sui Fong inquired, "Where are we? Vancouver is so different from Hong Kong!"

Adjusting the rear mirror and making absolutely sure that there was no traffic coming from behind, confidently, I changed lanes. Then I replied, "The airport is in Richmond, and we are going north toward Oak Bridge. On the other side of the bridge is Vancouver. Our house is on the west side of Vancouver not too far away from the bridge."

As the car was speeding along the road suddenly Sui Fong pointed ahead and exclaimed, "What is that mountain? It's so beautiful with the ranges glistening with snow. Don't they just remind you of the Dragon Hills in Kowloon back home?"

I looked toward the direction of her pointing finger and replied, "Oh! That's Grouse Mountain—a famous local skiing resort. We will go there for dinner one evening. The view from the mountain is quite spectacular. You will like it. It's like a sheet of diamonds and emeralds—in some ways it will remind you of the Hong Kong and Kowloon night lights."

Before we knew it we arrived home and I was backing my small car into the garage.

Standing by the stove stirring a pot of hot, spicy noodles, I said to Sui Fong, "As there are only two of us for dinner, you don't mind if we eat in the kitchen, do you?"

"Since when did we have to stand on ceremony?" Sui Fong asked while helping herself to a glass of water.

Between the two of us we finished all the noodles. "Boy! That was a terrific meal—Thai food, our favorite—hot and spicy!" Sui Fong exclaimed pushing away the empty plate. "This five-bedroom house is so spacious and elegantly furnished. I do like your choice of decoration. That gold vase standing in the corner of the living room really blends in with the carpet." Her dark eyes scanning the sparkling kitchen. She continued, "Melanie, you never fail to baffle me. How do you handle all the housework and keep a career going at the same time?"

Affectionately I smiled at my friend and grunted, "With great difficulty!" I sighed and continued, "In between serving my clients and taking care of the house keeping, sometimes I wish there were thirty-six hours in a day instead of twenty-four. Mind you, I do have a maid that comes in for a few hours each week to tend to all the heavy cleaning."

Sui Fong pushed her chair away, then stood on her feet and stretched her stiff limbs recalled, "After all these years, you still haven't lost your touch for cooking. Back in England, do you remember the days when you would use us as your guinea pigs? Experimenting on your cooking? Those times are still vivid in my mind. After you came to Vancouver I missed your cooking so very much."

I couldn't resist the temptation of teasing my friend, "You mean you only missed my cooking? How disgusting." I began to stack the dirty dishes and soaked them in the sink.

"You know what I mean...." moving closer to me, Sui Fong stammered embarrassedly.

It was Christmas of 1984, Sui Fong's first visit to Vancouver—my home for the last few years. I had managed to adjust and had taken to my new life style immediately. Life was so peaceful, unlike the nerve wracking atmosphere of Hong Kong. Vancouver was so green and spacious, not once did I feel claustrophobic. After dinner, Sui Fong and I adjourned from the kitchen to the living room. We paused on the threshold of the living room to admire the details of my Christmas decorations. I had refrained from buying tinsels and glitter and turned to nature for a decorative theme. Garlands and branches of evergreens and mistletoe tied with red and gold ribbons were much in evidence. A mixture of fruits, fir cones, and nuts was placed on the round coffee table that was placed in front of the settee. The Christmas tree glistened in the corner of the room with a numerous amount of prettily wrapped presents littered around the tree—a well-proportioned live pine. I have always had a passion for the fragrance of fresh pine. It added freshness to the house. I hated plastic Christmas trees. Sniffing the fragrances of the fresh evergreens, we walked across the room and settled in front of the fireplace. I sat on the carpeted floor with my legs crossed. With the burning logs roasting my back I nursed a mug of hot chocolate. Settling back in the corner of the settee to make herself more comfortable, Sui Fong sighed and said, "I do like your hair cropped short. It sort of makes your plump face look thinner.

"The years have been kind to you. Although in your early forties your face is hardly lined and a mischievous sparkle still twinkles in your eyes. I have noticed that you still dress casually. Nonetheless you are a picture of grace and elegance. No wonder Gavin still raves about your beauty."

Poking my waist and patting my plump face, I replied with a grimace, "I have added a few extra inches to my waist and a few unwanted pounds to my body. But you haven't done too badly yourself. We haven't seen each other for a number of years, and yet you still manage to maintain your youth. You certainly don't look like a mother of a twenty-year-old son."

Gazing at the snow drifting down slowly and fluttering against the window pane, absentmindedly Sui Fong wondered what Cedric was doing in Hong Kong. Then she sighed, "The years have dwindled before our eyes. Do you remember the days in England when you, Gavin, and I would chat until dawn?" There was a pause, then she continued, "Come to think of it, we have known each other for so many decades. I still find it difficult to believe that you are married to Gavin."

"Good old Gavin, my friend, my lover. Thirty years is a long, long time…as you know, we met when we were kids. Life is definitely intriguing with its twists and turns. Would you have believed that you finally made Hong Kong your home? It was so long ago when Raphael dated Lynette, and instead of those two getting married, Gavin and I are now married."

Sui Fong lazily lounged on the settee in front of the warm fireplace. She was admiring the elegant decor of the comfortable living room. Jackie, my teenage daughter, and her cousins were enjoying a session of karaoke in the family room—their singing and laughter echoed through the house. The two of us gazed into the burning logs, lost in our memories of nostalgic moments from the years gone by.

Breaking the silence, Sui Fong praised my daughter, "Jackie has definitely inherited your beautiful voice and charming manners."

I stretched my crossed legs and flexed my cramped muscles, then pointed my toes toward the roaring fire. I sighed and replied, "every day I thank my lucky stars for my terrific good fortune. Someone up there obviously is extremely fond of me and I am grateful for His attention."

Sui Fong absentmindedly fluffed the cushions and agreed with my beliefs. "Our relatives and friends back in Hong Kong all thought you were lucky. A few eyebrows were raised when you decided to immigrate to Vancouver and the announcement of your marriage to Gavin certainly caused a few tongues to wag."

I chuckled good-naturedly and wriggled my toasted toes, "I kind of expected those reactions. I guess my past performances had not contributed credit to my morals."

Leaning back on the cushions and adjusting her position in the settee Sui Fong interrupted understandingly, "You were not entirely responsible for your behavior. Destiny does sometimes dominate our lives."

I nodded my head in agreement, "I see your philosophy. When Gavin and my paths crossed again for the third time, I wanted to treasure the relationship that we had shared for so many years. I had all the intention of utilizing this unexpected chance and fabricate the most from this unpredictable opportunity. Mind you, much courage was warranted."

Sui Fong smiled sweetly while watching my face intensely. She said with seriousness, "To say the least…but aren't you delighted with all your accomplishments? You have made a name for yourself as an interior designer and you are the reigning queen of this magnificent home. Jackie obviously admires her stepfather! What more can you hope for?"

Rubbing my tired shoulders I agreed, "Absolutely! In your wildest imagination, would you have ever believed that one day I would pursue a career and be blessed with a superb husband? Without his patience and constant encouragement, undying devotion and endless consideration, it would have been impossible for me to attain such tremendous achievements."

"Fancy you being an interior designer, and a successful one at that. What was the incentive for the hard work?" Sui Fong searching my face inquired.

I put my head on my knees, thought for a moment and replied, "I love spending money, even better when I am spending someone else's money and get paid for doing it. Joking aside, when Jackie became independent life began to bore me. I wasn't contented with staying at home and attending to the tedious house work—preparing the food, washing dirty dishes and attending to the laundry. I definitely hated being a slave to the stove. I have a taste for elegance and beauty so I took a course in interior designing. Eventually I learned the ropes for the trade and I experimented with my own house. This experiment turned out to be the best advertisement for my career. When my friends liked what they saw they referred me to their friends and my career was mapped out for me."

Changing the subject, Sui Fong inquired, "Melanie, didn't you have any romantic feelings toward Gavin? In the early days didn't the idea of leaving England with him ever enter your mind?"

Attempting to provide an appropriate answer for my friend I took my time in finishing the drink in my hand, then pensively, I explained, "I have known Gavin for too long. He was always my friend, my companion and mentor—my guardian angel. Regrettably I took him for granted. Like an utter fool I was blind to his affection. Like all spoiled young people you know how spoilt we were—never had to work hard for anything. Everything was handed to us on a silver platter. I craved for excitement. Gavin was too stable and I resented it. Our relationship was too dull. Honestly, if I had married him instead of Marcus we would be divorced today. I was destined to walk one whole circle before I was reunited with the 'right guy'."

I removed myself from the carpet and screwed my nose. "I better clear the mess in the kitchen before we retire for the night. Tomorrow will be a long and exciting day for us!"

Sui Fong and I returned to the untidy kitchen. Dirty plates were washed, clean pots and pans were stored away. Fondly I put my arms round her shoulder and whispered, "Both Gavin and I really appreciate your presence at our fifth wedding anniversary reception. Our friendship is priceless—I wouldn't trade it for all the tea in China."

Sui Fong affectionately patted my hand. "It is my pleasure to be here. I only wish that Cedric could have joined us, but he is too involved with an extremely complicated case. It would be impossible for him to be away even for a few short days."

When the kitchen was sparkling clean again, Sui Fong stifled a yawn. "How time flies—look at the time! Jet-lag is catching up with me. My fatigued body is yearning for a comfortable bed. If you don't mind, I will retire to bed first?"

I gazed at the clock in the kitchen and exclaimed, "Goodness gracious! I am so selfish—you must be positively exhausted. You only arrived this afternoon and the plane journey from Hong Kong was not exactly short…twelve hours can sometimes be a life time. Please go to bed. I will wait for Gavin."

I returned to the living room and added more logs to the dying fire. Absentmindedly I poked at the burning wood. Sitting on the floor, crossing my legs, and cuddling a cushion I gazed into the flickering flame and my mind traveled back in time….

Three

I was grateful for my seat by the window...whenever I was bored with the lesson I could gaze out to the spacious concrete-paved playground. Born with a curious nature, I was pleased with the full view of the Headmistress' office because I was able to keep track of all the activities that generated from her room. Miss Lee's monotonous voice hummed on...I could hardly keep my eyes opened. Flexing my leg and jerking it up and down I waited impatiently for the end-of-lesson bell to go.

When Miss Lee started to write on the black board, I glanced out into the playground. Sister Rosemary, the Headmistress, strode out from her room in quick even strides. Someone had obviously rubbed her the wrong way. Her face was red. She was notorious for her Irish temper. Whenever she was about to explode, automatically her complexion would turn red. She looked around furiously tapping a stack of note paper on her palm. Her black and white starched habit never failed to fascinate me—there were absolutely no creases visible on the garment whether it was early in the morning or at the end of the day. With Hong Kong's humidity and heat I constantly wondered how the nuns could bear to wear their monstrous outfits. Purposefully, Sister Rosemary stalked across the playground while the rosary attached to her waist jingled with her every movement. The student who was in trouble with her had my full sympathy.

"Melanie, Melanie—stop your day-dreaming and concentrate!" Miss Lee sharply jerked me back to attention. Surreptitiously I stuck my tongue out and pretended to flip the pages of my detested mathematics book—stupid math. Whoever invented this boring subject should be shot. If only I could tear the wretched book into shreds and throw it into the harbor! Just watching the shreds floated away would give me ultimate pleasure and extreme satisfaction.

Eventually the much-appreciated end-of-lesson bell echoed throughout the school. Chairs scraped the concrete floor. Exhausted girls who had spent the entire day concentrating on their demanding lessons, were anxious to leave the classroom. Hurriedly, they gathered their books and rushed out of the room, pleased to get away from the daily restricted school's regulations. Students of different ages and sizes, commenced to file out of the imposing school gate in small groups.

I was one of those girls. My long, thick, beautifully shiny, black hair, although tied in a fashionable pony tail, was an added burden to my small framed body. Clutching my books, I briskly made my way to the tram station. Squinting my sparkling brown eyes, I averted my face to avoid the strong glare of the hot sun. My lovely oval face was dripping with sweat. I joined the long line of girls all waiting impatiently for their turn to board the stationed tram.

When at last I boarded the tram I quickly made my way to the upper deck. With a sigh I took the empty seat by the window. As the tram moved it stirred movements in the oppressively still air and a slight breeze soothed my hot and sticky body. After showing my monthly ticket to the conductor I gazed out of the window. The noisy Hong Kong streets and everyday activities never ceased to fascinate me. Pedestrians were incessantly in a hurry rushing to their destinations. On both sides of the road were enticingly decorated shops. The pavement's hawkers' wheel barrels displayed their latest merchandise tempting shoppers to squander their money. I could visualize the bulging wallets slowly reduced as purchasers peeled off dollar notes.

When the tram arrived at my destination, I hastily descended the steep and narrow stairs. Leaping off the tram I darted across the street and hastened into a tall concrete block of flats where my home was located on the twenty-first floor. Waiting irritably for the descending elevator, I waved at the old caretaker of the building. He was sitting on his reclining easy chair mopping sweat from his hot face and fanning himself.

When I opened the front door, the cool air generated from the air conditioner brought life back to my tired and exhausted bones. My dog, Lucky, a cute, white Yorkshire Terrier, barked and rushed toward me. The small animal jumped up and down to attract my attention. I picked my pet off the floor and walked into the living room. Our cousin Cedric was sprawled lazily on the sofa, while Mother was talking to him.

"Hello, Mummy! What is Cedric doing here?" I gave Mother a peck on the cheek and winked at Lynette.

Knitting needles clicked as Mother continued to knit her latest creation. For a brief moment, she removed her attention from the sweater that she was knitting and replied, "Cedric has invited Lynette to a party."

Interrupting his Auntie Wei Ling, Cedric explained, "My school friend, Raphael Fernados, will be celebrating his birthday this weekend. There is a shortage of girls so I am here to extend an invitation to your sister. Female cousins can come in handy at times."

I asked, "What about me?" I made myself comfortable on the floor with Lucky cuddling in my arms.

Lynette, pulling Cedric's sleeve to try and catch his attention, intervened, "Melanie you are too young to be invited!"

Cedric gave me a conspiring wink and responded cautiously, "I don't think so. Raphael has a few younger brothers and sisters and I am certain they will be delighted to entertain Melanie."

"What is the cause of all the commotion?" Alastair, the youngest member of my family, inquired, as he poked his head into the living room.

"I have been invited to a party!" Lynette gleefully and proudly informed my younger brother while giving him the victory sign.

Alastair entered the room and removed Lucky from my cuddling arms, while I kicked him on the ankle playfully. He muttered, "Parties—what a waste of time! By the way, Mummy, Uncle Edwin called earlier, would you like to return his call?"

My mother, Au Yeung Wei Ling lost our father in a car accident when Alastair was only one year old. Being a mother of three had been a strenuous responsibility. A few years ago while attending a dinner party, she was introduced to a middle-aged solicitor, Edwin, who was fascinated by her beauty and courage. Subsequently they began to see each other more and more and he, more or less, became part of the family....

During the next couple of days the household bustled with activities. Lynette searched her wardrobe repeatedly trying on different outfits endlessly. She couldn't decide which would be the perfect dress for the big occasion. The maid was instructed to iron one dress after another. Mother fussed over her hair, trying various hair styles. Lynette was beyond herself with excitement. The phone was continuously busy. She was constantly rushing to the phone communicating with her friends and exchanging ideas. The record player consistently blasted the latest hit songs. Lynette invited her friends to join her in practicing all the popular dance steps.

I secretly regretted having successfully obtained an invitation to the dance. Basically I was a very quiet and timid young lady and hardly welcomed the company of a crowd. How I was hoping that I did not have to attend the party! I would prefer to take Lucky for a stroll in the park or hide in my room to listen to my favorite songs. The pocket money that Mother gave me every week had been spent on the purchase of my records.

Anxiously and impatiently Lynette waited for Saturday to arrive while I dreaded every moment as the day drew nearer. When Lynette and I were properly dressed in the latest fashion for the party, Mother drove us to Raphael's house. Cedric was there waiting patiently for us at the entrance. Immediately we were introduced to our host Raphael. He was attractive, friendly and witty and wasted no time to flirt with Lynette. He was fascinated by her attractiveness—instantly Lynette was attracted to him too, and I was left to fend for myself.

The decoration in the luxurious flat captured my immediate attention; I admired the smart and modern furniture. The white comfortable settee, the floral wall paper, the magnificent rugs which appeared casually laid out on the floor. The well-lacquered dining table with matching chairs contributed to the elegance and beauty of the flat. The dimly lit room was filled with soft music and thronged with young people. Some danced, while others helped themselves to the variety of delicious food laid out on the dining table. Some gathered in small groups *tête-a-tête*. I felt uncomfortable and out of place. Fretfully, I wandered out into the balcony to escape from the crowd. It was twilight time and the salmon colored sky took my breath away. Raphael's residence faced the ocean, and the serenity of the sea was unbelievably peaceful. Humming to myself and tapping my feet to the rhythm of the music, I admired the unblemished view.

Suddenly I felt someone watching me. Timidly I turned my head and noticed a young man standing by the balcony door.

The newcomer with extremely handsome Latin looks and a dark complexion was absolutely gorgeous. His features were sharp and dramatically dominant. The intensity of his gaze attributed to my increasing discomforts. Not accustomed to this type of approach but dazzled by the young man's smile, I shyly extended my hand to him and stammered an introduction. "I am Melanie, Cedric's cousin."

Tongue-tied for a split second the young man gradually regained his composure. Smilingly he replied, "My name is Gavin—the birthday boy's younger brother…you must be Lynette's younger sister. To tell you the honest truth from Cedric's description of you I was expecting a little girl. No wonder I was quite taken aback by your appearance. Your exquisite features are kind of bewitching and I can easily be hypnotized by the charisma of your voice."

I must have been blushing badly; I could feel my ears burning and my complexion changing color. Thank God for my dark complexion and the dim lighting. I would die of embarrassment, if Gavin should see my face turning to the color of a beet root.

After a moment of brief silence, Gavin asked me, "Tell me for someone of your tender age why are you wearing black? I would have thought that red would be a more suitable color."

Without a moment's hesitation I explained, "Melanie was a Greek Goddess. She always wore black—I am rather attracted to the color. I am afraid I don't have a passion for bright shades." I removed some strayed hair from my face.

For the rest of the evening Gavin hovered by my side, following me around and making certain that I had enough food to satisfy my empty stomach and drinks to quench my thirst. Presently, Gavin and I were involved with discussions on various topics…eventually, my shyness evaporated and we conversed like two friends who had known each other for a lengthy period of time. Too soon the evening came to an end but before my departure for home Gavin promised to contact me shortly.

After a week of silence Raphael eventually called Lynette, "Have you made any plans for Saturday? Would you like to watch a movie with me?"

Lynette was delighted with the invitation and accepted it immediately.

After a brief hesitation, Raphael continued, "I have a slight problem. I am not supposed to go out without a chaperon; therefore, Gavin will have to accompany me."

Tapping her forehead with her fingers thoughtfully Lynette suggested, "Why don't you come to our home with Gavin. He can play with

Melanie while we go and watch a movie. You can collect Gavin on your way home."

Dubiously Raphael asked, "Wouldn't Melanie mind?"

Lynette playfully pulled the telephone cord and replied, "I will insist that Melanie stay home and wait for your brother. I think she rather fancies him."

"That would be terrific! I will see you tomorrow shortly after lunch." When Raphael hung up Lynette screamed and searched for me. "Melanie, Melanie, where are you?"

I was in my room struggling with my homework. "Raphael has invited me to a movie tomorrow but Gavin has to accompany him. On your behalf, I have invited him to spend the day with you. While we are out, you can keep him company. Please promise me you won't disappear before his arrival," Lynette insisted.

Closing the book that I was reading and stacking them neatly on my table, I implored, "Do I have to? I'd much rather be on my own or play with Yvette from next door."

Lynette kissed me gently on my cheek and pleaded with me, "Don't be such a stubborn old goat. You told me that you like Gavin. I am confident that the two of you will hit it off like a house on fire and certain that you will appreciate his company just as much as he cherishes yours." Whistling to herself without waiting for my reply, Lynette disappeared into her own room.

The following day to my own utter astonishment I truly looked forward to seeing Gavin again. When the front door bell rang, Lynette dashed for the door. Raphael and Gavin were smartly dressed. The elder brother gave Lynette a tiny bunch of daisies and the younger brother offered her a box of chocolate. My sister was delighted with their thoughtful gestures. Soon after their arrival Lynette left home with Raphael, and Gavin was alone with me. Too embarrassed to utter a word, I was unable to break the silence. When the front door bell was heard again, I jumped from the chair and excused myself. I was relieved to find Alastair with our neighbors' two children: Yvette and Raymond Tong.

Timidly and shyly I introduced Gavin to the newcomers, whereupon Alastair suggested going to the park to play. After leaving a message for Mother I put a leash on Lucky and the five of us ventured into the park. Groups of children were engrossed with different games. Dogs pestered the public—running around barking playfully. Constantly echoes of the bursting activities could be heard. We spent a glorious joyful afternoon together. When it was time for dinner, Mother invited Gavin to join the family for a pot luck meal. Apparently Lynette had called earlier begging permission to eat out with Raphael, and Mother thoughtfully granted them a few more hours. After an early dinner, Mother had to attend a party with Uncle Edwin so she left us to amuse ourselves. Alastair decided to play tennis with Raymond so Gavin was again alone with me. Shyly I invited him to listen to my records and a peaceful evening was whiled away chatting and listening to music. Both of us were delighted with the opportunity to get acquainted.

It was Friday again. I was wanted on the phone. Gavin's smooth deep voice was exceedingly delightful to my ears. I was hoping that he might call. "Did you have a nice week?" Gavin inquired.

Pulling a chair for myself and jiggling with the telephone cord I replied, "Yes, but I sure am glad that the weekend has finally arrived."

Gavin's deep soft voice drifted into my ears as he said, "Elvis Presley's new film *Blue Hawaii* is on. How would you like to see it with me? Perhaps tomorrow?"

Pulling a long face reluctantly I admitted, "I would love to but I am afraid I have squandered all my pocket money for the whole week...." I confessed. "I couldn't resist the temptation of visiting the record shop and I guess somehow my control went astray again!"

Chuckling to himself Gavin teased me, "It will be my treat, but for the remaining of the week I will starve—we will be in the same boat." He continued, "I will come and collect you tomorrow—most probably after lunch—the least I can do is to have lunch with my parents. By the way are you aware of the fact that your parents and mine play Mah Jong together?"

I was thrilled with the news and the invitation. The next day, up bright and early, I leisurely indulged myself with a shower and washed my hair. When the long hair was finally dried, I brushed it a hundred times in order to restore the shine. Then I tied it with a ribbon. I decided to wear my new blouse and skirt of virgin white. Satisfied with my own chic reflection in the mirror I waited for Gavin. When he finally arrived, I was so thrilled when he complimented me on my appearance.

Gavin and I both thought the movie was absolutely fabulous. I fell in love with my idol, Elvis, all over again. When we left the movie, continuously, I hummed the songs. Gavin asked if I were hungry. Shyly I pointed to the store and suggested, "Why don't we share a coke and a bun?"

On our way home Gavin and I passed a record shop. Insisting that I should wait for him on the street, he disappeared into the shop. When he emerged again, he surprised me with his recent purchase. The sound track of *Blue Hawaii* materialized on my hand and I literally bounced up and down. Screeching with joy and clapping my hands, I gave Gavin a bear hug. The record was his first contribution to my collection of records.

Four

Soon the summer holiday arrived. Gavin and I spent most of our free time together…never weary of each other's company. Gavin was my shadow; he was my companion and dear friend—the elder brother that I had longed for. Our lifetime friendship was developed and nourished during the lazy days of that interminable hot summer.

One morning, with fascination, I watched Alastair and Raymond challenging each other in a new game played with picture cards. Much as I wished to join them I was reluctant to let on that I did not know the rules of the game. Ultimately I turned to Gavin for advice. Immediately he offered his expertise. Soon after my plea for assistance he arrived with his personal collection of cards and patiently demonstrated his skills and showed me how to master the game.

"This game is awfully simple. The cards have pictures on only one side. Any number of players can participate. Each player will contribute a certain number of cards—the number will be decided by all the players. Then all the contributed cards are stacked faced downwards and put on the floor. The spin of the bottle will determine which player would start the game."

As Gavin proceeded, I watched and listened attentively. "Each player will take turns clapping his or her hands. The aim is to flip as many cards as possible from the stack. You are allowed to clap only once."

Impatiently I interrupted, "Do I get to keep all the cards that I have flipped?"

Gavin shook his head and replied, "No—only the cards with pictures facing upwards. The cards with the pictures facing downwards will be returned to the stack."

I countered indignantly, "That's not fair—it's difficult! To remove the cards from the deck and to flip them simultaneously would almost be impossible."

"That's the skill you have to master." With deftness Gavin clapped his hands and generated enough air movement to enable the cards to flip. He continued, "When the entire stack disappears then the player with most cards will be the winner. He would then be allowed to keep all the cards that he has won during the entire game. Now, let's see if you can do it."

Gavin stacked all the cards and encouraged me to clap my hands. Soon I became an expert. When Raymond and Alastair played the game again I confidently took my place as one of the contestants—to their utter disgust and amazement I was winning. Expertly I soon won most of their cards. During Gavin's subsequent visit I offered to divide my winnings with him but he declined.

I was reading in my room when Gavin arrived, "How would you like to take a ride on the peak tram? I have been informed that the stroll around the peak is really refreshing. The clean air will do you a world of good."

Presently the two of us boarded the Peak Tram. Slowly the moving vehicle climbed the steep hill. I was somewhat nervous with the height but Gavin recommended that I held my head high and stare out of the window instead of gazing downwards. Shortly the majestic view of the Hong Kong Harbor captured my attention and instantly my fear dissipated. All the passengers disembarked when the tram arrived at the Peak Station. Holding my hand, Gavin sauntered toward the walking path that circled around the peak. Birds chirped…a slight breeze stirred in the air. I adored the fragrance exuded from the greenery and blossoming flowers. Breaking the stray twigs from the trees, jauntily, I sprinted along the trail that would lead us toward the Lookout Point. From there we could see a full view of the magnificent harbor.

I marveled at the ocean—crossing ships that were anchored by Ocean Terminal. The leisure boats cruising along the shore and the ferries carrying passengers or vehicles crossed the busy harbor…the peninsula of Kowloon stretched far into the distance. I absorbed the scene with fascination. Engrossed with the panoramic view stretching my hands I pointed into the horizon and uttered softly, "Will it be possible for us to count the numerous concrete buildings that are built on the hillside? Imagine the exorbitant number of people residing on this tiny island. It is rather a scary thought! Mind you, in the evening when all the lights are glistening it is like a Fairyland. I am sure that it is even better than Las Vegas' lights. It is not surprising that Hong Kong is known as 'The Pearl of the Orient'."

As Gavin and I moved away from Lookout Point we walked on to the other side of the island. The tall buildings gradually vanished from sight. We decided to relax our weary limbs. Flopping on the grass, Gavin pulled out a handkerchief from his pocket and tenderly wiped my sweaty forehead. I returned my gaze from the horizon and dreamily questioned my companion, "Well, how does it feel to be sitting here looking down from Victoria Peak and see parts of Hong Kong resting at our feet?" Not waiting for a reply I boasted, "Did you know that one of the scenes from *Love is a Many Splendid Thing* was filmed here? I found the film really romantic!"

I pulled some grass from the ground and chewed absentmindedly. I remarked, "I rather fancy the other side of the island. This side is too congested, although magnificent with all the towering buildings and decorative ships. The Southern side is not yet developed and I hope that they won't develop this part of the island. I hate to see Repluse Bay, Deep Bay, South Bay, and Stanley Beach destroyed. The scenery is still unspoiled by mankind. I like to look at the mountains. The serenity of the calm blue sea is so soothing to my nerves. Usually only a few sail boats glide by. The contrast between this side and the other congested side is tremendous."

Pulling me onto my feet Gavin replied, "If you appreciate the southern side of the island so much we should move on. When we get to the other side, you can admire the view to your heart's content. If we complete the entire circle, I will contemplate tempting you with an ice cream."

When I had finished the promised ice cream, I licked my fingers. Gavin asked, "Do you want another ice cream?"

Sheepishly I hid my hands behind my back and shook my head. Gavin was baffled, "Then why are you licking your fingers?"

"Force of habit I guess. Let's go home. I am tired. I am sure Mummy doesn't mind you joining us for dinner tonight. I have some new records." I grabbed Gavin's hand and steered him toward the tram station and we returned home.

Bursting into my room, Alastair found me sitting on the floor scribbling away. My record player was softly playing my favorite songs. Grabbing every opportunity to tease me he said, "I see you are copying the lyrics of the songs again. You don't seriously think that our family will agree to you pursuing a career as a singer, do you?"

Chewing the rubber tip of my pencil and screwing my nose I grimaced and replied indignantly, "I can still learn to sing, can't I?" I returned to my scribbles and ignored my brother.

Irritably Alastair interrupted my train of thoughts again, "Ray, Yvette, and I have decided to visit the famous Tiger Balm Garden. Would you like to come with us?" My younger brother added as a second thought, "Gavin is welcomed to join us, the two of you are inseparable! I am not going to bother inviting Lynette. No doubt she has made other plans with Raphael...."

Curiously I inquired, "Why would you guys insist on doing something so boring? Can't you think of other entertainment that requires more imagination? What is there in the garden that is so irresistible?"

Alastair was exasperated, "Tiger Balm Garden is extremely popular with the tourists. Mr. Aw Boon Haw, the founder of the garden, would probably be turning in his grave if he should hear your rude comments. May his soul rest in peace! Did you know that he built this garden to promote Tiger Balm Oil? Try not to be so ignorant. Anyway, there are many gruesome statues for us to view and admire—I rather like them."

Turning off the record player I put away the records that were scattered on the carpeted floor. Glaring at my brother I countered, "I realize this herb medicine works wonders for muscle pains and itches. It's extremely popular with athletes but the smell of the ointment is positively repulsive. And you, brother of mine, fancy being attracted to those horrifying ghastly statutes. You do possess a warped mind! I will call Gavin now. Shall we say around two in the afternoon?" Then I pushed Alastair out of my room.

On Tai Hang Road outside the front gate of the garden the bus dropped us off. We had to climb a steep slope before reaching the garden. At the end of the climb I was huffing and puffing.

"Out of breath already? You should play tennis with us." Alastair suggested while inhaling in deep breaths.

Pushing Alastair away from me, I grumbled, "Stop picking on me—

I don't like tennis!"

Tourists of assorted nationalities wandered around admiring the different carvings on the side of the hill while hawkers tried to sell them postcards of Hong Kong. Pointing to the empty swimming pool, Yvette inquired, "I wonder why the Aw family doesn't make full use of the pool?"

Standing on tip toes, I took a peek at the empty pool. Immediately I had the answer. "During the evenings, when the garden was closed to the public, the grandchildren and cousins used to enjoy a dip after dinner. Unfortunately one of the cousins was infected by Polio. Subsequently the family ceased to utilize the pool—believe it or not—it might be just a rumor."

Gavin friskily yanked my pony tail, harassing me, and mockingly he asked, "How did you manage to invent such a strange tale?"

Twirling my pony tail and with a smug expression I retorted, "It is not a figment of my imagination. Our maid narrated the incident to me."

Laughing and giggling, we sprinted up the steps. Racing each other to the top of the hill. Different variations of carved figurines displayed scenes from Hell—I was disgusted and horrified. Tongues were extracted from the figurines' mouths to be chopped because they lied on earth; convicted murderers were thrown into a big pot of burning oil; thieves' hands were chopped off. The expressions on the faces of the figurines were positively creative and vivid with imagination extremely artistic but definitely ghastly. "No wonder some of my school friends labeled this place 'the nightmare garden'!" Shivering I caressed my trembling body with my arms and continued, "This garden does give me the creeps. It provides such an eerie atmosphere." Screwing my nose I commented, "Fancy having to live here, Yak."

When the children strolled passed a tomb, Alastair provided additional details. "One of Mr. Aw's sons was killed in a plane crash in Malaysia and his body was never recovered. His clothing and personal belongings are buried in this tomb."

A pagoda came into sight. Pointing at the tall building, Raymond contributed, "Mr. Aw's ashes are stored inside that small container. Can you see it?" We were curious. Alternatively we each took a peek.

Indignantly I stamped my feet. Screwing my eyes tightly and covering my ears with my hands I objected vehemently, "Oh, do stop your narrations. Both Yvette and I are scared out of our wits."

Raymond and Alastair winked at each other mischievously and chanted simultaneously, "Typical female behavior—you are frightened by almost anything."

We were exhausted and famished when we returned home. Mother invited Gavin to stay for dinner, while Raymond and Yvette returned to their residence. After a meal of delicious wonton noodles, I hinted that Lucky could do with a walk. With the small dog racing ahead, Gavin and I strolled into the park. Obviously the other children had returned to their homes because dusk was settling in. I loved it when the lawn was relatively noiseless. I felt as if I had the entire park to myself. We lay on the grass comfortably. I used my hands as a pillow and looked toward the bewitching sky all the while scrutinizing the twinkling stars hanging from the galaxy. "It's incredible. Can you count the number of stars in the sky?"

Gavin watched me, dumbfounded with my incredible comment. He inquired, "You don't really expect me to count the stars, do you?"

Watching the stars, I gestured toward the sky with my outstretched hands. I nodded my head somberly and answered. "Of course—I am counting."

Gavin removed his long body from the grass moved closer to me and watched me intensely with his attractive dark eyes. He was intrigued by my bizarre behavior. "I am perfectly happy and contented sitting here quietly and watching your eccentric performance."

I changed my position on the grass so that I could face my friend. I returned my gaze from yonder and watched Gavin's expression in the darkness while inquiring, "What is your ambition in life?"

Before Gavin could provide me with an answer, I continued, "For myself, I would love to be a cluster of clouds…floating aimlessly…without a care in the world—just following my destiny."

"Your wishes are beyond me. Fancy wanting to be a clutter of clouds. You never ceased to surprise me with your sentiments. What a gorgeous romantic idiot you are." Gavin exclaimed rolling over on the grass and holding his stomach to control his laughter.

Exchanging our dreams and discussing our futures…our whispers murmuring in the soft night wind…the minutes ticked away as we conversed late into the night before returning home.

Five

I was reading the newspaper and picking on my hard-boiled egg. Lucky sat by my feet hoping that I would feed him with some crumbs from my toast. Lynette was filing her nails while Alastair complained, "Lynette, do stop your filing—its disgusting! Bits of your nails are dropping into my bowl of cornflakes."

Lynette glared at her brother and threw her napkin at him. Mother walked into the dining room, while tying the belt on her bathrobe. She took a seat at the table and poured herself a cup of steaming hot coffee. While stirring the coffee, she suggested, "Children how would you like to spend the day at the beach? Perhaps a B-B-Que while we are there? It has been a while since we have had a family outing." When a response was not forthcoming from us, Mother counter-offered, "Oh, all right, I don't see why you can't invite your friends. Ungrateful brats." she snorted.

Instantly, we thanked Mother for her kindness and Lynette hastened to the phone. Dialing Raphael's number she asked me, "Melanie, while I am talking to Raphael, do you want me to invite Gavin?"

Busily flipping the pages of the newspaper and adjusting my uncomfortable position on the dining chair I answered, "Sure!"

While Lynette was calling Raphael, Alastair knocked on our neighbors' door with the intention of inviting Raymond and Yvette to join the family's outing. When Lynette was off the phone, to my utter disappointment I was informed that Gavin would be unable to join us due to a previous engagement. I was very disappointed. I left the unfinished newspaper on the dining table and withdrew into my room. When the bedroom door was closed behind me my lips trembled and my vision began to blur with threatened tears. I would rather stay at home and sulk because I was feeling so frustrated but I didn't want to distress my parents so I promised myself that I would not allow Gavin's absence to spoil the happy occasion. Hurriedly I stuffed my swimming costume, a towel and another change of clothing into my bag.

After a lengthy car ride, we left the city behind and drove toward the outskirts of town. Finally, our family and guests arrived at Shek-O. The scathing sun from the glaring blue sky showed no mercy. The reflection from the white sand was hurtful to my eyes. I retrieved my pair of sunglasses from my bag and stuck it on my nose. There was a fresh water pond on the right side of the beach with very shallow water. Young children were splashing water at each other. From the beach one could see a small hill jutting out in the middle of the sea. This was known as the Abalone Hill. Often I wondered about its name. Could we really find abalone along its shore? On the left was a small village. I had a fondness for the shops in the village—all kinds of junk food were tempting to the palate. I loved sucking the dried sour plums and the thousand-year's eggs with sour ginger were really delicious. Just the thought of them made my mouth watered. Two rows of canvas tents were erected for the convenience of the swimmers, for the purpose of changing and storing their belongings. The rental charge was very minimal; therefore, the beach proved to be extremely popular.

Almost all the tents were occupied. With great difficulty we managed to rent one.

The beach was crowded with people. Women and girls paraded their fancy swimming costumes wiggling their attractive bodies hoping to attract attention. Some swimmers were energetically swimming toward the rafts that were anchored between the beach and the hill. Their movements caused ripples in the brilliant blue sea. Some relaxed while floating aimlessly on the water while others splashed water at each other playfully. Children screaming with laughter bounced up and down while beach balls were thrown across the sky. Some lay on the warm sand and soaked up the sun, while sun tanning lotion was sparingly rubbed on relaxed bodies.

Hurriedly we unloaded our bags and belongings. After changing into their swimming gear, Lynette and the other kids hurled themselves into the welcoming waves. Soon they were swimming, spluttering happily and noisily in the water. With no desire to join them, I wandered along the golden shores of the beach searching for exquisite seashells.

Retreating from the throng of swimmers, I sauntered along the endless shore with the shifting sand moving softly beneath my bare feet. I was lost in my own thoughts, when a special sea shell caught my attention. Half of the shell was buried in the sand and the other half that was visible shone radiantly with all the colors of the rainbow. Immediately I craved to possess the glittering shell. With outstretched hand I tried to retrieve the shell from the sand. Instantly another hand seized the object from me. I almost screamed with irritation and frustration. I wasn't going to allow another person to take possession of the shell. After all I discovered the treasure first. My eyes sparkled with annoyance. I was curious as to who had the audacity to steal the beautiful shell from me. Defiantly I searched the stranger's face and found myself staring into Gavin's teasing eyes.

Patting the sand off my hand, I stood with my feet wide apart, put my hands on my hips, and screeched abrasively, "What the heck…?"

Clicking his tongue and wagging his fingers at me, Gavin reprimanded, "Mind your language young lady!"

Delighted to see Gavin but distressed by his mischievous behavior I demanded an explanation from him, "I thought you had made other arrangements, so why have you come to this beach? I suppose with the purpose to irritate me?"

Gavin knelt on the sand and retrieved the shell, rubbing it on his jeans. Thrusting the shell toward me he rebuked, "You didn't ask what my other commitment was."

Pushing the hair off my face and brushing the sweat off my forehead with the back of my hand, I responded indignantly. "So, tell me!"

Sheepishly Gavin explained, "I had previously promised to spend the day with my parents. I knew if I accompanied them I would be spending the day with you. Your parents and mine made arrangements to meet here, in order that their customary, weekly Mah Jong game would not be interrupted and we kids could spend the day on the beach."

I blew at the non-existent sand on the shell and frowned with disbelief. Squinting my eyes, I cross-examined Gavin, "You mean my parents are playing Mah Jong with Auntie Pearl and Uncle Joe—your parents?"

Gavin pushed the hair off his forehead and fleetingly touched the tip of my up-turned nose with the gentle touch of his fingers. Insolently he replied, "Right on! You were so involved with your own thoughts. As far as you were concerned we were invisible. Who do you think rented the tent next to yours?"

I stamped my feet on the sand and grunted, "Well, really, why didn't Mummy tell me? What about you, why did you lie? Your behavior is preposterous!"

Gavin kissed me gently on the cheek, while whispering against my hair, "Does the word 'surprise' exists in your vocabulary? By the way, to keep the record straight, I did not lie. I never lie. I am only guilty of not volunteering information." Extending his hand to me, he suggested, "Friends again?"

Shaking his outstretched hand and grinning again, I agreed, "Friends forever!"

We spent the next couple of hours searching for more sea shells. My happy spirit had returned with the sudden appearance of my friend. I was exhilarated, my laughter could be heard from a far distance. When we collected enough seashells, we returned to our tents. Two Mah Jong games were in full swing. Mah Jong tiles smashing against each other, creating a considerable amount of noise. Having greeted my parents and their friends, I went to change into my swimming costume.

"Do you want to join the others for a dip in the sea?" Gavin asked affectionately while opening two cans of Coke and giving one to me.

Squinting my eyes to avoid the bright afternoon sun, thirstily I drank from the can and replied, "I'd rather build a sand castle instead." So hand in hand we sprinted toward the water.

Aunt Pearl, Gavin's mother, watched us running toward the sea and commented to Mother and the other two ladies who were the third and fourth players of the game, "It's fantastic how those two youngsters are such terrific friends. One very seldom witnesses such intense friendship shared between two so young. They are very fortunate to have found each other."

Gavin and I flopped on the soft sand and construction of the sand castle commenced with intensity. An enormous amount of patience was required. Without the correct amount of water to moisten the soft sand it was practically impossible to build. Eventually the task was finally completed. A fine looking sand castle was standing on the sand by the shore. Proudly we marveled at our own creation and workmanship. Suddenly a big wave hit the shore and part of the castle disappeared with the gushing sea water. I examined the half-crumpled castle and exclaimed in an extremely pitiful voice, "I sincerely hope that our friendship will not vanish into the sea like this sand castle."

Gavin held me tightly and promised reassuredly, "Our friendship is built on much stronger stuff than sand. Please wipe that melancholy expression from your face. It's most unattractive. I would rather see your smiles constantly. I hope that laughter and smiles will accompany you for the rest of your life."

The smile returned to my face. Playfully I poked at the remaining portion of the castle with my toe. Gavin was pleased that I was smiling again. Pinching my cheeks he said, "That's better, I can see the attractive dimples appearing on your cheerful face again."

Happily I dashed into the water and Gavin dived in after me. Being a much stronger swimmer, he soon caught up with me with hardly any effort. Playfully he attempted to thrust my head under the water while I tried desperately to evade his grabbing hands. With our heads bobbing in and out of the water, giggling and screaming, we swam toward the other children.

In the sky, the great ball of fire gradually disappeared below the horizon. Twilight was settling in. I swam toward the shore and shouted, "My growling stomach tells me its dinner time. Let's start the fire for the B-B-Que and feed our famished stomachs."

With everyone's help, a fire was lighted, B-B-Que forks were washed and cleaned. Paper plates and cups were laid out on the table. We all crowded round the burning fire, and soon the steaks, pork chops, chicken wings, and sausages were sizzling. I pushed Alastair's fork with my own and complained, "You are burning the chicken wing."

Removing the burnt wing from the fire Alastair retorted, "Mind your own business, who needs your help?"

I released the steak from my fork and placed it on my plate. I took a mouthful and yelled at my brother, "My steak is absolutely delicious and perfectly cooked. I hope you will choke on your uncooked food."

Eventually when all the empty stomachs were filled, the boys dug a big hole in the sand with the intention of burying the rubbish. Suddenly Alastair and Ray grabbed my shoulders and pushed me. I lost my balance on the soft sifting sand and tumbled into the hole. Laughing gleefully, Alastair threatened, "Let's bury the rubbish with Melanie."

Immediately Gavin extended his hand to me, while wagging his finger at Alastair. "Don't be so nasty, Melanie could be badly hurt."

When I was lifted out of the hole, I scrambled after Alastair and Ray but each went a separate direction, and I stood motionless shrieking with frustration and indignation.

Gradually the blaze from the burning fire changed to a dying amber. We sat around the fire and began to sing. Alastair insisted that I should perform for them, "Melanie why don't you sing a song for us?"

I could feel my face turning red. Bashfully, I looked at Gavin appealingly, "I would do it only if Gavin agrees to sing along with me."

Gavin tenderly brushed my face with his finger tips. He replied gallantly, "Only if you insist—your wish is my command, but don't blame me if my voice should drown your singing."

After a brief discussion, we decided to sing Everly Brothers' latest hit song "Devoted to You." Together we sang in harmony, and our voices rang out into the night, "Darling, you can count on me, till the sun dries up the sea...."

When the singing subsided, there was a moment of silence. Then applause exploded into the night air. Clapping her hands with the others, Yvette praised, "Melanie you do have such an enchanting voice, I wish I could sing like you!"

Raymond playfully pulled Yvette's hair and intervened, "You are either born with a beautiful voice or you are not, and you, Yvette, I am sorry to say, were not gifted with such a voice. You can't sing, you croak!"

"What a ghastly thing to say to your sister." Gavin consolingly patted Yvette's shoulders and interrupted kindly.

Yvette smiled appreciatively at Gavin and pulled a funny face at her brother. Then she said, "I agree with Raymond's thinking, but Melanie sings with such emotion. That is not a gift."

"She's had enough practice." Teasing me and then changing the subject, Alastair continued, "Let's exchange ghost stories. I will start...."

I was terrified of the dark and the eerie atmosphere of the night petrified me. I didn't need horrifying ghost stories to accelerate my fear. Sitting stiffly and concentrating on Alastair's narration, I failed to hear the movement behind me. Suddenly two hands covered my eyes. Frightened I jumped and screamed. Then I heard Gavin's soothing voice, "Raymond, do behave yourself, you will scare the daylight out of the poor girl!"

I wrenched Raymond's fingers from my face, then automatically I hit him and he rolled on the sand—everyone bursted with laughter. I was glad that they all thought Raymond's action was funny. I didn't. Snuggling close to Gavin, I held his hand tightly for comfort and support. His closeness expectedly drove away some of my fear. Swiftly my anxiety faded and I almost enjoyed all the ghost stories that were told.

When the Mah Jong games finally came to an end, everyone assisted with the packing and we returned home with our parents, feeling exhausted but happy after an absolutely delightful day on the beach.

Six

Too quickly the summer holiday floated by while September arrived and schools reopened. With great determination and strong self-discipline, we forced ourselves to concentrate on our school work again. I returned to school with mixed feelings—excited because another new term was beginning and depressed, that the enjoyable summer holiday was over. When school resumed, Gavin and I were able to meet only during the weekends, but each day we would spend at least half an hour gossiping on the phone.

One evening, Gavin called and he inquired about my day, "Hi Melanie, how was your day? Did you have a nice one?"

Fuming with agitation, I kicked the legs of the small table where the telephone was sitting. I replied despairingly, "My day could have been much better if it wasn't for my loathsome math lesson; my tutor literally drove me to insanity!"

Gavin took note of my irritated tone of voice and asked with concern, "Are you having problems with your math? Finding the subject difficult to follow?"

Furiously I pulled at the telephone cord, and exclaimed vigorously, "Am I having problems? Are you kidding? This monstrous subject was invented to humiliate me; it not only instigates an obstacle for my progress in school, but it activates my migraine headaches!"

Cajoling me soothingly, Gavin said, "You must be exaggerating. You have an astute mind; also gifted with intelligence, so why should this subject create such a catastrophe for you?"

I sat on the floor dejectedly and rested the phone on my lap. I retorted, "I can read for hours. I absolutely adore English, but this other dreadful subject—I wish I could burn all the ghastly books pertaining to the subject!"

"Instead of gallivanting round town on Saturday, why don't we spend a few hours on your math? I bet you have a problem with understanding the formulas completely. With your intelligence, you shouldn't find the subject so overwhelming and demanding." Gavin concluded.

When Saturday arrived, Gavin set me in my room, going through the much hated math formulas with me. He asked me a few questions, and when the answers were coherent, he was quite positive with the opinion that I didn't fully understand the formulas, "You don't understand any of the formulas. Why don't I walk you through each formula systematically and see if you can't catch on?"

Shortly, to Gavin's disgust, I was yawning, dozing on my desk, and finding it a strain to keep my eyes open. Gavin implored me patiently, "Melanie, you are just not concentrating. You are deliberately putting up a mental block for yourself. Please let's try again!"

Fidgeting on my chair and doodling on the rough pad I whined with excuses, "I have exhausted all my brain cells; my fatigued brain is screaming for oxygen."

Patiently, Gavin utilized the next couple of weekends, coaching and drilling the complicated formulas into my confused brain. With stubborn determination, and much bribing, he forced me to concentrate; absolutely refusing a break for me until he was satisfied with my progress. Miraculously, my mental block slowly but surely vanished and the cobwebs in my brains untangled and disappeared. I began to see a light in the dark tunnel. To my utter astonishment, I was generating an interest for the hateful subject.

The Autumn term drew to an end and I received my much dreaded report card. Anxious over the results, with trembling hands I ripped opened the informative card. When I read the marks on my test results, I was absolutely exhilarated with the result of my math examination. I threw the card into air. Excitedly I called Gavin, "I received my report card today and guess what? You are not going to believe this; for the first time, I actually passed my math, and with flying colors, too! Thanks to you, your intuition, and your patience. Mummy reckons that it would require a miracle for me to pass the subject."

Gavin was pleased with my result, at least his effort was not wasted on me. "I am very proud of you. I knew you would eventually master this subject. I have always known that if you are made to understand the formulas, you are capable of solving the puzzles."

To my ultimate delight, as an incentive for me to work harder, Gavin gave me two records and Mother increased my pocket money.

Christmas was fast approaching. Everyone was in a mood for celebration, and the festive atmosphere was definitely apparent. We were extremely excited over our presents. Instead of spending my weekly pocket money on my beloved records, with difficulty, I saved for two whole weeks. When the Christmas holiday started, one afternoon, alone, I wondered around Downtown admiring all the enchanting Christmas decorations and exquisite lighting. Different shapes and sizes of Christmas trees were on displayed in every shop. Each tree was decorated with a different theme. Santa Clause and his reindeers, threaded with strings of lights, were hung from one building to the next. The colorful lights twinkled like stars in the sky. I watched and admired with fascination while constantly keeping my eyes wide open for the appropriate present to purchase for Gavin. I visited shop after shop, there was so much to choose from. Perhaps a shirt? Or maybe a tie? I found most of my choices too impersonal. It was difficult to make a decision. The overwhelming merchandise displayed in the shop windows confused me. After much debate with myself, finally I decided on a pen, but I hesitated with the inscription. Eventually I decided on just two simple but meaningful words—*Friends Forever.*

On Christmas day, my family was invited to Aunt Pearl and Uncle Joe's for lunch. With armfuls of Christmas presents we arrived at Gavin's home. I was once again impressed with Aunt Pearl's tasteful decoration of her home. Standing in the corner of the living room, the tall Christmas tree glistened with tiny colorful lights added festival atmosphere to the room. Presents were scattered around the tree. The aroma of roasted turkey drifted into my nostrils and my mouth watered. The dining table was laid out with all the appropriate festive food—there was even minced pie, my favorite. I was delighted with the different variety of food. After a delicious lunch, when all the presents were distributed, everyone excitedly opened them. Soon the room was littered with torn wrapping paper. Examining and admiring my presents, I made a mental note to thank the different people who had given me the presents. Amidst all my goodies, mostly, I loved the identity bracelet that Gavin had so thoughtfully purchased for me. Immediately upon opening the box, I insisted that Gavin should assist me with the clasp, and instantly the bracelet was sparkling round my tiny wrist. I marveled at Gavin's tasteful choice, "Gavin, what a lovely bracelet and my name is inscribed on the inside of the tag. How thoughtful of you." I hugged him forcefully.

"I am so pleased that you like it. I want you to remember me always. When I am no longer with you, hopefully the bracelet will remind you of me. As for the pen that you gave me, I will treasure it and it will accompany me wherever I go," Gavin blissfully replied holding my hand. Clinging to Gavin tightly, I sighed contentedly and faithfully gave my promise, "How can I ever forget you? I will never let you out of my sight!"

On New Year's eve, Gavin's family and mine decided to celebrate New Year's Eve at the Eagle's Nest. The elegant restaurant was situated on the top floor of the Hong Kong Hilton Hotel. When we arrived at the hotel, Uncle Edwin followed by Lynette escorted Mother toward the elevator. Alastair grabbed my hand and said, "Mum, Melanie and I would like to inspect the lobby, we will join you shortly in the restaurant."

Mother frowned disapprovingly, but Uncle Edwin nudged her shoulder and nodded his head with approval. Without providing Mother with another chance to protest, excitedly we sprinted toward the escalator which took us to the Mezzanine Floor—the hotel lobby. The lobby was bursting with activities; hotel guests were buzzing around, bell boys busily loading and unloading luggage from the trolley; front desk clerks with smart uniforms and pleasant smiles, patiently served the guests. I stood motionless and watched with fascination. After wandering around the lobby curiously for a while, Alastair pulled my sleeve and hissed, "We better make a move on and find the elevator for the restaurant, we don't want to get into hot water with the old folks, definitely not tonight anyway."

When we arrived at the restaurant, we were escorted to our table. Gavin's family was already seated and Mother beckoned us to join the party. The table was beautifully decorated; sparkling silver cutlery laid neatly on the table. The black color serviettes folded into the shape of swans were displayed on white fine bone China plates. The black table cloth was shimmering due to tiny pieces of silver tinsel sprinkled on the cloth. Sitting on the center of the table, the artistically arranged bouquet of fresh white roses added elegance and charm to the already tastefully decorated table. Candle flames flickered with the air movement in the dim lighting of the spacious dining room.

Through the floor length windows, I could see all the lights sparkling in the streets, and the peninsular of Kowloon stretching out across the harbor. The view was phenomenal. I couldn't help myself but stare. When I took my seat next to Gavin, he assisted me in adjusting the paper hat on my hair while commenting, "You do look ravishing tonight—reminding me of a fairy tale princess."

Bashfully, blinking my long eyelashes and beaming with sheer joy, I thanked him for the compliment.

While the five-course meal was being served, a band of four musicians enthusiastically played captivating music with sensational rhythm throughout the entire evening. The gentlemen were elegantly dressed in their dinner jackets and the ladies were dressed magnificently in the latest fashion ball gowns. Their expensive jewels were very much admired. Our parents joined the other dancers on the dance floor swaying to the rhythm of the rumba; moving their bodies sensuously while enjoying the cha-cha. Bending their bodies gracefully they danced to the tango. The ladies' dresses twirled while waltzing around the dance floor. Bodies twisting and turning to the lively rock'n roll music—a delight to the watchful eyes of the audience. I gawked with awe and admiration, wistfully hoping that I would one day be able to dance gracefully and expertly.

Soon the band began to play "Auld Lang Syne" and the countdown for the New Year started. We were too young to join the adults on the dance floor, so excitedly and impatiently we remained at our dining table. Amidst the noises of laughter and music the clock struck twelve. We leaped from our chairs, rushing to grab the colorful balloons that were released from the ceiling. Being so small framed, I had difficulty fighting for the balloons I was awfully grateful to Gavin when he put a few in my hand. Hanging on to our balloons, we embraced and wished each other a happy new year. With misty eyes, I held Gavin tightly and tenderly we kissed each other. Relishing the marvelous evening and memorable moments, we welcomed the dawn of another new year.

"Melanie, Uncle Edwin and I have been invited to play Mah Jong at your Aunt Wei Fun's home; Alastair will be joining us. He does appreciates an occasional weekend with Cedric. Lynette no doubt will be otherwise occupied with Raphael. You will be on your own again, do you want to invite Gavin for a casual meal tonight? Let Ah Ying know how many to expect for dinner. Ever faithful Ah Ying—wouldn't know what to do without her." My mother said to me while checking her handbag making certain that she had the car key.

Still brushing my long hair and checking my reflection in the mirror, I replied, "Alastiar of course enjoys his weekends with Cedric. Who wouldn't? Auntie Wei Fun spoils us rotten, she always caters to all our whims and demands."

Cedric's mother was my favorite Aunt—Auntie Wei Fun. She was Mother's elder sister. Cedric had one sister, Ardelia—who was a few years our senior and extremely independent. We all loved our Aunt Wei Fun because she was definitely a very kind person; her plump face and figure were always bubbling with joy. I could just imagine Alastair being fed with all his favorite food. Even if Aunt Wei Fun didn't do the cooking herself, undoubtedly she would instruct the maid to do it.

Breaking my train of thought, Mother inquired, "Would you like to come?"

Expertly I gathered my long hair and tied it neatly with a ribbon. Mumbling, I declined politely. As much as I adored Aunt Wei Fun and her enticing cooking, an evening with just Alastair and Cedric would positively drive me to an early grave. Maybe not to that extreme; nevertheless, I couldn't afford the risk of having my hair turn gray overnight.

Later toward the evening, Gavin arrived in time to join me for dinner, bringing with him a box of my favorite ice cream.

"Don't you agree with me that the New Year's Eve dinner was terrific?" Gavin asked for my opinion while helping himself to another plate of his favorite fried rice noodles—rice noodles stirred fried with sliced B-B-Que pork and shrimps, sprinkled with heaps of spring onion.

Spooning the last bit of noodle into my mouth and pushing the empty plate away, I secretly confided in Gavin, "I particularly admired the elegantly dressed ladies. They looked magnificent. When I grow older, I promise myself I will be dressed likewise. By the way, your parents and mine are such terrific dancers, I wish I could dance with their skill and grace."

A gleam began to shine in Gavin's attractive eyes, winking at me, with a conspiring tone of voice he suggested, "I don't see why not—we are going to be on our own tonight, why don't we practice? Between the two of us, we should be able to remember most of the dance steps; but if we fail to recollect, we can always make up new ones. For all we know, with enough practice and imagination, we may become expert dancers too."

When I finished my ice cream, habitually I started to lick my fingers. Gavin yanked the fingers from my mouth and smacked my hand, he reprimanded, "You are doing it again, don't lick your dirty fingers, it's most unladylike!"

I grimaced and cheekily stuck my tongue at Gavin, "Yes, Grandfather. God, you are perpetually so prim and proper. The ever perfect gentleman."

Gavin pulled me off the dining chair then he shouted into the kitchen, "Ah Ying, thank you for a delicious meal. I do love your cooking, and you always cook my favorite dish."

The plump form of Ah Ying appeared on the threshold of the dining room, wiping her wet hand on the apron, she beamed at Gavin. "It is my pleasure to cook for you. You are always so polite—never fail to compliment me, and kind words always linger on your lips."

When we returned to the living room from the dining room, Gavin put a stack of Mother's dance music on the record player. After a few hours of practice, through trial and errors, we began to dance with expertise, although at first a few toes were stepped on constantly. I was basically a great lover for music, and Gavin was born with rhythm in his veins. Dancing was no hardship to us. After our first evening of dancing, Gavin and I both fell in love with this newly developed hobby. From that evening on, whenever we were provided with a chance, secretly we would practice our dance steps. It didn't take us long to cultivate a taste for dancing and soon we were dancing superbly, and I believed that we made a stunning couple.

Seven

Together Gavin and I journeyed through the care-free golden days of our youth. We knew no fear nor regrets. There was no boundary to our happiness and no end to our joy. The minutes, the hours and the days fluttered away.

We strolled in the park together and we laughed in the rain together. How many sand castles were built and washed away by the ebbing tide? We swam in the sea and basked in the warm sun. We were seen in the cinema giggling and laughing. When we were in the library, we read and attended to our homework. Singing and dancing became our constant companion. Playfully we teased each other and exchanged our dreams. Countless jokes were shared. Too many nights we cuddled together and told each other ghost stories.

Laughter and tears escorted us. My world became Gavin's world. When I cried, he comforted me. When I laughed, he could feel my delight. Another summer came and swiftly departed. I hoped those heavenly days would ever end.

After the Christmas holiday, school reopened and we returned to school. One Friday afternoon, after school broke up, unexpectedly Gavin called me, "I have to come and see you after dinner tonight. Will you wait for me?" There was a strong sense of urgency in his voice.

Knowing Gavin as well as I did, I began to panic. If I could detect anxiety in Gavin's voice, then something was definitely bothering him. His emotions were normally well under control. But I was determined to sound light-hearted, so cheekily I teased him, "Don't sound so serious. It's not the end of the world, you know!" When I was off the phone, feeling jittery, I began to pace up and down in my room. Feeling frustrated with the unknown, I frowned and chewed my nails. I was petrified. I had a premonition that disaster would soon invade and disrupt my life. Impatiently I waited for his impending arrival.

When Gavin finally arrived with creased brows and a sad face he suggested taking Lucky for a stroll in the park.

I was dying with curiosity "You didn't rush over just to take Lucky for a walk. What is bothering you?"

He didn't answer me but took my hand and put the leash on Lucky. We left home and silently we walked toward the park.

When we arrived at our destination, we moved away from the evening crowd. Gavin located a quiet spot. Sitting on the grass, Gavin gazed at the horizon. With a dejected tone of voice he insisted that I should search my memory. "During one of our family dinners, do you remember my parents mentioning something about sending Raphael and myself away to further our studies?"

I screwed my eyes and tried to recall the incident before I responded. "I suppose so...our parents are always harping on the same subject. After all there is only one English University in Hong Kong. In order to obtain a recognized professional degree, ultimately we will have to go abroad to study. Why are you approaching this subject now?" Suddenly, I stopped talking and watched Gavin intensively. In the dark, his profile was hardly visible to me. The suspense was unbearable. "Gavin, tell me what is on your mind."

Gavin returned his gaze from the distance and took my hands in his. Softly he whispered, "You do know that I am very fond of you, and you have become my companion and younger sister. Together we are sharing a friendship that is extremely rare. Nothing on earth will ever destroy this rapport that we have between us."

The uneasiness that I felt was gradually increasing, I was experiencing a feeling of doom. My quivering voice was rising, and I beseeched him, "Gavin, please, don't keep me in suspense. What is going on? Please, I need to know the truth."

The pains in his eyes were not lost to me. I began to shiver and my hands were turning icy cold.

My body temperature was rapidly dropping. Suddenly, Gavin took a deep breath and he shared his troublesome thoughts with me. "My parents have decided that Raphael and I should further our study in England. We will be leaving Hong Kong at the end of June next year.

I couldn't believe what I heard. Frowning, softly I stuttered, "But…but…I don't understand. What are you telling me?"

Nervously, Gavin rubbed his nose with his fingers. Looking away from me he continued, "I will be leaving Hong Kong shortly. I don't know when I will be returning. We will no longer be together. In fact, we are going to be oceans apart."

I shook my head vigorously. Stammering, I whimpered, "You don't know what you are saying…you are lying. This is another prank of yours. Please don't harass me. I can take almost any joke but not this particular one. Please don't tease me—I cannot bear it. Don't be ridiculous, how can we be separated? We are the invincible Siamese Twins—we are bonded together forever."

Gavin was desperately attempting to comfort me by pulling me closer to him, but he was speechless for a moment, then he declared, "I had expected you to be disturbed by the news, but your obvious distress is penetrating into my inner soul." Crushing me into his arms and stroking my long hair tenderly, he repeated my name over and over again. "Oh, Melanie, Melanie, I would give anything to be able to erase this pain from you. I am afraid what I just told you is no prank. I have no other choice but to leave you in June."

I clung to him and stifled a groan with the back of my hand. I was stunned; physical pains attacked. I was incapable of any motion or reaction. Uncontrollable tears were streaming down my face and I began to sob. I clutched my stomach—a sharp instrument had stabbed my guts; a piece of my heart was sliced away by a sharp knife. The excruciating pain was intolerable. I rocked backwards and forwards unable to control my shaking body. In order to protect myself, my inner instinct for survival was triggered and my sorrow was converted to anger. Instantly I pulled away from Gavin unable to control my wrath I started to scream. The piercing sound sliced through the air into the darkness. Subconsciously I began to hit him. Beating his chest with both hands, I shrieked "You are lying—lying—I refuse to believe a word that you are saying. You gave me your word of honor that we would never be separated and that we would always be together. Don't you understand? You are a part of me. I refuse to let you break your promise to me."

Gradually, when my screaming subsided, I collapsed into the folds of his arms. Automatically, I brushed away the tears from my face and, simultaneously, I was hoping that I could push the pain away. Shielding my tearful face with my hands, I whimpered. Despite the fact that I wanted to apologize, the pain was so intense that I couldn't bring myself to look at him. Whispering I stuttered, "Gavin, I am sorry…so sorry….I didn't mean to hit you. Oh God, this has to be a nightmare I will wake up soon…."

Gavin's face was wet. Our tears mingled, and his controlled emotion suddenly snapped. Fiercely he held me closer to him and gently he lifted my face. Hoping to console me, he whispered, "All good things have to end eventually. Let's be grateful that we have had the opportunity of sharing two wonderful and unforgettable years together. Our paths will cross again. In order for us to survive this pain we must live with this belief. We will only be separated for a few short years. We will meet again. I give you my solemn oath. Please believe me." He buried my distressed face in his shoulders while stroking my hair continuously.

After a long while I removed myself from Gavin's embrace, pushing the hair off my tear stained face I moaned, "Who is going to walk Lucky with me? Who will assist me with my math? Where am I going to find another dancing partner? Will I be counting stars alone?" I threw a string of questions at him. Clinging onto Gavin again, I pleaded with him. "Gavin, please, please don't go. I can't bear this pain. My heart is aching and my migraine is hurting dreadfully. I can't seem to be able to stop the tears. This is a horrible feeling—I wish I could die."

Looking straight into my eyes, Gavin implored, "Melanie, please stop, your grief is tearing me apart." Then gently he brushed my trembling lips with his.

Slowly my sobbing subsided. When I raised my head again, Gavin quietly remarked, "I hate to see the sparkle disappearing from your watery dark eyes. It is devastating for me to see the dimples on your sweet face replaced by tears." Gently Gavin attempted to wipe the tears away, but this gentle action generated more tears.

Unexpectedly the agony that I felt suddenly switched to anguish. Roughly, I pushed Gavin away from me and I dried my own tears with the back of my hand. I yelled for Lucky. Hesitantly, I put the leash on him and said to Gavin, "I have to go home now. It is getting late Mummy will be worried."

Gavin was astounded by my sudden impulsive behavior. Mutely he followed me. When we were leaving the vicinity of the park, I mumbled to myself, "I am not a weakling and I refuse to cry. I have to find the strength to sustain this pain. Laughter and smiles will accompany me for the rest of my life. I can't cry and I won't cry!" Proudly, I lifted my head and straightened my slumped shoulders. I marched into the building but before I disappeared, I turned toward Gavin and stubbornly informed him, "Don't accompany me, I have to be alone. We have said our goodbyes, let's leave it at that. There is nothing more to be said." Without another backward glance I dashed for the elevator.

I was grateful to find myself alone in the elevator. Dejectedly I cuddled Lucky craving for comfort and warmth. The gentle dog licked my face playfully and lovingly. I took a few deep breaths hoping to control my shattered emotion. My heart was pounding at such a speed that my ribs began to hurt. When the elevator came to a stop, roughly I wiped my tear-stained face with the back of my hand. I took another deep breath, then I opened the front door.

Quietly I let myself into the flat. By then I had managed to dry my tears. I hoped that my distress was no longer apparent. Hearing a commotion from the living room, gingerly, I poked my head into the room. Lynette was sobbing in Mother's comforting arms, while Uncle Edwin was anxiously pacing up and down the floor. My presence went unnoticed. Alastair set on the floor gently tapping his tennis racquet on the side of the settee. When he finally saw me, he ventured to open his mouth to speak but Uncle Edwin stopped him by a flick of his hand. Swallowing the unspoken words, he motioned me to join the family, so quietly I entered the room.

My slight movement caused Lynette to raise her head from Mother's shoulder. Removing herself from Mother's arms, my sister saw me standing by the door. Immediately she screeched, "Raphael and Gavin are going to England to study in June. How could Auntie Pearl and Uncle Joe be so absolutely heartless? Don't they realize that they are definitely breaking my heart?" Her whining was endless and the annoying sound was like drums beating against my ears.

Suddenly Lynette's eyes blazed with anger. Wagging her finger at my direction she directed her anguish at me. "What is the matter with you? Don't just stand there—have you lost your tongue? Have you nothing to say? Aren't you going to miss Gavin? You cold and heartless creature!"

With her uproar I cringed squeezing my eyes tightly I fanned my hand in the air.

Uncle Edwin was appalled with Lynette's behavior. He ceased the pacing and protectively jumped to my rescue. Sternly, he reprimanded my sister. "Young lady, that is quite enough! We all have our own way of handling our grief and sorrows. Let Melanie be."

Upon hearing Uncle Edwin's reproach, Lynette resumed her crying. Mother signaled Uncle Edwin to terminate his criticism by putting her fingers to her lips. Although the raw pain that I was feeling inside was definitely disturbing; nevertheless, I held onto my pride with stubbornness. Mother realized that I would never display my sorrow in public. She smiled at me knowingly. She knew that I would always suffer in silence. Lynette and I were so distinctly different in character.

When I ignored Lynette, she started her yelling again. "Mummy, why don't you talk to Raphael's parents. You are such good friends. You have to help me!"

Gently stroking my sister's hair and patting her hand encouragingly, Mother consoled her. "Raphael has to further his study. You cannot be his stumbling block. You must be sensible. If your love for each other is deep enough, a mere separation will not alter your feelings for each other. When your Uncle Edwin had to obtain his law degree from England, we were separated for two years. Now we are together again. Have faith in your own feelings."

Lynette pushed Mother away and stamped her tiny feet. "I bet those were the longest years of your life."

Mother's eyes started to mist over. Biting her lips she replied, "I've had worst. I thought I was going to die when I heard of your father's accidental death, but I lived on."

Lynette stood with her legs planted firmly on the floor she glared at Mother and demanded an explanation. "If you have been through all the pain from a separation why do you want to inflict the same pain on us?"

Uncle Edwin shoved a handkerchief into Lynette's hand and interrupted, "Please don't hurt your mother unnecessarily. She doesn't deserve any of this nonsense. This is all part of growing up. We have, at one time or another, walked the same path and survived. I expect the same from you."

I was too heartbroken to cope with Lynette's unreasonable tantrum. She would have to deal with her own pain and carry her own cross. I smiled at my family and quietly returned to the solace of my own room. That night, sleep escaped me. Tossing and turning in my bed I became the victim of insomnia. Overnight I grew up having to swallow my first pill of disappointment. I was certain that through my entire life, there would be more sleepless nights, more tears and heartaches.

Bravely and silently, I tackled my sorrows and pain but I wasn't coping successfully. My appetite vanished and I was losing weight rapidly. Constant lack of sleep stimulated dreadful headaches—I was finding it awfully difficult to concentrate during the ever demanding lessons. My eyes were enormous black pools on my small face. My complexion turned ashen and sallow; the natural glow dissipated. I attempted to display a brave smile on my face but anyone could detect the sadness behind the restrained grin.

I spent weekend after lonely weekend alone in my room. I buried myself among my books; my records were my constant companion. They reminded me of much happier days. I took long and lonely walks with Lucky, discouraging all visits from Yvette. I refused all communication with Gavin. I was no longer available when he called. I declined all invitations for dinner or lunch from Auntie Pearl and Uncle Joe. On the few occasions that Gavin endeavored to visit my home, I would fabricate excuses and disappear into the haven of solace—my own room. With cold shoulders and icy silence I discouraged him to follow me. I was determined to keep my distance from Gavin and learn to survive without him and his support. I insisted that Gavin should become history. I could not allow him to perforate into my life again. The pain was never ending and endurable. I felt bitterness toward my destiny and decided that thoughtless fate had stolen away my happiness.

One afternoon, when I returned home from a stroll with Lucky, I quietly let myself into the flat with my own key. When I walked by the living room, I saw Mother and Uncle Edwin. I didn't mean to eavesdrop but when I heard my name being mentioned, automatically, I halted and took a peek into the room. Mother was offering Uncle Edwin a cup of coffee and then she took the seat next to his. She obviously wanted to confide in him with her next remark. "I wish that Melanie would rant and rave like Lynette. She is too young to shoulder her own sorrow. Her stubborn nature will ultimately be her downfall."

Uncle Edwin stirring the cup of coffee and leaning back on the cushion interrupted, "The two girls are so different, like night and day. Melanie maybe stubborn, but she is definitely not selfish. Lynette is self centered; therefore, she exhibits her feelings, hoping to gain sympathy. Melanie is too proud. She refuses to accept defeat or failure. To cry would represent the action of a coward. She would share her joy and bliss, but failure she would swallow bravely and silently."

Mother moved closer to Uncle Edwin on the settee and she nodded her head in agreement. Then she asked him, "Why do you think Melanie is so fiercely rejecting Gavin? She cannot really blame him for her suffering? I bet he is suffering just as much, if not more. She must be aware that he is genuinely very fond of her."

Uncle Edwin closed his eyes and thought for a while before he answered. "I truly believe that she is not rejecting him as a person, but she is protecting her own feelings. She is badly hurt and she resents the unfamiliar deflectable feeling of rejection. She is lost and absolutely confused. She has no desire to be hurt again. She knows that Gavin has no choice but to leave her in few months' time, she doesn't see the reason for prolonging the agony. She craves for a clean cut. In a way, she is extremely sensible if she can cut her loses now." Sighing deeply he continued, "But it is a shame to witness such a tremendous relationship going to waste."

Mother started to pace the room, then she stopped and shook her head, "I disagree with you. The relationship will not be wasted. I have this distinct feeling that their unique friendship will stay intact. No oceans or time could intervene—those two will remain friends forever!"

Edwin sighed and stretched out his long legs then he beckoned Mother to return to her seat next to him. When she resumed her sitting position, he put his arms around her shoulders protectively and said, "I sincerely hope that you are correct. In any case, I think Melanie will soon find herself again; she is young enough to bounce back into life. This in fact has been a terrific experience for her. Let's just hope that in the future, she is still capable of loving and sharing."

Massaging her forehead, Mother replied, "I don't think this ordeal will change her character; she is an extremely sensitive child with the capability to feel agony and ecstasy to their fullest."

Tears stung my eyes I couldn't bear to listen to the rest of their conversation. Quietly I sneaked into my room. I kicked the door closed and tumbled onto my bed. I crushed my head with the pillow so that my crying would become a muffle. Hoping to stifle my moans and groans, I bit fiercely into the quilt on my bed. Feeling frustrated, I kicked my legs in the air. Gradually, I felt released from my cooped up tension. Feeling absolutely exhausted and deflated I fell asleep. In my dreams Gavin and I were once again strolling along the golden shores of Shek-O beach, collecting sea shells and he was smiling into my eyes….

Eight

When I opened the door to the flat, I took a couple of deep breaths and shivered. The cool air penetrated into my bones and goose pimples appeared on my arm. Hong Kong's winter could be so cold. Swiftly I went into my room and unloaded the armful of books on my desk. I was relieved to be out of my uniform. I pulled a thick jumper over my head and wriggled into my jeans. I left my room for the kitchen while pulling up the zipper on my jeans.

I snooped around the kitchen hoping to find some left over from lunch, but Ah Ying was just too tidy to leave food lying around in the kitchen. I poured myself a cup of hot tea from the thermos and warmed my cold hands with the hot cup. By the time I walked into the living room, half of the cup was empty. Mother was sitting comfortably on the settee with her feet propped up on the stool and she was knitting away. Lucky spread her small body in front of the heater and was fast asleep, obviously enjoying the heat generated from the heater.

I flopped down on the settee next to Mother and gave her a bear hug. "It sure is nice to be home." I picked up the ball of wool from the floor and placed it in Mother's knitting basket.

Mother smiled at me lovingly, then she returned the knitting to the basket. "Had a rough day in school?"

I leaned back on the cushion and closed my eyes before my reply was forthcoming. "No…nothing worse than a normal day. Just glad to be home."

Lynette joined us and gave Mother a peck on the cheek, then she moved Mother's feet from the stool and sat on it. I opened my eyes slightly and smiled at her lazily. I closed my eyes again. Their chatting was having a hypnotizing effect on me and I must have dozed off.

Suddenly Lynette's question woke me with a jolt. My sister's sweet voice was murmuring, "Have you considered sending me abroad to study?" Softly she asked Mother.

The next moment, I was wide awake and waited for Mother's reply. She was flabbergasted with Lynette's suggestion. Hesitantly, she answered, "No, I can't say that I have, why?"

Lynette gracefully removed herself from the stool and pushed me further into the corner so that she could sit next to Mother. Tenderly she put her arms around Mother's shoulder and sweetly she said, "Auntie Wei Fun reckons that its about time Cedric should be sent away to study. We all have to leave home at one time or another…." After a slight pause, she continued, "You don't honestly think that I will stand a chance of enrolling into our one and only university in Hong Kong, do you?" Smiling brilliantly and watching Mother with her bewitching eyes, she suggested, "I can leave with Raphael."

Mother hesitated before she answered, "There is no doubt that you will have to study abroad, but now is not the right time, perhaps sometime in the future."

Lynette took Mother's hand into her hands and stroking it gently, she astutely interrupted, "But why not now? I am old enough."

From Lynette's tone of voice I could predict another tantrum from her. She begged, "Mummy, please don't be so cruel. You don't want to be the culprit for my unhappiness, do you? I promise that I will behave and I will never be the cause of any further distress to you. Just let me go!"

Lynette can be so convincing when it suits her intention and purpose. She can be perfectly persuasive. Charm exuded from her when she fluttered her long and thick black eye lashes innocently and sweetly. Mother became frightfully thoughtful for a while and then she decided to invite Auntie Wei Fun for dinner. Picking up the phone, she dialed Auntie Wei Fun's number. After chatted briefly on the phone, Mother instructed Ah Ying to expect her sister for dinner.

After dinner, I excused myself and disappeared into my room. After studying solidly for two hours, I needed to stretch my tired limbs. Rubbing my weary eyes, I decided to get a drink from the kitchen. I hadn't had anything to drink since dinner and I certainly could do with something hot in my stomach. The draft from the windows was chilling my bones. When I emerged from my room, I heard voices coming from the living room. Noiselessly and curiously I approached the room. The two sisters were relaxing and chatting amicably. Mother was sitting on the settee and Auntie Wei Fun occupied the single arm chair that was placed on the other side of the coffee table. Two steaming cups of hot liquid stood temptingly on the table. Auntie Wei Fun was busily cracking the hard shell of the dried melon seeds and extracting the dried nut from the shell. I didn't want to interrupt them but as soon as I heard Mother talking about grandma, my footsteps halted. Since my father's untimely death, there had been a rift between Mother and his family. My grandparents were extremely rich and my father was their only son. Overly superstitious, somehow they had blamed Mother for his accident. From time to time I secretly visited my grandparents. They were getting on to their elderly years I felt I owed them an occasional visit. Mother was speaking very softly, her voice was hardly audible, but I managed to grasp the gist of the conversation. Auntie Wei Fun put all the empty shells in the ashtray then she removed the cup from the coffee table and took a sip of the hot tea. When she returned her attention to Mother she said, "Wei Ling, you know, Lynette does make some sense. You will have to send her away soon."

Mother creased her brows and gazed around the small living room. With a heavy sigh she replied, "I know, but financially it will be an added burden to me. It has not been effortless to maintain this household…clothing the children and feeding them can be a cumbersome demand to say the least. Even though we have managed so far, sometimes I find the effort terribly strenuous. Also, I cannot turn to Edwin for assistance. After all, these are not his children. As for the children's grandparents, they are hopeless, stubborn old goats!"

Auntie Wei Fun returned the cup to the table, smoothing the crease from her dress. "Now that you have mentioned Edwin, I meant to discuss this issue with you before now. Don't you think its time that you should seriously consider marriage. You are not getting any younger. After all these years, I would have thought Edwin has proved to be a faithful suitor."

Mother removed herself from the settee. She moved over to where Auntie Wei Fun was sitting and patted her sister's hand tenderly while explaining, "There is never the perfect time. The children are still too young. I would like them to be a bit more independent before I can consider my own happiness…I owe it to their father's memories. Also,

I don't particularly enjoy unnecessary gossips. I don't want Edwin's family to feel that I am taking advantage of him, his kindness or his wealth."

There was a prolonged silence while Mother was pacing the room. When she stopped she stated, "I know I shouldn't deprive Lynette of a golden opportunity. I guess somehow I will have to find a way to support her lodging and school fees."

I could no longer retain my silence. Boldly I charged into the room, interrupted their conversation and confessed to my eavesdropping. "Mummy, I couldn't help but hear part of your conversation. Please agree to let Lynette join Raphael in England. They do share something that is beautiful and it's impossible for us to predict the future. Let's not spoil it for them. Together we will make it possible for you to afford Lynette's expenses abroad."

Auntie Wei Fun gave me an astonishing look and was grateful for my interruption. Immediately she agreed with my thinking. "Next year, after the summer holiday, I will be sending Cedric away, why don't you let Lynette leave with him? Raphael would have had a few months to find his bearings before the arrival of these two younger ones."

Mother returned to her seat, then she fluffed the cushions. Absent-mindedly she muttered, "I still feel that Lynette is too young to fend for herself. I don't have any relatives in England, and I hate the thought of her being on her own."

Auntie Wei Fun thought for a while then suddenly she exclaimed, "Wei Ling, don't you and Edwin have a friend in England? I think his name is Peter Chan. Ardelia met him while she was studying in London. Couldn't you contact him?"

Mother smacked her forehead with her hand. "Of course, Peter, how could I have forgotten him? He operates a chain of Chinese restaurants in London. Come to think of it he is still a bachelor. He might just consider becoming their guardian. I will write immediately."

Having put in my two bits of words, I kept my fingers crossed for Lynette. I kissed Mother good night, said good bye to Auntie Wei Fun and then I returned to my room and my never-ending homework.

It was Christmas Eve again. Somehow I just couldn't bring myself to be in a festive mood. As far as I was concerned nothing was worth celebrating. Although Gavin's impending departure no longer caused excruciating pain, the mere thought still created a dull ache. I declined an invitation for a pre-Christmas dinner with Auntie Pearl and Uncle Joe;

instead I decided to attend the midnight mass alone.

The church was crowded, packed with churchgoers. The air was stifling and I was cramped into a corner. Although I had the rosary clutched in my hands not a single prayer was said. I couldn't concentrate on what the priest was saying. The choir's beautiful voices were just humming noises irritating my ears. At the end of the service, absentmindedly I followed the crowd filing out of the church. When I emerged from the church, the temperature had dropped. Cold wind cut into my body. I pulled my collar and wrapped my coat tightly and snugly round my shivering body. I breathed in the cold air hoping to clear my confused brain, then briskly I walked home.

"It's too late for someone so young and beautiful to be walking alone." Someone patted me on the shoulder and nervously I jumped. The deep voice jolted my memories. How I had missed the sound of this particular voice. Gavin followed me from the church and caught up with me with his long strides. When he was walking next to me he muttered, "When you arrived in the church, immediately, I saw you. Your melancholy face and mesmerizing beauty definitely stood out in a crowd. Your image just took my breath away." He touched my arms slightly, then tenderly he complained, "You are much too thin." Gavin gazed into my eyes then he whispered, "I have missed you terribly, Melanie, an awful lot!" Gently Gavin lifted me off my feet and folded me into his arms. Gently he kissed me on the cheek. He whispered, "Merry Christmas, Melanie!"

Gavin's closeness and his gentleness plus the kind words cut right into my heart. I winced at his touch, my vision began to blur by unshed tears. I lost the strength to utter a word. I was drowning in the pools of his attractive eyes. Gradually I managed to force a tight smile. When I regained my composure, I resumed my walking. Gavin followed me and asked, "Are you still angry with me?"

Slowly I turned toward him and I responded dejectedly, "I was never annoyed with you. I was angry with fate. I don't like the hurtful feeling that is constantly churning in the pit of my stomach!" I pulled away from him and dashed into the darkness.

The following morning, the family gathered around the Christmas tree happily unwrapping our presents. Mother distributed the presents and put an unexpected present on my lap. The gift was wrapped with very pretty festive paper and tied with a gorgeous ribbon. Silently I took the gift and softly I asked, "Thank you Mummy. It's from Gavin isn't it?"

Mother nodded her head and I stared blankly at the present for a while. I unwrapped the present tenderly and read the card that was attached to the ribbon. To Melanie, Keep smiling, our paths will cross again. Friends forever. Love, Gavin. Caressing the record gently, sadly I thought to myself, another contribution to my collection.

Mother's voice brought my attention to the present. "I have some good news to announce. My dear friend Peter from England called last night, wishing us all a very happy Christmas...."

An electrifying tension shot through the room and all movement ceased. Lynette was holding her breath waiting impatiently for Mother to continue. "Peter has agreed to be Cedric and Lynette's guardian in England. He will be searching for a good school for Lynette." Wagging a finger in the direction of my sister, smiling fondly she concluded, "and you, young lady, will be leaving for England with Cedric after the summer holiday!"

Everyone spoke at the same time. It took Lynette a few seconds to comprehend what Mother was saying. She threw the unwrapped presents into the air and rushed into Mother's arms. Lucky could sense that something important was happening. She circled round everyone's feet, wagging his tail and barking. I looked at Alastair and he was beaming. I was so, so happy for my sister. Lynette was exhilarated with happiness, there was no way that she could control her pleasure. Shrieking with joy, she hugged every member of the family. I embraced Lynette lovingly and offered my congratulation and good wishes, "Lynette, I am so happy for you. I wish you all the happiness. Raphael must be delighted with Mummy's decision!"

Alastair winked at me and chanted cheekily, "Good riddance. Now we can enjoy some peace and quiet around the flat. Maybe we all will get a chance to use the phone." Lynette bashed our brother's head playfully and screeched, "I am sure you will miss me!"

Alastair pulled a funny face and stuck his tongue at Lynette. "Like hell I will!"

Mother was aghast with her son's foul language. She smacked him on the head with some torn Christmas wrappers and reprimanded, "Alastair, mind your evil tongue!"

Uncle Edwin moved closer to Lynette and she waltzed into his welcoming embrace. Kissing Lynette fondly, Uncle Edwin advised, "I hope you realize how many sacrifices your mother has made for you. I hope you will not disappoint her."

Screwing her nose, thoughtlessly, Lynette replied, "I don't see why Mummy should worry about money, she should just marry you!"

RETURN

I was stunned and disgusted with Lynette's inconsiderate remark. Indignantly I hissed, "Lynette, how could you be so insensitive to Mummy's feelings? She will not be marrying Uncle Edwin for monetary reasons. She will only marry him because of love."

Sheepishly Lynette lowered her head, obviously regretted her outburst. She removed herself from Uncle Edwin's arms and grabbed Mother's shoulder. All the while apologizing profusely, "Oh Mummy, I am so sorry, really. That remark was uncalled for, I don't know what caused me to say something so utterly stupid."

Too embarrassed to look at Mother and Uncle Edwin, Alastair and I started to tidy the living room, and soon all the torn wrapping paper was thrown into the rubbish bin, and the house was in ship-shape again.

Gavin's imminent departure was fast approaching. As the months turned into weeks, I was gradually regretting my recent atrocious behavior toward Gavin. I wanted to apologize to him before his departure but I didn't know how to handle the situation. I could not tolerate the thought of a two-year friendship being discarded overnight. When I received the invitation for Raphael and Gavin's farewell party, I jumped for the opportunity to renew our friendship, so I called him.

Fidgeting with the telephone cord, I sucked in a deep breath. Timidly I said, "Gavin…" then I had to pause to find the next word. Bashfully I continued, "Thank you for your invitation…."

I could detect from the tone of Gavin's voice that he was overjoyed to hear my voice. He insisted, "You will come, won't you? It wouldn't be a party without you."

"Of course, and Gavin, what are you doing this weekend? Can I buy you a cup of coffee?" I asked, all the while I could feel my face turning red.

Gavin teased, "Are you sure you can spare the money? Wouldn't you rather spend it on your record instead?"

I uttered a slight giggle and I heard Gavin breathe a sigh of relief. He responded happily, "My Melanie has been revived. I will come after lunch. Promise me you will reserve the entire day for me. I will even chip in with the expenses." His voice boomed over the phone with exhilaration.

When Saturday arrived, my door was pushed opened gently. I could see Gavin's smiling face in the reflection of my mirror. A smile blossomed on my face. I beckoned him to enter the room. Once again, just like old times, I set on the floor with my legs crossed and Gavin lounging comfortably beside me. The record player was playing softly. The Everly Brothers were singing our favorite song, "Darling you can count on me, till the sun dries up the sea," which brought back many memories. I started to sniff. Gavin folded me into his arms and comforted me, "Melanie, Melanie, please don't cry anymore I can't bear to see your distressed face again. You have lost enough weight already!" He implored me, "Don't you know, I have missed your laughter and your giggles. Please laugh for me again." Lifting my face with his hands, I saw his eyes were sparkling.

I wept uncontrollably. I brushed the tears from my face and murmured, "Gavin, I have been so beastly to you. I don't want to hurt you, I know you are not the cause for my ordeal, but I couldn't direct anguish anywhere but you. Please, forgive me. I have made myself ample promises not to cry again, but I don't know how I am capable of generating so many tears." Blowing my nose, I tried to catch my next breath. Words stumbled from my lips, and stammering, I proceeded. "I have been utterly selfish, instead of encouraging you to further your studies, I have been stewing in my own juice and drowning in my own sorrows. Will you ever forgive me? I have no defense for myself but the thought of not having you around me, supporting me…just the thought of losing you made me cringe. Can you understand this deflated feeling?"

Gavin squeezed my trembling body closer to his heart, then he coaxed me with his soft voice. "Hush, Melanie, Melanie, hush…." He lifted my tearful face and persisted, "You are not losing me. We maybe apart physically for a few short years but you will be with me constantly in my thoughts and in my dreams. How can I ever forget you?"

When my sobbing began to cease, Gavin insisted that I should close my eyes. He had a surprise for me. "Can you imagine the degree of our happiness when we do meet again? If we have not tasted the sorrow of parting how can we truly appreciate the sweetness of a future reunion?"

With my eyes closed I could feel a cold object being pushed gently into my palms. When I opened my eyes, he whispered, "Until we meet again."

Resting on my palm was a brown color jar, made of clay, with the word "memories" carved on the side. Gavin could sense my hesitation, he explained, "I want you to put the jar on your bedside table. Each morning when you wake up, look at it with a smile. Tears are definitely forbidden. Until we are provided with the opportunity to meet again, this jar will hold all our memories intact."

Clutching the jar tightly I buried my head into Gavin's shoulder. My voice was muffled. "What a lovely sentimental thought." I pretended to blow into the jar. "Is that how you reserve all the memories?" We laughed.

Mother escorted Lynette and myself to the farewell party. Immediately upon our arrival Mother and Uncle Edwin disappeared into the study to play Mah Jong.

Lynette circled round Raphael possessively. Proudly, she informed the other guests of her imminent departure to join Raphael on the other side of the world. All the girls were flocking around Gavin, demanding his attention. With perfect manners he attended to each of their needs. Dancing and chatting—being the perfect host. Suddenly I felt terribly neglected.

Music, laughter and chit-chat surrounded me, but I felt dreadfully lonely. Looking around me, I decided to go into the balcony. The view of the ocean and horizon stretching out in front of me brought on a heavy sigh. The same sea, the same sky, but a different me. I had matured, being forced to taste the bitterness of separation from a dear friend. I had known supreme happiness; I was therefore suffering from utter despair.

Gavin must have seen me disappearing into the balcony. He excused himself from the crowd and followed me. Quietly he sneaked up to me and kissed me gently on the face. The sudden action startled me and I gasped. Returning my gaze from the far horizon, I stared into Gavin's talkative eyes. They were saying a thousand words to me but not a sound could be heard. I lifted his hands onto my face and gently kissed his palm. With a silky voice I said, "Adios, my friend—my prayers will go with you."

When we returned to the living room, I promised myself to enjoy the rest of the evening. Tonight I would dance and laugh with Gavin. Tomorrow I could cry to my heart's content.

Gavin departed. I was in a daze for a while moving around like a zombie. Days glided by for me without meaning. I floated around the apartment gloomily. Gradually with tremendous self-discipline I pulled myself from my depression, and slowly my life fitted into a pattern. Slowly but surely my equilibrium returned.

The days turned to months and finally it was the eve of Lynette's departure. Mother was busy attending to Lynette's last minute packing. Suitcases were opened and stacks of clothing were folded neatly, ready to be put into the bags. Continuously, Lynette was wanted on the phone.

Her friends wanted to chat before her departure.

When it was almost time for bed Lynette bellowed, "As I will be seeing Gavin soon is there any message that you would like me to deliver, or maybe a present? I will gladly accommodate."

I paused before closing the book that I was reading, then I shook my head. At which point, Lynette snapped at me nastily. "No wonder Gavin used to compare you with a cat—distant, cold, absolutely unfathomable! Your action is really inexplicable. Why did people think that the two of you were Siamese twins? You can't even bother to write to him!" Slamming my door, she returned to her own room in a huff.

I set on my desk baffled with my own feelings and debated with myself. Surely I couldn't be guilty of all the charges that Lynette had just flung at me. On too many unaccountable occasions I had tried to put words on paper. I did want to write to Gavin but no appropriate words would emerged from my confused brain. There was so much to say but I didn't know how to start and when to stop. The size of the paper was just too inadequate. Slowly, with a pen in hand I made a desperate attempt to compose a letter. No suitable words appeared on the paper instead I was drawing trees… one tree…two trees. Soon the paper was filled with all shapes and sizes of trees. On top of the trees were clouds, countless clouds floating in the sky. When I finished, I put the painting in the envelop and sealed it. When Gavin open the letter he would understand the meaning behind the picture. A painting could paint a thousand words. Clutching the envelope I returned to Lynette's room and sheepishly requested, "If it's not too much of an inconvenience, please give this to Gavin."

Stuffing the envelope into her bag Lynette demanded, "Is that all? Just a thin envelope?"

I replied, "The contents of the envelope is enough. By the way thank you, I do appreciate your good intention." Quietly I returned to my room and I sat on the floor. I leaned against the side of my bed and I put my hands behind my head. When I closed my eyes, Gavin's smiling image drifted into my mind's eye. I whispered to myself, "When will I see you again?"

Nine

When Gavin left for England I absolutely refused to see him off. It was just too final. I couldn't bear to see him walking through the departure gate, not knowing when I would see him again. But when Lynette and Cedric were leaving there was no way I could have talked myself out of going to the airport.

Although Lynette and I were as different as night and day in character; nevertheless, we were sisters. We would always be bonded together. I wouldn't say that we were close but I would nonetheless miss her when she finally left home. With a heavy heart I left with the family for the airport.

There must have been twenty of us heading for the airport and only two of us were leaving. I couldn't understand why people enjoyed going to the airport to see their friends or relatives off. I hated it, too much tears, too emotional! Everyone seemed to be talking and moving at the same time. I was caught in the middle of this mad whirlwind and not liking it at all.

After an interminable wait, Lynette and Cedric's luggage slowly disappeared on the conveyer belt behind the check in counter. Mother and Auntie Wei Fun were beyond themselves with grief and worries. Mother fussed. She reminded her daughter to behave. "Stay with Cedric.

Don't wander off independently, and call as soon as you have arrived."

Lynette and Cedric waved to us one last time before they disappeared through the departure gate while Mother and Auntie Wei Fun were dabbing their eyes trying to control their tears. No one wanted to leave the airport until the plane became a spark in the sky.

Auntie Wei Fun, not wanting to return to an empty home, invited our family for dinner. After a delicious meal which none of us had the appetite to enjoy, Auntie Wei Fun and Mother adjourned to the living room for coffee. I followed them while Alastair took off for a tennis game with Raymond. The two sisters made themselves comfortable on the settee and as usual I sat on the carpeted floor watching the two adults with wide eyes and trying to act grown up by joining in their conversation.

Auntie Wei Fun looked at me with a baffled expression and inquired, "Melanie, why do you always sit on the floor?"

I blinked then bashfully I replied, "When I sit on the settee my feet don't usually touch the floor, so instead of dangling my feet in mid air, I find it more comfortable on the floor."

Auntie Wei Fun chuckled, obviously finding my explanation amusing. Then, brusquely, she turned her attention to her younger sister and said, "Wei Ling, now that your financial responsibility is heavier it would be advisable for you to economize. The tenants I have upstairs have bought themselves a nice flat and will be vacating the premise at the end of the month. Why don't you put your flat on the market and move upstairs? I will charge you a minimal rent."

Mother creasing her brows faltered uncertainly, "I value your good intention, but I can't take advantage of your generosity."

Auntie Wei Fun fanned her hand in the air. Gruffly she replied, "How often do I have to drum into your proud head that we are a family. Now that Cedric has left, I am on my own most of the time. As for Ardelia, between her career as a solicitor and her social life I hardly have a chance to see her. I would love to tend to your children and the task would be so much simpler if you were living upstairs. By the way, without Lynette's constant pestering demand for your attention you really should spend more time with Edwin. Why can't you give an old lady a chance to pamper her niece and nephew?" Turning to me, Auntie Wei Fun pleaded for my support with her eyes.

I was exuberant with the offer. I would love to be near dearest Auntie Wei Fun. Both Alastair and I would be spoiled beyond description. It was a marvelous idea! I couldn't wait for Mother to accept the offer. Skeptical to Mother's reaction, in earnest I begged. "Mummy, I think it's a terrific idea. I agree with Auntie Wei Fun. You should start to consider your own happiness. Please try and spend more time with Uncle Edwin. He does deserve your undivided attention."

The offer was irresistible to Mother. So without too much persuasion, she finally conformed. It was decided that Mother would list her property on the market, as soon as possible, and the family would move into Auntie Wei Fun's empty flat in Happy Valley, over looking the Royal Hong Kong Jockey Club.

Drenched in sweat, I was ferociously clearing rubbish from my room. I had packed all my personal belongings into boxes and was ready for the movers to transport them to our new home. It was absolutely inconceivable how I could have managed to accumulate so much rubbish. With stubborn determination I derived energy and strength to put everything in order. I did not have the foggiest idea as to what to keep or what to discard. Struggling to make some positive decisions I started to make mental notes regarding priorities. Every little thing brought back memories of my days spent with Gavin. I wanted to cling on to all my bits and pieces as souvenirs. Eventually, being a sensible girl, I only kept the vital ones.

Hefty movers were moving one piece of furniture after another. Swiftly and systematically they were emptying the flat. I had mixed feelings about moving. I felt sadness about leaving the home where I spent my childhood, but then life had to move on. I was happy to be moving into a much larger flat providing me with a more spacious room. Clutching my "memories jar," my collection of records, and my record player, I moved into my new home.

While I was engaged with unpacking boxes and rearranging furniture, Ardelia paid me an unexpected visit. I was delighted to see her as she was my idol. I craved to be a career woman like her when I grew up. Ardelia was the perfect example. Like her I would one day possess a sports car and be escorted by different young men to rounds and rounds of parties—my social life would be colorful. My admiration for my cousin was unfeigned.

In her business-like yet friendly manner Ardelia said, "Now that we are neighbors, I insist that you visit my mother and me frequently. I have been neglecting all my cousins. I must amend my ways. Mum told me that you are a gifted singer. So am I. We will have to sing together." I was embarrassed by Ardelia's remark. We chatted for a short while, then she returned to her flat leaving me in utter bliss and promises of a brighter tomorrow. A chapter of my life had closed when Gavin departed, but now a brand new chapter was opening for me. I promised myself that I would no longer brood but try to live my life to its fullest.

Alastair and I were delighted with our new residence. The flat was enormous; our rooms were spacious. I was able to walk to school but Alastair of course missed Raymond's company. It was no longer convenient or possible for them to meet after school each day. But the weekends provided ample opportunities for their much enjoyed tennis game.

Lynette's letters arrived persistently and Mother missed her company. She was anxious over her eldest daughter. Peter proved into a responsible guardian. Soon after their arrival Cedric and Lynette were enrolled into different schools and they seemed to have settled into their new environment nicely. Lynette wrote home and complained about everything—lack of freedom, foul food and bad weather. It would be too uncharacteristic of her not to complain. I did miss her, although I was happy that I no longer had to endure her tantrums.

Gavin sent one postcard from England but I did not reply and he didn't write again. Slowly I managed to find peace of mind. Although Gavin constantly invaded my dreams, I was able to cope with the missing pieces of my life. Auntie Wei Fun was absolutely tremendous. I relished all the comforts that my aunt was lavishing on me.

Delighted with the new environment Mother was soon feeling extremely relaxed. She was able to spend more time with Uncle Edwin. The days drifted by amicably and harmoniously for the family. One day Mother and I were window-shopping Downtown and someone called us, "Wei Ling…."

Startled to see Auntie Pearl, Mother waved, "Hey, Pearl, what a coincidence?"

"Hello, Auntie Pearl, how is Uncle Joe?" I greeted Auntie Pearl politely.

Hugging me Auntie Pearl exclaimed, "I haven't seen you for a few months and yet you have grown taller. You are transforming into quiet a beauty! By the way, I received a letter from Gavin and he told me that Lynette's guardian has invited him and Raphael for Christmas."

"That was awfully thoughtful of Peter. Lynette must be happy to be able to spend Christmas with Raphael. Don't you just miss them?" Mother inquired.

"When the boys first left home, it was positively insufferable. The flat was so empty and quiet. The worst is over now." Turning to me Auntie Pearl chided, "Gavin was complaining that he hadn't heard from you at all?"

At the mention of Gavin's name I frowned. Stammering I answered, "I have been occupied with my homework. In any case I have never been a great communicator. Next time when you write please send my love and tell him no news is good news." Hesitantly I turned my attention toward the shop windows hoping that my threatened tears would not be visible.

Although my head was turned away, I could hear Mother confiding in her friend. "It's more than a year since Gavin's departure. Edwin and I were hoping that time would ease the pain for Melanie. But just the mere mention of Gavin's name still induces tears. Mind you, they were extremely close. I suppose it was more or less our fault to have encouraged the relationship. I never realized such deep feelings were involved."

The two friends chatted for a while finalizing the arrangement for their weekly Mah Jong game. Then Mother and I said good-bye to Auntie Pearl.

Returning from school one afternoon, although my stomach was yearning for food, I could not resist going into the living room because I could hear voices chatting in English. Mother ordinarily did not entertain in the afternoon definitely not foreigners. I was unduly inquisitive. When I entered the room, Mother invited me to join her guest. "Melanie, this is Gi Gi. She is from England, a visitor to Hong Kong. Gi Gi and Uncle Edwin were friends when he was getting his Law Degree in London."

I extended my hand to the stranger. The lady was definitely European. She spoke English with an accent. Very smartly dressed—her black leather outfit was something that one would see in a *Vogue* magazine. Her cosmetic was applied artfully; there was a mystic air about her. On her feet were knee length Christina Keeler boots; numerous gold bangles were jingling round her wrists. I was impressed with her appearance.

"Melanie, Melanie, Auntie Wei Fun has prepared your favorite red bean soup. You better help yourself before I finish the entire pot." I could hear Alastair shouting from the dining room.

I excused myself and joined Alastair. Spooning the sweet soup into my mouth, I inquired about the mysterious lady who was with Mother. "Who is that lady? I must say, she looks marvelous."

"She is one of Uncle Edwin's friends. Apparently she came to Hong Kong hoping to marry one of Uncle's associates but the gentleman concerned is engaged to be married. His parents do not entertain the idea of a foreign daughter-in-law, so Uncle Edwin is stuck with her. By the way, between you and me, I don't like her." Alastair waved his hand toward the living room while whispering to me in confidence.

Enviously I replied, "I rather admire her smartness!" Then I held my head with both hands. Elbows resting on the dining table, I confessed, "I tend to agree with you, I don't think that I can trust her. Anyway she is only visiting town. Let's be courteous."

That same evening, after dinner, unexpectedly Ardelia came to our home. She found us chatting in the living room. She flopped on the settee and without mincing her words, she spoke quite openly to Mother, "Try to prevent Uncle Edwin from spending too much time with Gi Gi."

Mother was grateful to Ardelia and she shrugged her shoulders and replied, "Thank you for your advice, I do appreciate your thoughtfulness, but they are just good friends. The relationship shouldn't be too harmful."

Ardelia curled her feet on the settee and gruffly countered, "I have heard rumors to the contrary. I may be over reacting but preventions are always better then cures."

Mother changed the subject abruptly. Soon aunt and niece harped onto other subjects.

We were old enough to attend school unescorted; therefore, Mother hardly joined us at the breakfast table. Alastair was munching a piece of toast and started to gossip. "Are you aware that Mummy has not seen Uncle Edwin for three days? It's unusual for Mummy to play Mah Jong continuously for three evenings. I can smell trouble."

Stirring my cup of coffee I reprimanded my brother, "Uncle Edwin is obviously involved with complicated cases, so what is the big deal? Try not to make a mountain out of a mole hill."

Stuffing the last bit of toast into his mouth Alastair retaliated, "Uncle Edwin's chauffeur told Ah Ying that Uncle Edwin has been spending most of his free time with Gi Gi. She even accompanies him to court and every day she waits for him in his office."

Glaring at Alastair venomously I warned, "Oh, do keep your evil thoughts to yourself. I take the servants' gossip with a grain of salt. Please don't be a trouble-maker. It's advisable for us to keep our noses clean."

That evening Alastair and I had dinner with Auntie Wei Fun before we returned to our residence. Mother was out so we decided to do our homework together. I stayed in Alastair's room until it was time for bed. I heard the front door opening when I emerged from my brother's room. I could hear Mother whispering to Uncle Edwin so I disappeared into my room but before I could close the door I heard part of their conversation.

It was Mother's voice, "Edwin, I hate to be a nag, but is it absolutely necessary to be in the company of Gi Gi all the time? Doesn't she have other friends who could entertain her? This town is just too small for a scandal. People are already wagging their tongues. In any case, why can't I join you when you are entertaining Gi Gi?"

I could hear Uncle Edwin's defense. "Wei Ling, do be reasonable. Gi Gi is a stranger in town. Why is it so wrong for me to be hospitable? We have not been including you in our outings because your English is not too fluent. Gi Gi cannot comprehend our language and it would be too much of a strain for me to take up the role as an interpreter constantly. She should be leaving town soon." They obviously moved into Mother's room because their voices were no longer audible to me, but their conversation troubled my sleep that night.

Another month drifted by but Gi Gi was still in town. Tension was building up between Mother and Uncle Edwin. I began to despise the presence of the unwelcome woman. The intruder was the cause of Mother's grief and sorrows. Sometimes when sleep escaped me at night Mother's sobbing was slightly audible. I wished that I could erase away my mother's pain. If only the horrible Gi Gi would disappear. Lately, Uncle Edwin seldom visited our home and on the few occasions when he did, they would ultimately end the evening arguing.

One afternoon Alastair and I were enjoying our afternoon tea with Auntie Wei Fun. Mother was playing Mah Jong with Auntie Pearl. Unexpectedly Ardelia returned home early. It always pleased her to see us enjoying her mother's cooking. Nibbling the food Ardelia confided in her mother. "You know that Gi Gi is beginning to be a nuisance. I predicted disaster when she arrived into town. I hate to elaborate on the situation but her sole intention is to grab a husband and a rich one at that! I am afraid Uncle Edwin is the perfect victim. Mind you, I fail to understand his mentality. I haven't the foggiest idea what he could possibly see in that woman. The perfect gold digger and social climber. I wish Auntie Wei Ling would retaliate."

Mournfully I nodded my head and agreed with my cousin. I turned to Auntie Wei Fun and pleaded, "Auntie isn't there something that we can do?"

"Put a contract out to murder her!" Alastair banged his books on the table and growled.

"Alastair, you have been reading too many Kung Fu books—fancy killing people! Honestly!" Auntie Wei Fun wagged her fingers at her nephew. "I am afraid Wei Ling is in a dilemma! Gi Gi represents a breath of fresh air to Edwin. Her youth adds sparkle to his life. He is on an ego trip. I have no doubt that his feeling for your mother goes deep. Your mother on the other hand is a very proud person. She feels inadequate—being a widow with three children she reckons that she is not good enough for Edwin."

Alastair shot out of his chair and screamed indignantly, "I will be damned! That Gi Gi is so shallow. She purrs like a cat. She is catty too—cold and unapproachable. Mind you, she sure knows how to play up to Uncle Edwin. I could strangle her with my bare hands."

Wei Fun lovingly patted Alastair's head and chuckled, "There you go again. Learn to use your brains—not violence. Edwin will have to make a decision soon. This situation can't drag on indefinitely. It's inevitable that either Gi Gi or your mother will give him an ultimatum soon."

We heard Mother's voice. "I knew I could find the two of you here." Mother took a seat while I poured her a cup of coffee.

Alastair gave Mother a kiss and demanded, "Did you win?"

"Is that all you can think about—monetary monster?" I chastened my brother and pulled him back onto his chair.

Mother took a sip of the coffee then cleared her throat. Purposefully she declared, "I am glad that you are all here, I wanted to discuss something with you. I guess it has been apparent that Edwin and I are experiencing some difficulties. I have been doing an awful lot of thinking…" the family waited impatiently for her to continue, "Lynette has been writing home complaining as usual and I do miss her."

Auntie Wei Fun put more food on Alastair's plate then she interrupted, "Lynette's complaints are the least of your worries. Cedric criticizes but I just keep a deaf ear. What about Gi Gi's situation—any conclusion?"

Mother took a deep breath and revealed her intention. "Alastair and Melanie are getting to the age when I should consider sending them away. Nevertheless, I don't trust letting them go alone. Now that Edwin and I are caught in a stalemate situation, I think it's time that I should consider my family's future. Edwin is certainly very attracted to Gi Gi, and I am sure he finds her quite irresistible." I could detect the bitterness in Mother's tone.

Ardelia couldn't hold her tongue and cuttingly she remarked, "Uncle Edwin is an utter fool! I guess there is no fool like an old fool."

Defending Uncle Edwin Mother continued, "Don't be too harsh on Edwin. He needs time to find himself and so do I. Sometimes even love needs a holiday; therefore, I have been toying with an idea. For a while Edwin and I should stop seeing each other but Hong Kong is too small a place to hide. No doubt we will bump into each other constantly and it would defeat the purpose."

We all held our breath and waited for Mother's next sentence. "I have come to the conclusion that I miss Lynette and since these two younger ones are ready to be sent abroad to further their studies, I am thinking of consolidating all my savings and moving the entire family to England."

Everyone was stunned. Auntie Wei Fun was the first to regain her composure, "Have you told Edwin of your decision?"

Gloomily, Mother replied, "We are having dinner together, just the two of us. I will put all my cards on the table. I cannot tolerate his indecision and I have no desire to play a part in the "eternal triangle." It's absurd of him to think that he can eat the cake and keep it too. It's absolutely out of the question for him to keep the both of us."

The next morning, the family congregated in Auntie Wei Fun's dining room for breakfast and Mother gave us a detailed account of the discussion she had with Uncle Edwin the previous evening.

Mother broke the silence, "I guess you know that I wanted to talk to you...."

"I suppose so." Edwin confessed with earnest sincerity. "I guess I have been evading reality but before you continue there is something that I would like you to remember. I do love you, I have loved you since the first day I met you. For some unknown reason lately I find myself in a predicament and I need time to find myself again!"

Patting Edwin's hand Wei Ling shrugged her shoulders. She wished she could sympathize with him but anger clouded her mind and jealousy blinded her natural judgment. "I have decided to move the entire family to England." Dropping the bombshell she did not pause for Edwin's reaction, "Both of us need time. We have grown too accustomed to each other. Our love requires a period of interlude and this is the best opportunity. When I am gone, you will have time to reconsider our future."

Reluctantly Edwin agreed, "When I am in the company of Gi Gi I yearn for you, but when I am with you, her image clouds my mind. Wei Ling, try to understand my dilemma."

Wei Ling was hurt because of his weakness so she blurted, "Edwin, I will not even try to comprehend your feelings. When I love a person, my attention is never divided. We have been together for such a long time I am not willing to allow our relationship to go to waste. I am giving us more time to reconsider. Who knows, when I am no longer a part of your life, you may realize the significance of our relationship. I am not leaving your life for good. I will only be a plane's journey away, but life is just too short for indecision."

When Mother finished her narration, there were tears in her eyes. None of us could utter a word. It was obvious that Mother had made her decision and I was the first to support her. I was excited but distressed. I would miss Hong Kong my hometown. Nevertheless, the desire to reside in another country was overwhelming. I was in turmoil. Eventually I decided to be positive and refused to think on the negative side. I wanted urgently to help Mother. If a new environment would provide peace of mind for her then there was no turning back. We would make England our home for the next couple of years.

After school instead of returning straight home I made a detour. Soon I arrived at my grandparents' residence. Their house was in the Mid-Level, surrounded by a beautifully landscaped garden. I loved the garden. Endless beds of flowers blossomed in the summer. A fish pond was situated in the middle of the enormous, carefully manicured lawn. There was a Chinese gazebo built with green and red tiles. This Oriental fixture added extra charm to the garden. My grandparents loved animals and the dogs ran about freely. Whenever I visited them in the summer, I would sit in the gazebo and chat with them, breathing in the clean air.

When I rang the bell, I could hear the dogs barking behind the gate. When the gate was opened I played with the dogs for a while before I was escorted into the house. When I reached the family room, I found Grandma resting peacefully with her cat purring on her lap and Grandpa busily flipping the pages of the Kung Fu novel that he was reading. A slight glow appeared in his pipe each time he took a puff. Respectfully I greeted them with a slight bow of my head. Accepting a cup of tea from the servant, I inquired about their health. "Grandma, how is your cough? I hope you are still taking your medication." Turning my attention to

Grandpa, I teased, "Grandpa, I see you are still indulging in all your Kung Fu books. Try not to strain your eye sight." We chatted amicably for a while then I drew their attention to the purpose of my visit.

I held my grandma's hand and scanned her lined face. She must have been quite stunning when she was young. She still held herself gracefully. "Grandma, do you think Alastair and I are old enough to follow Lynette? I mean going to England to further our education."

Grandpa tapped his pipe on the ashtray and replied gruffly, "The thought has crossed our minds but your Mother is too stubborn to discuss this issue with us."

While stroking the cat on her lap Grandma intervened. "Don't you think you are too young to be granted such independence?"

Grandpa snorted and took another puff from the pipe, "Not if their Mother would accompany them."

Instantly I jumped to the opportunity, "What if Mummy should reside in England with us?"

Grandma leaned back on the cushion and sighed, "That would be excellent, but Wei Ling would never uproot herself—only wishful thinking!"

Excitedly I blurted, "She has decided to move the entire family to England. She is going to remove Lynette from the boarding school and we will all be attending the local private schools as day scholars. Boarding schools will be too much of a financial burden for my mother."

Narrowing his eyes, Grandpa grunted, "Money shouldn't create a problem. Our family can well afford to send you all to the appropriate schools."

Nervously I twirled my pony tail with my fingers. Frowning, I replied, "Mummy is too proud to beg for assistance."

I provided the perfect opportunity for Grandma to complain, "Pride has always been your mother's problem. Please tell her that although she is too proud to ask for our support, we, nevertheless, are insisting that we should be responsible for all your school fees. We will remit the money directly to the school. Make certain that you are put in the best school, especially Alastair—he is our only grandson."

I was exhilarated when I arrived home. I was also anxious that Mother might condemn me for my behavior. After dinner, I invited Mother into my room and insisted that she make herself comfortable on my bed while I sat on the floor. Timidly, I said, "Mummy, I need to talk to you…." Drumming my fingers nervously on the floor, I continued to confess, "I visited Grandma and Grandma today." I paused waiting for my mother's reproach, instead, she smiled at me understandingly and stroked my face fondly.

"Melanie, I am really not that naive. I am aware of the fact that secretly you do occasionally visit your grandparents and I am proud of you. The antagonism that exists is between your grandparents and myself. This rift should not involve the next generation."

Taken aback by Mother's understanding attitude, staggering, I continued, "I informed them of our decision to move to England. They were happy for us but they insisted that we be sent to the best schools and they were also persistent about being responsible for the financing of the school fees."

Mother watched my face and pensively she said, "Melanie you never fail to astound me. How old are you? How can you be capable of such thoughtfulness at your tender age? I never thought of letting them know of our decision. However, I am more than pleased with your grandparents' decision. I will not permit my pride to deprive you of the best. A good education is all that I can offer you. With a solid education behind you, you will never starve."

When Mother made a decision, she would not waste time to follow it through. Soon all our furniture was put into storage. Boxes and boxes of household goods were removed away by the movers. Once again I was packing. There was so much to attend to. Each night I was too exhausted for idle thoughts. As soon as my head hit the pillow I would immediately fall into a deep slumber.

I felt that my knowledge for the English language was definitely inadequate. There was too much for me to master in so short a period of time. I had a terrific appetite for knowledge. I was like a giant with an enormous stomach gobbling down any food that was visible. There was no end to my questions and when I couldn't find the answers from books that I read, I would ask. My brain was bursting with queries.

Ten

Mother's organization baffled me—how did she manage to move the entire family to England with such efficiency and where did she find all the energy? Her determination was admirable. I considered it a miracle that she did not suffer from a nervous breakdown. I guess the only sensible way for Mother to cope with the pain of leaving Uncle Edwin would be to keep herself utterly and entirely occupied—hardly giving herself a spare minute to ponder over her actions.

I was only allowed to bring with me on the plane all that I needed to settle into my new home. I was wracked with sorrow when I had to discard most of my souvenirs. I wrapped my Memory Jar with a blouse and stuffed it among my clothing. There was no way I would have parted with this precious gift from Gavin. While I was attending to my last minute packing I couldn't resist dashing into Mother's room and imploring, "Please Mummy let me bring my collection of records with me and also my record player. I really cannot live without them. Please, please...."

Mother was flustering around like a headless chicken. There was so much that awaited her attention. Her thoughts were consistently tormented and constantly she wondered if she had indeed made the right decision. Curtly she said to me, "Only if you are willing to carry them yourself. I have enough on my hands. Please don't trouble me with these trivial details."

Once again we found ourselves in the airport. Except this time I was leaving instead of seeing someone off. Passengers were continuously arriving and leaving. Uncle Edwin was awfully subdued. I guessed he was terribly upset with the fact that we were finally departing. Auntie Wei Fun was beyond herself with grief. I couldn't bear to watch her dejected expression. It was with great difficulty that I managed to kiss and hug her without bawling my eyes out. Alastair was very well behaved, for a change. Uncle Edwin folded Mother into his arms and wished her God speed. What more was there to say? Amid all the hustle and bustle the stewardess announced the departure of our BOAC flight that would transport us to England. Mother and myself, with Alastair tagging along, frantically waved farewell to our relatives and friends. Slowly and sadly we moved through the departure gate. Amidst a tremendous amount of confusion and tears we embarked on our journey to another country to begin a new life.

I sighed deeply when we finally settled into our appointed seats on the plane. Immediately, Mother seemed to relax and she closed her eyes restfully. No doubt she was absolutely and positively exhausted. She needed a moment of peace to gather herself together. As expected Alastair retrieved his comics and magazines from his bag and soon he was engrossed in all his reading materials. Eventually, he dozed off to sleep. Nothing ever troubled Alastair. As long as he was fed and was not deprived of his tennis games his world was at peace. He took almost everything with a pinch of salt.

It was fortunate that I occupied the window seat. I loved gazing out of the window and fantasizing. The engine exhilarated and roared into life. The giant silver bird was gaining tremendous speed toward the ocean and threading through all the tall concrete buildings. The plane was airborne and the island of Hong Kong became a dot in the ocean.

My dream of transforming into a cloud was more or less materialized. I was, in a way, floating in the sky but regrettably only toward one direction. I was leaving my beloved hometown and traveling with immense speed to another country. Amidst my fanciful thoughts I must have dozed off. Suddenly I was awakened by the announcement of our arrival at the Bangkok Airport in Thailand. We were on transit for an hour while the plane was being serviced and refueled. My legs were cramped and I was grateful for a chance to stretch my tired limbs. With Mother and Alastair together we followed our fellow travelers into the airport transit lounge. The air-conditioning was heavenly bliss cooling our hot and tired bodies. Somehow the cool air revived my spirit. Automatically I was gazing around the lounge with fascination. Filled with enthusiasm I dragged Mother with me and together we visited every shop in the lounge. I was terribly impressed with the display of silver goods. I admired all the sparkling jewelry with desire. Ultimately I decided that the identity bracelet that was given to me by Gavin so many Christmases ago was still the best. I would never trade it for all the silver from Thailand.

After an hour we once again boarded the plane. This part of the journey proved to be quite lengthy. After we were air borne for half an hour, a hot meal was served. I was intrigued with all the small trays that contained a three-course meal. Where was the kitchen? How was the food kept hot and where did the stewardesses make the tea and coffee? I was bursting with curiosity. When the food was consumed and the empty trays cleared away the activities on the flight ceased considerately. The lights were dimmed and our fellow passengers rested. I decided to explore the enormous plane. With curiosity I wandered along the aisle aimlessly and inquisitively I peeped behind every curtain. The restrooms were so small and yet so fully equipped. Tiny bottles of handcream and lotion were displayed on the small organized shelves. Little pieces of soap were wrapped individually for hygienic purposes. I was impressed.

I craved to talk to other passengers but was too shy, so when I had completed my unguided tour of the plane I decided to return to my seat. While gazing out of the window, an image of Gavin appeared among the cloud. He was waving and smiling at me. He had fulfilled his promise to me and our paths were soon to be crossed again. Would he be delighted to see me? Had his appearance altered at all? I realized that I had changed because lately I had been complimented repeatedly on my good looks. Was Gavin still fond of me? Would our relationship stay intact? Were we still friends? My thoughts were a tangled mess and I wanted so many answers to all my questions. Obstinately I was determined to revive our friendship if necessary.

While I was still day dreaming the plane landed at Frankfurt Airport, our last port of transit. Mother was asleep and was quite motionless. Alastair insisted on disembarking but I refused to wake Mother. She obviously needed the rest badly after almost killing herself with exhaustion attending to all demanding details prior to our departure. Sulking, Alastair returned to his seat while I flipped through my English book. I made a desperate attempt to memorize all the English words that were relevant to my limited English vocabulary. Mother's English was far from fluent. She would have to depend on me when we arrive in London. I was beginning to panic. My heart was beating so fast that I was beginning to feel nauseated. Although I was educated in an English school in Hong Kong and most subjects were taught in English my command of the language had room for improvements. I could read with no difficulty but my spoken English needed to be vastly improved and polished.

I said a silent prayer. "Dear God, please assist me when I have to converse with the Immigration and Custom officers. Please don't allow me to disgrace my mother. I wouldn't know how to handle such an embarrassing situation." I was so absorbed with my own anxious thoughts that I hardly noticed the bump when the plane landed at London Heathrow Airport. Almost shaking with apprehension I followed the other passengers and disembarked. Nervously I clung on to Mother for protection. When I eventually walked into the airport, gratefully all my anxiety evaporated. Instead I was impressed by the enormous airport. Never in my wildest dreams could I imagine such a massive building with so many activities. If I had thought the Hong Kong airport was congested it was nothing compared to this. I had never seen so many foreign faces and did not hear a word of Cantonese. I had never been exposed to so many English speaking people. The English were courteous, polite and perfectly mannered. No one was pushing or fighting. Joining the long line of passengers, we waited patiently for our turn to be interviewed by the Immigration Officer.

I was amazed and proud of myself. Eloquently I answered all the questions asked by the Immigration officer. The gentleman was kind and supportive. Instead of bombarding me with interrogation he was full of encouragement. The Custom Officers were just as pleasantly friendly and cooperative. They just waved the family through hardly noticing our luggage. With a big sigh of relief we struggled with our suitcases and moved onto the meeting lounge.

Among the sea of people I tried to find Lynette and Cedric. Lynette was the first person that caught my attention. She was frantically waving and trying to attract our attention. Mother was delighted to see Lynette. She dropped all the suitcases and rushed into her daughter's welcoming arms. Cedric pushed through the crowd and plastered his aunt with kisses. Standing from a distance was a gentleman of around thirty years of age and a bit on the plump side. He was grinning happily at the new arrivals. Mother dislodged herself from Lynette's embrace and beckoned the awaiting gentleman to join us.

"Peter, Peter, you have no idea how pleased I am to see you!" Mother was drying the tears on her face. Then pointing toward myself and Alastair she made the introduction. "This is Peter, my dear, dear friend. Lynette's guardian!"

Shyly I extended my hand and whispered a timid hello. Alastair grinned and greeted Peter enthusiastically. "Hi, I have heard so much about you. I bet Cedric and Lynette have provided you with enough harassment to last a life time!"

Cedric punched Alastair on the shoulder and then they embraced each other. Then Cedric pulled me into his arms and kissed me fondly. Together we gathered all the suitcases and moved toward the carpark. All the while chatting and exchanging news. I scanned the strange surroundings with amazement and curiosity.

Peter's car was too small to accommodate all the passengers and suitcases so it was decided that Cedric should accompany me and Alastair to find our own way home by taxi. Instantly I fell in love with the English taxis. To me they looked like toy cars. When all the suitcases were loaded into the trunk Cedric and Alastair occupied the passenger's seat in the taxi. I pulled the seat from the panel that divided the front of the vehicle from the passengers' seat and sat facing the two boys.

It was a new sensation to be traveling backwards and I wanted to open the window that separated us from the taxi driver. The vehicle soon pulled out of the airport and was speeding along the wet and slippery streets of London in a slight drizzle. The sky was oppressive with gray clouds and the weather was far from impressive. Nevertheless, I was overwhelmed by the fast-moving scenery. We drove past dozens and dozens of quaint little houses with well-attended gardens. Even in the midst of February, different color roses were in full bloom. The greenery took my breath away. Cedric and Alastair chatted endlessly, but their prattle was hardly audible to my ears as I was so mesmerized by the new environment and I fell under the spell of London immediately. I promised myself that I would soon get to know this new city like the back of my hand.

When the car drove past Buckingham Palace, my eyes nearly popped out from their sockets. I stared unblinkingly at the impressive palace. I had read about this amazing royal residence but to actually see it with my own eyes was an experience! The guards with their red and black uniforms guarding the palace gate looked like toy soldiers. I thought I had prepared myself with reading numerous books about London, but the books could not have described all the scenes to their perfection. I glared until the vehicle came to a standstill.

When we arrived at our destination the two boys unloaded the luggage and Cedric led the way to our new home. We walked through a short corridor that led into a good size living and dining room. The floor was fully carpeted. A big and comfortable settee was put against the wall on one side of the room with a coffee table placed in front of the settee. What caught my immediate attention was a fire place in the middle of the room with the chimney extended to the high ceiling. On the other side of the fireplace was a dining table and a few matching chairs. The carpet was a creamy beige color while the furniture was dark brown. The combination of the two colors added smartness to the room. Although the room was not luxurious it was, nevertheless, very comfortable. Immediately to the left of the dining room was the kitchen—sparkling clean and modernly equipped. Adjacent to the kitchen was the family room which opened to a garden through a pair of French doors. To the right of the living room were a few steps that led to the second floor of the house. There were five bedrooms—more than adequate for all the members of our family with a room to spare for guests. I snooped into every room marveling at their sizes and inquisitively opened all the cupboards and wardrobes. I was beyond myself with happiness. I had my own garden. I was already visualizing all the flowers that I would plant in the garden. Being a city girl I knew nothing about gardening, but I would soon learn.

After examining all the rooms on the second floor, I bounced into the living room again while Lynette was screaming for Mother to unpack our suitcases. Lynette wanted her presents. There was something for everyone. Suddenly Mother turned to Peter and inquired, "Will Raphael and Gavin be visiting later?"

I held my breath while Peter made himself comfortable on the settee before he replied, "They are usually not allowed to spend their weekends out of school. But this being a special occasion, they have applied for special passes. They will join us for dinner. I have reserved a table at Spring Garden tonight. Save the trouble of cooking at home."

"Is that your restaurant?" Mother inquired.

Peter nodded his head and Mother thanked him for his thoughtfulness then disappeared into Lynette's room while Peter turned on the television and was soon watching his favorite programs. Cedric disappeared into Alastair's room as there was so much catching up to do. I was happy to be left to my own devices.

I took my two suitcases into my bedroom and endeavored to unpack. Suddenly exhaustion invaded my tired limbs. I decided positively to leave my unpacking till later. Retrieving my dressing gown from one of the suitcases I indulged myself with a long leisure shower and washed my limp hair. When I returned to my room, my weary eyes refused to focus. With damp hair I curled into my comfortable bed. After such an interminable journey to be able to lie down on a proper bed was heavenly. Presently the voices from the next room faded and I fell into a much needed sleep.

When I opened my eyes again, the room had turned dark. For a moment I lost my sense of bearing and couldn't remember where I was. My mind was in a daze. When I heard someone knocking on my door, my disorderly mind began to untangle. Mother said, "Melanie, its time for you to wake up, we have to leave for the restaurant soon."

Immediately Mother's words brought my wondering mind back to the present and I jumped out of bed. All the fatigue that I felt earlier had deserted me and instead I felt excitement churning in my stomach. Frantically, I toppled my suitcases on the bed because I needed to search for the perfect attire for the evening. I would be seeing Gavin soon.

I stood in front of the mirror brushing my long hair and slowly my limp hair returned to life—the thick curly hair was shining again. The weather was cold enough so that I could allow my hair to cascade loosely onto my shoulder. Fastening a belt around my small waist, I was satisfied with my own reflection in the mirror. Lynette barged into my room unannounced. "Melanie, please do the back buttons for me?"

While attending to my sister's buttons, I couldn't help but admire my sister. She had matured. A touch of cosmetic was applied artfully on her face, which contributed to her attractiveness. Her choice of clothing was a great improvement, fashionable and tasteful. Her appearance reminded me of the models from fashion magazines. Enviously, I complimented her, "you look so smart! I do love your smart outfit."

Kissing me affectionately Lynette replied, "Before long you will be just as fashionable. It's sure nice to have you around again. I have missed you!"

Harassing Lynette I teased, "Have you been missing me or my services?"

Disappearing from my room Lynette laughingly chanted, "Both!"

When everyone was ready to depart for the restaurant the entire family crammed into Peter's car. Peter on the driver's seat with Mother and Lynette sitting next to him. The three of us were squeezed into the back seat. Being stuck between Cedric and Alastair, it was practically impossible for me to get a proper view of the streets. But I wasn't complaining. There would be plenty of time to visit the streets of London at a later date. In a way, I couldn't concentrate on the sights anyway.

Butterflies were fluttering in my stomach and I couldn't wait to see Gavin again.

Eleven

We were approaching the China Town of London. The streets were dirty and garbage littered the pavements. Most of the shops had Chinese names and Orientals were seen sauntering along the sidewalks. Peter parked the car on a back street and gestured toward a side door.

We proceeded along a short corridor and a door led us to the side entrance of the Spring Garden Restaurant. I was enchanted by the atmosphere of Peter's restaurant. It was unlike all the crowded Chinese restaurants in Hong Kong where all the tables were squashed together. The spacious room was scattered sparingly with small tables which accommodated two guests or more but not more than six. Centered on each table was a pretty arrangement of flowers with one candle glimmering in the dimmed room. Shadows flickering from all the burning candles added a utopian flavor to the atmosphere. Smiling, a waitress politely escorted us to another part of the restaurant. In the center of the room was placed a big round table with settings for eight people. An arrangement of roses was the center piece on the table. On one side of the room was a bar displaying various kinds of drinks ready to be served. Soft music soothingly drifted into my ears. The atmosphere of the room was enchantingly romantic and I loved it. Peter explained that this room was for big private parties.

Soon after we took our seats around the dining table, footsteps were heard running along the corridor, then the door was pushed opened and Raphael bounced into the room. Immediately he rushed into Mother's open arms and welcomed her affectionately, "You have not aged at all, still my gorgeous aunt!"

Mother shook her head and smilingly returned the compliment, "Still the perfect gentlemen with the ability to charm birds off a tree!"

Raphael kissed Lynette, then shook Alastair's hand vigorously. Turning his gaze to me he whistled and flirted with me. "You have turned into a ravishing beauty. If I wasn't involved with your sister I would be the next in line to pursue you."

I blushed and kissed him timidly on the cheek. Then I turned toward the door and waited breathlessly with great expectation. Presently Gavin walked through the door. He welcomed Mother in his quiet and gentle way and courteously greeted everyone in the room. Slowly he approached me and I stood motionless as I watched him moving toward me. Suddenly the entire room faded except for Gavin's handsome face. My vision began to blur with threatened tears. He was a dashing young man. He had grown taller but managed to maintain his slimness. His luminous dark eyes burned into my soul. Time was at a standstill for the both of us. He scrutinized me from head to toe. With a startled expression he walked toward me and sighed, "I have always remembered you to be beautiful in a childish sort of way. But now standing in front of me is a lovely matured young lady." He opened his arms to embrace me and I melted into his arms. Whispering in my ears he declared, "I have kept my promise. We are together again!" These few simple words washed away all the pain and bitterness that I had endured during the past few years.

During dinner Gavin sat next to me constantly attentive to all my needs. There was hardly a moment when there was no food on my plate. When my glass was empty, it was instantly refilled. I was spoiled all over again. I found it difficult to follow the chit-chat surrounding me. I was conscious of only Gavin's intense gaze upon my face. I was so delighted to see him that words eluded me. If he didn't know me better, he must have thought that I was pretty dumb.

Vaguely I heard Mother commenting on the food. "Peter I must say I am surprised with the standard of Chinese food in your restaurant. It is not bad at all."

Peter picked a piece of stir fried beef with his chopsticks and put it on Mother's plate. "Try this beef—specialty of the house. It is very popular with the English. The ginger and the pineapple fried with beef goes well with rice. I am fortunate to have found a good cook. He only recently immigrated from Hong Kong."

When dinner was over Peter invited Gavin and Raphael to spend the weekend with him but Mother insisted that Cedric and the two boys should be her guests for the weekend. The house was spacious enough to accommodate everyone. Cedric and Gavin took it upon themselves to escort me and Alastair home in a taxi so that the remaining party could travel home in comfort. After a delicious meal I was feeling exhausted again so I dozed in the taxi while my three companions chatted. When we arrived home, vaguely I recalled Gavin steering me into my room and soon I was tucked into bed. That night I dreamed of the park in Hong Kong and in my dreams I was sitting with Gavin counting stars again.

The following morning bright sunlight shone into my room but I was too lazy and too relaxed to open my eyes. The fragrance of fresh roses drifted into my nostrils and the petals of roses tickled my soft skin. Dreamily I blinked and saw Gavin kneeling by the side of my bed touching my face with a white rose and whispering into my ears, "Wake up sleeping beauty or you will sleep the day away."

I blinked again and stretched before I replied, "It wouldn't be such a bad idea!" Instantly my mind became alert and I jumped out of bed and rushed into the garden. Gavin chased after me with my dressing gown and shouted, "This is not Hong Kong. It is cold outside. You must remember to put on your dressing gown when you leave the warmth of your bed."

Wrapping the warm dressing gown around my cold shoulders, Gavin and I walked around the garden. I was admiring all the roses that were in full bloom. I remarked, "The roses are so beautiful. Did they come with the house or did Lynette plant them? One would hardly see roses like these in Hong Kong but then we didn't have gardens."

Gavin laughed while selecting a rose and stuck it behind my ears. "Are you kidding? Your sister hasn't the slightest inkling about gardening?"

Suddenly my stomach was growling. The aroma of delicious food aroused my appetite. "Who is cooking breakfast?"

"Cedric and Raphael have appointed themselves as chefs. Auntie Wei Ling, Lynette and Alastair made an early start for the super market. There is plenty of food, but if you don't hurry there might not be a scrap of food left for you." Gavin pushed me toward the bathroom.

When I was done with my toilette, I hurried into my room. I pulled a jumper over my head then dragged a hairbrush through my hair and stepped into my jeans. When I returned to the kitchen, I hungrily helped myself to a plateful of delicious scrambled eggs, sausages, bacon and toast.

"For someone your size you certainly have the capacity to retain a lot of food!" Raphael pulled my hair and teased me affectionately.

It didn't take me long to finish all the food on my plate and pushing the last bit of crumb into my mouth I asked, "Who is going to wash the dirty dishes? Goodness, we don't have Ah Ying with us anymore and Mummy is hopeless with domestic chores."

Stacking the dirty dishes and soaking them in the sink Gavin replied, "We just all have to chip in with our share of housework. I hope you realize you have plenty of adjustments to make."

Screwing my nose and pulling a long face I exclaimed, "But I don't have a clue or the foggiest idea of what I am supposed to do!"

"Cedric and Raphael did the cooking; therefore, it is our duty to do the dishes. Finish your food then I will show you how to wash the dishes and clean up the mess in the kitchen. Also I will demonstrate to you the skill of making a bed." Gavin said to me while rolling up the sleeves of his shirt.

Expertly Gavin explained the procedure of washing dirty dishes and cutlery. He washed all the dirty plates and cutlery, then he scrubbed the frying pans. Clean dishes were put away and the counters wiped dry. Soon the kitchen was sparkling clean again while I dried my wet hands on the hand towel. Then Gavin returned to my room and showed me how to make the bed. Within a short period of time my room was impeccable. Then we went to the living room. He started to fluff all the cushions and wiped the coffee table. I watched with fascination. I hadn't realized how domesticated Gavin was until then. The living room was in shipshape condition in no time at all. Later I was taught how to operate the washing machine and the dryer. When all the laundry was done Gavin even taught me how to do the ironing. The two of us spent the entire morning attending to all the housework. To my utter amazement I found myself enjoying the housework. I obviously had hidden talents that had not been discovered. I was determined to relieve Mother of all the trivial details of household chores. Later Lynette was delighted that I showed so much enthusiasm on the domestic side of things. She decided that I would make a much better maid than she would, and I was the designated person to attend to all the housework.

Overcome with the joy of seeing Gavin and sharing his company again I floated on air all day. The weekend fled by too swiftly for me. On Sunday evening, soon after an early dinner Raphael and Gavin returned to their boarding school.

Mother enrolled Lynette into the local private school. Frantically, with Peter's assistance, she investigated into all the possibilities of finding Alastair and myself appropriate schools. Her ambition was for us to resume schooling after the Easter Holiday. At the same time she was anxious to purchase a house so that we would feel more settled.

After numerous debates and arguments it was decided that it would be best for me and Alastair to continue our education in boarding schools. To my utter horror and disgust I was told that I would soon have a taste of boarding school life in a girls' boarding school in a small town in Cambridge. Alastair would travel to Sommerset to enlist into one of the top schools of the time. No wonder the school fee was atrocious!

When the problem of schooling was finally resolved, Mother devoted her days to house hunting. She met with difficulties. Either the houses were too small to accommodate the entire family or the price was too high. Shortly she became depressed and began to panic. In the midst of her apprehension Peter managed to discover a few houses that might be suitable.

Everyone had their own opinion of their dream house. After endless arguments and conflicting opinions, Mother decided on an older house. It was situated in Highgate, the northern part of London with the Underground station at close vicinity—therefore resolving the problem of transport. The house, although old, needed minimal renovations and decorations. The rooms were airy and spacious. Each member of the family was fortunate to have the privacy of their own room. There were two extra rooms for guests. The living room had a real fire place for burning logs and I adored it. Fancy having a blazing fire warming the room, absolutely fantastic. The kitchen was a good size room and modern. The garden was somewhat neglected but I was enthralled with the opportunity to attend to the garden. I wanted to learn all about gardening. There was just so much for me to grasp but I was confident of my own competence.

When all the legal documents were executed, the purchasing of the house was completed. Mother was relieved that there was enough money left to furnish the house. Shortly when all the necessary furniture was purchased and delivered, excitedly we moved into our new home. The kitchen was equipped with all the modern appliances and I was content. I intended to make full use of this part of the house. Hopefully the kitchen would eventually become my domain.

We decided to use the same colors from our flat in Hong Kong—black and white. We bought, more or less the same type of furniture. The settee and the two single chairs were upholstered with a back and white fabric. I made sure that all the black cushions were fluffed whenever I tidied the living room—they definitely added comfort to the settee. Every so often, I picked a bunch of white roses and arranged them in a black vase. I thought the black vase looked smart on the white coffee table. The white curtain billowed softly with the wind when the windows were opened which was seldom. We were still not accustomed to the cold and wet English winter. Most of the time we had our meals in the kitchen which was a blessing. It would have been difficult to keep the white dining table clean all the time. The black cushions on the dining chairs were such a contrast to the white frames, and they matched the black carpet tastefully. Different size black and white prints were mounted on frames and hung on the walls, and these were my favorites. The white washed walls no longer looked bare.

The family room was everyone's favorite. A big and comfortable settee was placed on one side of the room with the television standing by the opposite wall. A good size coffee table was put in front of the settee. This table was the home for all the magazines and packets of crisp and chocolate bars. A few leather bean bags were scattered on the floor to be used as extra chairs. I loved lounging on them because my feet need not dangle in mid air.

Easter holiday approached and Peter invited Raphael and Gavin as his house guests for the holiday. Cedric and the two boys found their way to Highgate every day and our house became their second home. Alastair with the help of Cedric and the two enthusiastic brothers monopolized the responsibility of all the renovations. Although, amateurs they performed diligently. Lynette relinquished her share of contribution to the restoration of the house because her obligation was to accompany Mother when shopping was required. Peter not having his own family appreciated invading our home. He was the designated chauffeur and advisor. Assisted by Gavin I was engaged in transforming the garden. Gavin taught me how to operate the lawn mover. All the weeds were extracted from the grass and an assortment of bulbs were planted. Potted flowers were on display and some reclining lounge chairs were purchased for the garden. While we were buying the potted plants I insisted on purchasing two big indoor green plants for the living room which added extra color and smartness to the black and white theme of the living room. Gavin was an expert on carpentry so he built a picnic table for the garden. Together Gavin and I decorated my room. Shelves were put on the wall to accommodate my books. My collections of souvenirs could also be on display. The Memory Jar was placed on my bedside table again. Gavin built a stand to home my beloved record player with ample space to store my records. Everyone was happy with the transformation of the house and all were proud of their own imaginative creation, invention and performance.

Gavin took me to the super markets and introduced me to the art of grocery shopping. When I was in Hong Kong, purchasing food was not my department but now I started to watch out for sales, and I was beginning to be an expert in buying cooking materials. Through experimentation and error, I slowly became an authority in cooking, and I loved my newly acquired skill. Mother was more than pleased to let me take over all the housework. With my systematic nature constantly the kitchen was spic and span, the bathrooms were sparkling clean, the laundry properly washed and ironed.

We adjusted to our new environment with no difficulty, although there were endless fights and arguments, not forgetting complaints as each expressed his or her opinion. But all in all Mother was delighted and contented with our performance.

Uncle Edwin's correspondence with Mother was far and few. When he did write, Gi Gi's name was never mentioned. Although exhausted when Mother retired to bed every night, I was positive that she still missed Uncle Edwin desperately. I was proud of Mother because she strongly attempted to eliminate the memories of the days gone by and managed to close another chapter of her life. I was sensitive to Mother's hidden sorrow and pain, so although I missed Uncle Edwin, I refrained from inquiring about him. I insisted that Mother be more involved with her favorite Mah Jong game, so consequently, most weekends, I would encourage her to accompany Peter to meet new friends. Eventually Mother's social life became hectic and soon she was invited to many Mah Jong parties—I considered Mah Jong to be the best cure for Mother's unhappiness.

Twelve

As the days drifted by I was exhilarated to be alive. Every morning I would wake up happy with my life. Blissfully humming my favorite tunes, I sprinted from one chore to another. Gavin became my friend and confidant again. The memories of Hong Kong began to dim and I no longer missed my hometown.

One afternoon Gavin invited me to watch a film with him. We arrived at Leceister Square Theater with plenty of time to spare so we walked toward Trafalgar Square. I was impressed by Lord Nelson's statue. Countless pigeons perched on his shoulders while a crowd sauntered around the square. Were there more pigeons than people? I wondered.

Thoughtfully I watched the pigeons fluttering their wings then settling on the ground hoping to be fed. "Gavin what do you think would happen to me if I caught one of these pigeons and cooked it?"

Gavin stopped walking. He was aghast with my suggestion. "You will be arrested!"

"But we eat pigeons back home, so what is the difference?" Baffled with Gavin's statement I countered.

Chuckling Gavin unwrapped a bar of chocolate for me and explained, "Eat your chocolate and forget about the pigeons. You are not supposed to eat these birds because their meat is too tough. The ones we ate in Hong Kong were especially bred for the purpose of eating. The folks back home do eat some weird things like pigeons and dogs. The English must think that we are primitives."

I stuck my tongue out and shrugged my shoulders. "In a way we Chinese sometimes can be quite uncivilized. I am glad our family doesn't indulge in this nasty habit of eating dogs. I think I will be sick if I were served dog's meat."

Laughing we went to see the film and the subject of eating dogs and pigeons was soon forgotten.

I woke up one morning and realized that I needed some Chinese cooking ingredients so I ventured into China Town myself. When I was finished with the shopping I decided to pay Gavin a surprise visit as his home was in the same neighborhood. When I arrived Cedric was in a hurry to join Alastair for a tennis game so he opened the door and I let myself in.

Raphael was emerging from the bathroom. Obviously he just had a shower because he was drying his hair with a towel while Gavin was reading the newspaper. Before I could let my presence be known Raphael said to Gavin, "Dawn is back in town. She called for you last night. Why don't you return her call? Since Dawn has been away you have spent enough time with Melanie. Now that Dawn is back in town its only fair that you should spend some time with her."

Immediately I coughed and knocked on the door. The two brothers were startled to see me.

Gavin beckoned me into the room and offered me a chair. I took the seat and curiously I inquired, "Who is Dawn?"

"She is the younger sister of Gavin's buddy from school. Gavin has been seeing quite a bit of her before your arrival. I think she is quite smitten with him. She just returned to London after visiting her grandparents." Raphael combed his wet hair with his fingers then explained further. "Gifted with a pleasant personality and dazzling good looks, Gavin is a very popular member of our school. He gets invited to spend many weekends with our school friends. Especially the ones with younger sisters. Not only is he favored by all the girls but even the parents like him. Dawn is one of Gavin's many admirers. Gavin has been dating this young lady for a while now but since your arrival he has unintentionally neglected Dawn. At the beginning of the Easter holiday she was out of town but now that she has returned she is of course anxious to see Gavin."

Folding the newspaper that he was reading Gavin interrupted, "Hey, when are you going to stop your chatting? I am sure that Melanie is not interested in my popularity with the girls. I will call Dawn shortly. If she has not made other arrangements I will try and spend the day with her." Then Gavin turned toward me and remarked, "I see you have been shopping already."

Pointing to my shopping basket, I explained, "I want to try out a new recipe tonight and was hoping that you may want to be my guinea pig, but if you are going to see your friend then maybe next time."

I hoped that my disappointment was not too obvious. We chatted for a while then I returned home.

I was astounded to hear of Gavin's liaison with another young lady, but I chastened myself immediately. Gavin was no longer a little boy. He had matured to be a nice young man. He should be socializing with other girls. I shouldn't quibble over his behavior. It was only natural for him to date. I was determined to be sensible and rational but the thought of Gavin being in the company of another girl troubled me.

After dinner Peter and Mother departed for their weekend Mah Jong game. Raphael and Lynette had been invited to a party. There was a film that Cedric and Alastair wanted to watch so they invited me along but I declined. I decided that a quiet evening on my own would be most enjoyable. I needed the time to myself. Easter holiday would be over soon, and I would be carted off to my new school. My anxiety over embarking on boarding school life was increasing. I was nervous and I needed answers to many of my questions regarding boarding school. I grabbed a book with the intention of indulging myself in some reading. I put on a thick jumper and relaxed on one of the reclining chairs in the garden. I read for a while but my concentration eluded me and soon I was gazing into the sky. Not a cloud was visible and the sky was clear. The air was crisp and absentmindedly I began counting stars again. Dreamily my mind wandered into the outer space.

"Melanie, how many times have I told you to lock the garden gate? Anyone could have entered the house unnoticed. London may be a safe town but not this safe!"

Gavin's reproaching voice startled me. Immediately my attention returned to the present. Amazed with his unexpected visit I asked, "I thought you were spending the day with your friend? What are you doing here?"

"I did spend the day with her but we had a slight disagreement. I thought that it would be best for me to leave her. No doubt she will come to her senses again tomorrow. Her tantrums don't usually last long."

Gavin apparently had no desire to volunteer further information.

Although I was inquisitive I refrained from requesting for more details. Instead I offered him something to drink.

"There is a chill in the air so why don't we adjourn to the family room? You make us a couple of hot chocolates and I will light the fire." Gavin held the French door opened for me.

When I returned to the family room, the logs were burning in the fireplace. I made myself comfortable on one of the bean bags. I cuddled a cushion and nursed my drink. Gavin sat beside me on the carpet and watched the fire.

Suddenly I broke the silence and requested, "Gavin can you tell me something about boarding school life? I am so ignorant and I feel extremely adequate. I have no idea what awaits me in the new school. I have only attended one school all my life and having to change school is scary enough without being a boarder."

Gavin smiled at me encouragingly and the shadows from the blazing fire flickered on his face. "Melanie, if I told you that boarding school life is enjoyable then I would be lying through my teeth. You will have plenty of adjusting to do. Much toleration is required on your part. Having to live with so many other girls can be most demanding. I am glad to say that your personality possesses all the proper ingredients. You are always willing to share and you are not selfish by nature. Boarding school life shouldn't create a problem for you."

I interrupted, "Why was Lynette so unhappy?"

"Lynette is a different kettle of fish. I am afraid Auntie Wei Ling has spoiled her rotten and to top it all your sister has a demanding character. She has to have her own way constantly; therefore, having to share meant hell for her. She retaliated against discipline and resented the lack of freedom. She will be happier attending a day school."

Shifting my body on the bean bag I put the mug on the floor, then I groaned, "I sincerely hope that your judgment on my character is correct. I am frightened but I don't want to voice my apprehension. I don't want to sound ungrateful. Mummy has made enough sacrifices for us already. I am grateful that I have been provided with this opportunity to have a marvelous education. I don't want to complain."

Gavin knelt on the carpet and pulled me toward him. I put my head on his shoulder. Instantly, my confidence was revived. Silently we watched the burning log for a while then Gavin suggested playing cards. Soon my concentration was evaporating and I was absolutely disheartened because I was unable to win any game. Yawning I stretched and complained, "I am tired and I don't want to play any more. You are too good for me!"

Gavin suggested that I should go to bed first. "Why don't I tuck you into bed and then I will wait for Raphael because I want to catch a ride with him."

I refused to go to bed, instead I returned the empty mugs to the kitchen. I rinsed the mugs before I joined Gavin in the family room again. I turned the television on and played around with the channels. Finally we found a channel that we both enjoyed and we settled down to enjoy the film that was on. The warmth and comfort of the room made it impossible for me to keep my eyes open. When Raphael and Lynette returned home I woke up. I must have fallen asleep cuddling the cushion while Gavin kept me company.

I had to leave for my school two days before Gavin's departure from London. On the eve of my departure Gavin came to visit me. He found me in my room with clothes scattered on the floor. The trunk that was to accompany me to school was opened with clothing half packed. I was almost in tears with frustration. Removing the stray strands of hair from my face I exclaimed, "I just don't know what to bring with me and I really have no idea how I am going to put everything in this small trunk."

Gavin removed the jumper that I was wringing with my fingers and soothingly he suggested, "Here let me demonstrate my skill in packing. While I am packing, I will tell you what are the essentials that you must bring with you to school."

Patiently Gavin folded all my clothes and packed them in the trunk. Simultaneously he advised, "You don't need too much clothing because you will be in your uniform most of the time. I suggest you bring a torch light with you. There will be times when you may need to do a bit of catching up with your school work when the lights are out. A hot water bottle is also useful. If the heating is not efficient then the beds can be quiet cold...."

Eventually when the tiresome task was accomplished we cleaned the mess in my room. When the room was in shipshape again, Gavin tucked me into bed and I didn't object. I was exhausted and grateful that I was still sleeping in my own bed.

Bending over me Gavin kissed me gently on the cheek and whispered, "You will be leaving very early tomorrow morning; therefore, you need a good sleep. Good luck and I will see you at the end of the term. In the meantime when you have time to spare do write to me."

Smiling, I nodded my sleepy head but before I fell asleep I saw Gavin turning off the light and closing the door quietly behind him.

Thirteen

The ringing of the alarm clock woke me from a troubled sleep. The sky was still dark so I switched on the bedside lamp and scanned the room with my sleepy eyes. The trunk was sitting by the door and its presence reminded me of my imminent departure for the boarding school. Reluctantly I removed my body from the warm bed and automatically I tidied my bed.

When I was dressed I walked into the kitchen and flicked on the lights. Peter would be arriving shortly as he was the designated driver to escort me to school. Hurriedly, I started to cook breakfast. Soon the coffee was brewing in the percolator and bacon was sizzling in the frying pan. I wondered who would be doing the cooking after I was gone.

Presently the household stirred into life. Alastair came into the kitchen rubbing his sleepy eyes. He poured himself a cup of coffee and asked affectionately, "All ready to leave?"

I picked on my food and replied sourly. "I guess so. I don't have any other choice."

Alastair put his empty plate in the sink and said, "Cheer up. It can't be that bad."

Grateful for his encouragement I forced a smile, "I guess not."

Lynette came into the kitchen and interrupted, "Of course it is bad.

I feel sorry for you Melanie. Soon you will know what it is like to be sentenced to prison."

Tears threatened to spill from my already misted eyes. Alastair patted my shoulders comfortingly and chastised Lynette. "Oh, do shut up. You are scaring Melanie out of her wits."

Lynette stared at Alastair and rebuked, "Don't say I didn't warn Melanie. Wait until you have to go!" Just then the front door bell rang and she ran to open the door. Peter joined us in the kitchen.

When Mother was ready to leave I said good-bye to Lynette and Alastair. With Alastair's assistance I stacked my things into Peter's car and we were on our way. The sky was gray and misty with a slight drizzle. Too soon the car left London behind. It was not exactly a great day for traveling and the weather somehow matched my depressed mood. I hardly noticed the scenery as the car sped along nor was I conscious of Mother's constant chatter with Peter.

After a few hours of driving we stopped for lunch. If I were in a better mood I would have enjoyed the old-fashioned, antiquated, archaic pub that provided us with an excellent lunch. My thoughts were so occupied with other tormenting thoughts that I could not activate my artistic mind to admire the quaint decorations surrounding me.

Toward dusk we drove into the vicinity of the school. The car seemed to be driving through endless miles of beautifully manicured lawns. Then the school appeared in the foggy distance.

When the car was parked outside the enormous house that was the school building, I was reminded of old haunted English houses that I had seen in the movies and I shivered. Peter retrieved my trunk from the car and he tugged a rope that must have been the front door bell for the door was opened instantly. We were ushered into the house by a girl of my age and dressed in a uniform which consisted of a white blouse and a blue pleated skirt.

An elderly lady with charming manners and a warm smile greeted us and beckoned us into a room. A fire was blazing in one corner of the room but I could feel no warmth. Extending her hand to Mother, the lady introduced herself. "I am Mrs. Babbington—Headmistress of the school. I am pleased that Melanie is joining us." Inviting us to sit on the settee in the room Mrs. Babbington offered each of us a cup of hot tea. I was grateful for the hot and sweet liquid because the tea somehow managed to relax some of the tension in my twisted stomach.

Mrs. Babbington returned her gaze to my face and gave me an encouraging smile. Then glancing at Mother, she said, "It is a wise decision on your part to send Melanie to our school. All the students are from neighboring towns. They have not had the opportunity of being exposed to the Oriental culture. It would be a tremendous asset for them to have Melanie around. On the other hand, your daughter will be provided with the chance to learn the English way of life, which I am certain is all new and fascinating to her. Granted enough time to settle in I am sure that Melanie should not have any problem with adjusting."

Without waiting for a reply Mrs. Babbington continued, "We do not encourage any contacts from home during the first ten days of school. We would like to give the girls a chance to settle down. No doubt there will be tears and home sickness to deal with for the first few days but eventually they soon take to this way of life. Every Sunday we encourage the girls to spend an hour on correspondence to their family and friends. No doubt you will be hearing from Melanie soon."

Mrs. Babbington paused and then looked at me. Her intense glare made me nervous and I cringed inward. Subconsciously I shifted my body and moved closer to Mother. Although, the Headmistress was smiling, her eyes did not smile. Returning the cup to the saucer, she stood and said, "I think it is time for us to show you Melanie's dormitory and then I am afraid you will have to take your departure, as supper will be served soon."

When we left the warmth of the room, my bones were chilled to the core. The old building was damp and the heating was inadequate. Because I grew up in the tropics I found it almost impossible to adjust to the damp cold English weather and I was cold most of the time. We climbed a flight of creaking stairs and then we walked along a corridor with doors on both sides. Through the doors endless cubicles could be seen. Mrs. Babbington turned into a door which led us into a cubicle. There were shelves on one side of the wall and on the other side was a small bed and a desk. There was a tiny wardrobe that was intended to accommodate all my belongings. The furniture was sparse but adequate. Definitely not luxurious but comfortable. A timid girl of my age was waiting for us in the cubicle and she was introduced to me. Anne was her name, and she would be my guide for the next two weeks.

When we returned to the front door I kissed Mother tearfully and thanked Peter for the ride. When Peter's car disappeared down the road, I returned to my room feeling absolutely desolate and lost. I caught my reflection in the small mirror and I was not surprised to see a crestfallen face with a forlorn look. Anne patted me reassuringly on my shoulder and invited me into her room. Obviously Anne had arrived at least a day earlier because her room was tidied and lived in. Her books were put neatly on the shelves. Her clothes were neatly folded and put in the wardrobe. There were photographs displayed on her desk. More books were scattered on the desk. Posters of her favorite singers were pinned on the wall.

Anne took my hand and encouraged me. "We all feel uncomfortable and dejected at first but the misery will soon vanish. In any case you won't have much time to feel sorry for yourself." Anne smiled at me then she continued. "My parents had to leave town for a short business trip; therefore, I was returned to school a day earlier. As a matter of fact I arrived yesterday. I am afraid I wasn't too diligent with my school work during the holiday so I am grateful for this extra day. I could do with some catching up." Inviting me to take a seat on her bed she sat on the only chair in the small room.

Fidgeting with the scattered books on the desk Anne peevishly informed me, "The detested morning bell goes at five in the morning. We have no more than fifteen minutes to attend to our toilette then we have to make our bed and tidy our room. Morning prayers are said in the chapel but no one is really awake until breakfast—which is served immediately after prayers. After breakfast, lessons commence without delay and no break until lunch."

I was horrified with the military schedule but I dared not voice my opinion. Depressingly I waited for Anne to continue, "We have one hour for lunch—big deal. School doesn't actually breakup until 3:30 in the afternoon. After we have rested for half an hour we have to attend to our afternoon sports lessons. These lessons are compulsory because they are part of our school curriculum. On the dot at 5:30 the supper bell will go and we are expected to finish our meal in half an hour. The food is edible which is a consolation. After supper there is one hour of prep. If you are fast you will finish all your homework within this hour otherwise you will have to forego the extra hour of leisure time before the 9 p.m. bedtime bell goes. When the bell goes, all lights are out and they expect us to sleep. To tell you the honest truth by the time the bedtime bell goes I am usually hungry again."

Disgustedly I screwed my nose because I couldn't believe my ears. No wonder Lynette absolutely detested boarding school. How was I going to get accustomed to this regimental life style? Anne sympathized with my concern and she watched me with her clear blue eyes, then she attempted to comfort me. "It's not as bad as all that. I may have exaggerated a bit. No doubt you will be adjusted soon—we all do. A bit of time is what it takes to break into the system."

Moving toward the door Anne gestured for me to follow her. "You had better attend to unpacking your trunk. When you have finished unpacking, I will show you where our trunks are stored."

I hardly had enough time to store away my trunk when the supper bell was heard throughout the entire school. Silently Anne led me to the dinning room. When I walked into the room, I could feel all the eyes watching me. Being the only Oriental girl, the others treated me like a specimen from outer space. I hung my head low but through the corner of my eye I could see that there were about twenty tables in the spacious room. Ten girls to each table. There were a few girls behind the food counter serving the food. When I took my seat next to Anne she whispered and contributed more information. "We all take turns in setting up the dining room and serving the food. Of course we take turns in doing the dishes as well. That I can assure you is the most horrible part but because there are so many of us we do it maybe ten times during each term. Ten times is bad enough already." She sighed then she shrugged her shoulders and pulled a long face.

I was unable to swallow the food that was put in front of me but I knew that it would extremely ill-mannered of me to leave food unfinished on my plate. With forced efforts I swallowed the food without tasting any of it.

After supper Anne took me into the Common Room with the intention of introducing me to some of the other girls. When I walked into the room, names and questions were thrown at me and I just blinked with apprehension. I was literally tongue tied. Anne patted my arms kindly and said to the other girls supportively, "Give the poor girl a chance. I am certain that in a few days time Melanie will remember all our names and she will be one of us." I smiled at Anne gratefully. I appreciated her rescue and support.

Eventually I was getting more accustomed to the hated bell that ruled our lives. I found that my command of the English language was far from adequate and I experienced difficulties following my lessons let alone chatting with the other girls. Consequently I lost my tongue for a few days. Slowly I was able to communicate with my fellow students but extra time was needed to cope with my school work. My days just flew by and I had no time for self-pity.

To my utter astonishment I was beginning to settle down. Not that I was really enjoying my life style but I began to enjoy the boarding school food. Roast potatoes with thin slices of roast beef and Yorkshire pudding. Fish and chips; spaghetti with meat balls; baked beans on toasts and mashed potatoes with minced beef. Although, I must admit on many occasions I did wish for a bowl of wonton and noodles and sometime I would crave for a bowl of steamed hot rice. Sometimes at night even though exhausted, I still couldn't sleep when my body hit the pillow. Tossing and turning my mind would wander back to the streets of Hong Kong. I was beginning to miss the noise and the excitement of Hong Kong. On numerous occasions my thoughts would bring me back to the house in Highgate, and I would miss Mother, Alastair and Lynette, always wondering what they were doing I longed to see them.

More often I found myself thinking of Gavin. Too many evenings I was so desperate for more time to attend to my forever demanding school work. During these times I was grateful to Gavin for putting the torch light among my belongings. This little gadget provided me with enough light to complete my unfinished homework. Every weekend I wrote to Mother diligently. I never complained but constantly reassured her of my progress. I had the tendency to write to Gavin when I had finished my letter to Mother. My letters to him were quite different from the ones to Mother. They were full of complaints and I voiced my anxiety and my fear. His responses were always encouraging and I lived for his letters.

One day after my lessons I was returning to my cubicle with Anne and a few other girls. Suddenly my path was blocked by a girl much taller then myself. With a nasty expression she snarled, "Hey you Chink! Why don't you learn to speak English properly?"

I was shocked beyond comprehension by this rude remark. The other girls grunted disapprovingly and they were appalled with the older girl's behavior. She was obviously a bully so everyone watched me and waited anxiously for my reaction. All the while suppressing my rising temper, I tried to ignore her. I wanted to by-pass the girl but she would not budge. I held my head proudly and with blazing eyes I hissed with dignity. "If you can speak my language with the same fluency as I speak yours then you can complain about my command of English."

There was utter silence then all the other girls giggled and some of them even applauded. Anne grinned triumphantly and she patted my shoulders with pride—obviously proud of my defensive action. Instantly the bully blushed and stepped aside. The other girls took the opportunity to insist that she should apologize to me. Not one to enjoy a scene, I shook my head and extended my hand instead and exclaimed, "Forget about the apology. It is only a trivial thing. Why don't we just be friends?"

The bully was taken aback by my reply and the snarl on her face immediately changed to a smile. She shook my outstretched hand vigorously and profusely apologized. "I am sorry for my obnoxious behavior and we will be friends! Maybe you can even teach me Chinese!" Everyone roared with laughter.

After this incident I was truly accepted as one of the girls. They no longer stared at me with animosity, instead I was greeted cordially and invited to take part in all their outings. My life was more bearable. My command of English improved tremendously. Not only was I forced to communicate in English, eventually I was beginning to think in English. The only time that I would use my mother tongue was when I wrote to Mother or when she called the school.

Fourteen

I was excited because the half-term break was fast approaching. I really was looking forward to a break of four days from my restrictive school life which I looked upon as an ordeal. Just before the short holiday I received a call from Mother. "Looking forward to your half-term?" Mother inquired.

"You bet I am!" I yelled into the receiver.

Then Mother's voice came on the line again. "Melanie how would you like to visit Alastair's school before you return to London? Your brother's headmaster would like to see me before Alastair leaves for London."

I was exhilarated with the invitation so I replied, "I would love to join you."

Mother warned, "Peter and I will collect you on Friday and from your school we will drive directly to Alastair's. It will be an exhausting journey because it is a long drive from your school to his."

I could not wait till the weekend and when it finally arrived I was up bright and early. Humming to myself I tidied my room and had a slight breakfast of hot coffee and cornflakes. Then I waited patiently for Mother's arrival. I sat by the window and watched for Peter's car. It was interesting watching all the cars that came to collect the girls. Finally

Peter's car pulled into the parking lot. Immediately I grabbed my overnight bag and hurriedly went to knock on Mrs. Babbington's door. I told her that I was leaving with Mother. I ran to Peter's car and rushed into Mother's open arms. Fondly I kissed Peter on the cheek. I was really happy to see her and Peter. Soon our car was speeding away to Alastair's school in Sommerset.

Breathing the air of freedom was a terrific feeling for me. I was delighted that I was no longer in the vicinity of the school. Sitting in the back seat of the car I was able to relax and enjoy the passing scenery. Mother turned round from the front seat and she remarked, "You have only been away for a few short months and yet you seem to have matured a lot."

Feeling confident, I chatted with Mother and Peter. With wittiness I informed them of my school life and narrated funny incidents that happened to me. Mother and Peter were both impressed and amused by my stories.

After a few hours of tedious driving we finally arrived at our destination. As it was in the middle of the night, Peter had to find a place for us to stay. Eventually he managed to locate a small pub which provided rooms and breakfast. When my head hit the pillow, I fell into a deep slumber grateful that I would not be awakened by the hateful morning bell. The sunshine shining through the flimsy curtain woke me. For a while I was disoriented because I had no idea where I was. When I looked around the unfamiliar room, I suddenly remembered that I was with Mother and Peter. In a few short hours I would be visiting Alastair's school. I heard a slight knock on my door. It was Mother urging me to join them for breakfast before we continued on our journey.

When we approached our destination I gazed out of the window of the car and I was captivated by the imposing sight of the school. It was fascinating. Nissen huts were scattered on the enormous school ground. At the end of the driveway there was a grand old house. Pointing toward the huts, I asked with curiosity. "Mummy what are those funny looking buildings?"

Smiling Mother answered, "Those are class rooms and this house is the main school building."

I was baffled. "You mean lessons in the huts? How unusual! What an experience—how fortunate for Alastair!" We parked our car in front of the old house. Gladly I stepped out of the car and stretched my cramped limbs. Then I checked my reflection in the car's side mirror and was satisfied with my reflection. My long black hair was gleaming brilliantly in the sunlight. My cheeks were rosy and I looked healthy.

A young man escorted us to the Headmaster who was waiting for us. I was impressed because he did not conduct his interview in his office but on the cricket ground. I had never seen so many young men and each time one of them looked at me I blushed. My eyes grew big and I could not remove my gaze from the cricket game and its spectators. Young men were running around with white trousers and jumpers. I was impressed! English school boys were such gentlemen. They were impeccably attired while playing a sport.

The Headmaster must have been over sixty-years-old. He was tall and wiry. He was attired in a tweed jacket and he wore gray flannels. The expression on his face was stern but his eyes smiled. Extending his hands to Mother he welcomed her. Immediately Mother introduced me. "Mr. Clark meet Melanie. She is Alastair's elder sister." Shyly I gave him my hand and looked into his smiling eyes.

Alastair appeared and beckoned me to follow him. I made a polite excuse and walked away with my brother. I followed him and instead of walking toward the cricket field he steered me toward another part of the school. We walked along a path with short scrubs on both sides. At the end of the path an enormous swimming pool came into sight. Pointing toward the pool I exclaimed, "You mean you have your own swimming pool?"

Proudly Alastair answered, "Yes and in the winter there is a cover on top of the pool—just like a big balloon. We can swim all year round."

Slowly we walked toward the pool and sat on a bench while my eyes searched the enormous ground and sighed, "You are lucky to be studying in this school. My school is indeed a prison. Sometimes the small town atmosphere suffocates me."

Nodding his head Alastair agreed with my statement and then he added, "Sometimes I do wonder whether this is indeed a boarding school. This place is so liberated. For a start, there are no uniforms for the girls. Our lives are not ruled by a bell. As long as we attend all our lessons and complete our homework we are at liberty to organize our own time. They encourage us to use our own judgment and initiative."

We chatted for a while then I decided to find Mother. When I approached the small group by the cricket ground, I could hear Mother inquiring about Alastair with concern. "How is Alastair doing?"

Chuckling Mr. Clark replied, "He is doing extremely well. I think he is improving especially with his tennis. He does get an awful lot of opportunities to practice."

I muttered cheekily, "Alastair and his tennis—he doesn't have to eat if he can play!"

When Mr. Clark heard my comment, he watched me with interest. He addressed me, "I am going to ask you a question. Try and provide for me the appropriate answer. Ten birds were perched on a tree and a hunter came along. Then he took a shot at one of the birds. How many birds were left on the tree?"

I was just about to answer 'nine' when I noticed the mischievous twinkle in Mr. Clark's eyes. Instantly I realized that 'nine' was too simple an answer. I pondered for a while then suddenly I got it and I snapped my fingers. I replied, "None! Sir."

The elderly gentleman roared with laughter and nodded his head with approval. I breathed a sigh of relief. I was expecting criticism and was gratified when I heard laughter.

Kindly Mr. Clark questioned me again. "Now why would the answer be 'none'?"

Squinting my eyes and twirling my curls I challenged his question with pride. "Sir! The birds are not stupid. They would fly away when a shot was heard. They would not hang around to be killed—would they?"

Satisfied with my answer Mr. Clark returned his attention to Mother. "Mrs. Au-Yeung, my compliments to your young daughter. She is not only gifted with a pretty face, she is also charming and she has brains too. I guess she has a sense of humor as well." After some consideration he gazed at me and suggested to Mother, "Have you considered sending Melanie to this school?"

Mother was startled. Hesitantly she answered, "I can't say that I have…. I know that this is a coeducational school but would Melanie be able to fit in?"

Mr. Clark moved closer to me and he put his arms around my shoulder. He replied, "I think so. She has all the qualities to be one of our students and we would love to have her!"

I held my breath and waited for Mother's answer. Never in my wildest dream did I expect to be part of such a terrific school. I couldn't believe my eyes when Mother nodded her head with approval. I nearly fell off the chair and I yearned to jump up and down. I was so happy I wanted to clap my hands.

Encouragingly Mr. Clark instructed, "We expect to see Melanie with Alastair when the summer holiday is over."

When I returned to school, I worked diligently. I no longer dreaded the lessons. I paid special attention and concentrated on all subjects. I intended to improve myself before I joined the new school. I would prove to Mr. Clark that I was a capable student and I had no desire of ever letting him down.

Fifteen

After the final examination was over there was another week before the end of the term. The minutes were like hours and I counted the days until I could leave for London. When the school finally broke up for the summer holiday, I experienced some mixed emotions. I was extremely happy that the summer holiday had started and I would not be returning to the same school. I was depressed because I was saying good-bye to fellow students with whom I had become friendly. I had grown especially fond of Anne, for we did share a few short months together. When I was on the train to London the depression feeling soon vanished and it didn't take long for me to get caught up with the holiday mood.

I opened the front door with my key and walked into a quiet house. No one seemed to be home. Struggling with my trunk, I tried to drag it into my room. A movement from the living room startled me. I was surprised to see a young woman emerging from the room. She had an extremely pale complexion, but she had lovely straight shiny black hair that was very smartly trimmed. The young lady had very attractive features and she was small like myself. She smiled at me and instantly I felt warm. The young woman moved toward me and smiled. "I am Sui Fong and you must be Melanie—I am Cedric's girl friend."

I grinned at her and said, "Oh I have heard about you! Alastair wrote and told me all about you. It's sure nice to meet you."

Cedric must have heard us speaking because he poked his head out of the family room and remarked, "So it's you. I see the two of you have met." Seeing the heavy trunk on the floor he reprimanded, "Why didn't you ask me to help you? The trunk is too heavy for you to move by yourself."

I struggled with the trunk and replied, "I didn't know anyone was home because the house was so quiet. As a matter of fact I am surprise to see you." Winking at Sui Fong I continued, "Sui Fong obviously is a good influence on you and she must have taught you some manners. I see you are no longer boisterous and rowdy, and I approve of the improvement."

Cedric threw the newspaper that he was reading at me while I side stepped and disappeared with lightning speed into my own room leaving Cedric to struggle with the trunk. Sui Fong followed me and suggested kindly, "Would you like me to help you unpack?"

Gratefully I returned her smile. "Thanks, awfully. I really appreciate your offer but I can handle unpacking. You can offer again when I have to pack at the end of the holiday. I think I will have a shower and then we can get better acquainted. I will tell you all about Cedric just in case he has omitted some truth about himself."

Cedric smacked me on the head and pushed me onto the bed. Giggling I teased, "Sui Fong you didn't know that you are dating a monster did you? If I were you, I would reconsider your relationship with this horrible young man!" Then I pushed Cedric and Sui Fong out of the room and closed the door. When I was alone in my room, I collapsed on the bed. I had really missed my own bed and room. With my hands cradling my head I gazed onto the ceiling and my mind was drifting. Suddenly I bounced out of bed and yanked opened my door. Loudly I screamed at Cedric, "Hey cousin, do you know if Gavin will be arriving in London soon?"

Cheekily Cedric replied, "You would like to know wouldn't you? But I am not telling you. Especially after the way you have mistreated me! All you can think about is your pal Gavin."

Sui Fong interrupted, "They have arrived. Both Raphael and Gavin will be staying with Peter for the duration of the holiday! I think he called earlier to say he is coming later."

Naughtily I stuck my tongue at Cedric and muttered to myself. "I hope he will come because I am going to cook for everyone tonight!"

Teasing me Cedric said to Sui Fong, "I wouldn't trust her cooking if I were you. She would only poison you!"

I picked up the pillow from my bed and threw it at Cedric. Mother

Return

appeared in the midst of our commotion. When I saw her, I threw myself into her outstretched welcoming arms. Removing the long hair from my face Mother complained, "When I heard the racket I knew instantly that you have returned home. It's sure terrific to have you back. We have missed you!"

Fondly Cedric cut in, "Auntie you may have missed her but I haven't!"

"Oh Sure! Not even my cooking?" With a loud voice I retaliated.

Chuckling, Mother intervened, "Melanie, I am appalled by your behavior. I thought you are a lady and ladies don't yell!"

"I am a lady. Really Mummy I am a lady!" I insisted. "Cedric always brings the worst out of me. When he is not around, I am usually much better behaved." I complained and returned to my room closing the door behind me. I was happy that I had my last say.

After I had my shower, I put the record player on. While my favorite records were playing, I sat in front of my mirror and proceeded to dry my hair. Gently my door was pushed opened and I saw Gavin's reflection. I dropped the hair dryer and comb immediately and rushed into his arms. He kissed my cheek tenderly and whispered against my hair, "It's sure nice to see you. Auntie Wei Ling told me that you are the chief cook tonight and I thought you might appreciate some assistance."

Soon I was dressed in my jeans and thick jumper. My long hair was tied into a pony tail. Like a breath of fresh air I sprinted into the living room and grabbed Gavin's hand. He followed me into the kitchen and helped me tie the apron around my slim waist. Searchingly I opened the refrigerator and checked to see what food was available. Soon the stewing beef was washed and marinated. I insisted that Gavin should cut the onions because the vapor from the onions always made my eyes water. Expertly, I peeled the carrots and the potatoes. Within half an hour the pot of stew was bubbling on the stove and the French bread was warming in the oven. After dinner Sui Fong offered to wash the dirty dishes with me and we chatted like old time friends while we cleaned the kitchen. A rapport between us was unfolded. Little did we know that our newly developed friendship would last a life time.

When the pots and pans were stashed away and the kitchen had resumed its sparkling condition Gavin made hot chocolate for everyone. Sui Fong left the kitchen with a mug of hot chocolate for Cedric. Gavin said to me, "Dawn will be leaving for the States in a few days. She would like me to spend the next couple of days with her. I am afraid I won't be able to see you until after she leaves."

I was disappointed and a sad expression fleetingly displayed on my face but almost instantly my expression changed and I smiled. "I understand. There will be plenty of time for us to be together. We will have the remainder of the summer."

Gavin touched my face gently and folded my small body into his arms. He removed the strayed curls from my face and he remarked, "I have always known that you are a thoughtful and understanding person. I am very fond of you."

Overwhelmed by Gavin's gentleness I stood motionless in his arms. Alastair charged into the kitchen and announced, "A very important game of Monopoly is just about to begin. Would you two like to join us?"

Reluctantly, I removed myself from Gavin's embrace and hand-in-hand we joined the others in the family room. As usual I was losing and my money was disappearing with speed. Thoughtfully, Gavin shared his money with me and I was able to finish.

During the next couple of days, when I had some free time, I would indulge myself with window shopping. I visited many shops with Sui Fong. Although Chinese by birth, she was born in London; therefore, she knew the city inside out. In the mornings I would attend to the garden and there was always an arrangement of fresh cut flowers from the garden displayed on the coffee table. I put a white rose in a small vase and placed it next to my Memory Jar on my bedside table. I was contented that I was responsible for the majority of the housework and Mother was more than pleased to have her little helper home from boarding school. I experimented on different recipes and the family constantly marveled at my skill.

Finally Dawn departed for her holiday and Gavin returned to my side. Gavin spent almost every day with me. Together we fed pigeons in Trafalgar Square. We visited Madame Tussaud's Wax Museum and admired the wax figurines. We fed ducks in Hyde Park and I enjoyed wondering around Battersea Park. We would watch a film or ride on the Underground train from one end of London to another. We were never tired of each other's company.

One afternoon Gavin and I ran out of pocket money so we had no other choice but to stay at home. The weather was warm and the sun was shinning. I sunbathed while Gavin read a book. We were enjoying the peaceful afternoon. Alastair was playing tennis with Cedric and Sui Fong patiently watched the game like a faithful puppy. Lynette, Raphael and Mother attended to the grocery shopping. I was lazily dozing off when I heard a slight noise from the family room. Gavin must have heard the noise because he put his book on the grass and remarked, "I thought we are the only living souls in the house. I better go and investigate. I thought I just heard a door closing."

Soon after Gavin disappeared through the French doors and before I could resume my position on the grass I heard Gavin shouting from the room. "Melanie, come immediately. I have a surprise for you."

I loved surprises so I jumped to attention while removing bits of grass from my swimming costume. I staggered into the family room through the French doors. I saw Peter speaking to another gentleman. The profile of the visitor was awfully familiar and when he turned around I was able to see his face. My eyes grew round and big. I opened my mouth but was speechless. The amazement on my face must have been hilarious because Gavin and Peter could not contain their laughter. Shortly I regained my composure and I screeched. In my hurry I neglected the small stool on the floor and I tripped. Fortunately Gavin came as fast as lightning to my rescue and I didn't further embarrass myself by falling flat on my face. Peter and the visitor were amused with my clumsiness. When I was steady on my feet again indignantly I exclaimed, "Uncle Edwin what are you doing here?"

Uncle Edwin grinned at me and replied, "I have just arrived from Hong Kong. Don't you want to see me?"

Putting my hands on my hips I turned to Peter and demanded an explanation. "Peter you knew Uncle Edwin was arriving. You must have collected him from the airport. Why didn't you inform us of his arrival?"

Shaking his head good-naturedly, Peter sighed in exasperation. "Don't you like surprises?"

"I love them!" Then I rushed into Uncle Edwin's arms while a peel of laughter echoed from my throat. Suddenly I groaned miserably. "Oh where is Mummy? When are they going to come home?" Breathlessly I continued to explain, "Mummy took Lynette and Raphael to the super market and they usually spend hours there!"

Uncle Edwin made himself comfortable on the settee and patted the seat next to his, telling me to sit down. "Why don't we all make ourselves comfortable and you can update me with all the latest gossips."

For the next couple of hours, words stumbled out of my mouth continuously. I refused to stop my babble. There was not a minute when I was at a loss for words. Uncle Edwin was engrossed with all my latest gossips. He remarked on my maturity and newly developed wittiness and confidence. I made him laugh and I made him sigh. Gazing out of the window and looking into the distance I described in detail the first few miserable months of boarding school life. Gavin and Peter only managed to put in a few words here and there.

Presently the sound of a car's engine could be heard backing into the driveway. When the door was opened, Mother came into vision with an armful of paper bags filled with grocery. Before anyone could utter a sound she looked blankly at Uncle Edwin then she blinked and their eyes met. Slowly the bags on her arms started to slide onto the floor and with a crashing sound, bottles of juice and milk were broken. Oranges and apples rolled all over the carpet. Cabbage and potatoes were scattered at Mother's feet. Ignoring the mess on the floor and without further hesitation Mother accelerated into Uncle Edwin's irresistible arms. I grinned blissfully because I was positively delighted for Mother.

Raphael and Lynette followed shortly. When Lynette saw Uncle Edwin she literally threw every shopping bag into the air. Her fast motions caused another thunderous crashing noise and more bottles and grocery were grounded with lightning speed. Reluctantly Uncle Edwin released Mother and happily folded Lynette into his arms then he greeted Raphael cheerfully.

Gavin and I cleaned the mess of broken bottles and bruised fruits. When the chore was accomplished and the excitement had died down I insisted that I would attend to the cooking for that evening. Like a busy bee I was buzzing around. With Gavin's help I cooked a very spicy and delicious curry lamb. Uncle Edwin loved curry. After dinner Peter thoughtfully invited all the youngsters for a few hours of bowling so that Mother and Uncle Edwin would enjoy a few hours of privacy. They definitely deserved the time to be together.

Sixteen

When Uncle Edwin had been in town for a couple of days, Cedric called and asked to speak to Mother. I was curious. When Mother replaced the receiver on the phone I asked her, "Cedric is usually not so charming to me—what did he want?"

Mother beckoned me to follow her into the kitchen and she replied, "He wants to bring Sui Fong's brother for dinner. He thought it was a good idea for Sui Bun to meet the family."

Mother had purchased some grocery and I started to put the food into the refrigerator. I asked, "What was your reply?"

Mother washed her hands and sat on the kitchen chair. "I told him that I am no longer the designated cook. But I told him that you wouldn't mind cooking for one more person."

I closed the refrigerator's door and sat on another chair. "Did you? I will have to charge Cedric for my service!"

Mother chuckled and replied, "You wouldn't. In any case Cedric did say that you are quite a little darling. He thought you were the perfect little home-maker."

"He can't bribe me with flatteries!" Then Mother and I discussed the menu for the evening meal. We decided that a roast beef and Yorkshire pudding would be nice.

Just before dinner was served Sui Fong arrived with her brother Sui Bun. The young man was extremely shy. His complexion was as pale as Sui Fong's. He was attractive and very smartly dressed. He brought flowers for Mother and two bottles of wine for Uncle Edwin. There was a big box of chocolate for the family. Secretly I approved of his good manners.

When Sui Bun was introduced to Lynette, immediately she was impressed by his charming and good manners. Throughout the entire evening, to Raphael's disgust Sui Bun dominated Lynette's attention. Lynette saw to it that Sui Bun's glass was never empty—his plate was heaped with food. After dinner Sui Bun invited the family to go dancing. Lynette was pleased as pie. Instantly she accepted the invitation because she always enjoyed a good evening out. Alastair preferred to play tennis so he disappeared. I was too young to go dancing so I stayed home with Gavin.

After the party left the house, Gavin followed me into my room. He made himself comfortable on the floor while I selected some records. Pensively he asked, "How did you find Sui Bun?"

I was searching for Elvis' new record so absentmindedly I replied, "He seems agreeable. Some girls would find him awfully attractive but he is not my cup of tea. My future boyfriend will have a dark complexion. Sui Bun has good manners. It was thoughtful of him to bring the presents for the family."

Gavin interrupted, "He can afford it. After all he is a few years our senior and no longer a student." After pausing for a moment he continued, "Lynette seems to be quite attracted to him."

Music was softly playing. I sat on the floor with my legs crossed. Supporting my chin with both heads I said, "I tend to agree with you. The instant they met I could sense a certain electricity sparkling between them. I hope this is not going to be the cause for the complications that develop through the eternal love triangle."

Gavin cradled his head with his arms and gazed into the ceiling. Then he protested, "What do you know about the eternal love triangle? You and your vivid imagination. You do realize that eventually Lynette and Raphael will have to go their separate ways! What they share between them is what the grown ups would call puppy love. Lynette will move on to greener pastures. It wouldn't surprise me a bit if the next guy in line for her is Sui Bun."

I sighed with my next remark, "I hope you are wrong! I would hate to see Lynette and Raphael breaking up. They have been going out with each other for so many years."

Gavin gazed deeply into my eyes and predicted, "We are too young to be involved in a serious relationship. We have a long way to go before we can even consider marriage. It will be sad when those two break up but it is inevitable!"

When Raphael returned with Lynette, Gavin kissed me good night and left.

After Lynette was introduced to Sui Bun she declined all of Raphael's invitation. She preferred to go out with Sui Bun. I was having tea with Mother and Uncle Edwin when Lynette joined us. She gave Mother a big bear hug before she took a seat. Mother was intrigued with Lynette's obvious affection. "Young lady, what have you got up your sleeves? Is there something that you want?"

"Well, as a matter of fact, I would like to discuss my future with you!" Lynette replied sweetly.

Uncle Edwin chaffed, "Your future is indeed a serious subject. Your mother and I are all ears. What do you have in mind?"

Scrutinizing Mother and Uncle Edwin, Lynette waited for their reactions. "It is obvious that I have always detested school. Now that I have passed my 'O' Level examinations would you be agreeable if I were to cease schooling? I would like to work for a while. I need time to find my bearings and I really don't know what I want to do."

Mother was appalled by Lynette's suggestion so she exclaimed, "What about your 'A' Levels and university? In any case I reckon you are too young to work. Who would want to employ you? A student fresh from high school with absolutely no working experience."

Uncle Edwin patted Mother's arm to calm her anxiety then he intervened. "Lynette, you know that your mother is right in her thinking. Aren't you a bit too young to venture into the business world. What do you know about making a living?"

Characteristically Lynette objected indignantly, "Oh, don't be so old fashioned! There is no written law that says we have to attend a university. As for obtaining experience—how will I do this if I am not given a chance? If a position was offered to me by a reputable firm would you allow me to accept?"

Mother was about to protest when Uncle Edwin interrupted, "If you really detest school then there is no point in us prolonging the agony. I can see your point of view—perhaps some working experience may do you a world of good. I want a promise from you. If in the future you should wish to resume your education you must do so! Anyway we will resume this discussion when you have been granted an interview for a job!"

Beaming with satisfaction proudly Lynette informed us. "I have been offered a position! I went for my interview this morning and I was accepted immediately."

Mother was surprised by the information. "You presumptuous little brat. Please tell us how you managed to wangle an interview?"

Proudly Lynette announced, "The receptionist in Sui Bun's accountancy firm has resigned. I happened to mention to him that I was seeking employment. He managed to pull some strings with personnel and I was granted an interview."

Accusingly Mother reprimanded Lynette. "I hope you didn't pressure Sui Bun into getting the interview for you. Knowing you, you are perfectly capable of twiddling people round your little fingers!"

Lynette exclaimed indignantly, "Of course I didn't! I passed the interview on my own merits. The personnel manager likes me and he recognized my potential. In any case anyone with a bit of brains can answer the phone and a mouse can do the filing. You just have to be charming to be a successful receptionist."

The following week Lynette started her career as a receptionist. Working in the same office as Sui Bun provided ample opportunities for them to meet. Soon Lynette and Raphael drifted apart. She no longer had the time or the patience for her childhood sweetheart. She found Raphael immature compared to Sui Bun.

One evening Gavin and I returned home from a stroll. When I opened the front door, I could hear Raphael and Lynette yelling at each other. Frowning I put my fingers to my lips and gestured to Gavin to follow me into the family room. I then closed the door. I didn't want to intervene; nevertheless, Raphael's raised voice could be heard through the closed door. "Lynette, do be reasonable! You just can't fall in and out of love so casually. You hardly know Sui Bun. What about us? We have had a few years behind us." Raphael was pleading.

"Raphael can't you understand? We have grown away from each other and we have fallen out of love. We are no longer compatible. What we had was just a passing fling. It wouldn't have lasted. You should realize that at our age it is impossible for us to have a lasting relationship." Lynette retaliated with a loud voice.

We could hear Raphael's agitated tone of voice. "Lynette you can't just throw our feelings overboard. Why can't we give ourselves another chance? Please reconsider your decision. I just can't bear the thought of losing you!"

Lynette was losing her patience and she argued, "Christ Almighty! Why can't I get it into your thick head that you are not losing me? I will always be your friend. Our relationship has come to the end of the road. I am closing a chapter of my life."

Raphael demanded an explanation from Lynette. "How can you just close a chapter of our lives with just a flick of your finger? What about my feelings? Have you only feelings for yourself?"

"We just don't click any more. Need I say more? You will find some other girl to replace me soon enough. Why don't we give ourselves a chance to try again? Let's cut all strings immediately. I want to finish our relationship now." Positively Lynette concluded the discussion with a final note.

Behind the closed door I was shaking. Tears were streaming down my face. One would think that I was the one that was being jilted. Gavin put his arms around my shoulder and soothingly he comforted me. "I guess this outcome is inevitable. It is hard for Raphael now but in time he will get over the rough patch. May the best man win and in this round Raphael happens to be the loser. Don't worry your little head off—things will take their natural course."

I sniffed and attempted to dry my tears with the back of my hand. I knew that Gavin was right in his thinking. I nodded my head in agreement. When the yelling had ceased Gavin managed to let our presence be known by opening the door, then he left with a broken-hearted Raphael.

Sui Fong found me in my room. I was concentrating on a pattern for a mini skirt. Lately I had been sewing a few new outfits for myself. Teasing me Sui Fong remarked, "The busy bee is making another new dress for herself!"

Smiling I put the pattern on the table and picked up the black material that was to be my skirt. I defended myself. "I have to be prepared for the new school. We don't have to wear uniforms so I thought I had better improve my wardrobe. I have no intention of turning up in school in rags."

"You will never be in rags. You are so talented. You can turn a piece of rag into a smart dress." After a moment of silence she continued. "I gather you have heard about Lynette and Raphael?"

Sadly, I returned the material onto the table and joined Sui Fong on my bed. Twiddling a lose thread from the bedcloth, I confided in Sui Fong. "Yes! In fact Gavin and I walked into their argument the other night. It was most embarrassing for all concerned. I do miss Raphael. He hasn't been around at all!"

Sui Fong watched me intensely then she implored, "I hope your family has no hard feelings for my brother. If I could predict the future I would never have introduced Lynette to Sui Bun."

I was aghast with Sui Fong's thinking. I took her hands into mine and reassured her. "Don't be silly—don't blame yourself. If it was meant to happen then there is no way we can prevent it. Why should we have ill feelings against Sui Bun? I think he is quite a likeable young man. I guess I am just used to Raphael. Give me more time and I am certain that I will be very fond of your brother. Hey, cheer up. Sui Bun will be given the opportunity to prove himself! We are all reasonable creatures—at least I would like to think so." I winked at Sui Fong's worried face.

Sui Fong was obviously grateful for my thoughtfulness. She kissed me on the cheek and murmured, "I knew you would understand. I hope that the other members of your family share the same opinion. What about Gavin? Raphael is his brother."

"I wouldn't worry. Lynette has decided to terminate her relationship with Raphael and it is her life. Sui Bun should not be considered the culprit. We can't condemn Sui Bun for Lynette's actions. He will be given a fair chance with the family. I do realize that because we are Chinese, our family's opinion is very important to us! As for Gavin he predicted the outcome and he does take everything with a pinch of salt. He is a true philosopher. Did you know that I nick-named him the 'old man'?" I was amused with my own remark so I laughed.

When I opened the front door of my house I said to Gavin, "I really enjoyed the film. It was nice of you to have invited me. In return I will cook dinner for you!"

Gavin chaffed, "Don't be such a cheek! You have to cook dinner anyway—as if you had a choice!"

We walked into the corridor and I was surprised to see a gilded bird cage sitting on the table.

"Look!" I said pointing to it.

Curiously I took a peek at the card that was tied to the cage with a pink ribbon. "To Lynette, with love, from Sui Bun." Playing with the card I commented, "How sweet!" Then I turned to Gavin and complained, "You never send me love birds!"

Gavin was offended and he countered, "What about all the records that I have contributed to your collection? Ungrateful creature!"

Inside the cage in one corner was a small container stuffed with cotton wool. Pointing toward the container I asked, "What in heaven's name is that gadget?"

Gavin looked over my shoulder and explained, "You silly goose—that is a small shelter for the birds' eggs."

Fascinated I ventured, "You mean Sui Bun actually expects the birds to produce eggs?"

Gavin retied the card to the ribbon and answered, "Obviously!"

Subsequent to Gavin's explanation an idea popped into my mischievous mind. Naughty thoughts were churning in my head. Without further hesitation I grabbed Gavin's hand. I struggled into my coat and insisted that Gavin do the same. Then I yanked opened the front door and skipped down the driveway. I raced toward the Underground station. When Gavin caught up with me, he demanded an explanation for my weird behavior. "Can you please tell me where we are going in such a hurry—where is the fire?"

When we reached the sweet and tobacco store by the station, I stopped for breath. Then I pointed toward the store and explained, "I want to buy some chocolates that are shaped like eggs wrapped with silver paper! I want to put the chocolate eggs inside the cage."

Gavin was bewildered with my bizarre suggestion. "You can't be serious! Will you stop and consider Lynette's reaction when she discovers that the eggs are not real? She will slaughter you mercilessly!"

Coaxing Gavin with all my feminine charms I implored him to become my accomplice. "Oh, don't be such a stuffed shirt and be a sport for a change! Surely even Lynette can take a practical joke. She will see the funny side." Then I entered the sweet store. Dubiously, Gavin heeded to my proposal.

I sprinted from the store with my purchase stuffed in my coat pocket. When we arrived home, we were panting and puffing. Briskly I opened the cage door and painstakingly I put the chocolates among the cotton wool. I embraced Gavin and gave him one of my elusive smiles and we quickly scrambled into my room with the door half opened.

Shortly we heard the front opened and Lynette's voice floated into my room. We peeked from my room and snooped through the half-opened door. We could see Lynette undoing the buttons on her coat with Sui hovering around to assist. Lynette approached the table and immediately the bird cage caught her attention. After she read the card she turned round and kissed Sui Bun. Sui Bun was beaming from ear to ear. He was more than pleased with himself.

When Lynette intensely scrutinized the cage, we tried to stifle our giggles. Then she screeched, "The birds have produced eggs!"

Sui Bun must have been flabbergasted with Lynette's discovery.

Gently he eased Lynette away from the cage and observed. Then he exclaimed in bewilderment. "There was no egg when I delivered the birds during lunch time. How could they have produced with such speed?"

I tumbled from the room and I was killing myself with hysterics. Gavin could no longer contain his laughter. Perplexed by our amusement Lynette pushed Sui Bun away from the cage then she opened the little door and took the eggs out. I was laughing and crying at the same time. I tried to wipe the tears from my face with the back of my hand. After examining the eggs, Lynette swiftly attempted to smack me, and I tumbled onto the floor. When Sui Bun took the eggs from Lynette, even he burst into uncontrollable laughter.

Laughing, Lynette pinned me on the floor and tickled my body mercilessly. She knew that I was extremely ticklish. Soon I was begging for mercy. I screamed for Gavin and Sui Bun to restrain my sister. Mother and Uncle Edwin returned home and they were taken aback by our peels of laughter. They entered the room and found Lynette sitting on me. We were killing ourselves laughing while Sui Bun attempted to pull Lynette off me. Gavin was sitting on the floor holding his stomach and trying to control his hysterics.

Mother inquired with wonder, "What are you guys up to? Aren't you too old to be playing on the floor?"

Lynette was up on her feet and rushed into Mother's arms. She wailed, "Your daughter has just played a practical joke on me and I was teaching her a lesson. She put chocolate-shaped eggs in my bird cage and I thought that my birds had produced them!"

Uncle Edwin grinned and said, "Melanie, trust you to do something like this. You do need a vivid imagination to perform such a trick!"

Seventeen

It was a Saturday afternoon—only three weeks before school started again. Clean laundry littered the kitchen table. Socks had to be matched; towels had to be folded; the blouses and skirts that required ironing were put in the ironing basket. I insisted that Alastair help me fold the laundry. Reluctantly he was matching the socks. Lynette came into the kitchen and informed us, "Uncle Edwin and Mum would like to see you in the family room." Then she walked away.

Hurriedly I removed all the laundry from the table and put them to the laundry basket. Then I carried the basket with me into the family room. I found an empty corner and sat on the floor. When I was comfortable in my crossed-leg position, I resumed the task of sorting and folding the laundry. Mother sat next to Uncle Edwin on the settee while Lynette and Cedric each occupied a bean bag. Alastair joined me on the floor.

I couldn't help but noticed that Mother's face was radiantly glowing. She was serene and contented. Since Uncle Edwin's arrival a month ago Mother's beauty had blossomed. When Uncle Edwin arrived in London he had rented a car so that although he stayed in a hotel near Peter's restaurant every day, he had no difficulty in communicating from the hotel to our home. His constant presence had been an added happiness for Mother.

Uncle Edwin tenderly took Mother's hand and said, "I regret to tell you that my holiday in England is coming to an end. When I leave for Hong Kong, I would like your Mother to come with me."

We were startled with the information but Mother smiled sweetly at Uncle Edwin then she explained, "Don't look so shocked. I am not leaving for good! I will only be gone for a few weeks. I think I deserve a holiday, don't you? I will be staying with Auntie Wei Fun. I would like Cedric to stay here while I am away and Peter has kindly offered to keep an eye on you all." She paused waiting for an objection.

Suddenly Alastair leaped from the carpet and yelled, "You mean we will be left on our own with no supervision?" Throwing the cushion into the air he shrieked, "Hurray! When are you leaving?" I kissed Mother tenderly and reassured her, "Mummy you do deserve a holiday. There is no need to worry about us. We are old enough to look after ourselves."

Mother smiled and replied, "I will be home in time to take Melanie to her new school."

Alastair pulled my pony tail and proudly offered, "Mummy, take your time. I can escort Melanie to school. She can catch the train with me."

"I am sure that you are quite capable but I really do not have the intention of leaving you for too long. The house may be burned down during my absence. The neighbors may complain about your noises and you will all be arrested and I will have to bail you out from jail!" Mother teased.

Lynette countered indignantly, "Oh Mummy. Don't exaggerate. What do you take us for? A bunch of brats from the streets?"

Uncle Edwin mocked, "Not a bad description." Then he spoke in a solemn tone and implored us. "Seriously, please promise to behave. I want your mother to have peace of mind while she is away."

We agreed unanimously to behave and we looked forward to our two weeks of independence.

Two evenings after Mother and Uncle Edwin had departed for Hong Kong, Sui Bun thoughtfully invited us for dinner. I was glad that I was able to relax and not trouble myself with the cooking. After dinner Sui Bun look Lynette dancing. Alastair, Cedric and Sui Fong departed for a few games of bowling while Gavin escorted me home. When we arrived home, we listened to records in my room.

Thoughtfully I confided in Gavin. "I hope that Uncle Edwin has finally gotten Gi Gi out of his systems. It would be nice if both Mummy and him should decide to give their relationship a chance." I brushed my hair while I persisted, "It was unfortunate that Gi Gi was involved. I am more than pleased that she is no longer in the picture."

Gavin stacked more records on the player and commented, "You do get over emotional. Auntie Wei Ling is mature enough to handle her own affairs."

I objected, "I know—Gi Gi's existence nearly jeopardized their happiness. How I had craved for this reconciliation between Mummy and Uncle Edwin."

Sighing in exasperation Gavin commented, "Melanie you are incorrigible! You are too stubborn and you believe that all your ideas are right. We all have our own lives to live."

Rebelliously I persisted, "I just want Mummy to be happy. She does deserve some happiness. After all she has been widowed for more than ten years. I have been pleased that she was dating Uncle Edwin for as long as I can remember. They are not young like Raphael and Lynette. They really cannot afford to waste too many precious years."

Hugging my knee I continued wistfully with enthusiasm, "I hope Mummy will marry soon! I would hate to see her growing old and still be on her own. We will grow up and eventually have to leave home." Miserably, I muttered to myself, "I would hate it if I had to be alone when I am old and gray." Then changing the subject I altered my mood. Smiling sweetly I asked Gavin. "I hear Raphael has found himself a new girlfriend. Have you met her?"

Thoughtfully Gavin responded, "Yes—attractive girl—absolutely adores Raphael. She worships the ground that he walks on. As far as she is concerned he is just incapable of any wrong doings." Gavin sighed and lounged on my carpet—using a few cushions for pillows. He made himself comfortable while I sat on my bed and cuddled my pillows.

After a brief moment of silence Gavin spoke again, "You know, Melanie, I came to the conclusion that it is much better for a person to be loved than to love!"

I watched his face and frowned. "What is the reason behind this belief?"

Gavin gazed out of the window and explained, "Raphael is the perfect example. He was so much in love with Lynette. Persistently, he tried his utmost to please her and adhere to all her whims and desires. Lynette in return took him for granted. It must have been difficult and trying for Raphael. Now Ronnie is nutty about him and one can see that he is enjoying the role as the recipient."

When I did not reply, Gavin returned his attention to me. I was cuddling my pillow and had closed my eyes. I was yawning. Getting on his feet Gavin offered to tuck me into bed and he would take his departure. But I insisted that he should stay with me until I fell asleep. So Gavin resumed his position on the carpet. It must have been the warm room and the soothing music because Gavin fell asleep before I did.

The sunshine woke us and Gavin sat upright with a jolt and exclaimed, "I must have fallen asleep. I have spent the entire night in your room. What would your family think?"

Then Cedric was knocking on the door. "Gavin, answer the phone. Your brother is on the line."

Gavin walked into the family room and I rubbed my sleepy eyes and followed him. When Gavin picked up the phone I could hear Raphael's bellow. "Last night Dawn called around nine. I asked her to call you at Melanie's but she refused. Then she called again around twelve but you still had not returned. This morning she rang really early and when I told her that you were still not home she was not pleased with the information. She slammed the phone on me. You had better pacify her because I can predict a storm brewing in the air."

Not waiting for Gavin to reply Raphael continued, "I don't really blame her. I would be upset if I were in her shoes. Anyway what were you doing at Melanie's?" Suddenly he stopped, then with a serious tone of voice he inquired, "You didn't do anything you shouldn't have done—did you? Auntie Wei Ling has just left town two days ago!"

Gavin was horrified with Raphael's insinuation so he hurriedly interrupted, "Raphael how could you insult Melanie? We spent a very innocent night together. We were chatting and she fell asleep and I did the same. For your information, I slept on the floor while she slept on her own bed! Please don't make a mountain out of a mole hill!"

"What about Melanie's reputation and Dawn's feelings? Have you no considerations at all? What would Melanie's family think?" Raphael's challenging voice echoed into the room.

With dignity Gavin spoke into the receiver, "Her family will be told the truth and I hope that they will have more faith in her than you do. As for Dawn, I will sort her out later. She does not have a hold on me. We are not going out on a steady basis nor are we engaged to be married! I do not have to account for all my actions."

Then Gavin hung up and suggested that I should return to bed. He left for home. Later I woke up and went into the kitchen searching for food. To my amazement Sui Fong was obviously waiting patiently for me. I found her pacing the kitchen and pensively drinking from the mug that she was nursing in her hands. When she saw me she grabbed my shoulders immediately and without mincing words she said, "I don't want you to think that I am interfering or probing but Cedric called me this morning and suggested that I should have a chat with you. He is rather concerned that Gavin had spent the night in your room."

I was astounded and innocently I gulped for an explanation. "Did Gavin really spend the night in my room? If he did then it was probably my fault. You see we were chatting and I dosed off. He suggested that I should sleep but I insisted that he should stay with me until I fell asleep. He must have fallen asleep too." I pulled Sui Fong into my embrace and assured my friend. "Don't worry! You can trust me—it was all very innocent. I wouldn't lie to you!"

Skeptically Sui Fong searched my face and commented, "The two of you are inseparable and really I won't condemn you if you did start an affair with Gavin. If it did happen I would like to be informed so that we can discuss birds and bees. There is a lot that you have to learn that you won't learn from school!" She gave me a conspiring wink.

I saw the funny side of the situation so I giggled and I implored her. "Sui Fong trust me—I am not denying the fact that I am extremely fond of Gavin. But what he feels for me is truly platonic. What we feel for each other is different from what you feel for Cedric. Gavin is my friend, my brother and my companion. I am still waiting for my knight with his shining armor to arrive at my doorstep—preferably on a white horse! When I do plunge into my first affair, you will be the first to know. You are very endearing to me and I would like to think that we can share all our secrets."

Sui Fong was relieved and the frown disappeared from her face. She looked me straight in the eye and advised, "Melanie you are maturing. Soon the inevitable will happen. We are living in the twentieth century. When it does happen I would like to think that fortunate guy is Gavin. He is so devoted to you!"

I was appalled by Sui Fong's suggestion. "Sui Fong you may think that we are living in the twentieth century. Our parents certainly don't! They still believe in being a virgin on a wedding night. Mother will slaughter me if she thinks that I am indulging in an affair with Gavin. Anyway it won't happen—I love Gavin like a brother." I paused, then frowning I hinted, "I think I have managed to convince you but what will Dawn think? I have a horrible premonition that I have given Gavin endless unnecessary problems. I wish that there was something that I can do to amend the situation!"

Sui Fong thought for a while then she snapped her fingers. "I have an idea! Why don't we invite Gavin and Dawn for tea? Surely when Dawn meets you she will see for herself that there is nothing between you and

Gavin."

I thought Sui Fong's suggestion was brilliant. Immediately I grabbed the phone and excitedly I dialed Gavin's number. When the invitation for tea was accepted I took a shower before their arrival.

Sui Fong answered the door bell and invited Gavin and his friend into the family room. When I joined them I smiled charmingly and extended my friendly hand to Dawn. She was fashionably dressed and exuded confidence. She was attractive with the aid of cosmetic artistry. Her blond hair was stylishly cropped. She returned my smile frostily and with aloofness she scanned my face. Animosity was burning in her cold blue eyes. When we had made ourselves comfortable—to our utter astonishment—Dawn rudely demanded an explanation from Gavin. "What were you doing in this house last night? Why did you spend so much time with Melanie while I was away? What about my feelings? Are you double-timing the two of us?" Gavin was bombarded with endless questions.

Gavin was appalled with Dawn's outburst and Dawn was evidently blinded by jealousy. Calmly Gavin explained, "I spent an innocent night in Melanie's room. There is no cause for such animosity. Melanie is my dear friend and she is like a sister to me."

Shrieking Dawn leaped from the chair. "You are contradicting yourself. One moment you are trying to convince me that your relationship with Melanie is purely platonic and the next minute I find out that you had spent the night with her. I always thought that Melanie was a well-behaved young lady with a good family background. Obviously I have been provided with misguided information!"

I did not like the way that Dawn was discussing me as if I were not in the room but I was too polite to protest. Anyway both Sui Fong and I were dumbfounded with Dawn's criticism of me. Gavin was devastated with Dawn's conviction so he quickly jumped to my defense and retorted, "Please don't insult Melanie and misjudge her unkindly."

Nervously Dawn started to pace the room and raising her voice she demanded, "Why are you defending her? I suppose you have to protect her honor. Maybe you did sleep with her!"

I could see that Gavin was desperately attempting to control his temper. With a restrained voice he insisted, "I did not sleep with Melanie—I repeat—I did not sleep with Melanie!"

By then Dawn was beyond reasoning and she screamed, "What is wrong with me? We have been seeing each other quite frequently. I thought that you loved me why didn't you take me to bed. Am I not good enough for you?"

I was too embarrassed to watch Dawn's expression. I must have been blushing at her outburst. Secretly I wished that I had not invited them for tea. It was definitely a wrong step on my part. I took a peek at Sui Fong through the corner of my eye and saw that she was staring at Dawn with wide eyes. With composed expression Gavin explained, "I am fond of you but I do not want to start a serious affair with you. We are too young to talk about love. I enjoy your company but if companionship is not what you are seeking then I think we should call it a day."

"Are you threatening me? Is this an ultimatum?" Dawn abruptly stopped her pacing and glared at Gavin.

Gavin attempted to reason with Dawn. "Don't be ridiculous. You are dramatizing the issue! I am merely making a suggestion!"

Dawn was obviously intimidated and annoyed by Gavin's unruffled attitude so she threatened, "Your suggestion is not going down nicely. Either you leave with me now in order to prove your innocence or you will never see me again!" She stormed out of the room without a backward glance and ran down the driveway.

I was surprised when Gavin sat on one of the bean bags instead of following Dawn. When the front door was closed with a loud bang I collapsed on the settee and covered my face with trembling hands. When Gavin regained his composure he sighed and apologized, "I shouldn't have accepted the invitation. I honestly believed that when Dawn was introduced to Melanie the two could become friends." He pointed his fingers at me, then he returned his attention to Sui Fong, "I have no right to subject the two of you to an ugly scene like this."

Sui Fong shook her head and with an understanding smile she reassured Gavin. "Don't feel too bad. Hopefully in a few days time Dawn will see sense again!"

Gavin started to pace the room then he stopped and confided in us. "In a way I feel relieved because I have cleared the air with Dawn. She is suffocating me with her affections. Her unreasonable demands are beginning to annoy me. I have no desire to be involved with anyone—especially not Dawn. She is fun to be with, but I am too young to be tied down. I need my freedom. I have a bright future ahead of me. I enjoyed Dawn's company while it was purely platonic and if that is not good enough for her then I am afraid we should go our own separate ways."

I was depressed by the confrontation—I detested scenes. I didn't want to be the cause for Gavin's unhappiness. Sedately I suggested a compromise. "Please don't argue with Dawn. We can stop seeing each other. I am satisfied with just phone calls."

Gavin's mood immediately changed. Chuckling he teased, "What are you trying to do to me—bankrupt me financially? Have you forgotten that every minute on the phone costs us money? Can you imagine? The phone bill will be phenomenal if we should sit on the phone like we used to do in Hong Kong."

The memory of Hong Kong reminded me of better times so I smiled enchantingly. With gentleness Gavin stroked my soft long hair. "Don't blame yourself—it is definitely not your fault. You are not the cause for the rift between Dawn and myself. I am just not ready for commitments. It is obvious that Dawn and I differ in our opinions. I am sad because a friendship has been severed but pleased that I have the courage to terminate this so-called affair. It is not healthy to drag it on. In time Dawn will find someone else and I wish her all the happiness. I am not the right guy for her." Grinning charmingly Gavin took my hand and kissed my palm. "In any case I really don't know what was the cause for the confrontation. School will be starting soon and I will not be seeing either of you for a while. When you attend Milford you will probably have a million boys falling at your feet and fighting for your attention!"

"I hope so! I don't expect anything less than a million." Cheekily I replied and winked at Sui Fong.

When Mother returned from Hong Kong she looked well rested and she was beautifully tanned. She was grateful that we proved to be responsible young adults and loved our independence. Not that she was expecting anything less then perfection from us. I was glad to have her home because I had missed her tremendously.

Eighteen

I was perfectly capable of following Alastair to catch the school train. When Mother suggested that she should escort Alastair and me to Milford we declined her offer. Exuberantly I arrived at Paddington Station with Alastair. The station was enormous with so many platforms—unaccountable numbers of trains arrived and departed. With difficulty we found the right platform for our departing train. It was a special train for students returning to Milford. Between Alastair and myself we struggled with our trunks and finally stored them in the luggage compartment. My excitement quickly vanished when I boarded the crowded train. I was almost paralyzed with anxiety. I did not expect to see so many young men—they were more or less Alastair's age group. There were hundreds of them. On board were also young ladies but their presence was far and few. Timidly I followed Alastair to find our designated compartment. I was happy to note that my younger brother was no stranger among these rowdy, young people—his popularity was definitely apparent. He greeted his friends joyously and introduced me to them. Nervously I returned their encouraging smiles.

When the train finally eased out of the station my nerves were calmed and I settled into the compartment comfortably. My eyes traveled up and down the moving train. The young ladies were magnificently dressed and their outfits were divine. Some of the girls were like models from fashion magazines. I admired their exuding confidence and vitality. I was in awe with my surroundings. The young men were all smartly attired in blue blazers and gray trousers. I was so intrigued with all the strange faces that I was incapable of concentrating on the murmurs around me. Everyone seemed to be talking simultaneously—exchanging gossips—variations of topics were discussed. The exciting and happy atmosphere was so exhilarating that I could hardly believe that I was on board a train en route to a school—maybe a summer camp was more appropriate. The few hours of traveling just drifted by so swiftly and soon the train was fast approaching our destination. Alastair left me for a while to chat with his friends. Just before the train pulled into the station he returned and I listened intensely to his instructions. "You realize that we won't be staying in the same house. All the boarding houses are scattered around the school. There is only one girls' house and it is "The Grange." When the train arrives in Bath, we will be transported to our houses by coaches. These same coaches will transport you to and from school every day. I have been assigned to stay in the house that is actually situated inside the school grounds; therefore, I don't have to undergo any daily traveling."

When the train pulled into the station at Bath there were six coaches waiting for us. When the train came to a final halt, instead of pushing and fighting, the students alighted the motionless train in an orderly manners. All the young ladies were assisted off the train and then the young men followed.

Alastair pointed to the coach that was marked "The Grange" then he gave me a peck on the cheek and said, "Sis., we have to part now. That is the coach that will take you to your house and my coach is this one here. Go to your house and unpack and get yourself acquainted with the other girls. I will see you in school tomorrow." Then he walked toward the coach that was marked "The House." I hoped my shyness and nervousness were not too obvious when I boarded the bus with false gaiety.

I took the first seat that was available to me. Another girl occupied the window seat next to mine. I watched her from the corner of my eyes and I realized that she was also uncomfortable. She was fidgeting and continuously folded and unfolded the handkerchief that she was clutching. Automatically I gave the girl a supportive smile and informed her, "I am new to the school and I don't know anyone!" Extending my hand, I introduced myself. "I am Melanie Au-Yeung from Hong Kong. What is your name?"

Bashfully the girl blushed and shyly she replied, "My name is Carol Parker. I am also new." She scanned the almost filled coach. "I hardly know a soul!"

I was relieved that I was able to find myself an ally. Abruptly I volunteered further information about myself. "My younger brother is the only person that I know from the school so we are more or less traveling in the same boat. We can certainly assist each other."

She said her name was Carol Parker. She nodded her head in agreement and smiling sweetly said, "I am so glad that I have met you. I no longer feel so lost and helpless." During the coach ride we chatted amiably and exchanged confidences.

When we finally arrived at "The Grange," the girls scampered off the coach excitedly. There were no designated rooms for us and we were able to choose our rooms and room-mates. All the other girls were returning boarders so they claimed their old rooms. There was only one room left in the attic so I invited Carol to share the room with me. Together we assisted each other with our luggage and we found our accommodation. I was pleased that our room was in the attic because the noise from the other rooms was hardly audible. There were big bay windows with pink curtains. Two comfortable beds were placed on each side of the room and plenty of wardrobe space was available. Also there were two work desks and there were more than enough shelves mounted on the walls for all our books. I was impressed by the space and I loved it. Instead of small cubicles it was lovely to share a proper room with Carol.

After we had unpacked, we decided to familiarize ourselves with our new home. We wondered around the house and found the Common Room. The room was spacious and comfortable. French windows surrounded the room allowing much light in and the room was extremely bright. There were many easy chairs and two big settee. A fair size television stood in a corner of the room. When we entered the room, we were greeted by many fellow students. The girls were friendly and of mixed nationalities. Quite a few of them were from the Orient. Some were Japanese, some Korean, and a few Filipinos, but there was only one Chinese girl. I smiled at her and she introduced herself as Jean Chan.

Jean invited Carol and me to share the settee with her. Then she remarked encouragingly, "You two must be new. In time you will get used to this mad house. You had better because this will be your home for the next couple of months. Really it is not too bad!"

I scanned the room, then I returned my attention to Jean. Smiling happily I said, "I am contented and satisfied with what I have seen so far. I went to a prim and straight laced boarding school. This is heaven compared to what I had to endure."

With dark laughing eyes Jeans responded, "You won't find too many rules and regulations. The school recommends self-discipline. There is no fixed time for you to get up in the morning just don't miss the coach. Make sure you arrive promptly for lessons and no one will complain. You are almost free to do whatever your little hearts desire."

I sat with my legs crossed then I put my hands on my knees and asked politely, "Are we far from the school?"

Gazing out of the window and pointing toward the manicured grounds Jean replied, "There is only one house on the actual school ground but there are five houses at close vicinity. All the girls stay in this one and the other four houses are for the boys. We have coaches that deliver us to school every morning and the same transportation return us in the evening. A few older boys are allowed to bring their own cars but they are prefects finishing their final year. By the way, you two must be famished. There is no proper dinner in the evening. You have to help yourself in the pantry. There is usually plenty of food."

I didn't want to interrupt Jean by telling her that I knew some of the rules. So attentively I listened and waited until she had finished, then we adjourned to the pantry. I was thrilled with my discoveries. The pantry had white washed walls and big French windows looked out into the beautiful garden. A table covered with a red table cloth stood in the middle of the room. There was so much food on display: fresh bread for sandwiches; varieties of cheeses and cold cuts; jars of jam; marmalade and peanut butter stood by a big dish of creamy butter. The green salad looked fresh and crunchy. A big basket that contained apples, oranges and bananas was put in the center of the table. I marveled at all the food. It was difficult for me to choose what to eat.

The concept of this school was entirely new and appealing to me. There was no room for criticism. My faith in boarding school was immediately restored. I was powerless to conceal my astonishment. I needed no persuasion to attend school the following day for I was truly looking forward to it.

That evening I had no problem with falling asleep. I loved my comfortable bed and my new environment. I was awfully grateful to Mother for providing me with this superb opportunity to further my education in such a prestigious school.

When the alarm clock woke me the next morning, I bounced out of bed immediately. Briskly I attended to my toilette then I returned to my room. I could not decide on what to wear. No Uniforms! How fantastic! I could not believe my good fortune. Carol was soon influenced by my enthusiasm and she began to relax. Her uncertainty was gradually diminishing.

Return

Impatiently, I waited for the coach and finally we arrived in school. When we descended from the stationed coach, many young men were waiting for us. Alastair was among the anxious crowd. I was delighted to see him. Enthusiastically I introduced Carol to him. When my excitable prattle eventually ceased Alastair escorted us to a small cottage that was adjacent to the main school building.

"Boys are not allowed into this house. It is called "The Cottage"—a hideaway for the girls. You will find a locker that is designated for you and you will find a time table and a map of the school.

"It's going to take you a while to find your way around. You go to different nissen huts for different subjects. There are five minutes between each lesson and that should provide you with ample time in-between lessons to find the appropriate hut. Good Luck! I will see you again at break time." He waved and blew me a kiss, then he walked away.

Accompanying each other, Carol and I found the locker room. After we had retrieved our time table and map we ventured into the enormous school grounds again. Regrettably Carol and I had different lessons so I found myself alone, searching for the right nissen hut. I stood outside 'The Cottage' and I saw groups of girls with a few senior boys strolling down the driveway. The junior boys were jogging on the side lane. Following the crowd I walked down the driveway then turned into a small path. Different color nissen huts with a number painted on the door were aligned on both sides of the path. Reading the numbers on the doors. I finally found the hut that I was looking for.

With determination and confidence I walked into the hut. As expected the hut was relatively small in size and only accommodated a few work desks. Five students occupied some of the desks and I stood by the door with uncertainty. An elderly gentleman beckoned me toward him. He was quite short and he had a big belly. He had warm smiling eyes and a pair of glasses were perched on his noise. I took a liking to him almost immediately.

"You must be the new girl from Hong Kong. Melanie is your name and you are Alastair's sister. Welcome to Milford and I am Mr. John your English tutor. Do grab yourself a seat and let's commence with the lesson."

The other students bestowed on me their welcoming and charming smiles. I found to my astonishment that I was the only female in this class. Shyly I took the first available seat. Mr. John pointed to the empty desk in front of him and said, "Do move up to the front because there will not be any more students joining us!"

He must have seen the astonishment on my face because he explained, "We usually have no more than five students in a class. On some occasions you may be the only student. Also, you have different fellow students for each subject. You are assigned to a class according to your standard and not your age. If you are more advanced in a certain subjects then you will be among senior students. If your standards are low you will be attending classes with much younger students."

    I nodded my head apprehensively. There was so much to remember. Soon I was involved with my lesson. So much individual attention was bestowed on me that constantly I had to master all my concentration. If my mind should wander then instantly I was jerked back to attention by Mr. John. My scattered brains would no longer be allowed to ponder. The days flew by with tremendous speed. I attended one lesson after another and I went from one hut to the next. Soon I was part of the fast-moving crowd. During the course of the first day I was late for only two lessons. I could not find the right hut but I felt no humiliation because each time I was greeted cordially by the tutor and no harsh words were used. At times the younger boys behaved atrociously because they spoke and laughed loudly in class. But most of the time all the students' manners were impeccable.

    At the end of the day I returned to the "The Grange" feeling absolutely exhausted. I flopped on my bed and exclaimed, "Wow! What a day! My brain will need a transplant soon. My head is a mess of cobwebs."

    Carol was feeling miserable. Limply she agreed, "You can say that again! So much was crammed into my mind that it will take forever for me to digest it all!"

    I hoisted my tired body off the bed, then I complained, "If you are exhausted, how do you think I feel? My command of English is so inadequate. It will take twice the time for me to understand, learn and remember. Anyway, let's cut the self-pity and feed our empty stomach."

    Later in the evening when we were ready for bed, I sighed with determination. "Now that I am no longer hungry I feel positively revived. I have decided that all beginnings are always tough. Tomorrow will be easier for us. After all, Rome wasn't built in a day. I should have more faith in ourselves. I am trying to convince myself that all the teaching is really for our benefit and I must not be intimidated by hard work. Hard work! That's all it takes!"

    Carol covered her head with the blanket and moaned, "I only wish I had your confidence."

    After a good night's sleep we felt rested and refreshed. Our energy was regenerated. Once again we were equipped and willing to face another day with anticipation. We had more time to roam around the 'The Cottage' so we visited each room. There were showers installed in the big wash rooms. Easy chairs scattered sparingly around the Common Room. This room reminded me of the Common Room we had in "The Grange," except there was no television. Next to the Lockers room was a walk-in closet to hang our coats. There was a room for cooking lessons and a room for sewing. Typing lessons were also available. When we returned to the Common Room, I was suddenly perplexed with a list that was pinned on the notice board. I signaled for Carol's attention. "Look at this piece of information—"The ten best looking boys"…how interesting!"

Jean hovered over our shoulders and chuckled. "I wouldn't bother with this list. It is last term's information—positively out of date. Next week there will be another up-to-date list posted. There will be a new one after the dance. By the way has anyone discussed the dance with you? It will be on this Saturday. We have a dance at the beginning of each term and one at the end of term."

I shrugged my shoulders and replied, "I will have to give it a miss. I rather fancy a quiet evening to get caught up with my work!" Returning my attention to Carol I suggested, "Carol why don't you go with Jean? You will enjoy it!"

Carol pulled a long face and protested, "Why don't you join us? It should be fun!"

Jean intervened, "I think the both of you should attend. It will be the perfect opportunity to meet guys!"

I laughed humorously, "I really don't have the spare time for boys. I have a more important date with my books."

When Saturday finally arrived I was relieved that I had the whole empty house to myself. After a quick meal of cold cuts and green salad I attacked my books diligently. I realized that I had to work extremely hard to be able to cope with the complexity of all the new subjects. The hours quickly drifted by and suddenly the girls returned from the dance. Laughter and giggles drifted to the attic. I closed the books and rubbed my tired strained eyes. Then I flexed my fatigued muscles. With starry eyes Carol burst into the room excitedly. She yelled, "I am so happy that I had decided to go and attend the dance. I met the most gorgeous boy and his name is Anthony Close."

I was impressed and inquisitive. So leaning on the closed door and squinting my eyes I teased her. "It didn't take you long to meet your dream boat. Are you in love?"

Carol threw her pillow at me and complained, "You should have joined us. There were so many nice looking young men. With your looks and charming personality you would have been most popular!"

Stubbornly I responded, "Boys are irrelevant and unimportant to me for the next little while. Let me get over the first hurdle by concentrating on my work then hopefully my knight in armor will appear."

Carol protested faintly, "You are ever so conscientious. I wish I could possess your diligence."

I laughed and countered flippantly, "When you have three foreign languages crammed down your throat simultaneously you will have my diligence and will power. Believe me—you will!"

Mr. John and I were the last to leave the hut. At the end of each lesson I usually liked to stay behind to help Mr. John tidy the room. My English tutor addressed me with firmness. "I am impressed with your improvement and your growing interest in the English Literature. You should also work hard with Latin. This subject will be a great help to you."

I screwed my nose and protested, "Latin is a dead language!"

"Nevertheless, a beautiful one." Mr. John replied positively.

I had to agree with him. "It is beautiful. As a matter of fact I no longer have a problem with Latin or French. My weakness is with math. I really don't know how my math tutor can tolerate my ignorance."

Patting my small shoulders encouragingly my English tutor and new found confidant comforted me. "You cannot be perfect on all subjects. You have to be contented with progressive improvement."

Suspiciously I inquired, "Are you sure that I am doing O.K.?"

Mr. John was beaming at me. "More than O.K.! You should try not to be so negative. You are too much of an idealist and a perfectionist. Perfection can be a heavy burden on your young shoulders. You have to learn to accept defeat. So you don't possess a brain for numbers—big deal—concentrate on the subjects that you like! I am certain that your parents don't expect you to be brilliant with every subject. You are not a born mathematician. You have to be a good manipulator to be good with figures. I have discovered that students who enjoy English Literature are usually dreamers. But mathematicians are practical and down to earth people. You definitely don't fall into that category." I was pleased with Mr. John's compliments and advice.

Nineteen

I couldn't believe that I had been in Milford since September. In another two weeks we would break for the Christmas holiday. That Friday we did not have any lessons but I persuaded Carol to return to school with me. I wanted to finish a dress that I was making and I wanted to use the Sewing Room.

When we arrived at school Carol and I went into the locker room. I opened my locker and to my surprise a big, brown envelope fell from within. Retrieving the envelope, I ripped it opened. A handful of photographs fluttered onto the floor. Carol was curious and she hovered over my shoulders while I was picking up the scattered photos. Then she exclaimed with astonishment, "Hey look—these are photos of you!"

I was baffled when I was flipping through the photos. I looked at Carol and inquired inquisitively, "I don't remember posing for any of these photos…when were they taken and by whom? Can you recognize the location?"

Carol took the photos from me and examined them carefully. Then she frowned and squinted her eyes thoughtfully. Suddenly she had answers for my questions, "I know when they were taken. I remember your outfit and I can recognize the rugby field. Do you remember accompanying me to Anthony's house to watch the Rugby match? I think it was last Saturday!" When she returned the photos to me she murmured, "They are lovely photos!"

The photographs were taken from different angles. My long hair was billowing in the wind and covering half of my face. I was laughing and I was gazing into the distance with a dreamy expression. Carol decided conclusively, "Well! Whoever took them was a professional—he used first class equipment and he knew what he was doing. You have yourself a secret admirer!"

"Don't tease! What nonsense. Me? A secret admirer? You have to be joking. Who would be interested in little old me?" I returned the photos to the locker and closed the little door.

Carol stood with her feet apart, one hand on her hip. She wagged her fingers at me and retorted, "Don't underestimate yourself! You have been too involved with your work. You don't have the faintest idea how attractive you are to the opposite sex. The boys are naming you the Ice Princess and putting bets on who you are going to date first! I don't think that you know how attractive you are—I would kill for your exotic looks."

I patted Carol's cheeks tenderly and chaffed, "You do exaggerate. I don't hear any complaints from Anthony."

Carol suddenly slapped her forehead. "Talk about Anthony! Let's try and solve this mystery. All it takes is some sort of detective work and we should be able to find the mysterious photographer. We will solve this mystery with our logical minds."

I tapped my feet while I was folding my arms. I challenged Carol's thinking. "I suppose you consider yourself Sherlock Holmes and who is Dr. Watson? May I ask?"

"Anthony, of course! Come to think of it all the boys that were present at the rugby match were from the same house. Anthony should know who is a good photographer and who would possess such expensive equipment. I will make a trip to the village and find out from the chemist who developed the photos!"

Affectionately I put my arms around my friend's shoulder and warned, "Don't create a fuss. This is awfully embarrassing."

Together we walked into the Sewing Room and Carol retorted, "I have a trustworthy personality. I will use all my discretion and my lips are sealed—have faith in your friend!"

A few days later, excitedly, Carol reported to me. "The chemist doesn't recall anyone asking him to develop your film. Only Theodore Rockfield is capable of developing films himself. He is the Head Boy in Anthony's house and he does have fantastic equipment. He has his own dark room. As a matter of fact he is the appointed photographer for the school magazine. He must be the guy that we are searching for!"

I tried to recall the name but I drew a blank. I insisted, "Hold your horses! We may be barking up the wrong tree and he is not our mysterious guy. Don't jump to conclusions. Someone might have borrowed his equipment and he might have developed the film as a favor!"

With a twinkle in her eyes Carol asked dubiously, "Your guessing is a bit far fetched don't you think? My instinct tells me that we have stumbled onto the truth. Theo has to be our guy. I am certain that he has developed a crush on you!"

Shaking my head I said, "You are so vulnerable! A few photos don't mean anything! I must get rid of this enthusiasm from your system."

We sauntered slowly out of "The Cottage". Someone called Carol. She turned. Immediately and excitedly she nudged me sharply. Then she muttered softly but urgently, "Talk of the devil! Turn your head casually—Theodore Rockfield, the photographer, is walking toward us with Anthony."

I did not see the loose stone on the ground when I turned abruptly. I tripped and twisted my ankle. Stumbling onto the ground I moaned, "Ouch! I have hurt my ankle!"

I was grateful for the hands that assisted me. When I removed the weight from my ankle, I fell into a pair of strong and comforting arms. Rubbing my painful feet, I attempted to thank the stranger who had assisted me. Lifting my head from his chest, I gazed into the stranger's face. His face immediately took my breath away! A pair of dazzling blue eyes were smiling at me. He had thick dark brown hair and perfect Adonis' features. Deep-set eyes, high cheek bones, and a firm jaw. Dark brown hair and clear blue eyes. What a breath-taking combination! My world stopped turning and I could hardly breathe. I stared into the handsome face and excitement churned in my stomach. All my good manners were forgotten.

There was a twinkle in his eyes and with a deep and gentle voice Theo asked, "Are you all right? Can you stand on your feet?"

The sound of his gentle voice jerked my attention to my aching ankle and I gasped, "I will try. By the way—thank you." I gave my rescuer one of my most charming and enchanting smiles. Regrettably, I removed myself from his comfortable and warm embrace. I clutched Carol's hand and limped away without a backward glance.

Carol put her arms around my shoulders and hissed, "Don't you just wish that Theodore is your secret admirer? I think he is just super. I drool each time he smiles at me."

I nodded my head and smiled wistfully, "He is extremely good-looking. By far the most attractive guy in the school. I am surprise that I haven't noticed him before. Anyway I don't think that I can be so lucky—he can't be the mysterious guy, and I don't really care."

Carol yelled and accused me indignantly, "You are such a hypocrite! Anyone could see that you were interested. You couldn't take your eyes off him. I do believe the Ice Princess is melting."

I put my fingers on Carol's lips and reprimanded her. "Don't shout. The entire school will hear you. I suppose it would be rather nice if he were indeed the guy who took the photos…anyway what do you want me to do? Should I feel honored?"

"Sarcasm won't get you anywhere!" Carol rebutted.

I thought for a while then concluded, "In any case it's too late. It's almost the end of the term."

"There is always next term." Carol gave me a conspiring wink.

During the next little while Theo's handsome face intruded my thoughts constantly. I would have liked to see him again but the opportunity of us bumping into each other never arose. Then it was the end of the term and the school closed for Christmas. Carol and I boarded the train for London. I was pleased that it was finally the end of the term and all the examinations and tests were behind me. As much as I liked the school I was truly looking forward to a restful and festive Christmas holiday. Uncle Edwin would be arriving soon and the family would be sharing a cheerful holiday together. Some of Alastair's chums joined us in our compartment and they were making arrangements to meet during the holiday. Holding hands, Carol and Anthony sat next to each other. I ignored the murmuring around me and gazed out into the horizon dreamily. Suddenly the door to the compartment was yanked opened and a deep voice informed us, "Fifteen minutes to our arrival! Get ready you guys!"

There was a slight pause. I returned my gaze from the distance and when I turned toward the door I was dumbfounded. I was mesmerized and hypnotized by blue eyes—eyes that were scrutinizing my face and were simultaneously smiling at me. Understandingly my companions uttered some feeble excuses and departed from the compartment. I was left alone with Theo. He closed the door behind him and took the seat next to mine.

I was melting by his alluring charm and charisma…the faint smile on his lips was so seductive. Tenderly, he inquired about my ankle.

I blinked shyly and when I was able to speak again I replied, "No permanent damage—I am walking again!"

The young man extended his hand to me and said, "I am Theodore Rockfield and you are Melanie the Ice Princess!"

I put my trembling hand in his and softly he inquired, "Are you returning to Hong Kong for the holiday?"

I couldn't remove my eyes from his dazzling blue eyes. Haltingly I murmured, "No. My mother lives in London and we have a house in Highgate. How about you? Where is home?" I wanted to know all about him.

Reluctantly he released my hand and crossed his legs adjusting his position. "I come from Surrey but my parents have a flat in London. My father travels to London quite often. The family will be spending Christmas in Paris!" After a moment's hesitation Theo asked, "Can I call you when I return to London?"

Hurriedly and excitedly I scribbled my phone number on a piece of paper and I replied with coyness, "That will be lovely. I will look forward to your call."

Suddenly, Theo jumped from the seat and said, "I have something for you." Then he disappeared into the corridor. When he returned he put a brown envelop on my lap and whispered, "Merry Christmas Melanie!" Then startlingly he kissed me gently on my lips and disappeared through the door again. I sat motionless. I was shocked and pleased that he had kissed me. I had never been kissed on my lips before and I rather fancied the feeling of butterflies fluttering in my stomach. Slowly, I woke from my daze and opened the envelope. Photos of myself were visible. Evidently my secret admirer was Theo. I was in high heaven and found myself floating on air. I was absolutely delighted with my discovery. I was still staring intensely at the photos when Carol and her companions returned to the compartment.

When Carol saw the contents of the envelope, she clapped her hand. Proudly and gleefully she exclaimed to the others, "See I told you! I was right! Theo is Melanie's secret admirer!"

There was a puzzle expression on Anthony's face then he remarked, "Melanie you are something! I have been in this school with Theo for four long years. He has hardly shown any interest in any of the girls—some of them were really striking, too!"

I was blushing and my face turned red. I was really embarrassed with Anthony's statement. Witnessing my discomforts Alastair teased, "Wait till I spill on you—the entire family will have an earful and no doubt Cedric will be pleased with news. He will have a terrific time harassing you…he does enjoy giving you a hard time!"

Fondly I smacked Alastair's head. I threatened, "Don't you dare utter a word to the family. If you do—I promise you—I will murder you. I won't have any hesitation or regrets when I mince your body!"

"I bet Theo will not be too impressed by your violence. In any case there is a price for everything—how much is your little secret worth!"

I shook my head in exasperation and playfully I slapped Alastair's hands…. I could still feel Theo's lips on mine when the train pulled into Paddington Station.

Twenty

I was delighted with the Christmas tree that Mother and Uncle Edwin had purchased. It was a live tree and fresh, about five feet tall, chubby and round—just perfect! Happily and excitedly I opened the boxes of newly purchased Christmas ornaments. Helpfully I assisted Mother with the decoration of the tree. Uncle Edwin was reading the newspaper and waiting patiently for us to finish hanging the ornaments on the tree so that he could connect and hang the strings of lights. Suddenly the front door bell echoed through the house. Mother asked me, "Are you expecting anyone?"

When Mother returned to the family room, she was holding and admiring a beautiful bouquet of white roses. She reprimanded me while reading the small envelope that was attached to the arrangement. "You really shouldn't encourage Gavin to spend so much money on you. This is terribly extravagant of him—this bouquet must have cost him a small fortune!"

I was puzzled by Mother's remark. "Gavin wouldn't spend money on flowers. He doesn't believe in spending money on perishable goods—flowers don't keep!" I removed the flowers from Mother and read the small card while Mother hovered around with curiosity.

Written on the card were a few simple words and yet they held so much meaning for me. I read again. "Wait for me, Love, T." I was delighted with Theo's unexpected thoughtfulness.

Wondering aloud I murmured to myself, "How did he know my address and how did he know my fondness for white roses?"

Alastair pounced in the room. When he saw the present clutched possessively in my hands he took the card from me and teased, "Penny for your thoughts! No need to look puzzled—I gave Theo our address. During last term he wangled from me enough information about you to write a book!"

I snatched the card from him and shrieked, "Christ! You awful traitor! You knew all the time that the mysterious guy was Theo. You were always aware that he was responsible for the photos. Why didn't you tell me?"

When Alastair saw the beautifully decorated tree he whistled and examined the ornaments, then he answered, "You didn't ask me, did you? You were so involved with your work. You hardly paid attention to what was obvious! Theo has had a crush on you from the first time he saw you. When he discovered that I was your brother, he befriended me instantly." Cheekily Alastair winked me.

"You are a devious monster! How could you? I should have guessed!" I wagged a finger at my brother accusingly then I disappeared into my room with the roses.

Throughout the day, repeatedly I played the song "White Rose from Athens" on my record player. The lyrics were so appropriate. Mother came into my room and found me sitting on the floor and dreamily gazing into the far distance. The pretty white roses stood attractively on my dressing table.

Mother touched the soft petals and sighed, "I guess your knight with the white horse has invaded your life. I just hope that you won't get too involved—I don't want to see you getting hurt. You are still so young."

Uncle Edwin followed Mother into my room and interrupted her reassuring, "Melanie may still be a baby to you but lately she has matured immensely. You can't be her guardian angel forever and worry over her. She has to lead her own life. No doubt she will appreciate advice, but please don't dictate her life. She is stronger than you think and she will handle her own life nicely. She may seem a bit weak in character at times but she does possess a strong mind. She is willful and stubborn. Don't be over protective."

Later Sui Fong gently pushed opened my door and found me deep in thoughts. I was thinking about Theo...his charming good looks and his beautiful blue eyes. When I felt her shadow on me, I returned my gaze from the window. I jumped to my feet and embraced her. "It's sure nice to see you. I have missed you awfully. I have so much to tell you!"

Reciprocating my warm hug Sui Fong said, "I am sure you have a lot to tell me! I missed you too. It's nice to have you home again!"

Blissfully I adjusted the already perfect arrangement of roses and asked, "By the way, any idea when Gavin will arrive in London?"

Sui Fong shrugged her shoulders then teased, "Cedric told me that he is arriving tonight. I thought you had replaced him with another person."

I pushed Sui Fong onto the bed playfully and we both stumbled onto the soft mattress. "You nit—one doesn't replace friendship. Gavin is such a dear, dear friend."

"What about Theodore? Also, a dear friend?" Sui Fong giggled and threw the pillow at me.

At the mention of Theo's name I blushed and retorted, "Alastair and his big mouth. I can kill him with my bare hands. Please stop your harassment. Cedric will have no mercy for me!"

We made ourselves comfortable on the bed, then we began to exchange the latest gossip. Suddenly Sui Fong's smiling expression turned serious and she confided in me. "Lynette is experiencing a lot of resentment from my mother. Those two just refuse to see eye to eye with each other. I have attempted to reason with my mother but she is so stubborn. Their utterly selfish behavior is making life awfully difficult for Sui Bun."

Immediately my sympathy went to Sui Bun. To have the two most important women in his life fighting constantly must be nerve wracking for him. I put my head on my knee, then I held my face. "My sister can be over bearing at times but she doesn't mean any harm. Mummy has spoiled her rotten and she is accustomed to getting her own way all the time."

Sui Fong sighed dismissively. "I wish I could defuse the stormy silence between the two women. Their dislikes for each is so obvious—they are absolutely beastly to each other. For Sui Bun's peace of mind I hope this feeling of utter resentment will terminate soon."

Acknowledging Sui Fong's remark I tried to judge the situation logically. "It must be awful for Sui Bun...I agree with you...their bickering has to stop. They must come to a truce. Perfectly childish behavior!"

Sui Fong conceded. "My mother tends to be overly possessive. I don't think that it's your sister's personality that triggers off Mum's resentment—it's not even a matter of personality clashes. Sui Bun is my only brother and Mother's security is threatened each time he demonstrates some interest for a girl. Lynette is too strong willed for her liking because she expects to have a submissive daughter-in-law. She won't be content until she is allowed to select a wife for my brother. I wish my father didn't die. It must be awful to be a widow!"

I slid off my bed gracefully. Stretching my cramped muscles I sighed, "I don't blame your mum or Lynette. I put the blame on Chinese culture. The women of your mum's generation have been trained to depend entirely on their husbands. They didn't know how to survive on their own. They were robbed of all their independence and their wings were clipped. Unfortunately, if their husbands should pass away before them they cling onto their sons like leeches."

"We are living in the twentieth century now. Mother will just have to adjust. She can't honestly expect her future daughter-in-law to behave the way she did. The frostiness between the two will have to dissolve soon. My poor brother is feeling positively rotten and he is getting the rough treatment from both sides. His nerves are really raw. I have an awful premonition for disaster."

I cupped Sui Fong's worried face with my hands and comforted her soothingly. "Sui Fong you are letting your imagination run wild—possibly over reacting—it can't be as bad as all that. Let's cross the bridge when we reach it."

The next day when I woke from my undisturbed sleep, I was bewildered by the scenery outside the window. The garden was covered by a blanket of snow. Frozen icicles were dripping from the trees. Excitedly I jumped out of my bed and reached for the telephone. Without further hesitation I dialed Gavin's number. After a few rings a sleepy voice answered.

As soon so I heard Gavin's voice I fired questions into the receiver. "You sleepy head! When are you coming to see me and what time did you get in last night? Why didn't you call?"

Gavin yawned and feigning irritation he rebuked, "Where is the fire and why all the excitement? Can't you ask your questions one at a time?"

I stamped my feet and pulled at the phone cord irritably. "Have you seen the snow outside? I wish you would come so that we can play with the snow!"

Chuckling Gavin teased, "It was snowing when the train pulled into London last night. The weather was awful and it took me a long time to find a taxi. When I arrived home it was rather late so I didn't bother to contact you. I knew that you would call this morning when you saw the snow. I was just waiting for your call…"

I thought Gavin was lying to me so I hissed into the phone. "Liar! You weren't waiting for my call but sleeping. Anyway are you coming or not?"

I could hear him shuffling out of bed while he muffled, "I will be at your service as soon as I can. In the meantime make yourself some breakfast while you are waiting for me."

"Yes, *Old Man* and stop nagging." I returned the receiver onto the phone and went to the kitchen searching for food.

Although I was dressed warmly, I was still shivering in the garden. It was extremely cold. The temperature had dropped drastically overnight. The cutting cold wind blew at my face mercilessly. I rubbed my gloved hand to keep the blood circulating. I decided to move about so I shoved the snow while Gavin built a snowman for me. I had never seen snow and I loved the feel of it drifting through my fingers. Naughtily I made snowballs and threw them at Gavin. Peels of laughter echoed from the garden. Soon Alastair and Cedric joined in the snowball fight. I rolled on the wet snow to evade the snowballs and ultimately I was soaking wet. Oblivious to the cold and the dampness I had a lovely time.

After a few hours of rumbling in the snow Gavin insisted that I should soak in a hot bath. When I was wrapped up snugly in dry warm clothes again I proceeded to prepare the evening meal while Gavin chatted with me.

Suddenly a loud commotion could be heard from outside the kitchen. Lynette arrived in a huff. Slamming the front door, she screamed at our parents crossly, "Sui Bun's mother is just too much—I couldn't control my temper anymore so I told her to mind her own business, and I told Sui Bun that I never wanted to see him again!"

With a soothing tone Uncle Edwin inquired, "You are going a mile a minute. Calm down and help herself to a hot drink. We are not going anywhere. You can tell us what is bothering you and what seems to be the problem that exists between you and Mrs. Cheng."

Gavin made Lynette a cup of hot tea and both of us joined them in the family room. Lynette accepted the tea gratefully, and she narrated the accident with her natural dauntless manner. "I had invited Sui Bun home for dinner tonight. He hasn't seen Melanie and Alastair since they have been home from school. He is always hinting how much he misses Melanie's cooking. Anyway after lunch he told me that his mother had called and insisted that he go home for dinner tonight. To my utter disgust and disappointment he agreed."

Pausing for breath and scowling Lynette continued. "When I asked him why he agreed to have dinner with his mother tonight, he told me that he didn't want to hurt her feelings. What about my feelings? This is really the last straw! I absolutely refuse to have anything to do with this dispirited weak character. He never has a mind of his own. Talk about a puppet on the string. He can be his mother's puppet but I won't! Why can't he just say no to his mother instead of kowtowing to her endlessly?"

Gavin decided that it was time for us to return to the kitchen, so we moved toward the kitchen discreetly, but we could still hear Mother's voice. "I can see your point of view and understand your frustration. Mrs. Cheng's possessiveness can be rather humiliating at times, but after all, Sui Bun is her only son. You can't condemn a person for being loyal to his mother. Lynette, you have to be more understanding and try to be reasonable. You can't just abandon your relationship with Sui Bun simply because Mrs. Cheng can be difficult at times..."

Lynette screamed reproachfully, "Be reasonable! I am absolutely sick and tired of this entanglement. There is certainly no end to that old woman's illogical demands. Sui Bun will have to replace me with someone who is willing to accept his mother for what she is—an old bag! I am just the wrong choice."

"Can't you learn to adjust? One has to give and take with every type of relationship. Try not to magnify the problem. Don't lose your perspective. You are no longer a little girl but a mature young lady. Don't make hasty decisions that you may regret later." I could hardly hear Mother's sensible advice to Lynette.

I thought both Mother and Uncle Edwin could do with a cup of tea. So I made a fresh pot and took it into the family room. Pacing the room nervously Lynette was squirming and quivering with aggravation. "Mrs. Cheng is constantly trying to provoke me. She distinctly and positively dislikes me. I will fulfill her wishes. I don't want to have anything to do with Sui Bun ever again!"

Hoping to convince Mother that she had made the right decision Lynette hugged her and implored, "Honestly, Mummy I have tried, but most of the time I am livid with resentment. I frankly do not see a future for us. We might as well cut our loses now...at least, hopefully, we can still be friends."

I returned to the kitchen deciding that I had heard enough because I was tense with apprehension. Frowning I confided in Gavin. "Only yesterday Sui Fong was so anxious over this problem. I never thought that the end would come so soon."

"I kind of expected this out-come! For once I tend to agree with Lynette. From what I have seen and heard so far, surprisingly, she has been bending backwards for Mrs. Cheng. We can't expect her to accept the older woman's constant unreasonable demands resiliently—it's too uncharacteristic for Lynette. You might able to tolerate Mrs. Cheng's unreasonable behavior but definitely not Lynette. Perhaps for a short period of time but to expect her to accommodate indefinitely will be a hoping for a miracle!" Gavin concluded.

I stopped chopping the onion for tears were streaming down my face. Gavin was alarmed. "No point in getting yourself so uptight and upset over Lynette's problem. It will resolve itself eventually." Gavin pushed a piece of paper towel into my hands.

I smiled and took the paper towel from Gavin gratefully. I blew my noise and explained, "I am disturbed but not to the point of tears. The onion is the cause of my tears."

I pushed the chopping board over to Gavin, gesturing him to take over the task. Gavin took the half-cut onion from me and made a comment. "Momentarily I thought you were crying for Lynette and Sui Bun—you are capable of doing it—you do possess such a kind heart. You have pity for almost anything."

Twenty-One

A week had passed by since Lynette's outburst. She had stubbornly refused to see Sui Bun. Unanimously we decided that it was best for the family not to interfere. After all Lynette should be mature enough to know her own mind. If she married Sui Bun, she would have to live with him and his mother—it was impossible for bystanders to make any harsh judgment or take sides.

The family was gathered in the family room after a delightful Christmas lunch. Instead of eating the traditional turkey we decided on steamed fish and shark's fin soup—authentic Chinese food. The fire was blazing in the fireplace...the warmth of the room and the flickering lights on the Christmas tree was having a mesmerized effect on me. My eyes were closing and I was dozing off to sleep lying on the carpet. Suddenly Uncle Edwin's voice jerked me back to attention. "Your mother and I are delighted to have the entire family with us today because we have a joyful and important announcement to make..." Everyone waited with anticipation for him to continue.

"We have decided to get married during the Easter Holiday. Hopefully your mother will return to Hong Kong to take up permanent residence with me!"

We were all stunned into silence by the news and the room was dreadfully quiet. Then suddenly everyone spoke spontaneously. I was the first to regain my composure. Happily and excitedly I jumped from the floor and pounced on Mother. "It's about time too. I was beginning to think that it would never happen. I am so pleased for you. Mummy, you do deserve some happiness!" Turning to Uncle Edwin, I kissed him briefly. "Well Daddy! Welcome into the family. How does it feel to be tied to three brats for the rest of your life?"

Uncle Edwin pulled a funny face and laughed. "The thought is definitely scary and absolutely mind-bombing—it's a frightful experience, but I am sure I will survive!"

Cheekily and with an assertive tone Alastair warned, "I wouldn't do it if I were you. You don't know what you have let yourself in for. But if you have truly decided, then what the hell? We are all fools at one time or another. Why should you be the exception? I rather fancy having a father for a change." He gave Uncle Edwin one of his bear hugs.

Having had time to review the situation, suddenly, Lynette demanded shrilly, "What about us? Who is going to take care of us when both of you leave the country?"

Cedric wagged his fingers at Lynette and chaffed, "We will change your nappies for you and we will be responsible for your milk bottles—not forgetting your pacifier, so that you won't be provided with an opportunity to suck your thumb…"

Lynette stamped her feet and smacked Cedric on his head while everyone cracked with hysterics. When the laughter subsided Mother said anxiously, "We are still pondering over the decision whether I should return to Hong Kong to reside. I would hate to leave you guys entirely unchaperoned. When we have found a solution, we will discuss the subject again."

Lynette turned timid and thoughtfully she ventured, "I have completed my schooling and have no immediate plans for furthering my education. Can I return to Hong Kong with you? Uncle Edwin…I mean Daddy, can you assist me in securing some sort of employment in Hong Kong?" She added in a matter-of-fact manner. "I am no longer a green horn—I am a trained receptionist."

Uncle Edwin immediately agreed with approval. "I think that this is an excellent suggestion. Melanie and Alastair will be in boarding school half of the year. They can return to Hong Kong for all their summer holidays and we only have to bother with the Christmas and Easter Holidays. In any case I don't see why they can't come back to Hong Kong three times a year."

I sprang from the floor and exclaimed, "That will be too extravagant!

I am certain we can find an alternative—something that is more economical and suitable. Maybe Peter will be kind enough to provide us with a home during the holidays?"

Mother answered thoughtfully, "That is a thought! But then it may be too much of a responsibility for him. We will see!" She added as a second thought. "Talking about returning to Hong Kong for the summer...Cedric's sister Ardelia will be getting married in the summer and she has extended an invitation for Melanie to be one of her bridesmaids. You will all be returning to Hong Kong for the summer!"

I was flabbergasted. I couldn't believe my ears—returning to Hong Kong for the summer and as a bridesmaid! I had to be dreaming! Mother smiled at me and I kissed her. Then I turned to Gavin. "What about you and Raphael? How are you going to survive without me for the duration of the entire holiday?"

"For your information," Gavin replied with equal arrogance, "we will be going to Hong Kong for the summer as well! So there you are—is my reply to your satisfaction?"

I nodded my head blissfully. Gavin and I will be visiting Hong Kong again—I just couldn't wait for the summer to arrive. The family meeting was finally concluded with an extremely cheerful note. Every member of the family was exhilarated with Mother's forthcoming wedding.

The following evening, unexpectedly, Lynette and I were alone in the house. I took the rare opportunity to talk to her about Sui Bun.

"Are you serious about breaking up with Sui Bun?" I inquired.

"We've never had the chance to enjoy a cozy *tête-a-tête*...why don't I make ourselves something hot to drink and you can start the fire in the family room?" Lynette walked into the kitchen.

When Lynette returned with a couple of mugs in her hand, the logs were burning in the fireplace. The burning logs dispatched a warm glow into the room adding homeliness and snugness to the atmosphere. Lynette gave me one of the mugs and sat in front of the fire. I sat next to her. She took a sip of the hot liquid and revealed her feelings. "I hope you don't think that I am being awfully heartless and selfish toward Sui Bun. Sometime one has to be cruel to be kind. I honestly cannot see a bright future for us. It's best that I cut all strings immediately."

Gazing into the fire Lynette proceeded pensively, "In all honesty, I am far from ready to settle down. Sui Bun is searching for a permanent relationship. In any case, even if I were ready I wouldn't be able to cope with his mother's persistent demands. Sui Bun and I will be fighting constantly. It's too demanding and nerve-wrecking for all parties concerned."

I searched Lynette's face and for a fleeting moment I thought I saw some sadness portrayed through her lovely eyes. I agreed with her thinking wholeheartedly. "It is a difficult task for two people to adjust to each others' habits. You don't really need a third party involved and interfering constantly. Sui Bun is heading for disaster if he doesn't put a stop to his mother's unyielding behavior."

Lynette smiled sadly and interrupted. "Precisely—that's exactly what I have insisted upon him. He has already lost me and who ever gets involved with him in the future will experience the same interference from his mum. No doubt, there are some submissive girls who can tolerate such absurd behavior but I really cannot cope. I need to breathe again. This relationship is suffocating me—returning to Hong Kong is the best solution for all concerned. I really have no reason to stay on in England...although, I have lived in England for so many years, but basically my roots are still in Hong Kong. I still look upon that enchanting city as my home and no other place can capture my heart and attention. Secretly I have missed Hong Kong terribly."

I was happy that Lynette had taken me into her confidence. Reassuring her that she had my complete sympathy and support, I said good night to her and returned to my room.

A few days later Sui Fong found me in my room. I was sewing rapidly with experienced skill. Making herself comfortable by sprawling on my bed Sui Fong begged, "I need a big favor from you!"

Removing my attention from the material to Sui Fong's face I inquired with intrigue, "Sure, what can I do for you?"

Sui Fong responded with a grimace, "Sui Bun has been quiet ill. As a matter of fact he has been off work for two weeks already...since Lynette's resignation. Mother is rather alarmed. I thought perhaps you could have a talk with him and put some sense into his thick head. He does admire your good sense of perception. He thinks that you have a logical head screwed on your shoulders."

"What a lovely compliment—I don't really deserve it. O.K. Why don't I visit him tomorrow and this will provide me with the opportunity to talk to him about Lynette."

"Sui Bun doesn't know that Lynette has decided to return to Hong Kong. I have decided not to tell him—the information may be too much of a shock for him."

I reprimanded Sui Fong for her childish action. "It's wrong to keep the truth from your brother. He is not a weakling but a grown man. He should be able to ride any waves deriving from life. I will tell him when

I visit him."

The following day I kept my promise to Sui Fong. Soon after lunch I found myself ringing the front door bell of the Cheng's quaint little house in Hampstead. I was admiring the immaculately manicured garden when Sui Fong opened the door for me. When I walked into the living room of the Cheng's residence I found Sui Bun gazing out of the window with a dejected and pitiful expression. His eyes had lost their normal sparkle. His complexion was dull and the natural glow on his cheeks was no longer apparent. The room was too warm and the television was on full blast, but Sui Bun showed no interest. Mrs. Cheng hovered protectively around her son. Sui Bun greeted me with a melancholy smile and my heart twisted with pain. I sympathized with him—caught between a domineering Mother and a demanding girlfriend. I returned Sui Bun's smile and greeted Mrs. Cheng with a cheerful hello. Mrs. Cheng offered me a cup of hot Jasmine tea then immediately complained, "I don't understand your sister's attitude. What has my son done to her? Why does she treat him so heartlessly? She refuses to see him and rejects all his phone calls. Has she no compassion at all?"

"Mother why can't you hold your tongue for a change? Melanie is here to visit Sui Bun. She does not want to listen to your criticism of her sister," Sui Fong chided Mrs. Cheng crossly. It was apparent that she was losing her patience and tolerance toward the older woman.

Ignoring Mrs. Cheng's rude outburst, I sat on the single armchair that faced Sui Bun and inquired, "Sui Bun I hope that you are not feeling too poorly. Maybe some fresh air will you a world of good. You shouldn't be cooped up in this room. The stale air will certainly do more damage to your health. You need some sunshine!"

Neglecting to acknowledge my rational suggestion Sui Bun blurted, "I miss your sister desperately. I really want to regain her favor. I don't want to lose her."

I attempted to soothe Sui Bun's hurt feelings and defended Lynette simultaneously. "You haven't lost Lynette. The two of you are still friends. She reckons that for a while it is best that you don't have any contact with her. Both of you need some time to recover your equilibrium. Lynette has made a sensible decision. She is really not the right candidate to be your future wife. There is definitely someone more suitable for you…given time and patience you will find the right girl and Lynette will become a fond memory…"

Sui Bun challenged my statement indignantly. "You are so young. What do you know about relationship between a man and a woman?

What makes you such an authority on this subject?"

Patiently I patted his hand and countered, "I may be young but I happen to know my sister only too well. Have you heard of an ancient Chinese saying—"A jungle cannot accommodate two reigning tigresses?" My sister cannot be domineered—she will always be her own master. Ever since she was born my mother has spoiled her rotten. It's awfully difficult for her to change now. She has tried to mend her ways—you may consider the change imperceptible but I must admit the improvement is colossal by her standard—she really cannot do more. Nevertheless, it's obvious that her progression is not good enough for Mrs. Cheng's standard. We all have our own expectations." You will be much better off with another girl with a timid personality and a demure nature."

Stubbornly Sui Bun persisted, "We should all strive to adjust to this predicament. Why can't Lynette give us another chance?"

I moaned, then coaxing Sui Bun with an encouraging smile, I cajoled again, "Sometimes we are all too set in our own ways. As the saying goes, "One can't really teach old dogs new tricks"—this is the perfect example. This situation is too tormenting for all parties concerned. Why don't you cut your losses now and thank your lucky star that you have been provided with another chance to find someone more suitable?"

Sui Bun was not convinced. He was awfully persistent. "There must be another way to handle this entangled situation."

I sighed inwardly. How could I tell this dejected young man that it was really a problem between him and his mother? Mrs. Cheng will always be determined to wriggle her way into her son's affair—resenting any girl who would get too involved with him. She intended to destroy any relationship that might threaten her security.

Furiously Sui Bun retaliated, "I will change and I will ignore Mother's demands. We will lead our own lives!" He bestowed his mother a disgusted look.

Tactfully and with haste I reminded Sui Bun of his responsibilities. "We all have our obligations. Mrs. Cheng is your mother and we mustn't forget our priorities in life. You can change your girlfriend but you only have one Mother."

Defensively Mrs. Cheng interrupted and challenged me, "Are you insinuating that I am the cause of this mishap and that I have been ill-treating your sister? Have I been so unfair to her?"

Exasperated Sui Fong pounced to my rescue. "Mother you should know where the limitation of interference should terminate. You have your own beliefs and we have our own ideas and dreams. We cannot all kowtow to your whims continuously. We live in a bureaucratic society—

we are entitled to our freedom. Traditionally we Chinese girls should all be yielding to our elders but we cannot accommodate to you blindly. Let this be a lesson to you. Next time round, do try and mend your ways."

I marveled at Sui Fong's boldness. If only Sui Bun had half of his sister's courage he might not have lost Lynette's affection. Who would ever know? I resumed my task of coaxing Sui Bun. "I am optimistic that you will feel better soon. For the time being I realize that it is difficult or almost impossible for you to accept the fact that time will heal all wounds. Raphael has survived...he is now dating another girl who absolutely adores the ground that he walks on and he is so much happier. In any case Lynette has decided to return to Hong Kong with my parents permanently." I thought I would drop the bomb gently.

Sui Bun almost leaped from his seat. He was horrified with the news. Gloomily he grumbled, "Lynette's decision is positively heartless and brutal!" When he sat down again he paused for a few short moments then he remarked decisively, "I will follow her to Hong Kong."

With undisguised disgust Mrs. Cheng screamed, "You must have lost your mind completely. That girl has bewitched you. How can you follow her to Hong Kong? What about your training as a chartered accountant? What about me? Don't you dare. I won't allow it!"

Sui Fong impatiently waved her hands to silence the two agitated parties. "Mother control yourself—this is just a jest on Sui Bun's part. He cannot be serious about following Lynette to Hong Kong. The whole idea is impractical and reckless!" Returning her attention to her brother Sui Fong scolded, "Don't be so thoroughly pathetic. How can you even consider following a girl to the other side of the world? Lynette has made a sensible and positive decision—let us support her. Hopefully we will all survive and learn from this little episode."

I could sense that Sui Bun was tormented with grief but his sister's outburst somehow defused his compulsive thinking. Gallantly, he agreed with his sister's wisdom and graciously, he thanked me for my sympathy. He assured me that he truly appreciated my caring. He guaranteed that I had found myself a true friend in him and if ever I required assistance of any kind he would help me with no hesitation. When I left, to my surprise, Mrs. Cheng followed me to the front door and thanked me. Sui Fong walked with me to the Underground station. Gratefully, she remarked, "You were marvelous—such tact and delicate diplomacy—you managed to convince Sui Bun that Lynette had made the right decision and at the same time you did not criticize my mother or rub her the wrong way. I am really grateful."

I purchased my ticket, then I kissed Sui Fong fondly on both cheeks.

"What are friends for?"

When I arrived home, I was mentally exhausted. It was such a demanding mission but I was delighted that I was able to contribute some comforts to the Cheng family. Secretly I wished that Sui Bun would learn from this bitter experience and be able to cultivate more firmness against his mother. Uncle Edwin and Mother were sitting in the family room chatting with Lynette. The threesome was discussing their traveling plans. When Lynette saw me, she looked at me anxiously and inquiringly. She knew that I had been to visit Sui Bun. I gave her the thumb of victory and winked at her conspiringly, showing her that my mission was accomplished successfully.

Uncle Edwin inquired, "Well, young lady. I heard that you have been visiting with Sui Bun and his family. I hope that you have been able to talk some sense into the young man."

Flopping on the floor I closed my eyes and took a deep breath. "I hope so, but somehow I have this wretched feeling that Mrs. Cheng will invariably be Sui Bun's stumbling block to his future happiness. He will have to learn to fight his mother." I paused then I chuckled and dramatized the situation. "Sui Bun actually threatened to follow Lynette to Hong Kong—his impulsiveness nearly caused Mrs. Cheng a major heart attack!"

Mother was staggered and appalled with my dramatized revelation. "Heaven forbid—you are not serious?"

I shook my head and laughed, "He did threaten, and Mrs. Cheng screamed. Between Sui Fong and myself, we told him that he was pathetic and irresponsible. We insisted that he should struggle on with his life in England, with or without Lynette. England is after all his home. Mind you, I reckon that he has managed to unnerve Mrs. Cheng with his empty threats. Let's hope and pray that Mrs. Cheng will mend her ways in the future." I shook my head dejectedly and muttered, "Between you and me and the four walls I doubt if Mrs. Cheng will ever change—she has been brain washed by the old fashion Chinese tradition!" I turned to Mother and said cheekily, "Thank goodness, Mother you have not been brain washed... I think all widows should remarry!"

Twenty-Two

"Melanie, Melanie you are wanted on the phone!" Alastair was yelling.

I didn't know that Alastair was home. Obviously he had returned from the library. I hoped that he had managed to borrow the reference book that I needed to finish my essay. I closed the book that I was reading. Instead of answering the phone in my room I joined Alastair in the family room. "Is it Gavin?" I wanted to know.

"Why don't you find out for yourself?" Then my naughty brother disappeared into the kitchen obviously searching for food. How could he eat so much? I wondered.

When I picked up the phone a deep voice asked, "Who is Gavin?"

I was motionless for a split second—absolutely mesmerized by the enchanting voice. When I was able to find my voice again I answered haltingly, "Gavin is a friend of the family. When did you return to London?"

Theo's attractive voice echoed into my ears. "I flew in late last night. I was hoping that you may be free to spend the day with me."

I was positively entranced by the invitation. Without any hesitation I immediately accepted wholeheartedly—his offer was too tempting for me to refuse. Theo's response was music to my ears. "Terrific! I will call for you in an hour's time."

"Shall I give you the address?" I asked excitedly.

"I have your address." Was his reply.

"Of course. Oh, by the way I really liked the roses that you sent me...so thoughtful of you, and I almost forgot to thank you," I muttered bashfully. When I replaced the receiver on the phone I could feel my face turning red and my eyes must be sparkling. Butterflies started to flutter in my stomach. My heart was beating so fast that my ribs hurt. I had to a take a couple of deep breaths to steady my trembling legs. I dashed into my room and yanked opened the wardrobe door. I was frantically trying to decide what would be the perfect outfit for my first date with Theo. After at least fifteen minutes of debate with myself I decided on a simple black wool dress. During the next little while I took exuberant care to attend to my hair and face. Finally I was delighted with my own reflection in the mirror. My face was glowing with radiance. Theo definitely had an intoxicating effect on me.

When I opened the front door, my heart almost leaped from my mouth at the sight of Theo's handsome face. He stood by the open door and shoved a bunch of white roses into my trembling hands. He looked so gorgeous with his blue blazer and an open neck white shirt. Smiling tenderly he pulled me into his arms and gave me a gentle hug. Then his lips brushed my face briefly. I was breathless and motionless. Theo had hypnotized me. When I was composed again I invited him into the family room and offered to get him a hot drink. I needed a few moments to catch my breath.

When I returned from the kitchen, I brought with me a vase for the roses that he had so thoughtfully brought for me. I found Theo scanning the room curiously. "Do you live with your parents?"

Lounging on one of the bean bags, I prattled away nervously. "My mother is a widow but she will be remarrying in a few months' time. Then she will return to Hong Kong with my stepfather. He is a practicing solicitor back home. For now I live with Mummy, my elder sister Lynette and Alastair. My cousin Cedric sometimes stays over. Then there is Gavin our family friend who visits us quite often. When Mummy is away, our guardian Peter keeps a watchful eye on us."

Theo gazed deeply into my eyes and asked curiously with tenderness, "Don't you feel homesick for Hong Kong?"

Returning his gaze boldly I shrugged my shoulders and replied, "I used to miss my hometown badly but it's not too bad now...at least my immediate family is here with me. I suppose I will feel desolate when my parents and sister return to Hong Kong. A final decision has not yet been made as to where Alastair and myself will be staying during our holidays. We may have to return to Hong Kong for all our holidays."

Theo returned the cup and saucer on to the coffee table then he asked, "What would you like to do—a drive perhaps or maybe watch a film?"

I felt so mature sitting next to Theo while he was driving his little white sports car. We drove to Hampstead Heath and parked the car. Although it was drizzling and the wind was bitterly cold I was oblivious to the bad weather. I felt ecstatic. We set in the warm car and chatted. Theo told me about his family and his childhood. His father was in the travel business with branch offices scattered all over England and Europe. Mr. Rockfield senior was obviously successful. Due to his business he had to do a lot of traveling. Occasionally Theo's mother accompanied her husband. Theo was the youngest son. He had an elder sister who was a devoted ballerina. Proudly Theo told me that she performed internationally and was hardly home. When she was home she would stay in their flat in London. I was fascinated with all the information. When I began to shiver from the dampness and the cold Theo took me to the El Sorano Coffee Shop on Hampstead High Street and I tasted the best cup of cappuccino. When we had finished our coffee, Theo drove me to the West End and we watched a film. When it was dinner time, we shared an excellent meal of pasta in a chic Italian restaurant. Obviously Theo was a regular customer because all the waiters knew him and we were escorted to a secluded table. I loved the intimate atmosphere—we were able to resume our conversation without too much interference from the waiters and other diners. When Theo finally returned me to my home, we made arrangement to meet again the following day. Theo kissed me gently on my lips and he sauntered back to his car. I watched until his car disappeared into the night.

I waltzed into my room humming to myself. When I was finally in bed sleep escaped me. I gazed out of the window into the garden. Stars twinkled in the clear sky and the moon was shining enchantingly—the entire universe was utterly beautiful. I was falling in love. The feeling was so strange and yet so captivating. Then suddenly my thoughts returned to Gavin, my ever faithful friend. He would be so delighted for me. When I was in Gavin's company I felt secure and I was comfortable. But with Theo I felt excitement and I was a bag of nerves—constantly in extreme ecstasy always wanting to reach for the moon. Theo made me feel beautiful and I wanted to scream on top of the highest mountain telling the whole world of my newfound love. That night I had marvelous dreams. Theo's attractive eyes invaded my unconsciousness.

The next day the persistent jingle of the phone woke me from my deep slumber. Sleepily I pushed the hair off my face and fumbled for the phone extension on my bedside table. Gavin's assuring voice asked, "So how was your date?"

When I heard Gavin's question, I returned to earth from outer space. Dreamily I replied, "News certainly travel fast—I suppose my brother has been babbling again."

I could hear Gavin's chuckle before he suggested, "I have to be leaving town in a few hours because I have been invited to stay with some friends for a few days. How about cooking some breakfast for me? I can be with you in an hour. I would love to hear about your latest romance." Cheekily he added, "I can just about spare you a couple of hours before my departure!"

I happily agreed and was cooking in the kitchen when Gavin arrived. The mouth-watering aroma of fried sausages and sizzling bacon drifted into the family room. I could hear Alastair saying to Gavin, "I can smell cooked breakfast—let's join the cook in the kitchen!"

After helping themselves to freshly brewed coffee Alastair paced the floor impatiently while I put the sausages and bacon on warm plates and Gavin sat on the edge of the table. Gavin watched me with interests, then he said to Alastair with a cheeky tone of voice, "Don't you think your sister is beautiful and oozing with confidence?"

Alastair winked at Gavin conspiringly and he mumbled with his mouth full. "Yeh! I think Theo is the cause for the improvement."

I untied the apron around my slim waist and threw it at Alastair. "You two are positively beastly and nasty to me—so sarcastic!" I yelled at them.

Later Gavin and I were alone in the kitchen. "Well young Melanie, I am all ears and waiting patiently for your confession," Gavin teased.

I replied indignantly, "I have nothing to confess! I have been dating this most gorgeous young man Theodore Rockfield. This strange feeling that I feel inside is so alien but terrific... I feel as if I can conquer the entire world with my bare hands." Pushing the empty plates away I continued, "I know this all sound immensely daft to you but I seem to be contradicting myself continuously. I am in heaven one moment and yet I feel sad the next—I just can't describe this weird emotion persistently churning inside me. I feel so vulnerable, no longer my own master. I am swaying with the wind." Humming to myself, I waltzed around the kitchen.

Gavin suddenly snapped his fingers and said that he had found the perfect solution for my dilemma. "I suggest a cold shower. The shock may bring you back to earth! You possess all the symptoms of a love-sick teenager." Then with a serious tone of voice he advised, "Be careful—don't go too overboard—it's not healthy or wise to be floating on air."

I cupped his serious face with my hands and groaned, "Oh! I do hate your disturbing imperious lectures. Let your hair down for a change—live—don't behave like an old man. Life is full of excitement. Go for it. I absolutely detest it when you are so sensible all the time! Be a dare devil. Who knows what tomorrow may bring."

Gavin persisted, "We are too young to be involved with any type of serious relationship. If you climb too high, the pain will be unbearable when you fall. I am really and truly delighted for you…but I don't want to see you hurt. I would hate to see a tearful Melanie. We are bound to be hurt at one time or another but to what extent is up to us. Up to a point destiny does control our lives but chances are there for us to grab and risks are there for us to take. Tears and laughter usually go hand in hand. If you laugh too much, you will ultimately cry just as much."

I hugged Gavin tenderly and he reciprocated. Gently I murmured into his hair, "You are full of wisdom…" Then laughing I disentangled myself from Gavin's embrace. Wagging my fingers at him I yelled, "and full of bullshit!" I was in hysterics with hiccups while Gavin was horrified with my naughty behavior.

"I am disgusted with your foul language. Obviously Auntie Wei Ling is wasting her money. She truly believed that this school with such an exorbitant fee would turn you into a lady. She would be so disappointed with your performance."

Happily Gavin and I cleaned the kitchen, then he left to visit his friends. In the meantime I waited impatiently for the arrival of my dream lover. When Theo finally arrived, I invited him for dinner.

Uncle Edwin and Mother were playing Mah Jong at Peter's while Lynette had gone out with some friends. Alastair was out playing tennis with Cedric. No doubt Sui Fong, the ever faithful spectator was with them. It was nice that we had the entire house to ourselves.

When I extended my invitation for a home cooked meal, Theo was dubious about accepting. He had dated numerous girls and all those girls refused to venture into the kitchen. I was nervous but soon my anxiety evaporated because Theo was sitting in the kitchen and seemed enthralled with my efficiency. Vegetables were chopped, meat was marinated, pots and pans were clanging. I moved from the stove to an open drawer; I was washing the chopping board while the steaks were sizzling in the hot frying pan. Appetizing aroma filled the air. Plates and cutlery were placed on the table. Soon an appetizing meal materialized. When the elaborate and delicious meal was consumed I meticulously cleaned the kitchen. Theo was fascinated and he marveled at my speed and efficiency. I strove for Theo's approval and I craved for his compliments.

While the coffee was brewing Theo returned to the family room and more logs were added to the blazing fire. When I rejoined Theo with the freshly brewed coffee, he insisted that I sit next to him. Then he sent me to heaven with his next remarks. "Melanie I have fallen under your spell…your exotic beauty has a hypnotizing effect on me. I have never dated an Oriental girl and the experience is intriguing and captivating. I am more than impressed by all your hidden domestic skills, and I am also aware that you are a conscientious student. If you feel the same for me then I am really a very lucky guy and I count my blessings. These newly discovered emotions frighten me. Before I met you I had no wish to be involved with anyone on a permanent basis but I find it impossible to resist your charm. I have decided to listen to my heart and let destiny guide me—I will throw all my cautions to the wind."

I was stunned by Theo's frankness and was caught speechless. I gazed into Theo's adorable blue eyes and I smiled blissfully. Then I surrendered into his inviting arms…

Twenty-Three

It was decided that Mother and Uncle Edwin would return to Hong Kong after school reopened. Happily, Cedric agreed to baby-sit the house during the absence of my parents. Lynette was no longer working so Mother wanted to take her back to Hong Kong as soon as possible. The threesome would not be returning to England until the Easter Holiday. Mother was adamant with her wishes to have a quiet and small wedding in England. Gavin accompanied us to the airport. I was more accustomed to my parents' constant traveling—the airport no longer activated unnecessary grief for me. I was able to wave happily when my family walked through the departure gates. When we left the airport Gavin caught the first available train and returned to school. Cedric and Alastair went to watch a film, and I went home to a relatively noiseless house. I was feeling a sense of loss as I did miss my family. Although I was depressed nonetheless I was excited about returning to Milford. In order to suppress the feeling of loneliness and desolation I spent the afternoon cleaning the house thoroughly. After a simple meal I took meticulous care in packing my trunk. During the holiday whenever I had spare time on my hands I had been making new clothes for myself. I loved smart clothes. With my increased interests in fashion I was also aware of my looks. Experimenting with cosmetic became one of my favorite hobbies. I realized if I were able to apply make-up artfully it would definitely add to my attractiveness.

Excited over the forthcoming term I boarded the school train for Sommerset. Carol was delighted to see me. She was full of fascinating adventures for my attentive ears. She had spent the entire Christmas holiday as Anthony's house guest and she was full of praises for his family. I was happy for my friend's newfound happiness. I really couldn't complain. I wasn't doing too badly with my love life. Although Carol's excited chatter was constant, my thoughts were drifting. I waited impatiently for the appearance of Theo.

"Melanie, you are not listening!" Carol pulled my hand and demanded my complete attention.

Carol's shrill remark brought me back to the present. I smiled at her serenely. "What did you say…?"

"Obviously I have been babbling to myself for the past twenty minutes. What happened to your concentration? Does it have wings?"

The door to our compartment was pushed opened. Expecting to see Anthony, Carol was surprised to find Theo standing by the open door. Smartly attired as usual he approached me and kissed me tenderly. I couldn't help but inhale his masculine, musky smell. Carol was astounded with this display of affection between Theo and myself. Puzzled she stared at us with her big brown eyes.

"I have to attend to some tedious details so I have to leave you for a while. Will you be O.K.?" Theo asked affectionately while touching the tip of my nose with gentleness.

Carol couldn't contain her insolence so she remarked, "How do you think Melanie existed before your gallant invasion into her life?"

I shooed my friend into silence by nudging her shoulder. Lovingly I gazed into Theo's eyes and reassured him demurely, "Don't worry about me. This chatter box with her interminable jabber will keep me entertained until we arrive." I winked at Carol and chuckled.

Carol waited until Theo had disappeared through the door then she protested, "Is there something terribly important you have neglected to tell me? I thought I was your friend and confidant—obviously I was wrong in my thinking—our friendship is not that significant." Carol glared at me then she mimicked Theo's tone of voice and repeated, "Are you going to be O.K.?"

Killing myself with hysterics and sighing in exasperation I begged my lovely friend to be reasonable, "Carol, you are absolutely impossible—the ultimate limit!" Do you realize that since the train has pulled out from the station you have not stop pattering for one minute? Whatever happened to that shy little girl who couldn't find her tongue? Have I been provided with a chance to say a word?"

There was a moment of silence then Carol giggled, "Well! I am waiting...I haven't uttered one tiny word for over a minute!"

I replied shyly, "I have seen Theo a few times during the last week of the holiday...."

Carol curled her arms around me and commanded, "And...I am still listening!"

"There is nothing more to confess!" I insisted returning her embrace.

"Oh sure! Then why did your eyes follow Theo's back with such longing? Why did your face glow with radiance when he appeared? Why did you blush when he spoke to you? You were so jumpy and nervous. Each time someone pushed open that door you get tense." Carol's interminable questions were like a machine gun firing at me continuously.

Amused by Carol's inquisitiveness I tried to reason with her, "Are you quite finished with all your why's and but's? There is nothing more to tell. Do stop your gibbering and admire the scenery. Can you believe that the sun can shine in January? Whatever has happened to the snow?"

Carol ignored my diversion and screamed indignantly, "You liar! The entire school will hear of your romance with Theo tomorrow. The Ice Princess has finally melted and trust Theo to be the cause of it. You will be the envy of all the girls." Carol hugged me forcefully. Then whispering she murmured, "I am delighted for you. I am also proud of you. You do deserve the best."

When the train finally arrived at its destination Theo reappeared. He escorted me to the waiting coach then murmuring endearments into my silky long hair, he kissed me gently on the lips. I was embarrassed by his demonstration of affection for me. I blushed and swiftly disappeared into the coach with Carol following me and grinning like a Cheshire cat.

The next morning Carol and I found our way to "The Cottage". When we walked through the door, all conversations ceased. It was so apparent that the other girls were talking about us or rather about me. One of the prefects, Diona, sneered at me and imparted a disgusting look toward my direction. With a sway of her long blonde hair she marched out of the room. With Diona's sudden departure everyone spoke spontaneously with enthusiasm. "Is it true that Theo is dating Melanie?" I could hear Josephine ask Carol.

"Of course!" Carol proudly replied while reviewing the new time table.

Jessica remarked, "Diona is not pleased with this new development. We all know that she has been trying to attract Theo's attention ever since her first day in school. Theo ignored her, but he had not been dating another girl so she had no reason to fret. Now that Melanie is in the picture it will be a different story."

Sally interrupted. "I can guarantee that Melanie will be in for a rough ride this term. With Diona's insufferable behavior and vindictive nature she will make certain that her rival will be provided with extra duties in order that she would not have any spare time to spend with Theo."

Alice predicted with sympathy, "Diona can make life awfully miserable for Melanie—after all she is a prefect. I can tell you now—that is exactly what she is going to do."

Carol decided superciliously, "We will cross the bridge when we come to it. No use crying over spilt milk. What's done is done. We can't force Diona on Theo or destroy his affection for Melanie. In any case why shouldn't he date Melanie? There is positively nothing wrong with my friend. He has made a splendid choice and I am proud of him."

Mr. John was delighted to see me again. "How was your holiday? You look marvelous. I bet you spent an enjoyable Christmas with your parents—have they returned to Hong Kong?" I hope you are prepared to endure another term of hard work!"

During the lesson Mr. John was disturbed by my abnormal behavior and loss of concentration. Discreetly I stole too many glances at my watch. I was not fully alert and on a few occasions my mind wandered off the subject that we were discussing. Mr. John had to repeat his questions to me. Before the end of the lesson, Theo was already waiting for me outside the hut. Mr. John saw him and immediately guessed the reason for my distraction. When the other students filed out of the room, Mr. John detained me. "Melanie, Theo obviously is very much attracted to you and you to him. I am happy for you. All young people need some outside diversion and stimulation to improve on your work. Theo is attractive but notorious for his lack of interest in his school work. His only fondness is in sports. I hope that he will not be a bad influence on you or prove to be a hindrance to your work. You are conscientious and you have tremendous potential. I am convinced that if you are provided with proper guidance you are destined to have a superb career. Don't disappoint me or yourself."

I was eager to join Theo. With determination I mastered all my concentration and listened to Mr. John's advice. The discussion among the girls in 'The Cottage' had disturbed me and I needed reassurance from Theo desperately. When Mr. John dismissed me I swiftly gathered my books and waved at my tutor. Immediately, I sprinted out of the hut.

When I was in the company of Theo my feelings of inadequacy evaporated and I no longer lacked any confidence. My desolation disappeared. Chatting happily we strolled on the lawn. We were so comfortable with each other. After a while we sat on the grass. I pulled some grass from the ground and chewed absentmindedly. The bitter taste was refreshing and gratefully I counted my blessings.

From the beginning of the term, I spent all of my spare time with Theo. It was heavenly to have him with me constantly. I loved to be with him but I wanted to work diligently as well. As predicted by everyone, Diona's nasty and jealous nature soon surfaced. I was put on extra school duties and when Diona was challenged on her decisions she was prepared with perfect explanations.

"Why do I have to supervise the younger girls during their prep time?" I asked defiantly.

Sweetly and craftily Diona justified her action, "You are extremely good with the children. You have so much patience with them and they just adore and admire you. I would have thought you would be the perfect choice."

Carol was disgusted with Diona's attitude. "What is this nonsense? Cooking experiments after classes? Trust that she-devil to assign this project to you. She said that you are a renowned cook; therefore, you would be the perfect leader to experiment with the other girls." With conviction Carol complained bitterly to me and I groaned inwardly—I didn't need another project. I needed time!

I was desperate for more time. Increasing volume of extra duties; ever demanding school work and Theo's demand for my time made life extremely strenuous for me. There were too many evenings when I had to work until late at night. In the mornings exhaustion prevented me from pulling my fatigued body out of bed. Soon dark circles under my eyes were visible and I was tired constantly. Although, determined to work diligently the standard of my work deteriorated rapidly. Mr. John was no longer able to retain his apprehension.

"Melanie, do you mind staying behind for a bit after lesson? I need to talk to you." Mr. John asked kindly.

Listlessly I agreed and flopped on the chair with a thump. I was surprised that Mr. John had not expressed his concern earlier. I was too ashamed to look at my tutor, so with downcast eyes I waited dejectedly for his criticism.

Mr. John started to pace the room with his hands behind his back. Eventually, he broke the silence and smiling kindly. He approached me diplomatically, "Are you finding your work too difficult?"

I blinked back threatened tears. I was mentally and physically exhausted. Overcome with frustration I craved for reassurance and guidance. I had to confide in someone and my kind tutor was my best choice. "I never seem to have enough time to attend to my school work. Diona is making life miserable for me because of my involvement with Theo. She has forced enough extra responsibilities on me to last me a life time. Theo is not showing any understanding to my problems instead he gets upset with me when I can't spare more time for him. I have been working at night when I should be sleeping. I am so tired!"

"There has to be a solution to your dilemma. You have to be firm with Theo. If you only have two hours to spare each day you can only allow him one." Mr. John advised compassionately. Due to his generous nature and perceptive mind I could no longer control my tears. The dam was broken and I bawled my eyes out. Between tears and sobs I emphasized on my increasing anxiety. "Diona is asserting her authority as a prefect profusely and unfairly. She reckons that I am the cause for her unhappiness. She truly believes that if weren't for me, Theo will be dating her. She is so wrong in her beliefs. Before I joined the school, Theo showed no interest in her. Why should he feel different now? She is also deviously sly. She has all the appropriate justification to cover up her devious action. One couldn't really point a finger at her. Life can be so unfair— I am disappointed."

Mr. John extracted a tissue from the box of Kleenex and shoved it into my clenched fingers. I accepted gratefully. Blowing my nose, my sobs began to subside. I was gradually regaining my composure. Promptly my kind tutor with superfluous kindness attempted to soothe the turbulent thoughts that were thundering in my clustered brain. "Melanie you must remember that life is never fair. You have to find the proper solution to balance out the unfairness." His wise words were to remain with me for the rest of my life. His wise perception on life was having a positive effect on me. His sedate manner and sensitivity to my depressed and dejected mood was like a strong dose of hope injected into my veins.

Hugging me fondly he allured me to smile again. He advised supportively, "Fate brought you and Theo together. Treasure this terrific opportunity, but you can only appreciate each other if the relationship does not create too much stress. How can you burn the candle from both ends? You have to diversify your attention from him and give yourself time to work. There should always be a right time for everything. You have to be firm with Theo's persistent demands."

Instinctively I jumped to my defense, "I do try to justify my actions with him but our viewpoints are perpetually clashing. He does not believe that a good education is an asset to his future. He was born with a silver spoon in his mouth. He will eventually inherit his father's successful travel business with no hindrance. Whereas, I consider a good education a definite must to my future career. My mother was a young widow. She has striven to provide the best for us. We never really lacked material things from life, but I hope I don't have to depend on her forever. I rather fancy my own success and independence."

Triumphantly, Mr. John beamed with his next remark. "I have always detected a strong personality in you. You believe in your own principles and you work toward them. I am extremely proud of your attitude and courage. Ignore Diona's malicious and childish conduct. Look upon it as an added experience in your life. Turn the table around. Instead of believing that she is ill treating you tell yourself that she is providing you with an opportunity to learn. As for Theo, he will eventually understand. If he doesn't then I am afraid he is not the perfect Prince Charming for you. Frivolous criticism should be ignored. Remember that you were born with exquisite looks and you are gifted with an even temperament. You also have a brilliant mind and plenty of intelligence is tucked into that tiny head of yours. Don't let it go to waste."

I was grateful for Mr. John's encouragement. After our discussions my confidence soared again and my spirit recovered quickly. I had to divide my free time evenly between my studies and Theo. But which was my priority? I failed to find the answer.

Twenty-Four

It was the last week of March. We had returned to school for almost two months. Theo and I were sharing a cup of coffee during our break. He finished his coffee and threw away the paper cup. Casually he said, "My parents called last night. They are coming to visit me this weekend. I would very much like you to come with me for dinner and meet them."

His voice always sent a shiver through my body, and my legs would turn to jelly each time he looked at me with his clear blue eyes. I would love to meet his parents but the end-of-term examinations were approaching too quickly and I needed the forthcoming end-week to revise. I decided to decline the invitation. "I was prepared to spend the weekend on my revision…."

Theo took my hand and playing with my fingers he interupted, "How boring. Do your revision next weekend. After all my parents don't visit every weekend. I thought you told me that you would like to make their acquaintance. This is a good opportunity."

Craving for his understanding, I implored him with my eyes. "I am awfully sorry but I have a very important test next week. It's impossible for me to postpone my revision, till next weekend."

Theo watched me intensely and his blue eyes turned to ice. Acidly he demanded, "What is more important? Meeting my parents or your wretched books?"

The tone of his voice chilled my bones. My anger was rising so I retorted defiantly, "I am afraid my wretched books will have to come first! I can meet your parents on another occasion but if I fail my test I will not have a second chance to rewrite."

Theo scowled and confronted me, "Are you insinuating that your books are more important than our relationship?"

I was outraged. I scrambled to my feet and retorted, "If you put it like that—then, yes! My books are more important!" I felt like screaming, "My education is important to me and so are you, but I can replace you—please don't make me choose!" I bit my tongue and kept the thought to myself.

Throngs of students were walking past us and they watched us with curiosity. Theo realized that I could not be bullied into changing my mind because I could be perfectly stubborn. I had a submissive nature but if I were forced into a corner I wouldn't hesitate to retaliate. Immediately he changed his tactic. With a provocative smile that almost always swayed my decisions, he cajoled, "Please Melanie, you are over conscientious! You won't fell any tests. Study on Friday evening and Sunday. I really would like you to meet them."

I was in a dilemma. I could never resist his charm. My resistance was slowly crumbling. "This is all ludicrous. Why are we arguing? You and my work are just as important to me—I will compromise—I will have dinner with your parents on Saturday and study during the remaining of the weekend."

When I arrived home, my excitement was gradually changing to anxiety. I had wanted desperately to meet Theo's family. Needing reassurance I called Theo, "Do your parents know that I am Oriental?"

Theo chuckled. He obviously thought my question was unnecessary and silly. "No! But is it important that they should be forewarned?"

Dubiously I responded, "Maybe you should warn them first."

Pensively Theo replied haltingly, "Racial discrimination has never been an issue in my family...but then I have never dated an Oriental before. I honestly don't know how my parents would take to the idea." After a moment of silence he continued decisively, "Surely they are sophisticated people—after all my father is in the travel business. They should be open-minded. This is not the nineteenth century." He consoled me...or was he trying to convince himself?

I could detect hesitation in his voice. I was worried. I had hoped that Theo had warned his parents. I didn't want him to take their opinions for granted, but I didn't want to insist. I decided to call Sui Fong. When she answered the phone and heard my voice she exclaimed, "Melanie, are you all right?"

I was nervous. Pushing my hair behind my ears and with forced gaiety I laughed, "Don't panic! I just need to confide in you!"

"Momentarily you had me worried. You hardly ever call from school. What seems to be the problem?" Sui Fong detected the nervousness in my voice.

"I have been invited to meet Theo's parents on Saturday," I blurted.

Sui Fong was relieved. "So? It should be a happy occasion for you—why the fuss?"

Frowning I countered, "Theo hasn't told his parents that I am Chinese!"

Peels of laughter echoed over the phone. "We are living in the space age. There isn't such a thing as racism anymore. Once upon a time I admit that mixed marriages were not too popular but today—it is perfectly acceptable!" Sui Fong reassured me with her confidence.

I moaned and confessed, "I am utterly nervous. What if they don't like me?"

Sui Fong responded encouragingly, "You are not a monster. To the contrary—you are an enchantment to the eyes. You will sweep them off their feet. Just be your normal charming self, and you won't have a thing to worry about."

Meekly I replied with doubts, "I hope you are right. You are such a dear friend. I do appreciate and treasure our friendship." That was not the first time or the last that I had to take Sui Fong into my confidence.

Saturday approached too quickly. By the afternoon I was flustering like a chicken without its head. An assortment of clothing was scattered on my usually tidy bed. Carol attempted to calm my increasing anxiety but with no success. I just could not decide on what to wear. Finally I wore one of my many black dresses. It was extremely flattering to my slim figure. I piled my hair on my head hoping that the sophisticated hair style would add maturity to my outlook. I was not impressed with the reflection in the mirror, so impulsively I removed the bobby pins from my hair and let it cascade down my back. Eventually assisted by a pair of hair clips my hair was pushed behind my ears. Experimentally, I added more color to my cheeks with blush. Then I used beige color lipstick. The faint color blended in nicely with my dark complexion. After too much fussing I looked chic but demure I was ready for Theo to escort me to the restaurant. When Theo's car was parked outside the house I kissed Carol briefly and implored her to wish me luck, then I jumped into the waiting car.

When we arrived at the restaurant, candles flickered on each table and cast shifting shadows in the dim light. A roaring fire was burning in the fireplace but the flame was unable to provide me with warmth. My hands were icy and my body trembled with anxiety. Theo squeezed my hand reassuringly and with wobbly legs I followed him. An attractive elderly gentleman beckoned us toward his table. Sitting by the table and nursing a glass of red wine was a glamorously attired lady. Mrs. Rockfield must have been in her late forties. A burgundy color wool dress molded her slim body. A heavy gold chain caressed her neck and matching earrings glistened on her ears. Her hair was stylishly trimmed and slightly tinted. Her sharp features were attractive but harsh. Her thin lips were painted the same shade as her dress. I was immediately overwhelmed by her elegance and overpowered by her distinct aloofness. She embraced Theo and kissed him fondly but when she saw me the smile on her face froze. Disapprovingly she scrutinized me from head to foot. I had the distinct impression that she disliked me instantly. When I returned her frosty smile my heart sank to the pit of my stomach and my uneasiness increased. Shyly I smiled at Mr. Rockfield hoping for a better reception. Theo was a young replica of his father. I saw where Theo had acquired his good looks. The suit that Mr. Rockfield wore was evidently custom made. His initials were discreetly embroidered on the cuffs of his white shirt. The diamond stud gold cufflinks shone magnificently. Timidly I took a seat and smiled charmingly at the couple. What else could I do but smile? Mrs. Rockfield ignored me and although her husband's manner was impeccable his eyes generated no warmth. Perceptive to my discomforts Theo gently gripped my cold fingers under the table. Son and parents exchanged the latest family gossip, and the mother made certain that I was not included in their conversation. I could hardly swallow the food that was ordered for me. Awkwardly, with the assistance of the fork I pushed the food around the plate. When the half empty dishes were cleared away Mrs. Rockfield reluctantly addressed me. "So where do you come from?"

In a whisper, I politely replied, "My home is in Hong Kong."

The mother squinted at me distastefully, "How often do you go home?"

"I haven't been back since my arrival in England almost a year ago," I answered with restrained politeness.

"What about your parents—don't they worry about you?" Mr. Rockfield inquired and watched me with his unsmiling eyes.

I shrugged my shoulders and returned his gaze boldly. "They do. But they believe that a good education is more important than keeping me at home with them."

Mrs. Rockfield startled me with her next question, "What are their views on mixed marriages?"

The unexpected question caught me off guard. She was obviously trying to make a point. I started to blush but I was seething inwardly so I answered with equal coldness. "Racism is not a problem at home—Hong Kong is extremely cosmopolitan."

Hoping to improve the embarrassing atmosphere, Theo interrupted, "Mother, Melanie is a good cook. She is extremely gifted."

Mrs. Rockfield was horrified and appalled with her son's remark. Disgustedly she waved her beautifully manicured hand in the air and retorted, "We have maids to attend to the household chores. Your sister or any of our friends' daughters would never dirty their hands in the kitchen."

I refused to acknowledge her irrational statement. I clamped my mouth tightly but I was shaking with anger. I returned the older woman's antagonistic stare with equal hostility. The unpleasant evening ended in disaster.

When Theo was driving me home, I could no longer maintain my poise. I was humiliated to the point of tears. Instead of snuggling close to Theo, frigidly, I sat away from him and my eyes were fixed in the far distance. The weather was gloomy and so was my spirit. Premonitory fear of his parents' rejection of me had materialized. Although we lived in a modern society there were some who still lived in the conservative past and believed in the old tradition that the East and the West should not meet. Silently Theo saw me to the door and gently kissed me. Without a backward glance I disappeared into the quiet house. I welcomed the stillness because the hurtful feelings that I felt inside added turmoil to my distressed thoughts. I was disgusted with the Rockfields' abusive behavior. I flung my coat over my shoulder and took off my shoes. Dejectedly I climbed the stairs and gently opened the door to my room. To my relief Carol was asleep—I was not in the mood for her endless questions.

That night I must have cried in my sleep. Carol was staggered with my appearance the next morning. My eyes were red and swollen and my face was puffy from crying. I greeted my friend with a grin. Carol sensed my unhappiness and I was grateful that she did not intrude on my privacy. She knew that if I had wanted to talk I would confide in her. At the first opportunity I went into the telephone room and dialed Sui Fong's number.

When she answered the phone, my depression had converted to indignation and resentment. I hissed into the receiver, "You should have seen the way Theo's parents scrutinized me last night—they made me feel so small and inadequate. You would think that the mother was interviewing a maid. What a degrading ordeal! I don't think I ever want to see them again!"

Sui Fong was startled by my outburst. "Your meeting with them was obviously a flop. Are you overreacting? You might have mistook their aloofness for nastiness. You can't expect every family to be as friendly as yours."

I yelled into the phone, "I was not mistaken! I would have displayed more consideration for my maid servant. They squashed me like one would crush an ant crawling in the dirt. The mother was positively horrid. Every sentence that she said to me was laced with sarcasm and insults. If Lynette thought your mother had mistreated her she should have been in my shoes. Your mother is a darling compare to those two morons!"

Sui Fong was curious, "How did Theo react?"

I shrieked, "He just kept quiet—absolutely lack of backbone—worse than Sui Bun!"

"Calm down—he might have been too polite or embarrassed to react. Give the guy more credit. Take a couple of deep breaths and you will feel better. If and when you do get another chance to see them again treat them with dignity. Don't degrade yourself to their level," Sui Fong advised positively.

I did feel better after I was able to let off steam. I managed to dedicate a few hours on my work. Although my concentration swayed a few times, I was nonetheless determined to bury myself among my books. Books were my greatest salvation. Whenever I felt depressed, I generated great comfort from my readings. Shortly after lunch Theo arrived with a bunch of flowers for me. I suggested strolling in the garden. I expected our discussion to be too private for all the curious ears in the house.

"I am appalled with my parents' atrocious behavior—especially my mother. Please accept my sincere apology. I wish to God I could have prevented their vindictiveness. I hope they have not done too much damage to our relationship. I realize that you would be too proud to tolerate such barbaric behavior."

I ignored his apology and retorted with coldness, "No apologies on your part are necessary. You cannot be responsible for their actions."

Theo pulled my rigid body into his arms and pleaded with sincerity, "I should have warned them of your nationality. It might have been too much of a shock for them. Be generous—give them time. They will change their attitude and repent! They did not actually say that they did not approve of you."

I screamed with hysterics, "Some thoughts do not have to be put into words. Their action was crystal clear. They resented me because I am Chinese! They did not even bother to give themselves an opportunity to get to know me as a person! I was condemned because of the color of my skin. I am sorry for my hysterics but I am just not accustomed to this kind of rejection. It's beyond my comprehension. When I was in Hong Kong we looked upon foreigners as people—people that we would treat with respect." Tears sprang from my eyes and I trembled. I covered my face with my hands hoping that I could erase his parents' images from my mind.

Stroking my hair tenderly Theo muttered into my ears. "Please believe me I do understand your feelings but remember you are dating me—not them."

I removed my hands from my face but I couldn't control the suffocating sobs. "Of course I am dating you, but your parents' approval is vital to our relationship. Their resentment toward me can be excruciatingly painful for us. It could also be damaging to our relationship." Then I related Lynette's ordeal with Sui Bun's mother and Theo listened with attentiveness. When we returned to the house dejectedly I said, "Let's forget the incident. What's done is done. Hopefully in time their attitude toward me will alter." I was trying desperately to convince myself.

During the remaining of the term. We did not talk about Theo's parents or their attitude again, but I could feel a thorn had been wedged into our relationship. Or was it purely my imagination?

Twenty-Five

Furiously I flipped the pages of the thick dictionary. I was determined to find a correct word for the sentence that would start the essay that I was writing. No inspiration arrived and it seemed impossible for the right word to surface. I was agitated—I had to finish the essay and I was losing valuable time. Vaguely I heard someone call me and said that I was wanted on the phone. I hoped that the call was important as I just couldn't afford to waste any more precious time. I threw the dictionary on the desk and ran down the stairs dashing for the telephone room.

Theo's commanding voice requested for my presence at the match when I answered the phone. "There will be an exciting rugby match played in our house this afternoon. It will be interesting to watch our house's team play against your brother's team. The coach will be coming by your house to collect spectators. I don't want you to miss the bus!"

I had no other choice but to complete the essay so regrettably I had to decline his invitation, "Theo I am awfully sorry but I must give the game a miss. I still have an unfinished essay on my desk waiting for my immediate attention."

"With your intelligence you don't need too much time to finish it. Attend to it after the game. I really would like your support. You know I always play better when you are watching." Hoping to sway my decision

Theo resolved to flattery.

I didn't want to disappoint him but my conscience took command of my confused mind so I insisted, "I really have to work—please don't be difficult."

I could hear Theo's agitated voice and sternly he remarked, "I am not accustomed to rejections and I don't like disappointments. You will regret your decision should you defy me!"

He should know better than to threaten me. I did not take to intimidation too well. I murmured my reply with distaste, "Please don't force an ultimatum on me. I am afraid this time my essay will have to come first."

I was so involved and distraught by our argument that I failed to notice Diona hovering by the door and eavesdropping on my conversation. I was determined not to give in to Theo so I insisted that he would have to play the game without my physical support and returned to my room. The coach arrived and departed without me but through the window I saw Diona disappearing into the bus. By that evening I was exhausted but my essay was completed to my satisfaction. The neatly typed pages lay on my desk ready for submission. I was rubbing my tired eyes and massaging my cramped shoulders when Carol burst into the room.

"I wasn't aware that you had an argument with Theo and that he had terminated his relationship with you!" Carol wanted me to confirm the rumor that she had heard during the rugby game.

I was baffled and intrigued by the information. Frowning I informed her, "We had a slight disagreement over the match but nothing as serious as termination of our relationship. At least I wasn't aware of it. How did you find out?" I wanted to know.

"From a reliable source—of course! During the game Diona broadcasted Theo's decision and he wasn't denying it! As a matter of fact she followed him around like a puppy and he was showering her with too much exaggerated attention."

I was more than distressed by the news. I crumpled on the bed and murmured philosophically, "It's only a matter of time that our relationship will end—it was obviously not meant to be a permanent affair. Theo and I are just too different in personality. He is exhausting me with his persistent demands for attention. I just don't have the energy to cope with his demands and orders…I feel so drained!"

Overcome with misery I sat on the bed and rubbed my forehead hoping that the severe headache would disappear. Sweetly Carol attempted to console me, "Diona is probably spreading malicious rumors in retaliation. I wouldn't lose any sleep over her viciousness. For now I recommend a hot drink and a good night's sleep. We will handle her tomorrow!" Carol was always so full of confidence. I only wished I possessed half of her positiveness.

During the night, I tossed and turned—sleep was evasive. When I managed to fall asleep, nightmares intruded my restless sleep. The next morning before the sun shone through the window I was up and immaculately dressed. With my usual well-groomed appearance bravely I went to the pantry for some unwanted breakfast. The thought of food repelled me but I needed some solid substance in my churning stomach. I knew only too well that a tough and demanding day awaited me. When we arrived in school, my bravery almost crumpled. Theo was waiting for the bus but not for me. He ignored me completely and affectionately greeted Diona. Together they strolled away into the distance. I was more annoyed than hurt by Theo's obvious rejection. I blinked back my tears.

Crying was pointless and tears were for the cowards. Summoning all my courage I maintained my composure and intended to survive the day with or without Theo. Clutching my books, I headed for Mr. John's hut instead of going to "The Cottage". I had no time for sneers and sniggering from Diona. I had no intention of providing the other girls with an opportunity to hurl questions at me. I didn't have any answers myself.

The weather was muggy and rain was imminent. Hurriedly and alone I moved lifelessly along the sidewalk toward my destination. Usually pampered by Theo's devotion I felt distinctly lost. Troubled and harassed by my own anguish and grief I began to run. By the time I reached the hut, I was almost breathless. Mr. John greeted me with sympathetic eyes—news certainly traveled fast in this wretched school. I was grateful that I was able to hide in the haven of the hut for more than fifteen minutes before the arrival of the other students. I needed some time by myself to regain my composure. Patting me gently on my trembling shoulder my tutor reminded me with kindness, "Remember that your first hurdle is to pass all your exams next week. The termination of your relationship with Theo will provide the perfect opportunity for you to concentrate on your studies."

I wriggled in my seat uncomfortably and clumsily I fumbled with the books on the desk. My mind was in turmoil. With a forlorn expression and in a frenzy I moaned, "Why do I have to choose between Theo and my studies? Life should not be either black or white—surely there must some shades of gray somewhere. Is it too selfish on my part to want him to meet me halfway?"

Mr. John perched on the edge of my desk and took my cold hands in his. Watching me intensely he said, "This is not going to be the first time or the last that you will have conflicts with Theo. Although he is a charmer, he doesn't like rivalry especially when his rival is a stack of books and notes. His pride is hurt because your first choice is your books! Life is a kaleidoscope. Who knows what tomorrow will have in store for us? You should not be deprived of a true and understanding relationship. Theo will have to be more sympathetic to your predicaments, or another person with more understanding and sympathy will enter your life, and the necessity of having to choose will no longer be an issue and Theo will lose you."

I realized that there was an awful lot of truth in Mr. John's reasoning but presently my life was at a standstill. My beliefs were lopsided. I couldn't see the silver lining in the cloud. Silently I pleaded for help but Mr. John could offer nothing further to ease my sufferings.

When it was time for me to leave the haven of the hut for my next lesson, my thoughts were like a willow swaying in a storm. During the next in-between classes break I dodged confrontation with the gossipy girls. Instead of returning to 'The cottage' I strolled toward the swimming pool. That area was usually relatively quiet during the winter seasons. The sun was shining and there was a warm breeze blowing in the air. Although spring was just around the corner, I was numbed to the warm air. Pulling my coat around me tightly I hoped for support and comfort. With my head bowed low, I hurriedly moved along the narrow path to the empty benches. Someone suddenly took the seat next to mine and gripped my shoulders. Nervously I jumped. Alastair squeezed my icy hands tenderly and I was grateful for his encouraging smile. I almost collapsed into his embrace—I wanted so much to cry on his shoulder.

Alastair was disappointed with Theo but he remained calm and collected and insisted that we gave Theo the benefit of the doubt. Cautiously he remarked, "Diona's vicious gossips can be deceptive and frivolous. She is notorious for her devious personality. I would like to believe that Theo is not so heartless. There must be a logical explanation for his actions. Be patient—give him a few days to find himself then I expect the two of you to further discuss your disagreements. In the meantime consider your exams as your top priority. I know you won't let Mum or the family down. We have terrific faith in you. You have brains and intelligence. No force on earth should be an obstacle to your studies. You are not only talented, you possess an inner strength and can be an extremely brave girl." He circled my shoulders with his strong arms and cajoled, "Come on—give us a smile!"

Gavin's words from long ago suddenly drifted into my mind.

"Laughter and smiles should accompany you for the rest of your life—big girls don't cry!" A slight grin began to appear on my pathetic face. Combination of Alastair's kind comforting words and Gavin's wish restored faith in me.

During the bus ride home I finally saw Carol. She flopped on the seat next to mine while I closed my eyes and sighed. I was exhausted—mentally and physically. Carol was inquisitive but I silenced her with my next request, "Let me rest peacefully for a while. We will talk in the evening—I promise!" I crossed my chest with both arms.

That evening when we had finally tugged ourselves into bed Carol approached me persuasively, "You know—we have to talk—you can't bury your stubborn head in the sand and refuse to budge."

I appreciated Carol's thoughtfulness so I murmured, "There is really nothing to discuss. Theo decides that he wants to end our relationship, then so be it. I can't dissuade him. It's wrong of him to make me choose between his affection and my studies."

Carol demanded righteously, "Did he tell you that he wants to give you up? Did you hear it with your own ears?"

I sighed dejectedly, "Sometimes action speak for itself. I am not an idiot."

Carol growled with her next remark, "It is absolutely crucial that you should demand for an explanation—you owe it to yourself."

"If he wants to talk then he will contact me. In the meantime I refuse to make an utter fool of myself."

Carol glared at me across the room and shrewdly she recommended, "I can understand why your pride is hurt. He openly snubbed you in school today but sometimes you can afford to swallow some of your pride. Don't you think that you deserve to know the truth?"

I was depressed—I was tired—I felt indignant. Carol somehow was capable of provoking me.

Suddenly instead of drowning myself with self-pity, I was angry and enraged. Utterly furious with Theo's contemptuousness I roared explosively, "Obviously our affection for each other is all irrelevant to his Lordship. I cannot continuously indulge him with his sumptuous whims and demands. I already have to battle for his parents' approval—which for your information, is not forthcoming. I now have to fight for his affection! But at what price? No man is worth all this bother."

"There is potential in your relationship with him," Carol said. He adores you and your feelings for him are pretty obvious. You have to be patient with him. He is spoilt and accustomed to having his own way. Give him a chance. He will eventually come to his senses."

I growled vehemently into the darken room, "I am not English but Oriental. Diona is English so she should be the perfect choice for his parents. To top it all she has the same bitching characteristic as Mrs. Rockfield. They are perfectly compatible. Diona will definitely not be discriminated by the color of her skin. I have my own pride and my own beliefs. I was willing to meet Theo halfway but if he cannot accept me for what I am then our involvement is not worth a penny!"

Diplomatically Carol intervened, "I am not asking you to swallow your pride entirely. I am only begging you to grant him the opportunity to provide you with an explanation. If he tells you truthfully that he prefers Diona to you then by all means forget him. I can guarantee my support for your action one hundred percent. Unless you get the answer straight from the horse's mouth don't let the relationship go to waste. I can't bear to see you suffer due to unnecessary malicious gossip!"

I pleaded with Carol. "Try to understand. I am suffocating and feeling claustrophobic. I can't tiptoe around Theo constantly. I have my own identity. This should be a give-and-take situation and not dispensing consistently on my part!"

Carol waited for me to calm down, then she said, "I am glad that I am able to force the anger from you. It's uncharacteristic of you to dwell on self-pity. It's assuring to know that you are capable of ranting and raving. I know you only too well—give yourself a few days—you will fight for your own rights."

I bounced out of bed and dashed over to my friend's bed. I clasped her shoulders and with assertiveness I reassured her. "I am really indebted to your camaraderie. When Theo is ready to talk, I will oblige. I only wish that I had half of your confidence and was more positive with my thinking. If I feel that I am fighting a losing battle then I will automatically beg-off from my liaison with him."

Carol kissed me gently on both cheeks and smiled. "I know you won't give up. You will talk to him—I know you will!" she insisted. I felt better after Carol's encouragement and reassurance. I was able to sleep as soon as we had concluded our discussion.

I was not provided with the opportunity to talk to Theo before or during the examination period. I ached for his company constantly and I missed him miserably. Every morning I woke with a dull pain in my stomach. I was persistently unhappy. Grateful to my pride and determination I stubbornly devoted all my waking hours to my revisions.

Miraculously I passed all my exams and tests with flying colors. There was only another week to the end of the term and I was looking forward to the tranquillity of my own home and privacy of my own room.

I was beginning to feel excitement for the forthcoming wedding of my mother to Uncle Edwin. They would have returned from Hong Kong when I arrived home. Relieved that the much dreaded exams were behind me I was able to breathe properly again. I decided to enjoy a moment of privacy and peace by the cricket field. Deeply absorbed with my train of thoughts I failed to notice that someone was following me. Lazily I sat on the grass. Habitually I chewed on some grass and thoughtfully tried to decide what to wear to the wedding. Suddenly my view was blocked by a shadow and a deep voice remarked, "I see you still like the bitter taste of grass."

Surprised and excited to hear Theo's much missed voice I lifted my head and gazed into his enchanting blue eyes. Feeling rebellious and indignant I replied to his comment with defiance, "Some things don't change!"

I was still annoyed and upset with him. Anguish burned inside me. The dull ache in the pit of my stomach had been replaced by resentment and indignation when he had not attempted to contact me. His silence humiliated me. For the past weeks I was so involved with my own studies I was oblivious to his activities, so I took it for granted that Theo had replaced me with Diona.

The next instant he warmed my cold heart with one of his bewitching smiles, "Do you mind if I sit with you for a while?"

With an impersonal gesture I moved my body slightly. My cutting reply oozed with sarcasm, "This field is not private property although at times I wish it were."

Unprepared for Theo's tender voice my resistance began to tumble and his attractive silhouette caused my heart to pound persistently against my ribs. It was with tremendous effect that I was able to maintain my composure. Theo said, "You really remind me of a cat. If you are rubbed the wrong way then you are ready to pounce and stretch. But if you are stroked tenderly then you purr. I do admire this extraordinary characteristic in your personality. You are soft and yet determined. You have guts and you are bullheaded but positively adorable. Are you gracious enough to grant me an audience while I share my thoughts with you? Or are you going to condemn me further without providing me with a chance to explain? Do you intend to cut me off completely and remove me entirely from your world?"

I refused to acknowledge his questions although I desperately wanted him to encircle me in his arms and assure me that all our misunderstanding had resolved itself. When an answer was not forthcoming from my tight sealed lips he leaped at the opportunity to continue,

"When you chose your essay to the rugby match I was disappointed and my pride was hurt. You obviously considered your school work more important than my company. I was too arrogant to accept the fact that I was forcing you into a corner with my persistence. Then Diona told me that you wished to terminate our relationship. I was hurt beyond description. Recklessly I fell for her trap and accepted her advancement on the rebound. Repeatedly Anthony suggested that I should talk to you but I was too proud to listen to him. I was too dumb to realize that Diona could be a two-faced snake. Carol told me that you hardly ever spoke to Diona so why would you confide in her? Carol's remark made a lot of sense and immediately I knew I was wrong. I wanted to beg for your forgiveness but I was so lost and ashamed. I didn't know how and when to approach you. Through an act of desperation I asked for Mr. John's and Alastair's advice. Both were of the same opinion that I shouldn't confuse you further until your exams were behind you. At first I wasn't sure if they had provided me with the best solution to my dilemma but eventually their advice began to make sense, so I held my tongue until now." He gripped my hands and continued, "Can you ever forgive me? Let's give ourselves another chance. We have to learn to communicate with each other and let's not allow our pride to take command over our common sense in the future."

I wanted to scream and let the whole world know that I was happy again. I didn't know how I managed to contain my utmost ecstasy to myself. Blissfully I murmured, "I guess I am not entirely blameless. I should have taken Diona's words with a pinch of salt. Our pride has deprived us of a few weeks of happiness and caused us enough heartaches. We have to learn from our mistakes. Malicious gossips can wheedle its way into our minds and plant seeds of suspicion into our heads."

The horizon was slowly changing to the color of dying ember. I looked toward the sky and secretly I thanked God for this second chance. I couldn't resist Theo's inviting lips anymore so I kissed him repeatedly on the mouth and all the while I mumbled, "Let's not fight anymore—it's too damaging to our feelings for each other." Theo returned my kisses passionately and bruising my lips, he agreed.

I floated on air for the remaining of the school term. Diona realized that her devious scheme had failed and ultimately she faded out of the picture. She accepted defeat and canceled all my extra duties. Relieved from all my after lesson activities I was able to spend more time with Theo and once again we were inseparable. Our relationship survived the first storm and blossomed. I could not believe my good fortune. I was pampered by Theo's faithful and devoted attention. I returned from hell and was no longer subjected to self-inflicted pain. My sad and dejected expression was replaced with a constant self-satisfied grin. My days were filled with pleasurable and memorable moments with Theo. I was contented that we were beginning to understand each other.

Soon it was the end of the term again. Theo would be visiting Europe with his parents. His absence from London suited my holiday plans marvelously. I would be too occupied with my family, and I would have no choice but to neglect him. Feeling refreshed and prepared for a terrific holiday, joyfully, Carol and I boarded the train for London. Tactlessly Carol jeered at me teasingly, "Positively ungrateful! I am positive that my interference has contributed to the happy ending for the love birds, but I don't even get an invitation for dinner to repay my kindness."

Theo chuckled while fondling my long hair. The silky hair sifted through his possessive fingers. I gave him an elusive and loving smile and gazed into his seductive eyes devotedly. I loved his masculine smell so I moved closer to him possessively. Reciprocating my affection Theo kissed me warmly, then chivalrously he arranged for us to meet Carol and Anthony in London when he returned from his holiday.

Twenty-Six

When the train pulled into Paddington Station, hurriedly everyone began to scramble off the train. Carol blew me a kiss and then she disappeared into the crowd with Anthony. Pushing his way through the throng of passengers, Alastair finally found me standing on the platform clinging onto Theo who had a connecting train to catch. I hated saying good-bye to Theo but I did want to see my parents. Alastair grabbed my hand and yelled so that Theo could hear him—the noises were deafening our ears. "I am afraid I have to take Melanie home now. No doubt we will be seeing you soon!"

I had to be content with another lingering kiss from Theo, then Alastair and I were on our way to the Underground station. Alastair bought the tickets then we boarded the train. When we were changing trains at Tottenham Court Road Station, I dashed for the first train that was available. Alastair pulled me back and pointed to the signboard, then he mocked, "Wrong train—this one goes to Hampstead! What happened to your common sense?"

I looked at the signboard and turned crimson. Vaguely I muttered an explanation, "I must have misread—it's dark in here!"

The train was relatively empty. It was only three in the afternoon, not quiet rush hour yet. Alastair found a seat and reserved one for me. Soon

I was absorbed with the different advertisements that were on display. Casually Alastair attracted my attention by nudging my shoulder. "Missing Theo already?"

Annoyed with Alastair's harassment I crisply rebuked, "Do you have to be so blunt and nosey? For your information, I was only looking at the advertisements!"

Alastair winked at me and retorted cheekily, "You are not a very good actress. Who do you think you are kidding? You just can't wait until he comes back to London. The only drawback with holidays is that the two of you will be separated!"

I shrugged my shoulders in exasperation. Alastair was such a tease, and he loved bullying me. But I absolutely adored my younger brother. Feigning annoyance I ignored him and his taunting. I was at the crest of divine happiness. Permanently dwelling in delightful thoughts, it was difficult for me to contain the ecstasy that I was feeling inside without letting the entire world into my secret.

When the train arrived at Highgate Station, cheerfully we ran from the station to our house. When we arrived home, as expected, we were greeted by a housefull of people. Mother lavished me with welcoming kisses while Uncle Edwin hugged me protectively. Lynette shrieked with joy. I was impressed with Lynette's fashionable outfit—she was positively trendy wearing a skin tight mini dress of bright red. I guessed that Mother must have gone overboard with shopping when they were home—who could resist shopping in Hong Kong? My theory was proven accurate. Mother delivered into my room a crammed suitcase. New clothes and accessories bursting the seam of the case. I couldn't retain my excitements. I pounced on Mother and showered her with kisses and hugs. I was intoxicated. I had never seen so much new clothes. I couldn't believe my eyes and good fortune. I most certainly would be the envy of all my school friends. Kneeling on the carpet, methodically I extracted each piece of clothing from the case. After examining them I folded the variety of jumpers, cardigans and blouses. Then I put the folded garments in the drawer and hung all the dresses in the wardrobe. I would iron them at my leisure. I experimented with the assortment of beautiful hairclips on my long hair, then I tried on the different pairs of earrings while scanning my reflection in the mirror with approval. Absolutely dazzled by all my new treasures, I repeated continuously, "Mummy, this is positively sensational, the ultimate limit, what utter bliss. How can I ever thank you?"

All the excitement had a dizzying effect on me. I felt light-headed and exhilarated with joy. When Lynette entered my room with a string of beautiful shiny pearls dangling from her manicured fingers, my attention was once again perked. Gingerly and caressingly I removed the pearls from her outstretched hands. Tenderly I touched them and looked at Lynette enquiringly. She surprised me with her next words. "I have an identical one. We are to wear the pearls on Mummy's wedding!"

Immediately I put the necklace round my neck and squawked, "You are kidding! You are not serious—you are pulling my leg. I have to be dreaming! Are they honestly mine for keeps?"

Lynette kissed me gently on the face and chuckled, "Why would I lie? Of course they are yours—and don't forget to thank Uncle Edwin. He picked the necklaces himself." I leaped into air and gave my sister such a fierce hug that I almost suffocated her.

Pulling away from my forceful grip Lynette took hold of my hand and teased, "Where do you find the strength? They obviously feed you well in school! I could hardly breathe when you were hugging me."

Contentedly I stored away the empty suitcase. Shortly I emerged from my room and oozing with confidence and charm, I sauntered into the family room with my new black jeans and black oversize jumper. My hair was clasped with a pair of gold and black hair clips. My enormous round eyes were emphasized with thick mascara. My dainty lips were painted with the fashionable pal beige lipstick. I thought I was positively attractive, even to my own eyes.

When I strolled into the room to join my family, all eyes turned toward me. Sui Fong rushed into my open arms and praised, "You look smashing! No wonder you are so popular in school!"

Turning scarlet I retorted, "Sui Fong please don't tease! I get enough of it from Alastair and Cedric!"

Mother and Uncle Edwin looked at me with renewed interest. Then Mother patted my shoulder and admiringly she exclaimed, "We have only been away for a couple of months and you have matured! I can't see the timid and unsure girl anymore but standing before me is a prim and proper young lady!"

I thanked Mother for her compliments and told Uncle Edwin how much I adored the pearl necklace. Then I searched the room and inquired, "Does anyone know when Gavin will be coming?"

Cedric mocked with a naughty reply, "I thought you had forgotten him!" I hurled the cushion that I was cuddling at my teasing cousin.

Mother intervened, "Melanie, behave yourself. For a moment you had me believe that you are the perfect lady. Ladies don't use violence."

"Yeh! Ladies don't use violence!" Alastair mimicked Mother and chanted. Then he stuck his tongue out at me playfully.

The quiet house on Highgate took on a new face. Laughter filled the air and the melancholy and rejected atmosphere was no longer apparent. I was delighted that I was able to take over the kitchen again. I cooked a hot and spicy curry chicken for dinner. Then immaculately and systematically I cleaned the kitchen with speed and efficiency. The door bell rang when I was stashing away the last plate. Shortly Gavin appeared on the threshold. I flew into his welcoming arms and clung onto him affectionately. Gently he pushed me away and scrutinized my face and remarked, "You are definitely one of the most attractive and loving girls that I have met. It doesn't seem so long ago when I found you in your little black dress standing on the balcony of our apartment in Hong Kong."

Sui Fong came into the kitchen and we sat around the table and exchanged all the latest gossips.

"So you have survived another term! I heard you had a few rough rides!" Gavin said affectionately.

Frowning, I answered, "To say the least!"

Sui Fong patted my hand and reminded me, "Be thankful that the arguments and misunderstandings are all water under the bridge now. You shouldn't have further arguments with Theo."

My lovely eyes were turning misty while I blinked my long eye lashes and stuttered, "Theo's parents still won't accept me, and I don't think they are likely to change their minds. Theo and I haven't actually ironed out all our differences. Constantly I have this suspicion that I am living in a fool's paradise. When we are together things are fantastic but when we are apart I have doubts about our future. I have this horrible premonition that I am hovering on the edge of disaster. Cupid is continuously missing his target with his arrow!"

Gavin took my hand into his and assured me comfortingly, "Melanie you are reading too many trash novels. Why do you worry about the future? You have to live for today. Let fate take you for a ride—we are only young once! We can afford a few bumps in life. If and when things do go wrong for us, we possess enough stamina to bounce back. You have survived the last little incident with Theo and Diona without too much damage."

I was puzzled so with inquisitiveness I asked, "How come you are so up-to-date with all my news?"

Sui Fong volunteered, "Cedric and your friend here do communicate occasionally. Don't let them fool you—men are the worse gossips in the world!"

"You do intimidate our good natures! We just happen to care!" Gavin clicked his tongue and defended himself and Cedric.

"Or nosey!" I laughed.

Gavin insisted with seriousness, "Melanie, you are made of strong substance. Don't let the Rockfields' atrocious behavior throw you off-balance. Be optimistic. You are dating Theo and not his parents. If you and Theo are compatible, don't allow the parents to interfere!"

There was silence while I chewed on Gavin's sound advice. Casually Gavin clasped his hands behind his head and leaned back on his chair. Automatically I warned, "Gavin don't do that! You are tilting the chair and you will lose your balance and topple over."

Gavin eased the chair onto the floor and chided, "The ever thoughtful Melanie! I thought we were discussing your problem and not my acrobatic acts!"

I returned to my problems and said, "The proper and clever course to take would be to ignore Theo's parents. Sometimes ignorance can be bliss. But then what about the differences between Theo and myself? He still resents it when I spend too much time on my books."

Creasing his brows Gavin was worried. "Theo's attitude is absurd. He can't be so stubborn and unreasonable. I can understand his resentment if you are spending time with another young man but surely not when you are only studying."

Sui Fong hesitated before interrupting, "That was the cause for their previous argument. Unfortunately their disagreement provided the perfect opportunity for a third party to intrude."

"That little episode was quite a performance!" I said. "I would not welcome another replay. I was merely functioning for more than a week. There were times when I thought the sky was crashing down on me. The pain was so intense and I felt so insecure..." The thought of it made me shiver and I was unable to finish my sentence.

Gavin immediately interrupted my unfinished sentence. "Was the argument absolutely necessary? Surely confrontations are sometimes unwise."

Sui Fong watched my face regrettably and intervened, "You are such an expert on human relationships. You would make a perfect diplomat. Melanie should have consulted you instead of maintaining her silence. I didn't get to hear about the incident until Alastair told Cedric. As a matter of fact I didn't contact Melanie because I didn't want her to think that I was prying."

Hoping to regain my composure I started to make coffee for everyone. I scooped a spoonful of coffee grounds into the percolator and put the sugar jar on the table. Then I took the bottle of milk from the refrigerator. I confessed, "You should have called! I desperately needed a shoulder to cry on but I was too embarrassed to scream for help. I was utterly lost and alone. It was like a hurricane attacking my confused mind. I couldn't think straight! The cause for the argument was silly and immature—pride and lack of communication!"

Gavin held my chin and assured me soothingly, "You silly goat—you should have called. Promise me you will whenever you need a shoulder to cry on—what are friends for?" Then changing the subject he asked, "What are your plans for tomorrow?"

Sui Fong gazed at me and waited for a suggestion.

I asked Gavin, "What do you have in mind?"

Gavin poured the coffee into the mugs and replied, "I need some assistance and suggestions! I would like you two to select a wedding present for Auntie Wei Ling and Uncle Edwin."

"I need help too! Why don't we snoop around the shops tomorrow? We should be able to find something suitable—three brains are better than one!"

Considerately I asked Gavin, "I suppose you would like to sleep in tomorrow?"

Gavin agreed positively, "You are right. You are so capable of reading my mind—no wonder we are buddies."

Turning to Sui Fong I requested, "Before we meet Gavin, will you accompany me to King's Road?"

Sui Fong was appalled and baffled by my request, "You are not serious! You have received a suitcase full of new clothes! What more do you want to buy from Kings Road?"

Warming my cold hands with the cup of steaming hot coffee I explained. "I am running out of cosmetic. There is a store in Kings Road that caters to customers like myself—with not too much money to spare. Anyway what is wrong with window shopping? I may have a suitcase of new clothes but I still need inspiration to put an outfit together smartly!"

Sui Fong smiled approvingly, "You are right—let's visit Kings Road tomorrow."

Gavin moaned, "Women! I will meet you girls for brunch and no earlier."

Twenty-Seven

The following morning when the alarm went, I pulled myself out of bed with no difficulty. I made a cup of instant coffee for myself, then I left a note for Mother. I remembered to wear comfortable walking shoes, then I ventured into town to meet Sui Fong. Feeling adventurous, we caught the Underground train to Kings Road. Immediately upon our arrival we were impressed by the trendy people hurriedly walking along the street. Mini skirts, laced-up boots, natural color body stockings, see-through dresses, and shirts for both sexes captured my interests and attention. Influenced by the Beatles, young men had long hair. The popular Beatles' songs blasted from almost every shop. It was indeed the trendy part of London.

The shops displayed enticing merchandises. Sui Fong and I could easily be induced to spend extravagantly. We sauntered along the street assessing our spending money. Vulnerable to spending, I could easily go wild squandering away my limited amount of pocket money. We had to restrain ourselves from going overboard and over-spending. Eventually and fortunately for our pockets we located the cosmetic store before too much damage was done to our money. Gingerly we pushed opened the door and instantly we marveled at the immense quantity of make-up on display. With curiosity I inspected the variety of choices. I tested different shades of blush, then I smudged various colored eye shadows on the back of my hand. All the while I admired the glittering colors of lipsticks and nail varnishes. Then I signaled for Sui Fong to join me when I stumbled upon a fantastic collection of false eye-lashes. Feeling adventurous, I bought a pair. I promised myself that I would perfect the art of using these false lashes if they should improve my looks. Selecting a light beige shade of lipstick that was popular and then I found the matching nail varnish. Sui Fong was more conservative with her taste. She preferred a classic shade of pink lipstick. Satisfied and delighted with our purchases, reluctantly we left the cosmetic store.

Returning to the crowded street I examined my reflection in the store window and snorted disdainfully, "I am really at a disadvantage with my wavy and curly hair. I do admire your straight black hair—it is so fashionable! I wish that there was something that I could do to straighten my hair!"

Sui Fong patted my curly hair and giggled, "A lot of girls would kill for your curls. We are such dissatisfied creatures. We should be contented with our own natural hair."

As we walked passed an antique shop, Sui Fong's attention was caught by a set of trays displayed in the shop window. Pointing toward the store window she insisted that we should take a closer look at the trays, so she pushed me through the door. Sui Fong was interested in a set of small tortoise-shell trays. Reflected by the sunshine they shone beautifully. Exquisite in design they were absolutely gorgeous. Sui Fong yearned to purchase them for Mother and Uncle Edwin.

I admired the trays but I grunted with conviction, "They are stunning. But I am sure that the price is more dazzling."

Sui Fong was thoughtful for a while then she replied, "We won't know until we find out!" She attracted the attention of the shop owner who offered to give Sui Fong a discount. Appreciatively, she touched the trays lovingly and hoped that she was able to afford the price. She was certain that Mother would share her enthusiasm over the uniqueness of the collection.

The shop owner who was aware of Sui Fong's obvious attraction for the trays, suggested a bargain. "You can have the set for five quid! I really cannot go any lower!" He pushed the trays into my friend's hands.

Sui Fong was in heavenly bliss! The price was definitely within her budget. Searching for her purse, she paid the five pounds. Clutching her newly acquired treasure she bounced out of the store and I followed, sharing her enthusiasm. Hurriedly we walked toward the Underground station. I glanced at my watch and cursed, "Blast! It's past twelve! We must have lost track of the time. Cedric and Gavin will skin us alive! By the time we arrive at Peter's restaurant it will be past twelve thirty!"

Sui Fong looked at her watch and responded confidently, "We will call from the station. They should expect some sort of delay when we are on our shopping excursions. I don't think they would mind too much. Anyway there are two of them—it's not as if they had to wait alone."

We scrambled into the restaurant. Hesitantly we apologized and immediately the food was ordered. I bestowed to the two young men one of my most enchanting and charming smiles. "I do apologize. We were delayed by the heavy traffic and...."

Cedric drumming his fingers impatiently on the table intervened, "Don't tell fibs—what traffic? You didn't drive—it's impossible for you to encounter traffic jams when you travel on the Underground."

I smiled sheepishly and confessed, "Oh, All right. We were delayed because the stores were fascinating!"

Gavin's anger softened when I blinked at him pleadingly, "At least you are honest with us. I hope you have not spent all your money. Let's eat and be on our way."

"Where are we going?" I asked with my mouth full of delicious fried noodles.

Cedric spooning more noodles onto his plate suggested, "I suppose you two wild creatures would rather fancy an afternoon at Harrod's. Hopefully we can find something for Auntie Wei Ling."

Excitedly Sui Fong exhibited the box that was prettily wrapped. Proudly she described the present. Cedric was dubious with her choice. "Are you sure Auntie Wei Ling will appreciate the trays?"

Pushing the empty plate away I interrupted, "Most definitely! Mummy will love them! She does have a craving for small antique articles. I doubt it if this rare and striking collection of trays can be found in Hong Kong. The daintiness of the trays is positively attractive."

Gavin frowned and complained, "Now what about Raphael and me? We must find something soon."

I poured hot Jasmine tea for everyone, then I assured him. "We are bound to find something suitable in Harrod's."

"By the way, girls," Cedric warned. "We are just going to search for a present for Auntie Wei Ling. You are not to buy anything because the prices in the store are just too exorbitant for our budgets."

When we were at the store, I couldn't stop staring at all the expensive merchandise that was on display. Dreamily, I wished that I could afford to purchase the smart and chic outfits. The costume jewelry glistened in the display stand took my breath away. I marveled at the collection of fur coats. Impulsively I chanted, "Can you just imagine me wearing one of these gorgeous coats on a cold winter day? I will have to visit Montreal one day—that's where they make the most fantastic coats."

Horrified with my obsessions for the fur coats, Cedric quickly diverted my attention by steering me toward another department. All the while reminding me, "We are here to shop for a wedding present! Will you stop your day dreaming? Fur coats—indeed!"

We visited department after department and we were unable to find anything suitable. Gavin was disheartened. Lamely he moaned, "What can you buy for a couple that has almost everything? It has to be small so that they can take it back to Hong Kong without too much trouble—any suggestions, girls?"

We looked at each other blankly, then we wandered into the gambling equipment department. An assortment of playing cards, sets of small roulettes, liars die, and dominos were displayed attractively. Suddenly my eyes twinkled because I was attracted by a box of chips. The box contained three different colored chips. The white chips shone like Mother of Pearl. There was nothing unusual with the red chips but the dark purple ones were unique. I had never seen such a outstanding color on any of Mother's Mah Jong chips. Pointing toward the box I exclaimed, "I have found the perfect gift! Mummy will love this set of chips and the size of the box is positively small enough for her to take home. Aren't the extraordinary colors of the chips unusual and fabulous? And chips are definitely essential to her weekly Mah Jong games. She will be pleased with our choice!"

All their attentions were turned to the chips. Unanimously we agreed with my choice. Gavin patted my shoulder and complimented, "What a brilliant suggestion! It's something that both Auntie Wei Ling and Uncle Edwin can use!"

Gavin paid for the present. Positively satisfied with our purchases we returned home and I sneaked the presents into the privacy of my own room.

A few days passed since our shopping expedition. It was a Monday afternoon when Mother received an excited phone call from Sui Fong. Enthusiastically she insisted that Mother and Uncle Edwin should wait for her. Apparently she had thrilling news for the family. An hour later an extremely excited Sui Fong arrived. She charged into the family room where we were chatting. Releasing herself of her warm coat Sui Fong reported, "I have found the perfect solution regarding the problem of a home for Melanie and Alastair during the holidays."

Lounging on the floor she continued to ramble, "My mother has decided to move to the flat on top of our grocery store in order to save traveling time. Sui Bun has agreed to accompany her. There is not enough room to accommodate me. In any case Mother doesn't consider it inappropriate for me to live above the store. If I live in an empty house, Mother will be worried for my safety. This morning Sui Bun came up with a brilliant suggestion. He would like Cedric to move in with me and during the holidays Melanie and Alastair can come and stay with us." Sui Fong waited impatiently for my parents' reactions and approval.

Frowning Mother answered dubiously, "I am not so sure that Cedric should move in with you. Wei Fun might object. My sister is rather old-fashioned in her thinking."

Cedric held Sui Fong's hands lovingly and suggested, "Why don't we call Mother and ask for her approval? That is if you have no objection to the two younger ones staying with us."

Immediately a call was put through to Auntie Wei Fun on the other side of the world. When she answered the phone she was anxious, "Is something wrong? Is Cedric ill?"

Mother replied reassuringly, "There is nothing for you to worry about! I need to discuss something important with you; therefore, the necessity for the long distant call. I didn't mean to alarm you." Cautiously and respectfully Mother repeated Sui Fong's suggestion.

There was a slight pause then Auntie Wei Fun replied skeptically, "What would people say? There are bound to be unnecessary and malicious rumors." My dear aunt expressed her concern while we waited impatiently for her to continue. "What about Sui Fong's reputation? After all she is not married to Cedric. They are not even engaged."

Mother negotiated on our behalf. "Up to a point I can understand your concern but this is London and the English way of living is entirely different from ours. One could say that we are living in an open-minded society so I wouldn't pay too much attention to malicious gossips."

Clearly I could hear Auntie Wei Fun's objection. "Nevertheless, we are still Chinese. We have our own traditions. Cedric and Sui Fong have been dating for a long while now and from what I can gather they seem to be extremely fond of each other. Cedric actually suggested returning to Hong Kong with her in the summer so that she will be provided with an opportunity to meet the other members of our family. I suppose they could announce their engagement in Hong Kong and we can legalize the situation."

When Mother replaced the receiver, she repeated Auntie Wei Fun's wishes. Sui Fong started to blush and Cedric jumped onto his feet and grabbed his girlfriend's shoulders and exclaimed, "We can have a double celebration in Hong Kong—our engagement and Ardelia's wedding!"

Although, happy for Sui Fong and Cedric I was flabbergasted. I wasn't too happy with the suggestion so I asked, "I don't want to be a wet blanket but aren't you two rather young to be married?"

Alastair growled at me and responded, "Who is talking about marriage? We are discussing an engagement."

"So? What is the difference? Engagement ultimately is followed by a wedding." I glared at my brother.

Alastair sighed wearily, "Of course. A wedding would be inevitable and unavoidable but it wouldn't be for another few years down the road."

Uncle Edwin had so far reserved his opinion. Suddenly he spoke, "Will you two stop your bickering—anyone would think that it's you two who are getting engaged. We are discussing Cedric and Sui Fong's future so let them voice their own opinion."

Bashfully Sui Fong lowered her head and murmured, "I have no objection to our getting engaged. No doubt Mother and Sui Bun would be pleased with the piece of good news! As you know my mother can be quiet old-fashioned in her thinking as well."

Muttering to myself I said softly, "I guess Sui Fong is destined to marry Cedric one day. Their devotion for each other is so obvious. I really can't imagine Sui Fong dating anyone else." I was a great believer in romance and happy endings. It was my turn to tease Cedric so I asked, "Are you going to go on your knees and propose?" Demonstrating my happiness for Sui Fong I embraced her and congratulated her. I was the first to welcome her into our family.

When Gavin was leaving the family room to join me in the kitchen Mother stopped him and said, "I am taking Melanie out for dinner tomorrow evening. Why don't you join us? We would love to have your company!"

Smiling at Mother charmingly Gavin accepted the invitation.

I was delighted with my parents' invitation for dinner. I was also happy that the invitation was extended to Gavin. When I was dressing for the occasion, I was furious with myself. Criticizing my reflection in the mirror while twiddling the curls on my long hair, I murmured scornfully at my own image. How I wished that there was something that I could do to get rid of the miserable curls. Suddenly I thought of a way to deal with my blasted curls. Hesitantly I removed the iron and the ironing broad from the kitchen then I assembled the equipment in my room. I filled the spraying bottle with clean water, then I hurriedly returned to my room. I closed the door and with a mischievous grin I lay my long hair on the iron board. Fumbling for the spraying bottle, I sprayed clean water onto my hair then gingerly I began to iron my mop of curls. When Gavin opened my bedroom door, he was horrified with my actions. He couldn't understand what I was trying to do so he yelled at me, "Melanie, whatever are you trying to do? Whatever possessed you to iron your own hair?"

I took a peek at him and rebuked, "Can't you see? I am trying to get rid of these horrible and unfashionable curls! I want my hair to be straight and fashionable like Sui Fong's."

Gavin gaped at my actions. He was shocked with my stupidity and vanity. Straining my arms, I tried to reach for the spraying bottle. "Don't just stand there and gawk! Help me spray my hair—I can't see properly!"

Seizing the bottle from my hand Gavin started to spray water on my hair and complained simultaneously, "You are such a dissatisfied creature! There is absolutely nothing wrong with your natural curls—I like them."

While my hair was sizzling under the hot iron I protested, "You have no sense for fashion. Curls are definitely out of style. Straight hair is indisputably in!"

"So some girls have straight hair, some have curls—why the big fuss?" Gavin demanded.

When I was finally satisfied with the improvement to my hair I flipped my hair back and smiled at my own creation. My long hair was glittering with a shine and cascaded down my back without any curls. This new hairstyle added a few years of maturity to my young and attractive face. When Mother saw me she asked, "Melanie, what has happened to your hair?"

Gavin interrupted, "Auntie Wei Ling you wouldn't want to know."

Our small party arrived at the quaint and chic Italian restaurant. Red table cloths added gaiety to the atmosphere. Shadows of candles standing in wine bottles as candle holders flickered on the wall. The waiters were friendly and a quartet serenaded the diners with their songs and melodies. I fell in love with the romantic environment. Scanning the room with curiosity, I wasn't paying attention to what Mother was saying so she patted my hand and requested, "Melanie, stop your day-dreaming and order the food!"

During dinner we chatted casually. When we were enjoying our desserts and coffee, Mother said to me, "Melanie, soon Edwin and I will be leaving you and Alastair to fend for yourselves in this foreign country. As usual, I am doubting my own judgment. Alastair will be able to look after himself because he has a carefree nature and nothing really bothers him. But you are a different kettle of fish. You have many good virtues, but your stubbornness is not one of them. Also, you never speak your mind. You tend to suffer in silence. Sometimes I wonder if you are aware of the evils that abound us in our society. You are innocent and naive. I am afraid that you will be hurt badly!"

Gavin comforted Mother with his next remark. "Auntie Wei Ling I can understand and appreciate your concern for Melanie. But I think she possesses a deeper character than we undrstand. Most of the time she portrays herself as a dreamer, but her head is really screwed on her shoulders properly. We should give her more credit."

Uncle Edwin agreed with Gavin's beliefs, "Wei Ling, Gavin is right! Melanie does use her head. She just doesn't want to voice her opinion."

I was indignant so I complained. "Hey guys! Your attitude is definitely unethical. You are discussing me as if I am not around."

Gavin attempted to comfort Mother. "What did I tell you? Melanie is not always so submissive!"

I could understand Mother's concern so I tried to explain my behavior. "Mummy, I just feel that there should be a time and place for everything. I get upset and annoyed, but then I reason with myself. Life can sometimes be so short, so why let a bit of disappointment ruin my day?"

Mother, frowning asked, "Don't you ever want to share your disappointment or unhappiness with anyone. At least talk about it!"

There was silence while I was trying to think of a way to define my logic. Tapping my forehead with my fingers I tried to explain. "Life is so unpredictable! You are with me now but soon you will be residing on the other side of the world. It wasn't so long ago that I had lost Gavin's friendship, but now we are together again. Who can predict what tomorrow will have in store for us?" Pausing for breath I gulped down some ice water from my glass then I continued. "As far as I am concerned life is not an eternal problem for us to solve but an exciting adventure for us to experience! We all make mistakes, but why waste time crying over spilt milk? I believe there is bound to be a better tomorrow and there must be a silver lining in every cloud. Why worry others with my problems? I believe they will eventually sort themselves out! If I remind myself continuously of my beliefs it shouldn't be difficult for me to overcome any obstacles in life."

Without providing Mother with a chance to interrupt I stumbled on, "The world is not a stage although there are some that believe that it is! Our life is real—we live and survive in it! There should not be barriers to our happiness or sorrows. Admittedly sometimes we do have to battle with our own beliefs but if we are true believers in ourselves then no mountain is too high for us to climb, so why should a few tears bother us?"

Removing a nonexisting fluff from his lapel Uncle Edwin sighed and looked at Mother, "Wei Ling obviously your anxiety for Melanie is unnecessary—she is no longer a baby."

Like an on flowing river I couldn't contain my thoughts, "At times I do feel disappointment because I am only human, but I don't feel cheated out of life. I am not naive enough to think that life is a bed of roses, but most of the time I would like to believe that it is! Sorrow and pain are inevitable at times, but then I don't think that we should be too discouraged by disappointments. We are young enough to maintain the stamina to fight for our beliefs! I refuse to behave or act like a coward. With enough gumption I feel I can manipulate my own destiny and solve my own problems."

I hoped that I had managed to reassure Mother with my outburst because after listening to me she concluded, "Melanie, I guess you are indeed growing up. I shouldn't be too overly protective. You do have your own theory and you will attempt to abide by it. I guess I have misjudged your courage. I thought you were too weak to voice your opinion or share your distress. But should you ever need a shoulder to cry on or need an understanding ear you know where to find us."

Uncle Edwin remarked, "I am happy that we are able to have this discussion. Now, hopefully, your mother's mind will be more at ease when she leaves you."

The food was terrific, and I was happy that I was able to talk openly with my parents. I hoped that I would be able to talk to them again in the future with such frankness!

Twenty-Eight

After so many years of courtship, Mother and Uncle Edwin finally married in Caxton Hall on a bright and sunny day shortly after Easter. The couple was exhilarated because all their children were present at their wedding. Many guests attended the marriage ceremony. Peter proudly gave the bride away. Mother looked beautiful in her cream Thai silk suit. Her face shone with happiness. I was not dressed in black but wore a smart, light-blue mini dress with matching blue pumps. My pearl necklace proudly caressed my slim neck and I blinked my false eye lashes each time I smiled. Peter's present to the happy couple was a dinner and dancing party to be held in his restaurant. There was no shortage of delicious food, and champagne flowed from unaccountable bottles ceaselessly. The guests danced continuously to the music of a five-piece live band that Peter had hired for the special event. When the musicians took their break Gavin and myself were the designated disc jockey for the evening. Amidst the flowing wine and happy laughter the guests danced late into the night. When we were relieved of our disc jockey duty Gavin and I danced—our practiced steps never faltered and I was told repeatedly that we were a smashing couple. Waltzing around the room with Gavin's tender arms around me there was no limit to my happiness.

When Mother and my stepfather returned from their honeymoon after spending one glorious week in Paris the house on Highgate was sold. All the legal papers were completed and signed. Father returned to Hong Kong while Mother with our assistance packed all our furniture and shipped the containers to Hong Kong. Alastair and I moved our personal belongings to Sui Fong's house. Finally an overly exhausted Mother returned to Hong Kong to join her husband and started her new life as Mrs. Edwin Ho. Lynette returned to Hong Kong with Mother and started her new career as a secretary with an import and export company. Apparently she loved her new position and her busy social life.

When all the excitement was behind me, I was able to relax. Gavin was to spend the last week of his Easter holiday with friends, but before he left he visited me in my new home.

"Hey, you two, I am awfully grateful for your assistance with my move. I wouldn't have managed on my own—I really appreciate your helpfulness!" I smiled at Gavin and Sui Fong sweetly. We were sitting in the kitchen enjoying the cheese cake that Gavin had brought.

Savoring the delicious cake Gavin chaffed, "Aren't we polite."

"I am not a selfish, demanding, lousy little creature! Why shouldn't I be polite? I don't usually take anything for granted—do I? Why can't you accept my gratitude graciously?" I demanded while licking the last bit of cheese from my spoon.

Sui Fong was putting the remains of the cake into the refrigerator. She was disturbed with my outburst so she intervened, "Melanie, you are overreacting. Gavin is only teasing! Let's enjoy some peace and quiet. When Alastair returns with Cedric from their tennis game we will have to suffer the running commentary of their accomplishments!"

Always sensitive to my temperaments Gavin asked, "Obviously something is bothering you! Do you want to talk about it? You are not missing your parents already are you?"

I grunted a reply irritably, "Of course my parents' departure is depressing, but I happen to miss that damn house in Highgate...don't get me wrong, Sui Fong, I am not being ungracious to your hospitality, but I just feel so..."

"Do continue! We are listening!" Gavin prompted.

I held my chin with both hands and rested my elbows on the kitchen table. I screwed my eyes and continued. "I am not just missing the house and my parents. I have other things on my mind."

Sui Fong stacked the dirty plates into the dish washer and guessed, "You are nervous because school is going to start soon and you are thinking of Theo again. Am I correct?"

I sighed and nodded my head. "I guess you are right. I am scared of seeing him again and yet I am excited. His ego has to be boosted all the time and my patience is running very thin. I am awfully fond of him but I also resent his arrogance. I am contradicting myself constantly and my conduct is most neurotic! His persistent demands on my time while we are in school is most irritable."

Gavin smiled at me encouragingly, "Try to take a day at a time! Don't make mountains out of mole hills!"

Sui Fong paced the kitchen with her hands behind her back then thoughtfully she asked, "Have you consider terminating the relationship with him?"

"Have I? All the time when I am not with him. But when he is with me I can't resist him. I seem to lose all my common sense." I covered my face with my hand and moaned.

The front door opened and closed. Sui Fong disappeared into the living room. Fondly Gavin pulled my hands away from my face and kissed my cheeks tenderly. Assuredly he said, "Give it another try this term. If things don't work out then you can seriously consider terminating the relationship. If your involvement with him does go sour, you have the summer holiday to look forward to—a few months in Hong Kong will do you plenty of good. In any case, this will be Theo's last term in school. It will be easier for you to get over him when you are no longer studying in the same school. Hopefully, out of sight—out of mind."

I shrugged my shoulders and sighed, "Most of the time-absence makes the heart grow fonder. Believe me I know." I gazed deeply into Gavin's eyes.

"Don't be so pessimistic. Where is your fighting spirit? Cheer up kid! I hate to see you feeling so depress." Gavin pulled me into his arms and whispered against my hair. "Give us a smile!"

I was grateful for Gavin's faithful support. I would rather lose Theo's affection than lose Gavin's eternal friendship. Platonic relationship and trustworthy friendship were so rare and difficult to find.

Theo called three days before school started. I had left my new number with the Rockfields' butler. Theo was surprised that I had moved and I was glad that he was visiting London the following day and would be in town until we returned to school.

When the door bell jingled shrilly I bounced down the stairs and rushed to open the door. Theo folded my slim body into his strong arms. I was feeling delirious with happiness. The pungent smell of Theo's aftershave lotion penetrated into my inner soul. I had missed him desperately. Clinging onto his arms, I ushered him into the living room. Sui Fong offered Theo a drink of orange juice and then she left the house. She had previously arranged to meet Cedric in town. Before she closed the door she yelled from the threshold, "Melanie, I nearly forgot to tell you. Cedric and Alastair are going to the bowling alley so don't bother with dinner. I think we will grab a quick bite at Peter's" She disappeared out of the door.

I was overjoyed to see Theo. He was disturbed with my blanched pallor and the dark rings surrounding my eyes. He tenderly inquired, "Melanie, are you ill? You look exhausted!"

I smiled and promptly reassured him, "I just haven't been sleeping properly. I guess I am still trying to get used to my new surroundings. Also, I miss my parents horribly and I miss my old house. The combination of the two have been exhausting and traumatic for me. I feel so alone and depressed. I suppose I am suffering from the anticlimax from the excitement of the wedding!"

I invited Theo into my new room and he was impressed. The room was impeccable. I was systematic and organized. Not a jumper or a hairbrush was out of place. There was a home for all my belongings. Tenderly Theo embraced me and his lips searched mine urgently. He then pushed the bedroom door closed with his leg. We stood in the room locked in each other's tight embrace and savored our tender kisses. Accidentally I lost my balance and our entwined bodies tumbled onto my patchwork quilt....

When I opened my eyes again the room was dark and Theo's naked body was snuggled closed to mine. Dreamily I yawned and stretched. My movement woke him and immediately he searched for my lips again. My lips were bruised and my flesh was tingling. I could still feel his gentle touches caressing my body. The feeling was so sensational that I wanted to remain in his arms for the rest of my life. I was desperately in love with Theo and my anxiety and apprehension over our relationship vanished.

Leisurely, Theo removed his body from my clinging arms. Tenderly he stroked my long hair and whispered against my ears, "I am awfully sorry. I guess I got carried away. I hope there are no regrets!"

I put my fingers on Theo's lips to silent him. "Please don't apologize! I am in ecstasy—I yearned for this to happen. I feel so much closer to you now. Just promise me that nothing will ever come between us!" I hugged him tightly.

That night Theo did not leave the house until late and I fell into a deep slumber. I did not wake again until the sun shone brightly into my room. Lazily I opened my eyes and then I closed them again. I wanted desperately to savor our passion all over again. When my stomach growled I remembered Theo and I had missed dinner and I was starving.

Humming happily I found my way to the kitchen. The aroma of coffee was so tempting—sniffing I poured myself a large mug. Then I discovered freshly baked croissants. When I was savoring the last taste of strawberry jam in my mouth Sui Fong entered the kitchen through the back door.

"Good morning! I bought some fresh milk!" Cheerfully she poured herself some coffee and joined me for breakfast. She scrutinized my face and there was a twinkle in her eyes. Her eyes told me that she knew. "Is there something that you wish to confide in me?"

I blushed and reluctantly I stammered, "I suppose you guessed? Well, it happened…and I feel so terrific and yet so strange!"

"I guess it was the inevitable. I don't blame you. As a matter of fact I am really happy for you but please take precautions. Auntie Wei Ling will kill me if you become an unwed mum." Sui Fong warned me.

I was horrified with Sui Fong's insinuation so I protested. "Heavens forbid! I will be careful! I have no intention of getting pregnant!"

For the next couple of hours we chatted. I loved chatting with Sui Fong. She was so knowledgeable and somehow we understood each other. When I was emerging from the shower Theo arrived. When I opened the door, I was still drying my long, wet hair. Shyly, I invited him into kitchen. He produced a box of chocolate eclairs. Sui Fong thanked him for the cakes and helped herself to one. Quickly she disappeared into her room. I made us a pot of fresh coffee and hungrily I ate the mouth-watering cakes. Water was dripping from my wet hair and I shivered. Theo encircled my shivering body in his arms and asked tenderly, "Are you cold? Do you want to change first?"

Licking the chocolate off my fingers I smiled, "I am not cold! I am just divinely happy and contented with life. I am floating on air but I suppose I will have to return to earth in two days time!"

"Why in two days time?" Theo was perplexed with my statement.

I kissed Theo and clinging to his inviting arms I murmured, "School will start in two days time or have you forgotten?"

Theo smacked his forehead with the palm of his hand, "Of course! How stupid of me!"

When I mentioned school, Theo became thoughtful. A shadow crossed his handsome face. He took my palm and kissed it gently. Struggling with his emotions he pleaded with me, "Melanie, there is something that I want you to know…my parents think that we have broken up and that we are just casual friends. For a while, please keep our involvement a secret from them. Give me some time and I will break the news to them gently."

I pulled away from Theo. Frowning I said, "In other words they are still prejudiced against me!" After a slight pause with a hurtful voice I asked, "Have you considered my feelings? How do you think I feel? I am not some back-street mistress! I want you to be proud of me. I am not ashamed to be seen with you—we have nothing to hide."

Theo drummed his fingers nervously on the kitchen table and fretted. "I can understand your apprehension and sensitivity. Their stubborn attitude is a nuisance, but please, I just need some time. I promise you we will have their blessing before long!"

I wished that I could believe him.

Although I felt unconvinced, his bewitching eyes soon melted me. My rising anger was defused. His voice had a drowning effect on me and I was no longer the master of my own mind. I was a slave to our increasing passion. My thoughts were disoriented.

Another ecstatic afternoon was spent in Theo's loving arms. His passionate touches and tender promises destroyed all my common sense. That evening, in the stillness of the kitchen, I tried to gather my scattered and confused thoughts. I sat alone, motionless and was crying softly when Sui Fong returned home. She was alarmed to find me huddled in the dark room. Switching on the lights Sui Fong offered me a glass of water. Wiping the tears from my melancholy face she sighed, "Theo must be the cause of your tears again?"

It must have been Sui Fong's kind words and soothingly voice. I exploded. Clenching my fist I muttered, "I just want them to give me a chance—they don't even know me as a person! Am I asking for too much? Why should they condemn me because I am Chinese?"

Sui Fong shook her head with sympathy then she inquired. "I suppose you are talking about Theo's high and mighty parents?"

I was choking with unshed tears. Coughing I spluttered my reply. "He wants me to keep our affair a secret from his parents!"

"What is Theo's priority and where is his integrity? How can he be so inconsiderate toward your feelings?" Sui Fong thundered. Fuming she exclaimed, "Look! To hell with his parents! It would be nice to have their blessing but if it's not going to be forth-coming then ignore them! You are dating the son and not the parents. Forget them. I am certain that in time Theo will force them into accepting you. How can you keep your involvement with him a secret? Can anyone wrap fire with a piece of paper? It's unreasonable and utterly cruel!"

I started to sob.

When we returned to school, I unintentionally started to neglect my work again. I was constantly in the company of Theo. I just could not resist him and I was available whenever he wanted to see me. Rapidly my school work deteriorated and my marks were not improving but slipping rapidly. I was agonized with my failure, but I was helpless to control my emotions and actions. Theo was an addictive drug and I couldn't bear to be separated from him.

Parents' day was swiftly approaching. As the days drew nearer to that weekend, Theo was constantly agitated. I could detect his increasing nervousness. One afternoon after lessons I implored, "Theo, something is bothering you! Do you want to talk about it?"

Gazing into the distance Theo absentmindedly replied, "I still haven't been able to convince my parents to accept our relationship. Will you pretend that we are just casual friends? When they come on Saturday I don't want them to ask any unnecessary questions."

I was upset but I didn't want him to feel my antagonism or resentment for his parents, so I lied. "Is that all that is bothering you? If it pleases you so much, of course, I will not let the cat out of the bag. I am not happy with your request but I will comply. I can be an obedient girl." I forced a smile on my face and pretended that his unreasonable request was acceptable.

The weekend finally arrived. I was far from idle. Due to the absence of my own parents and my ability to cook I was kept busy supervising the baking and the making of the snacks. When all the cooking was finished, I breathed a sigh of relief. I was actually looking forward to a delightful afternoon. When I emerged from "The Cottage," Carol waved at me frantically beckoning me to join her. I made my way over to where she was standing and briskly she introduced me to her parents. Then I smiled at Anthony's parents. Anthony's father complimented me graciously, "I have heard so much about you. You are very attractive and I can see the reason for your popularity with your fellow students. It is our pleasure to have made your acquaintance."

Shyly I bestowed to the older gentleman one of my most fetching smiles then bashfully and sweetly, I responded, "Sir! The pleasure is mine!"

Carol's mother marveled, "What charming manners."

"Have you tried Melanie's cooking? The food is delicious and artfully prepared. You are a very talented young lady." Anthony's mother added putting a small sandwich in her mouth.

From the corner of my eyes I located the Rockfields. I saw, to my horror, a lovely blond girl dressed in a smart Laura Ashley outfit kissing Theo possessively. I winced inwardly. Clenching my fists to control the pain and the anger I smiled bravely. Reluctantly, I removed my gaze from the couple. Ignoring the burning pain in my stomach, I chatted pleasantly with my friends' parents.

Eventually I made an excuse and moved on to mingle among the crowd. Jean wanted me to meet her parents because they had just arrived from Hong Kong. I searched for her and inadvertently I came face to face with Mr. Rockfield and his party. Hesitantly I greeted Theo's parents with a slight nod of my head. The father beckoned me to join them and reluctantly I obeyed. Mrs. Rockfield coldly introduced me to the girl who was clinging onto Theo's arms. "Melanie, come and meet Theo's girlfriend, Sue." I flinched but bravely I smiled at Sue and the mother cuttingly continued. "Hopefully they will be announcing their engagement soon. Sue has been joining us for all our holidays abroad and she is such a charming girl! When they are engaged, then a chaperon will longer be necessary and they can enjoy the privileges from our travel agencies. No doubt they will like traveling on their own with no supervision."

Staggered by the news I almost fainted. If looks could kill, I would have killed Theo but he turned his face away. Somehow I found the strength and managed an impersonal but polite smile. Then I extended my congratulation to Sue. She was beaming with joy! Carol and Anthony were walking toward me and unfortunately they heard the entire conversation. Disappointment showed on Carol's face and she was appalled with Theo's deceptiveness and selfishness. I was grateful when they gave me a knowing and supportive smile. Carol moved closer to me protectively and squeezed my icy hands reassuringly. With a forced smile affixed on my face I excused myself. I refused to be humiliated by the dreadful threatened tears. Vigorously I ran to the cricket field leaving the laughter and happy chatters behind.

When I was certain that I was alone, I collapsed on the grass. I welcomed the ominous silence that surrounded me. The minutes or the hours drifted by. I had lost count of the time. I sat on the grass motionless. I took a few deep breaths and willed myself not to cry although I yearned to scream and rave. I had to discipline my tortured emotions. My pride was hurt badly but I would suffer in silence. Theo nor his parents would never be allowed to see my tears. Clearly he had been two-timing me! I was disgusted and disappointed with his behavior, but I was adamant to cope with my own despair. My sorrowful thoughts were in chaos. My heart was turning numb. It was kinder for Theo to stab me with a knife then to cheat on me. The excruciating pain was dreadful and I yearned for a hole in the ground to bury myself in. The humiliation was intolerable—I had been utterly stupid—the urgency to our keep our relationship a secret—Theo's increasing tension and agitation. Why was I so blind?

Vaguely I heard the sound of crunching gravel. Carol and Anthony had found me siting on the grass cuddling my trembling body. Carol cradled my shivering body and suggested soothingly, "The crowd is thinning out—most of the parents have left! Melanie, why don't you cry? Don't hold the tears back. It's not good for you!"

Anthony was stunned by the sadness that was obvious on my face. My gaiety had vanished with the wind. Gravely I fumbled with my cardigan and I yearned for extra warmth. Will I be able to feel the warmth of the sun again? I asked myself bitterly. Suddenly the blowing wind brought a whiff of Theo's aftershave lotion into my nostril and my body tensed instantly. I braced myself for further lies.

Theo knelt on the grass in front of my crouching figure. He tired to take my hand but I pushed him away. He was whispering but I couldn't hear a word that he was saying. I covered my ears with my trembling hands. Vehemently I yelled, "I don't ever want to see or talk to you again—I don't believe you can be so deceitful!" I wanted to slap Theo's handsome face—I wanted to scratch his eyes out but I controlled myself.

"You two-timing bastard! Haven't you lied enough?" Anthony challenged Theo with wrath.

Carol stamped her feet indignantly and screamed, "You don't deserve Melanie's affection! You deceitful and conniving creature! I curse the day that you were introduced to her!"

Suddenly my composure snapped. I sobbed uncontrollably. "I have amended my ways according to your demands. Extracting minutes from my tight schedule in order that we can be together. I have ruined my studying routine to make myself available to you—to accommodate your pleasure—what more can I do?"

When my whimper gradually subsided I said with clarity and conviction. "You have destroyed my faith in human relationship. My devotion to you was absolutely abused. You have had your fun. Now will you leave me alone?"

Anthony emphasized elaborately on my wishes, "Theo, you heard her—leave her alone—lie to someone else. Find your casual fling with another girl, but don't hurt the poor girl again. She deserves better treatment than this intolerable, inexcusable, deceitful behavior. How can you justify your own action? How can you even ask for her forgiveness?"

"Will you guys give me a chance? Will you listen to me? I have forewarned Melanie of my parent's dislike for her. How can I make you understand? I really love Melanie—I wasn't fooling around with her! My parents prefer Sue, and I have no other choice but to obey them. My father can tighten the purse string and where will I be? I am too used to a good life and I can't survive without all the fine trimmings of life! It's too much of a sacrifice!" Theo seized my hand and continue to plead and beg for my understanding. "Melanie, forget my family and Sue! When we are together we are happy—aren't we? Give me another chance?"

I laughed hysterically. "Are you asking me to ignore your parents and forget that Sue existed? Do you think that I am a creature with no feelings? Even a dog has feelings! How can you even suggest that I should tolerate another woman in your life? Don't ask or expect the impossible. I am not a miracle performer!"

I pushed Theo away and instantly jumped on my feet. Without a backward glance I ran away.

I buried my grief in my books, I found some sorts of comfort from them—at least they would not lie to me or hurt me! Sui Fong called. She was distressed and alarmed by Theo's behavior. I sounded distant and dejected on the phone but I reassured her that I would survive—I had to—I had no other choice! Sui Fong obviously was worried because she called again and again. On two occasions even Cedric came on the phone. With his wittiness and amusing humor he actually extracted a few giggles from me. Carol and Anthony were true friends. Their support was a great comfort to me. Alastair and Mr. John showered me with extra attention. When I was a victim of insomnia instead of counting sheep, I began to count my blessings. I was surrounded by true friends. Unyieldingly I refused all calls from Theo. Beautiful bouquets of white roses were delivered but I threw them away immediately. Unopened letters were returned to the sender. Theo waited for me every morning, but stubbornly, I refused to acknowledge his presence. Theo no longer existed—only a bitter taste from the ordeal lingered. Slowly but surely the excruciating pain was replaced by a dull ache. Although my eyes no longer sparkled, at least I was capable of smiling again. Due to sleepless nights and loss of appetite I was losing weight pitifully. It was a nasty experience and I paid dearly for it.

Finally the much longed-for call came. Gavin's comforting voice was music to my ears and the soothing tone finally broke the dam of my restrained emotions. Uncontrollably I sobbed into the phone. I wanted him to hold me in his arms and I craved for his tender, loving care, but we were miles apart. When my sobbing subsided, I haltingly attempted a feeble chuckle. Sniffing, I snorted, "I needed that! I just couldn't cry! I will get over this and the next time around hopefully I will have learned from my mistakes. When Cupid shoots his arrow again, I will be prepared and better equipped for deceptions."

Gavin's soothing voice echoed over the phone. "I feel awful for you! I am proud that you seem to be able to look on the brighter side of things and that you can treat this mishap as part of experience from life. I know your stubbornness will provide you with the strength to survive this storm. Don't let Theo's deceitfulness spoil your carefree personality. When life gives you a wave, ride it to the end. I know you can do it!"

After a moment of silence I remembered to extract a promise from Gavin, "When you have the opportunity to talk to Cedric again, please insist that he mustn't tell my parents. I don't want to cause undue pain and unnecessary worries for them. There is nothing that they can do—this nasty experience is a cross that I must carry myself!"

I was grateful to Gavin's faithful devotion, encouragement and constant support. Before I ended our conversation I managed to contrive a chuckle. "My studies have been badly disrupted. I am glad that I have been able to catch up." Sighing deeply I continued, "I guess I have to close another chapter of my life. At least I have the forthcoming long hot summer to look forward to—can you believe we will be returning to Hong Kong soon?"

Gavin replied encouragingly, "That's my girl! You have the right attitude. Before we know it we will be strolling on the white sands of Shek-O beach or fighting over a seashell!"

That night I fell into a dreamless sleep—nightmares no longer haunted me. My broken heart was slowly mending and healing. Time was indeed the best healer. When school closed for the summer, I buried Theo with all my broken dreams. In time, he might only be a vague memory. I hoped that one day I would be able to forgive him and look back into this particular chapter of my life with no bitterness but fond memories of golden days.

Twenty-Nine

Alastair was struggling to heave my ridiculously heavy suitcase onto the rack in the train compartment. Complaining bitterly he demanded, "What in heaven's name have you got in this suitcase? One would think that you have a few bars of solid gold stored in it!"

Carol nudged my shoulder then she gave me a conspiring wink and teased, "Clothing! Of course! Your sister's wardrobe for the entire summer!"

"Really! Women! I refuse to believe that you won't shop in Hong Kong. Why do you want to bring so much with you? We are supposed to be traveling light. Why do you think our trunks were sent directly to Sui Fong's house? Honestly!" Muttering to himself, Alastair hauled his own much lighter suitcase onto the rack. Then exaggeratedly he collapsed onto the seat and pretended to wipe non-existent sweat from his forehead with the back of his hand.

I patted him lovingly on his arm and mocked, "Alastair, surely a tiny bit of work is not going to kill you. Just pretend that you are smashing the tennis balls across the tennis court then you won't feel so much resentment." Everyone laughed and my brother, feigning annoyance, glared at me.

The door to the compartment was pushed opened and Theo walked in. The laughter immediately ceased by his sudden unwelcomed appearance and there was an embarrassed silence. Carol gave me a puzzled look, then considerately she and the other occupants of the compartment excused themselves. To my disgust I was left on my own to face my tormentor. I shoved my body closer to the window. I wanted to disappear because I didn't fancy another confrontation—I hated scenes. I wished they hadn't left me—I was not going to enjoy this conversation. My heart thumped persistently. Hoping to regain my composure I gazed out of the window into the far distance and pretended to admire the view from yonder.

Theo silently slid into the seat across from me and said, "Melanie, can you ever forgive me?"

It was impossible and impolite for me to ignore him so I returned my gaze from the moving scenery. My eyes rested on Theo's handsome face and I smirked, "I don't know what you are insinuating—there is absolutely nothing to forgive. What happened between us is water under the bridge so it's absolutely irrelevant for us to brood on the subject further."

Theo gently removed a strand of stray hair from my face and gently touched my cheeks with his finger tips. Self-defensively I cringed from his touch. To my utter disgust and horror Theo was still capable of causing ripples in my heart. "Melanie, I am truly ashamed of my devious and disgraceful conduct. Since we have gone our separate ways I have had time to contemplate on my own feelings—I have missed you tremendously—please give us another chance!"

I sat motionless and with aloofness I replied, "I am afraid your flatteries no longer have any effect on me. I have been exposed to the ugly and sordid side of our relationship. I no longer have the intention of paddling though my life with lies and deceits." Smiling sweetly at the attractive face I added, "Theo you know, there is a very old wise Chinese saying. "Once a mirror is broken even though it's mended the cracks will forever be visible." Even if I agree to give us another chance, I will never be able to trust you again. I long for a perfect relationship—I cannot tolerate flaws in any involvement." Pausing to provide myself with a chance to take a deep breath I continued. "I am ashamed of my own stupidity and naïvete—our so called love affair revolts me—I can't justify my own recklessness! I no longer wish to live with self-disgust."

Theo winced with my cutting remarks. "Melanie, aren't you overreacting a bit? It was just a small lie on my part! Surely we are allowed a mistake here and there?"

My eyes flashed with anger. Decisively I yelled, "You and your inflated ego—just a slight misconduct! Is that what you call it? Your flippant remarks nauseate me. I was your toy—a new challenge—a China doll that you could display in public when it suited your purposes, but obviously not good enough for you to bring home. What do you want me to do? Hang around until you are tired of me or until you have finished messing around with my emotions and then discard me like a broken piece of China? What about my pride and the humiliation that you have inflicted on me?" Unshed tears threatened. I was shaking with the intense anguish that was burning inside. Inwardly, I scolded myself. "I can't cry because I don't have any more tears! I am through with self-pity!" I inhaled deeply to steady my unstable emotions.

Theo took my hand and pleaded, "Are you trying to convince me or yourself that our relationship meant nothing to you? Could you erase our feelings for each other with a flick of your fingers? Melanie, look at me! Don't I mean anything to you any more?"

Calmly and coldly I replied with firmness and aloofness, "I don't want to live with charades—I have my own identity! You were my world and I loved you. I trusted you and worshipped you. I craved for your love and devotion to be reciprocated, instead I received a pack of lies. I am not a subordinate to your precious Sue! I want to live again—I need to rebuild my confidence again—I don't want to live in world of shattered dreams! If we call it a day now, perhaps one day we could still be friends."

Theo shoved a large brown envelops into my trembling hands. With fierce force I ripped open that envelope. Photographs of myself scattered on the floor. Laughing bitterly, I bent my aching body and retrieved every photo from the floor. I opened the window of the moving train, then I tore the photos to shreds and sprinkled the tiny fragments out of the window. I turned triumphantly and remarked, "Gone with the wind! Our so-called love and devotion destroyed, flying away with the fragments of the photos!"

Theo accepted defeat and dejectedly left the train compartment. When I was alone I panted and I wanted to scream with frustration. My love and devotion for Theo had turned to hatred and resentment. I had to control my increasing temper. I refused to allow him to spoil my holiday in Hong Kong. I closed my eyes and I willed my anguish to vanish. I insisted that I deserve a fabulous holiday. I refused to allow him to intrude into my life again.

Alastair and I had arranged to meet Sui Fong and Cedric in Peter's restaurant. Gavin and Raphael would join us for a meal before our departure to the airport. It was decided that Peter and Sui Bun would drive the six travelers to the airport. We were catching an evening flight to Hong Kong.

When we arrived at the restaurant, Cedric was waiting for us. Searching the room I inquired, "Where is Sui Fong?"

Cedric replied, "She still has a few things to purchase. She won't be here until lunch time!"

"Good! We have a few hours to kill so why don't we knock a few balls around?" Alastair searched for his tennis racket.

Cedric agreed enthusiastically. "What a splendid idea! Melanie, we will leave you on your own for a few hours—don't get into mischief!"

When the two of them disappeared out of the restaurant, I pondered for while not knowing how I should kill the next couple of hours. I caught my reflection in the mirror and I flinched! I was disgusted with myself. My hair was disheveled and there were bags around my eyes. I looked utterly tired and haggard. The bouncing young woman was no longer apparent. Instantly I made a decision. I discovered a solution to get rid of my misery and lift my spirit. Grabbing my handbag, I sprinted down the street. Soon I found myself gazing at all the sleek outfits that were displayed on the shop windows. Defiantly I pushed the door opened and ventured into the shop. Finally, when I emerged from the shop, a few shopping bags were clutched under my arms. Then I sauntered down the road. Curiously gazing around me, a chic beauty salon caught my attention. Determinedly I entered the salon. When water was dripping from my long hair and I was sitting on the chair, facing the mirror, I confidently instructed the stylist. "Please cut my hair to shoulder length. Then I would like to have it straightened. I would like a side parting so my hair caresses one side of my face."

The friendly stylist was appalled with my instructions. Admiringly he fingered my long wavy hair and inquired, "Are you sure of your decision? You have such beautiful long curly hair!"

Stubbornly I smiled adamantly and insisted, "Absolutely no regrets—just cut it—I am also in a hurry because I have a plane to catch." I was amazed at my own determination.

After a couple of hours I was impressed with the expert stylist's new creation. My long hair was scattered on the floor. Then my hair was blown dry. Expertly he used curling tongs to straighten my hair and I adored my new image. I bounced off the chair, then happily I thanked the young man and gratefully gave him a hug.

Before I returned to the restaurant I made another detour into the chemist. A pair of curling tongs and a bottle of beige nail varnish were purchased. Hastily I returned to the restaurant and locked myself in the ladies. When I reappeared again, the waitress was overwhelmed with the transformation. With the aid of a natural color body-stocking to hide my bra and panties. I was dressed in a fashionable, chic see-through light beige mini dress. The short and daring length of my dress flattered my slim and well-shaped legs. On my dainty feet I wore a pair of size five flat heeled shoes that matched the color of my outfit. The stylish dress complimented my slim figure. My eye brows were artfully shaped. My big eyes were emphasized with brown eye-shadow and black eye-liner. My eye lashes were thickened with mascara. A light shade of lipstick was painted on my smiling lips. One last thing was missing! Impetuously, I searched through my shopping bags.

Finally, I found what I was looking for—the bottle of nail varnish that matched my lipstick. Pulling a chair up to one of the dining tables, I commenced to spoil myself with a manicure that added the final touch to my new appearance. When the last coat of nail varnish was finally painted on my petite nails, I was satisfied with the new Melanie.

Gavin and Raphael arrived with Alastair and Cedric. Shortly Sui Fong pushed opened the door, her last minute shopping clutched under her arms. She gave Cedric the bags and asked him to put them in her suitcase. No one noticed me sitting quietly in the corner of the restaurant. The waitress was busy putting food on the table when Sui Bun arrived with Peter. Cedric and Alastair changed from their tennis shorts to hipster bell-bottomed jeans.

Cedric asked, "Has anyone seen Melanie? I knew I shouldn't have left her on her own. She is going to be late!"

Hiding in the dark corner of the room I coughed to attract their attention, "I have been sitting here for the last fifteen minutes enjoying all the activities!"

All attention turned toward me and instantly they glared at me. They were speechless and dumbfound by the gorgeous transformation. Raphael whistled and Alastair barked, "What happened to your hair?"

"I decided that it was time for me to invent a new Melanie so I decided to get rid of my hair."

Sui Fong moved closer to me and scrutinized my face. She couldn't believe the hilarious expressions on the guys' faces. Approvingly she intervened, "Don't be stupid! Melanie had her hair cut and styled!" Cupping my face with her hands she shrieked, "I love it—it's absolutely terrific—you look dashing. I must say your new image is positively dazzling. You are going to be the crave of Hong Kong."

"Melanie you never fail to amaze me! You were left on your own for a few hours and what did you do?" Nodding his head with approval and admiration shining from his eyes Gavin remarked, "Positively a much improved transformation—I am impressed!" He embraced me encouragingly and whispered cheerfully, "Personally I am awfully proud of you—you look splendid—positively gorgeous!"

I hugged Gavin tightly and was beaming with joy. For a fleeting moment Theo was far away from my thoughts while I lapped up all the compliments that were bestowed on me.

Thirty

We were dropped off at the airport and we thanked Sui Bun and Peter for the ride. Assisting each other we checked in our numerous suitcases and eventually boarded the crowded plane. Cedric, Sui Fong and Alastair took up one row of three seats while Gavin, Raphael and I occupied the next row. When all the passengers were finally seated and settled the plane gradually took off and headed toward Hong Kong. I gazed out of the window while two stewardesses demonstrated the use of the oxygen masks. My thoughts automatically drifted back to the last time that I had boarded another plane to journey to England. Although, only over a short period of time my attitude toward life had altered tremendously.

I left Hong Kong as a timid and shy little girl—lacking in confidence and craving for knowledge…I was returning as an attractive matured young woman oozing with confidence. The bitter pill of disappointment that I had recently swallowed contributed to my maturity.

The light began to dim and the sound of chatter was replaced by a low hum of noises. A sudden nudge on my arm yanked me from my reminiscing and I returned to the present. Opening my eyes I turned my head and saw Sui Fong beckoning me to join her. "I am too excited to sleep. All the commotion is subsiding. Do you want to join me in the back so we can chat?" She pointed to a few empty seats in the back of the plane.

I climbed over Gavin's outstretched body and joined Sui Fong. When we took up the empty seats and were snuggled warmly with blankets Sui Fong inquired, "I don't want you to think that I am prying but do you want to talk about Theo? I think that its time that you should get it out of your system."

Shrugging my shoulders I smiled pathetically. "I guess so. I have to talk about it sooner or later—until I can voice what is in my mind I can't really get him out of my system."

Sui Fong patted my knees tenderly. "You know he will never be entirely out of your system."

Curling my legs onto the crammed seat I agreed. "I suppose not. When we were on the train traveling to London, he approached me unexpectedly. My heart shriveled when I saw him. Somehow he still has an invisible hold on me."

Sui Fong replied in a soft soothing voice. "First love never dies—as the old saying goes. The worst is behind you now. You have recovered splendidly, considering the shock and humiliation you had to endure."

My whisper was muffled by the humming of the engine and my words were a slur. "Sometimes I feel that I have dipped my fingers into borrowed time and that Theo was just a figment of my imagination. Whenever I saw him in school the pain became physical again. The first few mornings when I saw him waiting for me by the school bus I literally retched with misery. The dejected feeling that constantly suffocated me was frightening. I never thought that I could recover from it." I pulled the blanket up to my neck and shivered.

"I can share your feelings—you must have felt worse than a wounded animal. You need time to heal and regain your confidence," Sui Fong advised while looking out of the window into the black horizon.

"My pride was hurt beyond description. I was misled by Theo's camouflaged charm. He was, in fact, really shallow. His deceitfulness was disguised with charisma and I was overwhelmed by his potent appeal. I felt robbed as if I had been robbed of all my dignity and self-esteem." I thought for a while then I continued. "I could have fought for his parents' approval if Theo had stood by me and supported me. Instead he lied and expected me to tolerate Sue—that was really asking for the impossible!" I quivered at the disgusting thought.

"Theo was obviously not in tune with your personality." Sui Fong concluded decisively. "He can't really expect you to tolerate another woman in his life unless you didn't feel enough love for him!"

I rested my chin on my knee and sighed, "I am amazed with his stupidity. I had dropped enough hints. I have always made myself clear that I would only date a one-woman man. He had undermined my integrity. I would have thought that he should be aware of my thinking after Diona's incident. Anyway I am glad that it's all behind me now—a good lesson taught and learnt. I hope that I will be wiser next time." After a moment of peaceful silent I continued. "Sui Fong I do envy you! Cedric is your first boyfriend and shortly you will be engaged to him. It's all smooth sailing for you! Why can't it be the same for me?"

Sui Fong responded with conviction, "Fate and destiny. We are each destined to follow different roads in life. Hopefully this experience will make you a better and wiser person!"

"At times I do wonder, can we really alter destiny? Or can we fight for our opportunities?" I held my forehead and wondered aloud.

Sui Fong chuckled. "The hen or the egg first? Life is a mystery! We seem to be fumbling through life and eventually we hope to obtain the proper answer to all our queries."

Haltingly, I confessed to my trusted and dear friend. "I must be a glutton for punishment—mine was the perfect case of masochism. I had a premonition of Theo's infidelity! When his father introduced Sue to me, it was a scene of déjà vu. I was hurt but not too surprised."

Sui Fong pushed a strand of stray hair from my face and teased, "Are you certain that you are not embellishing your imagination?"

"Whatever! I am only glad that the blizzards in my mind are slowly subsiding and changing to a gentle breeze!"

There was a rustle in the dark and Gavin perched himself on the arm of Sui Fong's seat. "I thought I should check on the two of you—you have been gone for a while."

I stretched and beckoned Gavin to take the empty seat next to mine. He slid into the seat, then he released the small table and propped his elbow on it. Gazing at Sui Fong, he asked kindly, "Feeling the excitement yet?"

Sui Fong laughed nervously, "I am glad you call it excitement. I would say a thousand butterflies are fluttering in my stomach. Do you realize that I will be meeting Cedric's family in a few hours' time? It's positively scary!"

"You don't have a thing to worry about." I boasted. "They won't eat you alive! I assure you that they will absolutely pamper you. Auntie Wei Fun is adorable. She spoils us rotten. I personally guarantee their devoted attention—you will charm them off their feet!"

"Sui Fong, Melanie is right. She is not exaggerating. Auntie Wei Fun is indeed a darling." Gavin winked at Sui Fong in the dark then suggested that we should return to our seats.

We amused ourselves playing cards—sometimes I would read and doze off using Gavin's shoulder as my pillow. For once I was pleased with my petite size because I was small enough to sleep on the crammed seat with no difficulty. Although the flight was interminable, we managed to while-away the long hours contentedly enjoying each other's company reminiscing old times and guessing into the future!

The plane finally touched ground in Hong Kong Kai Tak International Airport. Assisting each other with our luggage, we sailed through immigration and custom without encountering any difficulty. When we reached the arrival lounge I was overflowing with emotion and was almost in tears. Sui Fong was nervous and I thought her knees were knocking violently. Gavin suggested that both over-emotional females should inhale a few deep breaths before we met our family.

Sui Fong shrieked, "This tension is unbearable—it's a horrifying experience—I can't bear it!" She covered her face with her hands. Cedric removed her shaking hands tenderly and kissed her lovingly on the lips. He whispered, "You are not facing a firing squad. They are only my relatives—they don't bite." I winked at my friend encouragingly and patted her shivering shoulders.

Relatives and friends greeted our smiling faces. We radiated with determination and self assurance and we proudly represented the young generation of the 60s returning from abroad. We were all attired in the height of fashion and a few astonished heads were turned admiring our trendy appearances. We were the envy of many on-lookers. Our confidence was unmistakably apparent. I was the first to fling my arms around Mother trying awfully hard to stifle my tears.

Auntie Pearl rushed into Gavin's open arms while Uncle Joe embraced Raphael. Auntie Wei Fun secretly brushed a tear of happiness from her smiling face. Sui Fong was introduced to her future mother-in-law and then Auntie Wei Fun kissed Cedric lovingly. Father crushed Alastiar with a bear hug and kissed me. When Ardelia finally had a chance to welcome me home she mocked with pleasure, "I think I had made a mistake by asking you to become one of my bridesmaids because you will steal all the lime-light from me!"

"Where is Lynette?" I asked anxiously searching for her among the sea of faces.

Father replied, "She is waiting for us at home because she is supposed to be supervising the cooking and making sure that your rooms are ready!"

I was overwhelmed and surprised. "Since when has Lynette turned domesticated?"

"Since the day she met her current boyfriend!" Mother replied while circling my shoulders with her loving arms.

Alastair mischievously asked, "Are you serious? Are you telling me that Lynette is finally ready to settle down with one admirer?"

"Who knows?" Father rolled his eyes and responded wittily while slapping Alastair's shoulder.

After we had gathered our belongings in a midst of confusion, we departed for the parking lot. Uncle Joe brought his car around and Gavin kissed me lightly on the cheek and disappeared into the waiting car. Sui Fong followed Ardelia to her car while Auntie Wei Fun happily chatted with Cedric. Father and Alastair stored our luggage in the boot of his car and we left for home. When we arrived, before I had time to admire my new accommodation, I dragged my overly heavy suitcase into my newly designated room and yelled for Lynette.

"I can hear you! There is no need to shout!"

I couldn't believe my ears! Lynette was asking me not to shout when I was the one who had to tolerate her constant screams and yells when we were in England. I ran into the kitchen and hugged my sister. Ah Ying's kind face was a welcoming sight. I was definitely home—faithful Ah Ying was cooking for me again. Then I was introduced to the young maid who was Ah Ying's assistant. I was glad that our old and devoted servant no longer had to attend to all the housework.

Finally, dinner was over and the dirty dishes were cleared away by the maid—I was glad someone else was attending to the dirty dishes instead of me. I was still buzzing with excitement and sleep eluded my exhausted body. I dialed Auntie Wei Fun's number and requested to speak to Sui Fong. When my friend answered the phone I asked, "Well? How is it so far?"

Sui Fong giggled and whispered, "Your information was one hundred percent correct! Auntie Wei Fun is fantastic but I still have to endure the family lunch tomorrow when I will be introduced to the rest of your family."

I could already imagine all the aunts and uncles fussing over us. I chuckled, "There is no point in stalling. You might as well get it over and done with. I don't see an alternative for you—of course you can always postpone the lunch to a later date. I will be your supportive prop and I can guarantee that the lunch will be an eye-opener for you."

"Very well for you to mock. You are part of the family." Sui Fong hissed into the phone.

I clicked my tongue and teased, "You will soon be part of the family."

"I have this distinct feeling that you are being absolutely beastly to me," Sui Fong said.

With consideration I replied soothingly, "Far from it! I am just about to outline our itinerary for tomorrow!"

Sui Fong flustered, "You mean I have other commitments after lunch? More relatives?"

"Let's analyze the situation…" I replied with a serious tone of voice.

My friend was in a frenzy and all her resolves melted. She moaned, "I can't endure more of this excitement."

"Sure now? No regrets!" I warned. Then I smugly continued, "After lunch I was going to offer to show you my Hong Kong and we could indulge ourselves with some serious business like s-h-o-p-p-i-n-g!"

Sui Fong yelled happily, "This is the best suggestion that I have heard so far. You have yourself a date!" An excited and tired Sui Fong hung up.

When I was finished talking to Sui Fong, I was hoping that Gavin would call. Almost spontaneously the phone jingled and I heard Gavin's much welcomed voice.

Laughing I said, "Talk about telepathy—I was just hoping that you will call." Exultantly I repeated to him my conversation with Sui Fong.

"You are a bundle of joy. You must be recovering from your tormenting experience with Theo. Your sense of humor has returned—trust you to scare Sui Fong out of her wits. By the way, when are you going to see me?" Gavin was delighted with my joyful voice.

"After my shopping expedition with Sui Fong—maybe we can meet for dinner," I replied.

Gavin chaffed, "I suppose I will have to settle for second best. Shopping will be my rival while we are here in this shopping paradise!"

"But of course." I wished him a goodnight and returned to my room.

The next morning I opened my eyes and lazily I stretched and looked around my unfamiliar surroundings. The humming of the air-conditioning sounded strange to my ears. I was disoriented—I couldn't remember why I was sleeping in this strange room. Then the annoying sound of the vacuum cleaner and the muffled voices of the maids jolted my memory. I was back in my own hometown again. I gazed up at the ceiling and was immediately engulfed with nostalgic thoughts. The ticking of the grandfather clock in the corridor reminded me that I was wasting my morning in bed. I bounced out of bed and opened the bedroom door. I peeped out from my room. Father was visible from the dining room and he was reading the *South China Morning Post*—obviously enjoying his coffee.

I rushed into the room and pounced myself on him. He scooped me into his strong arms and gave me a peck on both cheeks. "Good morning Daddy and what a beautiful morning!"

Father looked out of the window and he agreed. "It is definitely a good morning. I am delighted that the family is together again—we have missed you."

I blew him a kiss and responded, "And I have missed you!"

I sprinted into the balcony. The flat faced the south side of the island. The aqua-marine ocean stretched endlessly into the horizon. The reflection from the brilliant sun sparkled in the sea. A few sail boats sailed on the calm water. I loved the serenity of this quiet side of the island. I flexed my legs and twisted my slim waist and inhaled the fresh sea air. I promised myself that I would visit Stanley Beach soon—I could just walk there! The magnificent view of the green mountains and the calm blue sea never failed to take my breath away. Fleeting memories of Theo invaded my peacefulness, so I shook my head fiercely because I wasn't going to allow sad memories to spoil the enchanting morning. I was determined to store his image into the back of my mind. Standing on the balcony, I returned my gaze to the decor of the living room. On the mantelpiece photographs of myself and my family were prominently on display. The ivory curtains matched the light beige upholstery of the settee and armchairs elegantly. The varnished and polished wood floor shone with the sunlight. Mother's artful taste attributed to the grandeur and comforts of the room tastefully. I could smell a peculiar aroma, so screwing my nose disdainfully I sniffed. Curiously I ventured into the kitchen. Ah Ying was stirring a pot of broth. I inquired, "What an unusual smell—what are you cooking?"

Smiling the elderly cook explained, "I am making chicken soup with Ginseng. Your mother reckons that the entire family will benefit from the dried herb. The chicken is used to dilute the bitter taste of the herb." The cook wiped her wet hands on the apron then offered a seat to me. "So—little one—I hear you are a very good cook! Your mother is always boasting about your talent. You will have to demonstrate for me. We can exchange ideas."

Bashfully, I confessed, "Most of the time I don't know what I am doing. I am no expert—you will have to teach me—there is still so much for me to learn." I started to lift the lids off all the pots on the stove. Suddenly I discovered my favorite chicken and abalone congee bubbling in a pot. "I never get a chance to cook this super congee. It's just too time-consuming but I love it!"

With an ever-smiling plump face Ah Ying chuckled. She took a bow from the cupboard and filled it with congee and offered it to me. Greedily I sat on a kitchen stool and began to spoon the steaming hot porridge into my mouth. Alastair, rubbing his eyes, appeared on the threshold. Scanning the kitchen he sniffed grudgingly, "I suppose Mummy will insist that we all eat that smelly chicken soup! What a dreary thought!"

I winked at my brother lovingly. "Doesn't the smell remind you that you are really home and Ah Ying is cooking for us again? I am having congee. No doubt Ah Ying will be generous enough to feed you…trust you to appear where there is food."

Dreading the boring lunch with the family, Alastair and I left home with Mother, and she drove us into Causeway Bay. When we arrived at the Chinese Recreation Club, Alastair drooled with envy when he saw club members playing tennis. Mother suggested, "Cedric can give you a game after lunch! I will book a court for you!"

Frowning, Alastair inquired, "What about Sui Fong? Surely Cedric wouldn't want to neglect her. After all it's her first day in town!"

Proudly and confidently I interrupted. "I have made arrangement to show her around town—we can meet for dinner!"

Alastair rolled his eyes into the sky. "Poor Cedric. When you are through with Sui Fong, Cedric's pocket will be relieved of half of his money!"

Cheekily I rebuked and blackmailed him, "I am only doing the two of you a favor—do you want to play tennis or not? Would you rather I cancel my arrangement with Sui Fong so that Cedric can keep her company?"

The restaurant was crowded with people, their voices were bold and brash. I cringed because I was no longer accustomed to the shouting. We barely reached our table when I was besieged by outstretched arms. My relatives welcomed me exuberantly. Muttering polite replies, I inched my way to Sui Fong's table. My friend was overjoyed to see me. I was amused with Sui Fong's apparent discomforts. Determined to rescue my friend from our various uncles' and aunts' clutches, I slid into the empty seat next to the nervous Sui Fong and whispered, "Did you sleep well last night?"

Sui Fong grabbed my hand and sighed gratefully, "Yes, and thank you. I thought you were never going to show your face. I didn't know that you have so many relatives."

I intentionally shocked Sui Fong with my next words. "Wait till you meet the rest of the family at Ardelia's wedding."

"You mean there are more relatives for me to meet?" Sui Fong was startled.

I muttered, "What do you think?"

Eventually all the relatives took their seats and Sui Fong was staggered by the number of tables that our family occupied. She counted her fingers and recoiled. Four tables with twelve to each table. She was horrified. "How am I going to remember all their names and how they are related to Cedric. I am positively petrified." Sheepishly she turned to me for help.

I patted her knee and confessed in a whisper, "Don't worry! I don't know half of their names and I don't even try to remember how they are related to me. Life would be so much simpler if we could address them as Auntie so and so and Uncle so and so..." Pointing to the elderly gentleman sitting next to Auntie Wei Fun, I said, "He is Cedric's Koufu—which means he is Auntie Wei Fun's brother."

Peels of laughter and chatter echoed throughout the overly congested restaurant. When the food was served, I peeped at all the tiny baskets that were put on the table. Sui Fong had never been exposed to so many different variations of dim sum, steamed pork dumplings, spare ribs cooked with spicy sauce, Deep-fried prawns on a piece of small toast, deep fried squid and minced fish meat stuffed in green peppers, or sweet delicate egg custard tarts, which were one of my favorites. Sui Fong was fascinated. So much food was put on her small plate. I didn't know what to put in my mouth first—everything looked so appetizing.

When lunch was almost finished Ardelia nudged my shoulders and whispered, "If you can spare me an hour or so after lunch I must insist that you go to my seamstress and try on your gown. We are running short of time!"

I was excited with her suggestion so turning to Sui Fong I requested, "Do you mind if we go to the seamstress before we shop?"

Sui Fong was delighted with the invitation so she nodded her head while wiping her lips with the napkin.

When it was time to leave, Ardelia gestured for Sui Fong and myself to follow her. Soon her sport car was weaving among the heavy downtown traffic and speeding toward our destination. Ardelia screamed on top of her voice hoping that I could hear her. "You have such adorable parents. They insisted on selecting your gown. I had to adhere to their wishes so I hope that you are agreeable with their choice. I must compliment Auntie Wei Ling on her good taste—your gown is indeed lovely."

When we were ushered into the elegant shop, I was relieved that the cool air generated from the air-condition system was able to cool my hot and sticky skin. I marveled at the yards and yards of satin and silk that were on display. The mannequins looked fabulous parading variations of wedding gowns and bridesmaids' dresses. Finally I stood in front of the full length mirror. I was stunned with my own dazzling reflection. I had on a two-piece brocade dress. There were pearl buttons on the front of the jacket and it was over a floor-length straight skirt. On the hem of the skirt were three rolls of tiny pearls. The skirt added shape to my slim body. The jacket complimented my slim waist and the floor-length straight skirt added a few inches to my height. The light peach outfit flattered my tan complexion. Sui Fong whistled when she saw me. The seamstress' assistant was busily pinning the dress that would eventually mold my supple figure to perfection. I was speechless—I wasn't even sure that it was Melanie who was smiling back at me. I stood on tip toe so that I was almost as tall as Ardelia. "I have ordered matching heels for you. I am afraid they are four inch pointed heels. You are the shortest of the four bridesmaids. so you need the extra few inches." Ardelia informed me and I was grateful for her consideration. What did it matter if my feet would ache on the wedding day?

I was on cloud nine. I couldn't wait for the wedding. "Ardelia, I don't know about you, but I can hardly wait for the big occasion!"

My cousin was influenced by my happiness and excited enthusiasm. Excitedly she smiled bewitchingly. "I think I am more nervous then excited. There is just so much tedious details that I have to attend to— I never seem to have enough time on my hands and the days are flying by too swiftly!"

"Well you have two volunteers at your disposal—you can count on our complete support!" I promised and Sui Fong's head was nodding up and down in agreement.

Thirty-One

Ardelia volunteered to drive us to our intended destination but I refused politely. I insisted that Sui Fong should experience a tram ride. We waited until Ardelia's little red car drove into the distance then I grabbed Sui Fong's hand and we sprinted across the street to the tram station. While we were waiting for the tram, I mopped my forehead because I was drenched with sweat. The afternoon sun was dehydrating me. Squinting at the dazzling sunlight, I put on my sunglasses.

When the tram was crawling along the track, I staggered onto the upper deck with Sui Fong following behind me. I suggested that she should take a window seat. I sat next to her. Gazing out of the window Sui Fong asked curiously, "I thought we are going to do some shopping but I don't think the tram is moving toward the direction of Central Hong Kong. Cedric told me that all the shops are downtown."

I informed a curious Sui Fong, "I don't like buying from the expensive shops in town—you will find better shops of the same kind in London. I rather fancy bargaining with the hawkers on the street. We will find a better bargain if we shop in North Point."

Slowly the tram crawled toward North Point and enthusiastically I became a tour guide. I pointed toward a store that sold Chinese herbal tea. I told Sui Fong that I would make her sample a cup of the tea that tasted foul and bitter. She stuck her tongue out with disgust and giggled. She was appalled when she saw the store that sold cooked food. All the cooked meats were on display by the store window and many hungry flies were attacking the food—she was horrified! Sui Fong was fascinated with the passing scenes and her questions were interminable. Finally the tram came to a halt and we found ourselves standing in the crowded street of North Point. Sui Fong covered her nose with her hand and grunted, "What a ghastly smell!"

Screwing my nose I assured her, "You will forget the smell when you see all the nice things that we can buy!"

There were many hawkers on the street with their barrels of merchandise. I sprinted from one hawker to the next hoping to get the best bargain. Although I had been away from Hong Kong for a while, I had not lost my touch for bargaining. I just loved to do it—it gave me a great sense of satisfaction when I thought I had found a bargain.

At first Sui Fong was terrified and intimidated by the harsh expressions on the faces of the hawkers so she clung to me for her dear life. She was brought up in England so all the hustling and bustling from this alluring Oriental city petrified her. I reminded her that were purse-snatching thieves who roamed the crowded streets, picking their victims and she should be careful with her purse. Sui Fong grabbed my hand and frowned, "Maybe we shouldn't shop here—I am scared!"

I assured her of our safety. "Don't let the hawkers bother you with their stern faces. The Hong Kong people are not half as friendly as the English. This is a stressful town. Too many people living in too small an island—they are really quite harmless!"

Slowly Sui Fong conquered her fears. She followed me and marveled at the prices of the merchandise. We bought beautiful silk blouses; we tried on belts and we purchased handbags. We tried on costume jewelry seeking each other's advice. We were having a super time. Soon we were burdened with so many bags and boxes that we found it difficult to catch a ride on the bus. We decided to spoil ourselves with a taxi ride. With soaring spirits we returned to my home. Colorful blouses, belts, skirts, and earrings scattered on my bed, squatting on the bed Sui Fong marveled at our purchases. She was surprised and amused when she counted the remaining of her money, "How could I have bought so much and still have money left?"

I was sitting on the floor with my legs crossed and sipping a life-saving ice lemon tea. "The trick is to shop from the hawkers and learn the art of bargaining."

When Mother returned from town she heard our voices, pushed open my door and joined us. Clicking her tongue she reproached us humorously, "I sincerely hope that your ambition is not to buy up all the goodies that you find and clean up all the shops before your departure for England!"

"Mummy! What an outrageous suggestion, but a tempting one! I don't think that I have enough money to clean up the stores unless you increase my pocket money!" I replied cheekily and beamed with happiness and excitement.

Alastair pushed his way into my room and heard our conversation. He exclaimed in feigned horror, "Mummy, don't you be so foolish. I wouldn't increase her pocket money because she will clean you up in no time! Melanie is a real glutton when it comes to shopping—she is like a piranha—she will swallow all your money and won't even spit the change!"

Sui Fong was disgusted with Alastair's imagination. "What a revolting thought! Only a warped mind will conjure up such a comparison—really—Melanie and piranhas."

Laughing I threw the pillow at Alastair and said, "He is just jealous!" Mother was delighted with our laughter and quibble. Looking at her watch she exclaimed, "We should be leaving for Aberdeen soon—we are having dinner with the Fernados." Cedric followed Alastair into my room and asked, "What is the cause for all the commotion?"

Alastair pointed to all the goodies on my bed and warned his cousin, "If you don't put a stop to their spending you will leave town a pauper—don't say I didn't warn you." Sui Fong tossed my brother a look of exasperation and smiled sweetly at Cedric.

Half an hour later we piled into Mother's car. Father would go with Lynette on their own from town. Soon we were speeding toward Aberdeen. Tai Pak Restaurant was floating magnificently on the sheltered harbor. Bright lights glistened in the darkness. We scrambled onto the small sampan that would transport us to the floating restaurant. Sui Fong was so thrilled that she refused to sit but stood gazing out into the water. She was appalled and fascinated by the boat people. She couldn't believe that the small junks floating on the dirty water were homes for so many. She asked, "You mean these people actually eat and sleep on these tiny boats?"

I nodded my head and replied, "We just don't know how lucky we are—we shouldn't really take our good fortunes for granted."

Uncle Joe greeted us at the entrance to the restaurant. We followed him to our table. He asked Mother in a whisper, "How does it feel to have the monkeys around again?"

Smiling at her friend, Mother replied, "It's noisy and expensive but absolutely heavenly!"

"Pearl shares the same thoughts! It's terrific to have the boys home again. Life is awfully dull without them—I don't know if Pearl can ever part with them again!" Uncle Joe was shaking his head.

Mother frowned. "The thought of them having to leave again at the end of the summer holiday can almost choke me, but I try not to provide myself with the opportunity to ponder on the thought!"

When Auntie Pearl went to pick the fish for our dinner we followed her. I had forgotten the freshness of the seafood that was available in Aberdeen—fishes swam in the water and shrimps jumped. I made a pig of myself during dinner. When I sucked on the fish head, Sui Fong watched with horror. The fish eyes were delicious and the cheeks were so tender. The steamed prawns just melted in my mouth. I picked at the meat in the lobster with such expertise that Sui Fong followed my every movement. After dinner the parents chatted over cups of hot jasmine tea. Sui Fong and I made an excuse and walked to the open area of the restaurant and stood by the rails admiring the lights from the island.

"Hong Kong is unique—I don't think that it's possible for me to find another city like this. I can't believe that I am actually here—I have to constantly remind myself that I am not dreaming!"

I could hear a movement behind me and I heard Gavin's voice, "You are not dreaming. You are standing on Hong Kong soil!"

"Floating on Hong Kong water." I corrected Gavin's remark cheekily.

I took Gavin's hand and sighed joyfully, "Oh Gavin! I can't believe that I am visiting Hong Kong with you again. The future is so unpredictable! God knows where we will be this time next year—I hope we will still be together!"

Gavin gazed into my eyes and whispered, "I don't think that I would want to look too far ahead into the future. As long as I am with you today and we are happy then I am contented!"

Looking at the starlit sky I exclaimed, "I hope we never have to be separated by oceans and continents again!" I clung onto Gavin's warm body.

Gavin stood between Sui Fong and myself and he put his arms around our shoulders. "Don't wonder about the future—just live for now—don't ponder into the unknown. We shouldn't feel dejected or distraught because of something that is beyond our control—we are on holiday now so let's be festive!"

Suddenly lightning bolted across the sky and thunder exploded. Rain began to pour. I had a premonition of disaster. The future was unpredictable like the weather—the sun could be shining brightly only hours ago then a storm erupted...what about our future? Unpredictable like the weather?

When we arrived home, to my surprise, a bouquet of white roses was waiting for me in my room.

The scent from the flowers was overwhelming. I took the small envelope from the flowers and read the card, "Please give us another chance to pick up the tattered pieces of our relationship." Theo was trying to salvage our relationship. The fragrance from the roses reminded me of the pain and sorrow that I had endured. I didn't want to be hurt again. I longed for love, tenderness and understanding. While I was dwelling in my thoughts the phone rang and I heard Gavin's voice. Relieved to hear his voice I laughed hysterically but my laughter was soon replaced by heart breaking sobs. Gavin was stunned by my hysterics and demanded an explanation for my abnormal behavior.

"An arrangement of white roses came for me when we were having dinner.... I guess I still miss Theo terribly! The flowers reminded me so much of him. How am I ever going to get him out of my system? Obviously I am not over the worst yet!" Hoping to erase the pain for me Gavin attempted to console me but no tender words could erase the dull ache from my heart.

During the next couple of weeks I was caught in a whirlwind of social events—I was riding on a merry-go-round and I didn't want the carousel to stop—I was having too much fun. Delighted to be occupied continuously every moment of the day, I hardly had time to rest or think. I was lapping up all the attention bestowed on me. I loved my social life!

I was the designated organizer for Cedric and Sui Fong's engagement party. I attended to all the minute details. I enjoyed the role of the decision maker. When the restaurant for the reception was finally selected, the invitation cards were printed. Sui Fong loved the two dainty gold hearts that were engraved on the white cards—the design of the card was elegant and chic. Although, the party was to be a small family affair, nevertheless, fifty guests were invited. Together Sui Fong and I complied the guests list and every detail was attended to with great care. I accompanied Sui Fong when her engagement ring was selected. A small solitaire pear shaped diamond sparkled on a plain gold setting.

When the last stamp was affixed on the invitation cards, Sui Fong and I decided that we deserved a break. Accompanied by Gavin and Cedric we left our flat and strolled to Stanley beach. We sat on the soft sand and watched the ocean with the waves kissing the shore. I marveled at the clear cloudless sky. Twinkling brightly the stars were smiling at me. I could hear Gavin's voice in the dark. "Sui Fong, now that you have had a taste of Hong Kong let's share your opinion of this place with us."

I returned my gazed from the twinkling stars and waited for a response from my dear friend.

Objecting strongly Sui Fong replied, "It's unfair for me to comment or make a rash judgment—I hardly know the place!"

"You must have some impression…." Cedric insisted.

Resting her elbows on her knees Sui Fong answered, "It would need plenty of adjustment on my part if I were to live in this wonderland. I have this constant feeling that Hong Kong is not real—the people are not practical—as a matter of fact I don't like some of their attitudes. Compared to the English they tend to be very rude and unfriendly with no compassion for others. It's a selfish town. There is too much money to be made only if you have the right influence and connections, so consequently the rich get richer and the poor get poorer! The rich ladies can be vulgar and loud—it is off-putting at times!"

I interrupted, "I tend to agree with you—these rich old girls can be awfully intimidating. On the other hand, honest ordinary people do exist in Hong Kong." Gesturing to the other people strolling on the beach who did not belong to the world of the rich and famous.

Thirty-Two

Ardelia's wedding was fast approaching. Although I was not directly involved with the organizing of the important event, I participated in the rehearsals. On one of these occasions I was introduced to the groom's parents. They had recently arrived from England to attend their son's wedding. My heart ached when it was so obvious that they just loved and adored Ardelia…happy and successful mixed marriages could exist. I reminded myself repeatedly that I had made the right decision to break up my relationship with Theo. I believed that his parents' rejection of me was discriminating and insulting.

It was a perfect day for Ardelia's wedding. The air was warm but not too hot or humid. A much welcomed breeze brought comforts to the guests. When the numerous guests began to arrive in church, my knees began to knock. Nervously I straightened my skirt for the umpteenth time and constantly I removed non-existing fluff from my jacket. Powerless to control my increasing tension I caressed my pearl necklace playfully. I pleaded for assurance from Sui Fong, "My knees are rattling and I am so scared. Can you imagine the consequences if I should trip on the carpet and fall flat on my face when I am walking down the aisle…Lord! Give me strength!" I rolled my eyes toward the ceiling.

Reassuringly, Sui Fong insisted that I should take a few deep breaths. "Don't panic! If I didn't know any better I would think that you are the bride instead of the bridesmaid!"

The church was beautifully decorated. The altar was covered with so many different shades of roses. Candles flickered brilliantly while the organ softly played. Cedric and Alastair were attired in their best suits with a red rose stuck in each of their lapel buttons. They were two of the ten ushers. When the bridal car finally arrived, Ardelia was escorted out of the car by her father—my Uncle Sheldon. Ardelia looked magnificent. Her off-shoulder satin wedding gown with bell sleeves had a sweetheart neckline and was accented with tiny pearls along the hem of the skirt. Her diamond necklace accentuated her slender neck. Her face was glowing and her eyes were sparkling. She was composed and was a picture of serenity.

The priest signaled for the wedding party to proceed with the ceremony, and the cute page boy and the lovely flower girl bravely marched down the aisle followed by the bridesmaids. I was not provided with another moment of hesitation. I inhaled deeply and with my head held high and my eyes fixed on the elegantly decorated altar, I followed the wedding party. A gorgeous Ardelia slowly drifted along the red carpet in the arm of Uncle Sheldon.

My eyes started to mist over when the bride and groom took their wedding vows and exchanged rings. It was such an emotional sight when the groom lifted Ardelia's veil and they kissed tenderly. The wedding march was played and the happy couple left the church.

The wedding party finally returned to the Hilton Hotel. Collapsing on the chair in the dressing room, I was able to relax and breath properly again. The tension evaporated and I was awfully proud because I did not make a fool of myself during the church ceremony. I was delighted that the ordeal was behind me and I was determined to enjoy the reception to the fullest. Rounds of applause exploded in the crowded ballroom when the speeches were made and the bride and groom were toasted. When the music started Gavin escorted me onto the dance floor. We did not return to our seats until my four inch high heels were killing my dainty feet. Gavin mingled around the guests and I was pleased to be left alone for a while.

It was obvious that the wedding reception was a terrific success. All the guests appreciated the delicious food, the flowing champagne, and lively music. I left my table and sneaked to a quiet corner of the ballroom. Thinking that I was alone I grabbed a chair and flopped in it gratefully. I kicked away my shoes and rubbing my aching feet I hummed to the music. I was startled when a hand appeared and retrieved the shoes from the floor. A voice remarked, "I suppose these can be extremely uncomfortable!" He was hitting the heels on the palm of his hand.

Frantically I attempted to grab my shoes from the stranger. I was caught unaware in such an embarrassing situation. Apologetically I murmured haltingly, "I am not accustomed to wearing such high heels…I didn't know anyone was watching." I muffled a chuckle covering my mouth with the back of my hand.

"With or without your shoes you are a dream. How did you learn to dance with such grace? Your steps are so practiced for someone so young"

I was flattered by the compliments. I was bewitched by the stranger's charm and attractiveness. Holding my breath my face was red as a beet root. Twitching my handkerchief nervously I whispered, "Please give me back my shoes! If Mummy catches me without my shoes she will be most upset…extremely unladylike."

The shoes were not forthcoming but the stranger extended his hand instead. "I am Marcus Kwan and you must be Edwin and Wei Ling's daughter Melanie from England!"

Unaccustomed to conversing with such an elegant and mature gentleman I stuttered, "Yes! Do I know you?"

Smiling enchantingly, Marcus replied, "No…." Teasingly, he bargained with me, "These shoes will be returned to you if I have your promise to dance with me."

Nodding my head mutely I followed Marcus onto the dim dance floor. Waltzing in his warm embrace, I missed a few steps. He had a hypnotizing effect on me. Marcus was one of the most attractive men I had ever encountered. I didn't want the music to end—I wanted to linger in the arms of this gorgeous stranger. But when the music finally stopped, reluctantly, I returned to my seat, but my eyes followed him while he disappeared among the guests.

When I heard Sui Fong's soft teasing chuckle behind me I twisted my head and with a dreamy expression I smiled at her and marveled, "Wow! What an attractive man—I wouldn't mind spending the remaining of my life waltzing in his arms."

"I am sure you would—you were definitely the envy of all the ladies when you were dancing with him. I must agree with you—I do admire his charisma and his magnetism to the eye."

I was captivated by Marcus and curiously I asked, "Who is he?" My eyes were searching for him again among the crowd.

"I know you will be interested in him and you are dying to find out all about him so I have taken the liberty to gather all his vital information for you. Marcus Kwan is a solicitor—a junior partner in his father's firm of solicitors. His father, Jeffrey Kwan, for your information, is a good friend of Uncle Edwin. By the way, he is married and thirteen years your senior. Don't have any fancy ideas about him." Sui Fong winked at me and warned.

I awarded Sui Fong with a bewitching smile and shrugged my shoulders, "Oh well! Now I know how Cinderella felt when the clock struck twelve!"

Determined that Sui Fong's engagement party would be a great success, I adopted the attitude of a mother hen. Ferociously I insisted that all final and minute details were checked and double checked. I was not satisfied until the last floral arrangement was put on the center of the elegantly decorated dining tables. Gavin and Raphael were delegated to collect Peter from the airport. When the last name card was placed on the table, I returned home to change.

I piled my clean hair on my head and my face was caressed by curls. I sprayed my favorite perfume behind my ears and rubbed some on my wrist. I stepped into my shimmering black dress and clipped on black earrings. My enormous eyes smiled back me in the mirror and when I was satisfied with my dazzling appearance I returned to the restaurant. When I arrived, the room was already swarming with close friends of the family and relatives. Again checking the name cards with my list I was surprised to find Gavin's card was replaced by Marcus'! Searching the room frantically I caught Sui Fong's attention.

"Why am I sitting next to Marcus and where is Gavin going to sit?" I exclaimed.

Sui Fong replied insolently, "Last minute changes! Auntie Wei Fun thought Gavin should be put at the same table as Peter. After all Peter hardly knows a soul and Marcus' wife is out of town so I have decided to spoil you with a treat and the treat is Marcus—any complaints?"

"You could have warned me!" My heart was beating so fast I shrieked.

Sui Fong gripped my trembling shoulders. "Calm down! Marcus is only human—no big deal—although utterly gorgeous!" Changing the tone of her voice Sui Fong solemnly advised, "You mustn't have any wistful ideas! To you Marcus should only be an elusive dream. He is beyond your reach! He is married—in other words, untouchable!"

A thousand ants nibbled at me and I was unable to concentrate on Alastair's well-prepared speech. I fidgeted listlessly. Constantly I wriggled on my chair. When the applause subsided and the food was served, I pretended to be composed and collected. I decided to act my part as one of the hostesses and smiled charmingly at the guests sitting with me at the same table.

"So we meet again!" Marcus directed his attention at me. Bashfully I nodded. Normally I was witty and possessed a terrific sense of humor—words never failed me but on this occasion I lost my tongue. I couldn't help but stared at Marcus' mature handsome face. Searching my brain frantically I tried to find an intelligent and appropriate topic for conversation. I heaved a sigh of relief when his attention was diverted from me when one of the other guests inquired about his wife.

"I hear Carmine is taking a holiday in Europe." Without allowing Marcus to reply another guest remarked, "Lucky soul—she is always traveling!" Another alluring lady with her deep, sexy voice purred, "With a handsome husband like Marcus I wouldn't be traveling!" She winked at Marcus flirtingly and everyone laughed.

Ignoring the laughter Marcus whispered into my ears, "What is the name of the perfume that you are using?"

"*Ju Reviens.*" I muttered in a tiny voice. I had to find something clever to say otherwise he would think that I was dumb.

"This fragrance will always remind me of you! Perhaps one day you will return."

I was startled by Marcus' remark and it almost choked me. I returned Marcus' gaze boldly. Watching his handsome face I responded confidently, "One day! But definitely not in the near future. I won't be coming home until I have finished college. It's too expensive for my parents. It's really extravagant and unnecessary."

At the end of the party before Marcus took his departure he kissed me briefly on my cheek and whispered, "Don't forget to return...." Was he hinting something to me?

When I returned home that evening, I retreated into my room. Lying in bed, Theo invaded my thoughts briefly. Lately I was able to think of him without any more pain. To my utter surprise Marcus' attractive face materialized. I smacked my own forehead and whispered to myself. You are an extremely attractive and alluring creature but you belong to someone else and to another world.

I cuddled my pillow and fell asleep peacefully with a smile on my face.

Thirty-Three

Sui Fong was playing Scrabble with Cedric and Alastair. I lounged on the settee and frowned. I was feeling restless. "Has anyone seen or heard from Gavin lately? Come to think of it he hasn't called for over a week. As a matter of fact not since the engagement party!"

Without removing his eyes from the scrabble board Cedric replied absentmindedly, "I understand Gavin's elder brother has arrived from Canada. I guess he is busy showing him around!"

I was baffled. Even if Gavin was kept busy with family commitments, he never failed to contact me by phone. I reminded myself to call him the next day. Consulting my watch I suggested, "It's still awfully early! Can I interest anyone in joining me for a stroll on the beach?"

Alastair growled. He was obviously losing. "Why should we keep you company? Can't you see that there is a serious game in progress?"

Cedric flipped the pages of the dictionary and intervened, "Alastair, do shut up and concentrate! Melanie, we will have to give your invitation a miss tonight because I have a feeling that for a change I am going to slaughter these two!"

When the three Scrabble players refused to accompany me to the beach I shrugged my shoulders and decided to spend the rest of the evening with my books.

"Melanie, you are wanted on the phone!" Mother yelled from her room.

I answered the phone and unexpectedly heard, "Melanie, I am sorry that I had disappeared for a couple of days but my brother is in town. Dad said that I could use the car tonight so would you like to take a drive to Shek-O Beach?" It was Gavin.

"Shek-O? One of our favorite haunts! Come to think of it, we have been too occupied to visit our favorite beach. I will be ready in fifteen minutes. I will wait for you downstairs." Humming to myself, I dashed into room to change. To spend an evening strolling along the shores of my favorite beach and lying on the soft sand was a most welcoming pleasure. I told Mother that I was going out with Gavin and fifteen minutes later his car arrived. Kissing him briefly on the cheek I said, "I have missed you!" In the dark Gavin's smile was hardly visible.

Perplexed by his silence I inquired, "Is something troubling you? You are awfully quiet and subdued!"

The car pulled into the parking lot of the deserted beach. Only a few cars were visible. I yanked opened the door and rushed onto the beach with Gavin following me. Approaching the water I took off my sandals. The cool water was refreshing. Splashing the cool sea water onto my bare arms, I laughed. Gavin watched my silhouette and sighed, "Was it only yesterday that we were playing on this beach—selecting sea shells and exchanging our dreams? That happy little girl who I used to play with has transformed into a beautiful and mature young lady. I really couldn't bear the thought of having to leave you again!"

Gently caressing my face with his finger tips, Gavin pulled me into his arms. Enjoying the warmth of his protective arms around me I whispered, "Your behavior is weird tonight! Something is positively bothering you!" I searched his face in the dim moonlight.

For the second time that evening he ignored my questions. Hand in hand we strolled along the beach and every so often I bent my body and picked tiny pebbles to throw into the ocean. I stopped walking and watched the pebbles disappear with the ripples into the water. We must have been walking for half an hour when Gavin halted his steps and hesitated. Mournfully he whispered into the wind, "I am desolate—I honestly don't know how to soften the brutal blow!"

When I heard his extraordinary remark I was baffled and frightened. Stamping my feet I demanded an explanation immediately, "Gavin, what are you talking about? I don't understand a word that you are saying."

He pulled me into his arms with such force that our bodies collapsed onto the soft sand. Still lying on the sand he took my face into his trembling hands and murmured against my hair, "I will not be leaving with you!"

The waves were splashing against the shore and the sound of the rushing water made it almost impossible for me to hear Gavin's muffled voice. "That's O.K. You will probably want to spend a few more days with your brother. School starts again before the university reopens. If I should return to school before your arrival I will see you at Christmas."

Gently he pushed me away and watched my face intensely. In the darkness I thought I saw tears glistened in his eyes. "Melanie, you don't understand. I will not be returning to England."

I was removing the sand from my body—suddenly I stopped. The sand was sifting through my fingers. My eyes gleamed furiously in the dark. "What did you say? What do you mean? You will not be returning to England?"

Gavin pulled me into his arms again and mournfully he mumbled a reply, "Mother had been terribly depressed with our absence from home. Constantly she had expressed her wishes to emigrate in order that the family could be together...it was unanimously decided that our whole family will emigrate to Canada." Gavin continued.

There must be something wrong with my hearing—what was Gavin saying? What he was saying had to be a nightmare—I smacked my forehead forcefully hoping to knock some sense into my confused head. I screamed, "It cannot be a unanimous decision! What about your desire? Don't you want to finish your education in England?"

"I have no intention of complicating matters for my parents so the simplest way was to agree with the family." Gavin explained haltingly.

My temper was rising. I yelled into the sky with bitterness, "It all boils down to the fact that you are leaving me again! Why are you insulting my intelligence? Why can't you just tell me that we are going to be oceans apart? Don't you have enough human decency to be honest with me—I am old enough to handle disappointments!"

I was furious. I pushed him away and I covered my face with my hands. My fury exploded! Compounded with disappointment and disillusion with life I jumped onto my feet and rushed into the open sea. Gavin grabbed my trembling body. Crying and sobbing hysterically I hit him continuously on his chest, "I hate you! I hate you! I don't ever want to see you again!" Repeatedly I yelled into the ocean.

He cradled my rocking body in his arms. In a flutter he murmured, "Baby, please don't cry!"

Slowly he pulled me out of the water and because of my struggle together we collapsed on the soft sand. Removing a strand of wet hair from my face, Gavin was horrified with the utter disappointed expression on my face. He buried my wet face in his heaving chest. "It is not within my power to change our destiny! You will always be my beloved and your memory will eternally be cherished by me!"

He paused for breath and then he continued, "My infinite love for you will never cease! Continents may separate us but my thoughts will be with you always!"

I wailed, "I don't want to become your memory! I want you to be able to come running when I need you! Who will be my mentor and advisor when I am no longer able to touch or feel you? Your undying love for me will be meaningless when we are no longer together!"

I was agonized with excruciating pain. Gavin was lost for a reply. To my utter amazement he started to kiss me. Our bodies entwined and we rolled on the sand. I was breathless and surprised by his sudden passion. Finally he stopped kissing me and our lips parted. We stared at each other and we both realized that we could no longer look upon each other as platonic friends. We loved each other but we were about to lose each other again. Hoping to restrain his emotion, tenderly, he pushed me away and gazed into the distance.

"Melanie, life is not a piece of smoky glass! We have to be certain of our directions in life! We have to follow our own destiny and we cannot fight fate. Who knows—we may meet again one day. So many years ago we were forced to part by unforeseen circumstances and today we are together. Tomorrow we will be separated but..." Gavin was unable to finish the sentence. He was choking with his own emotions.

I was at a loss for words. My mind was confused—I couldn't think straight—I was in turmoil. I hated destiny and fate. Grudgingly I walked toward the parked vehicle. I willed myself to organize the cluster of mixed emotions that was churning inside me. I craved for the solitary of my own room and I insisted that Gavin take me home immediately. We drove in silence and when we reached home Gavin forced me to look at him. He watched my face with such intensity that I cringed. He wanted to imprint my tearful face into his memory forever. Wordlessly he kissed me fully on the mouth, and I ran into the building.

I slammed the front door and ran toward my room. With the door closed behind me I knelt on the floor. Burying my face on the bed, I moaned. Oh Lord why are you so cruel to me? How am I ever going to survive this loss? Life is unfair! Why did I take Gavin's devotion for granted? Why have I been so stupid? Why was I so blinded of his love for me?

I could find no appropriate answers to my questions....

❧   ❧   ❧

Noontime was approaching and there was still no movement from my room. Mother was worried. Silence replaced the constant music that habitually filled my room. Normally I would be up and about excitedly making arrangements for the day—me being the perfect organizer. Gingerly Mother pushed opened my bedroom door. She found me gazing intensely at the ceiling. My eyes were red from crying and my face was puffy and swollen from a sleepless night. Mother was devastated. It was painful for her to witness the withdrawn, motionless, dejected slim figure lifelessly lying in bed. Discreetly I was dabbing tears from my face. Making room for herself on my bed, protectively, Mother kissed me gently on the cheek and offered her sympathy with her eyes. "Would you like Ah Ying to prepare a breakfast tray for you?"

Shaking my head I attempted a feeble grin. "Mummy I am suffering from a dreadful headache—food is the last thing that I will need for the next little while." Gavin is what I need—not food! I said to myself. Sensitive to Mother's affection for me I assured her. "I should be up shortly!"

I heard Mother speaking to Sui Fong on the phone. "I suspect Gavin has told Melanie of his family's decision to emigrate to Canada. As predicted, Melanie is devastated! Why don't you come over immediately? She may not want to discuss the matter but having you around will be a comfort for her."

I tried to suffocate myself with the pillow and sobbed into the soft material. Then, I heard Mother confiding in Father. "I am unnerved by Melanie's silence! Surviving this great loss will require plenty of determination on her part. Their friendship is so rare and to lose each other again would create tremendous misery for them both. I hope that Melanie has the strength to survive this ordeal—I feel so, so sorry for her."

Vaguely, I heard Father's reply, "When the two were separated previously, admittedly Melanie was younger and was able to bounce back into life. She is still young—she should be strong enough to endure another storm. We will lend her a helping hand and offer our support…we will just have to stand by her."

Mother sighed understandingly, "I only wish that Melanie will rant and rave. I can deal with hysterics but her silent grief is awful. I am grateful that Cedric and Sui Fong are on their way over now."

Shortly the door bell chimed. Immediately Sui Fong came into my room. I could scarcely move when I saw my friend. Flatly I acknowledged her presence. Without mincing words she insisted, "Melanie, you will recover from this loss! You have done it before and you will have the gumption to do it again!"

Hearing Sui Fong's encouraging remark my composure collapsed. Struggling to control my emotions I whispered, "I am exhausted and mentally drained. It's only been a few months since I broke up with Theo and now I have to endure this pain of losing Gavin. I feel so strange...I can't feel anything at all. I am just numb. I find if difficult to think. I feel utterly empty." Sighing, I continued haltingly, "I should be happy for Gavin because he has been provided with an opportunity to emigrate to another country with his family. He no longer has to suffer the pain of being separated from his family, but selfishly I resent his parents' decision. Oh God! How I hate good-byes. I hate the oceans and the continents that separate us. I hate the boats, the trains and planes. They provide the means to make these heartbreaking separations possible. Why were they ever invented?" I demanded unreasonably.

"Extra effect will be required from you to see this rough time through. I agree this is an enormous blow for you, but you must handle this crisis bravely. Think of the good times that you have had together and these treasured memories will be a comfort to you." Sui Fong's voice was soothing and comforting to my ears, but I was smothered with my own grief and her wise words were lost on me.

I picked up the Memory Jar from my bedside table, fondling the rough surface of the clay. "Why do I have to store memories in this jar time and time again? Why can't I be like you? You met Cedric...you fell in love with him and will be married when he becomes a solicitor! Is it not possible for me to lead a smooth and happy life?"

How could Sui Fong provide answers to my questions? Nonetheless, she spoke in a soft voice. "Through our long voyage of life unpredictable destiny awaits us. It would be impossible for me to feel the jubilation of reunion with a loved one because I have never been exposed to the experience of being separated from someone that I love. In a way this experience will make you a better and wiser person."

Fresh tears sprang from my eyes and I remarked bitterly, "This experience I can do without—thank you very much—I would rather not taste the jubilation of reunion. I hate good-byes! My relationship with Gavin is sacred. He and I together, we shared something that was unique. I know I will never be able to replace him. What we feel for each other is beyond description."

Sui Fong wiped away the tears from my face. "All the more you should treasure his memory. Hopefully, one day you will be able to think back and relish all these priceless memories."

"And in the mean time, what do I do—stew in my own juice of sorrow?" I demanded.

Sui Fong replied, "You have to make every effort to enjoy the remainder of your holiday. Gavin would hate it if you should ruin your holiday! Who knows what will await you when you return to England! Look, you have obviously endured a sleepless night so why don't you have some hot soup. Try to sleep for a few hours. Auntie Wei Fun is expecting me to accompany her for a few hours. She is insisting that she wants to buy something for my mother and would appreciate some suggestions from me. Why don't we plan something for this evening?"

I was grateful that the flat was once again quiet. Ah Ying was absolutely adamant that I should have some food in my stomach so she made congee for me. I forced myself to eat the hot broth before returning to bed. Drifting in and out of a troubled sleep I dreamed of Gavin, then Theo's face invaded my confused dreams. When I floated into consciousness again, I found Gavin sitting on the floor by my bedside.

"When did you arrive?" Dejectedly I asked.

"I called earlier and Ah Ying told me that you were resting so I came over." Gavin replied tenderly pushing a strand of hair from my face.

Slowly I removed my tired limbs from the bed. Distressed by my disheveled appearance, unbrushed hair and swollen eyes, Gavin inquired caringly, "Melanie, are you O.K.?"

Suddenly my anger flared again. "What do you expect? Should I be jumping with joy? I will survive—I have done it before—I will do it again."

Instantly, I regretted my outburst. Collapsing into Gavin's protective arms I whispered, "I am sorry—I shouldn't be screaming at you—I know you feel just as bad as I do—I don't know what has come over me."

Fondling the Memory Jar absentmindedly Gavin suggested, "Melanie, we have shared too many tender moments together, and what we share between us is unique...I don't want us to part in bitterness." He returned the jar on the table and put a stack of records on the player.

My uncontrollable tears started to spill on my face and my body started to shiver. Sobbing I covered my ears with my shaking hands and whimpered, "I don't think I can bear to listen to these records again—please turn the God damn thing off!"

After a moment of silence abruptly I gathered all the records from the floor then I went into the kitchen. Shortly I returned with a big cardboard box. I put all the records into the box. "Look, why don't you take these records home with you? When you listen to these songs, hopefully, they will remind you of me."

Gavin was surprised with my strange behavior. "You don't honestly think that I can forget you do you? I don't need records to remind me of you. In any case, how can you bear to part with the collection. The records have followed you all over the world!"

"Don't you understand? It hurts too much for me to listen to them again! If we do meet again then you can return these records to me, but until then, they are yours. I want the person—I don't want memories." I crumpled to the floor.

Gavin pulled me into his arms and he was lost for words. He wanted desperately to comfort me but he was speechless. Tenderly he stroked my disheveled hair. I knew that if I just moved my head slightly our lips would meet and I desperately wanted him to kiss me but I was afraid of my own weakness so I moved away from him. Clenching my fists I inhaled a few deep breaths and with incredible will power, I pushed the box of records with my legs toward him. "Take them! This will be an incentive for you to return to me—now you owe something…"

We could no longer control our emotions. Swiftly we moved into each others longing arms and our lips met and lingered. After a long while Gavin pulled away from me and said, "God knows I want to be with you forever but fate wants it another way. I give you my solemn promise that I will make every effort to keep in touch." Then our lips met again. Abruptly Gavin pushed me away and said, "Melanie I have to stay away from you! I don't want us to do anything that we will regret later. When I return to you again, we will have something to look forward to…that is if we still feel the same way for each other."

"Empty promises. I know our paths will never cross again. We were blessed with a second chance to be together. We should be grateful for the happy times. We are just not destined to be together." I was disappointed with destiny. "If only I had the power to fight fate then we would never be separated again, but I am not a miracle performer!"

Sniffing I continued, "Please take the records—a farewell present from me. Even if they are to remain with me I will avoid listening to them. I don't want to be reminded of golden days gone by. I have to look into the future. It's pointless and stupid to live in the past. You represent my yesterday and so do the records. Let them be a tribute to our relationship."

I was so adamant with my decision that Gavin didn't have the heart to refuse me so he promised to treasure the collection of records.

It took me a few sleepless nights and a few unhappy days to recover from my depression. Fussing was the last thing that I needed from my devoted parents. I did not want sympathy. I was determined to overcome my own sorrow. Suffering in silence I dealt with my own grief. Although smiling constantly my exquisite and delicate features were melancholy. My eyes had lost their sparkle. Operating like a zombie I was disoriented—my body was functioning but mentally I was consistently in turmoil. The family bestowed undivided attention to me and they kept me busy continuously with social activities. Mother urged me to go on shopping expeditions with Sui Fong. Even Lynette was exceptionally considerate to me and insisted that I should be introduced to other young men. Alastair was sensitive to my depression, purposefully providing various entertainment for me—his beloved tennis games were neglected for a while. With the family's support and devotion my depression faded away. I was grateful for their love and attention. I really appreciated Sui Fong because she literally sprang to attention whenever I needed company.

It was our last day in Hong Kong. In the morning, accompanied by Sui Fong, I visited all my aunts and uncles, not forgetting my grandparents. Then in the evening Mother invited a few close friends and relatives for dinner. They were sad that Cedric, Sui Fong, Alastair and I were leaving the following day. After dinner, Cedric, Sui Fong and Alastair played Scrabble. I insisted that Mother should play Mah Jong. Our farewell dinner party should not be a sad occasion for my parents. I would miss home desperately. I could not resist the phenomenal view from the balcony, so I leaned on the rail and counted the stars again. Discreetly Gavin joined me in the dark. I could sense his presence before I was able to see him.

I pulled him into my arms and with my hand circling round his neck I gazed into his eyes. I smiled enchantingly and chuckling, I chided, "I have been wicked—I carved your face into my memory—I have cast a spell on you! No girl will ever fall in love with you because you belong to me and you have to return to me!"

Gavin was pleased that my sense of humor was returning. He kissed me briefly on my lips then he put my head on his shoulder. Enjoying our closeness I murmured cheekily, "Seriously. You will need my permission to go on dates or your future girlfriends will be turned into ugly ducklings and you will long for my beauty. Therefore you have no choice but to communicate with me."

Intensely Gavin gazed into my eyes in the dark and whispered, "I do believe I can detect jealousy on your part, and I am flattered. I will not disgrace myself by dating ugly ducklings—I will wait for the white swan." Tucking a piece of hair behind my ears, he kissed me.

When he finally released me from his embrace he murmured, "I promise that you will never be far from my mind. It will be a difficult task to replace you—in fact I can say that it is practically impossible!"

I wagged a finger at him and accusingly I complained, "Don't lie! You will forget me when I board that wretched plane tomorrow!"

"I guess we have always been a bit in love with each other, but we were too naive to recognize our own feelings. At least now we are aware of it! Even though it is a bit late in the day for us but then who can predict our future." Gavin muttered.

I gazed into the far distance wishing that I could take a peep into the unknown. I agreed with his thoughts wholeheartedly, "Quite so! Who knows what tomorrow has in store for us—you may just return to me again!" We were locked in each other's arms hoping that tomorrow would never come and we didn't have to say good-bye!

Thirty-Four

I returned to England. Before school reopened, on a few occasions, Theo called me. With polite charm and aloofness I refused all invitations to see him. Struggling to regain my equilibrium, I came to the conclusion that it would be wise for me to disassociate myself completely from him. I was satisfied that he should remain only a memory from my past. I still had a soft spot for his handsome face and suave manner, but he was a devil in disguise and his deceits had left a permanent scar in my soul.

I missed Gavin desperately. He called a few times after he had arrived in Vancouver but with the static on the line he was barely audible. I insisted that he shouldn't waste money on long distance calls. They were meaningless and only increased my longings for him. His letters were far and few. Casually and unintentionally the communications between us diminished. Optimistically I looked forward to a better and happier future.

I shrugged the past away with determination. With vengeance I dedicated all my time and energy on the ever-demanding school work. I devoured all the knowledge that was constantly poured into my brain. After a while even Gavin became a faded memory from golden days gone by. I was able to think of him without jeopardizing my peace of mind. My young zeal revived and the brutal blow of my loss was no longer a vivid pain. Instead of drowning in my own sorrow and feeling destitute I started to take on life with a completely different outlook.

I became pensive and no one would describe me as a bundle of joy. My teachers, especially Mr. John, were impressed with my rapid improvement. I winced at the very thought of any close association with the opposite sex. Casual dates I accommodated, but I refrained from any serious involvement with the numerous interested parties. I needed time to recuperate from my bitter experience.

Sui Fong was intrigued and horrified with my blasé attitude toward life. Disdainfully she scolded and reproached me, "Melanie, you are still so young! You can't just lose interest in the opposite sex! Do you intend to become a nun?"

Staggered by Sui Fong's reproach, I attempted to psychoanalize my own feelings. "Sui Fong, I have taken a grasp of my own life again and it wasn't easy. I have debated with myself endlessly and each time I came to the same conclusion—I am afraid of defeat and I don't want to be hurt again. Now it's not the right time for me to be involved with anyone because I have lost faith in any kind of serious involvement. In any case, the boys from school no longer interest me. They are extremely naive in their thinking. The school may be prestigious but the products are just too immature for my taste!"

Sui Fong was startled with my thinking, "You know—your perspective of life is far from healthy—we all need extra spices to stimulate our existence."

"Dating is an extravagance that I cannot afford. I am lucky that I have survived from my ordeals and I feel refreshed now. I swear I would not allow further involvement to complicate and cluster my simple life. It took iron will-power to sustain my sanity. If I permit myself to stray with my wild young ways again, I may never be able to recuperate. I feel absolutely marvelous now. It's a terrific feeling and I love it."

The months and years drifted by swiftly for me. I grew to be a sober young lady, no longer chagrin with fate. I graduated from Milford. After obtaining a diploma from the secretarial college that I attended I was ready to rejoin the exciting Hong Kong society. Frequently I would glance back at my younger days and was able to relish my memories of the past.

Thirty-Five

It was the end of another era for me. I completed my education in England and fulfilled my parents' and grandparents' wishes. It was time for me to return to Hong Kong. I knelt by my open suitcase attempting to pack my belongings. Pensively, I gazed out of the window into the far distance...my mind saturated with nostalgic thoughts. I savored the few years residing and studying in England. Absentmindedly I played with the catch on the suitcase. A sharp pain jerked my attention back to the room and the open suitcase. Blood was oozing from a gash on my finger, obviously I had cut myself while fidgeting with the catch. Clumsily I wrapped my injured finger with a handkerchief. I sat on the floor feeling depressed and frustrated with the unaccomplished task of packing. Activated by the pain from the wound my thoughts drifted to Gavin. Although his image only invaded my mind infrequently...somehow I still missed his tender loving care and thoughtfulness. If Gavin were here, he would have warned me about playing with the catch and attended to the bleeding wound. Yesterday was gone and tomorrow was out of sight. I had to accept the present. Reluctantly and rapidly I erased Gavin from my thoughts and willed myself to concentrate on my immediate problems of tedious packing.

Sui Fong gently pushed open the bedroom door. Frowning at the mess of clothing scattered on the floor she inquired, "How is the packing coming along? I was curious because not a sound could be heard from the room, so I thought you could do with some assistance."

With the sound of Sui Fong's voice I spun around. Demonstrating affection for my friend, impulsively, I hugged her. "I am going to miss you so, so much!"

"You will be equally missed. There are no if's or but's because you must return home. It is pointless and unreasonable for me to dissuade you otherwise and you will leave with our blessings." She gave me a peck on both cheeks.

I dreaded farewells. Each time I had to say good-bye to my loved ones my heart would be pierced by sharp pains. "I guess this is the fate of all foreign students studying abroad. Invariably we have to return home...it's impossible for us to change tradition. There is really nothing to detain me and I can't just sit around and allow my life to wilt away. I really belong to Hong Kong." Desperately I attempted to convince myself.

After a moment of silence I grunted, "I will miss Alastair and Cedric's endless mischievous pranks. Also, I am awfully scared for my own future. I do envy your stability. In two years, if all goes well, Cedric will become a lawyer and both of you will be married and return to Hong Kong. I only wish I know what awaits me. Hong Kong's life style frightens me. I respect the people there but I have my own principles and, as you are aware, I am also very opinionated. I hope I can still fit into their society. My feelings are so mixed and the excitement of living in Hong Kong does lure me to return, but I will be leaving a country that I have learned to love. I dread the thought of having to start a new chapter of my life."

A few hours later I finally accomplished the tiresome task of packing. After dinner Alastair and Cedric decided to stay home. Lighting the fire in the living room Sui Fong suggested that we all could do with something hot to drink. Sitting in front of the blazing fire I cuddled myself and hugging my knees I sneezed and exclaimed, "I am freezing and yet the room is so warm!"

Cedric tousled my hair and responded, "It's just your nerves—you are jittery about return to Hong Kong!"

The staccato of burning and crackling wood provided the only sound in the room. Silently we gazed into the glowing logs and indulged in our own thoughts. I sighed wistfully, "If only you guys are returning with me—wishful thinking on my part!"

"Don't feel too bad! This is only a temporary separation. In a few short years we will all be together again. The fascinating Hong Kong life style will keep you so occupied that you will hardly be provided with an opportunity to miss us. In any case, Alastair is leaving with you so you won't have to endure the interminable journey alone."

Clinging to Sui Fong I pleaded profusely, "Promise me that you will write religiously. I would hate it if communication between us should cease."

Alastair poked the burning logs and teased me. "Don't feel so wretched. Unfortunately, this is all part of life. We won't forget you! How can we fail to keep in touch? I am not going to pretend that I am not curious with all the current events and gossips in Hong Kong. You are going to be our grapevine. I have a suspicion that you have enough suitors to occupy all your free time but you will have to be responsible to provide us with all the juicy details!"

I grimaced and threw a cushion at my brother. "You don't mince words, do you? Do you have to be so blunt? Don't be ridiculous—you are raving crazy if you seriously expect me to tell tales on myself and give you a chance to hassle me. I should really be thankful to my lucky star that you won't be around to chase all my suitors away!"

"Don't be too harsh on your brother. You have tolerated his mischievous behavior for so many years you might as well be prepared to live with his misgivings for the remaining of the summer holiday until he returns to the university in the fall," Cedric chuckled.

Sui Fong added, "Alastair does sometimes, only sometimes, possess some honorable attributes. If he wants to be, he can definitely be a respectable delightful young man."

"What have you done for Sui Fong that you deserve such praise from her?" I inquired with humor.

Alastair tapped his lips with his fingers. "My lips are sealed and I am not telling. Let's wish Melanie a successful future in Hong Kong. If you should become a wall-flower we will send our sympathy but if you should find your Prince Charming we will refrain from teasing you. Hopefully we will be able to marry you off in the near future."

I strove to smack Alastair but he moved out of my reach. When I finally caught his hand, I playfully punched him in the stomach and writhing on the floor he mourned with feigned pain.

Sadly I watched the blazing flame and whispered, "I have been too spoiled by your attention and care. With a faint whistle you will jump to my attention. Who will comfort me when I want to cry or when I need to consult a friend—who shall I turn to?"

Overwhelmed by my obvious grief, Alastair countered, "My precious Melanie, you have sufficient intelligence, so if the occasion should arise that you do require our support, I trust you will no doubt have enough common sense to contact us. With sheer luck our assistance will not be required until we all return to Hong Kong. In any case, with your shrewd head you will be able to squirm your way out of any predicament." Alastair paused then added, "I assure you, you have nothing to fear. According to the stars no strange man will cause any unnecessary heartaches for you. Your faith will not be destroyed."

"Since when have you learned the art of fortune-telling?" Sui Fong chided, and everyone laughed at Alastair's strange remark.

Alastair and I arrived in Hong Kong. We were exhilarated to be home and reunited with our parents. Although I was delighted with the reunion, I was exhausted. I had hardly slept a wink during the entire journey. My thoughts were with Sui Fong and Gavin. We were, once upon a time, the greatest of friends. There were no secrets between us and we were each other's confidant. Sharing each other's dreams and supporting each other...unfortunately we were destined to be separated by three different continents.

Through a cloud of confusion, tears and laughter, we were escorted to the waiting car. Mother was astounded with my tired face. "Did you not manage to sleep at all on the plane? You look positively washed-out!"

Conscious of my disorderly appearance I patted my disheveled hair and smoothed out my crumpled dress. "I was too occupied with eavesdropping. The couple sitting behind us was involved with a most interesting conversation. I couldn't help but listen." I lied. I didn't want Mother to know how much I was missing Sui Fong and Gavin.

"She was also upset because she was leaving Sui Fong." Alastair opened his big mouth.

I chided, "You are such a brat! Did anyone ask for your opinion?"

Father, chuckling, winked at his wife lovingly. "Now we know they have indeed returned home." Alastair stuck his tongue out at me while I wagged a finger at him.

Mother sighed in exasperation. She was aghast and amused with our behavior. "Melanie, do behave yourself—you are almost nineteen. I was married to your father when I was your age. As for you, Alastair, will you stop bugging your sister?" Happily the family returned home.

I was delighted to be home. I had missed my family during my years of absence from Hong Kong. I rushed into the kitchen and hugged Ah Ying. I was happy that the old faithful servant was still in my parents' employment. My appearance induced her to tears and she dabbed the corners of her eyes with the apron and beamed. "I have made your favorite chicken congee!"

Again I embraced Ah Ying and exclaimed, "You are such an old dear and I have missed your cooking!" Then I waltzed into the living room, touching every object with fondness. Each item stirred a chord in my memory and I was enthralled that I was finally home to stay.

When I pushed open my bedroom door, I was thunderstruck. Sitting on my dressing table was a bouquet of white roses. They were not fresh flowers but made of fine bone China. I snatched the card and ripped opened the envelope. "To your bright future and may laughter follow you for the rest of your life —love, Gavin." I was so overwhelmed with emotion that tears streamed down my face and with trembling hands I touched the figurine lovingly. Mother followed me into the room. She was startled with the tears on my face. "Last month Auntie Pearl called from Vancouver and in the midst of our conversation I informed her of your arrival.... I guess she must have told Gavin and this arrived two days ago." She pointed toward the flowers.

I collapsed into Mother's arms. Drenching her elegant outfit with tears I muttered despondently, "I really would like to know when this ache and yearning for Gavin will vanish—I still miss him an awful lot!"

"I am certain that he feels the same for you. Auntie Pearl told me that he would lock himself in his room for hours and listen to your records...."

This information activated fresh tears and I sobbed. "We have to concoct a solution that can wipe out memories for us. We have to terminate our yearning for each other once and for all...." I stamped my feet and threw my hands into the air.

Soon numerous invitations poured in for me and I was never without an escort. Suitors were attracted to me like bees to honey. Although flattered by all the attention I never exploited my popularity. I did not take my dazzling looks for granted. I was so natural that people often wondered whether I was aware of my extreme attractiveness. I refused to stand on ceremony and I hardly declined any dates. I floated flirtatiously from suitor to suitor. Life to me represented a whirlwind of parties. Being an accomplished dancer, I never failed to have a partner. With innocent sophistication I shimmered in a crowd and my popularity increased rapidly. I was the envy of many young ladies. I possessed a warm and genuine personality. I was never conceited. To my Mother's utter disappointment I hardly responded to any of the young men's advances and this behavior baffled many of my friends, especially Mother.

≥● ≥● ≥●

One afternoon Mother found me sunbathing in the balcony and she joined me. Lounging on the reclining rattan chair she said to me, "Melanie, your blasé attitude really puzzles me. Are you not interested in any of the young men who have been hovering around you? Are you never going to settle down?" She smiled at me and shook her head.

My hair framed half of my face. I held my head with my hands and leaned toward her. Softly I replied, "Mummy, beneath all this jovial exterior I am still shadowed by the past. I am bewildered by all the attention and all the dates...constant celebrations of I don't know what! I find all the young men relatively shallow. I enjoy dancing with them. I appreciate their dinner invitations, but I can't communicate with them. Clearly there are differences in our thinking and beliefs. My open personality either fascinates or horrifies them. Some find me too conservative and yet others consider me too wild. I cannot deny the fact I was momentarily smitten by this mess of shimmering tinsels that represent our glamorous society, but I find it all a phony. It's fabulous to be pampered and spoiled but nothing is real. I can't seem to be able to develop a closeness with any of my new friends—men or women. I am lonely. I guess I am so different from them. I am searching...but I don't know what I am looking for. Somehow I prefer older men. Anyway I am perfectly content with my care-free ways, but I must seriously consider a career for myself. Summer holiday should be over for me."

Although Mother was touched by my frankness she was, nevertheless, adamant that I should not go overboard with my illusions, and be more realistic with my thinking. "Melanie, this is reality. You cannot dwell in the past. Undeniably some of your suitors are a bit immature, but most of them are healthy young men with good education and compatible family backgrounds. This extra-ordinary thinking of yours will destroy any opportunity for a solid relationship."

I was on my feet. I cupped Mother's beautiful face with my hands and implored, "Mummy, Mummy, I am not even twenty years old. You sound as if I am an old spinster. I have all the time in the world to find Prince Charming. I just haven't met him! I don't want to marry just yet—I have the whole world in front of me. I have too many tomorrows. Don't be so persistent and please don't fret—when the right guy comes along you will know. I promise. In the mean time I want a good job, and I think I will start looking tomorrow!" I was very determined.

True to my words, the following morning, I bounced out of bed bright and early. I joined Father for breakfast. Instead of my habitual attire of either swimming costume or jeans, I wore a pretty dress. He was impressed. "Who is the lucky man that is taking you out. He must be special."

"He is very special." I teased and kissed his forehead fondly, "The employment agent!"

Father was surprised, "Are you serious about a job? I know enough people to pull some strings for you."

"Thank you for your offer but I am determined to give it my best shot, and I don't want strings pulled on my behalf. If I need assistance, I will scream."

A few hours later the employment agent was impressed with me. My resumé was neatly and systematically typed and lying on his desk for his review. After glancing briefly at the document he watched my intense face. Dressed chicly I exuded self-confident and exhibited charming manners. "Melanie! What a lovely name and very becoming. Now let's get down to business…you are looking for a position. What sort of a position?"

Frowning I shrugged my shoulders, "I have always been fascinated with law. My father is a lawyer. I would love to be a lawyer's assistant."

Without any reservation the agent declared, "This is an extremely realistic town. No one wants to waste time on training inexperienced staff. They rather offer a bit more salary and engage someone with experience. In other words they don't bother with graduates."

I was appalled and disgusted with the information. "This attitude is ludicrous. We have to start somewhere. If we are not provided with the opportunity where do we begin?"

The agent intervened kindly, "I am afraid we are living in the midst of an extremely practical society. Sometimes we can bend the rules—very seldom—experience is definitely and ultimately compulsory. Unless of course someone can pull some strings for you."

I was fuming, "In other words I have to know the right people or I will be unable to obtain a position."

"Young lady, can I make a suggestion? Perhaps your father can be of assistance. Maybe one of his lawyer friends is willing to take a chance on you."

That same evening I discussed my dilemma with Father and he promised to try and solve my problem. The following day Father called excitedly, "Melanie, you are in luck. One of my old and dear friends, Mr. Pickering, is searching for a young assistant and he has accommodatingly granted you an interview. Be in his office by four in the afternoon."

I scribbled the address on the pad by the phone, then enthusiastically I prepared myself for the important appointment. Alastair sauntered into my room and collapsed on my tidy bed. "So, what is this rumor that I have heard about you looking for a job?"

I pushed my brother off the bed and attempted to straighten the crumpled bedspread, "Get off my bed or I will strangle you!"

Alastair spanked my bottom playfully while I screamed. Mother heard the commotion and intervened, "Are you two going to behave? Alastair let your sister be. Melanie stop yelling. Our neighbors will think that you are being murdered."

As soon as I was introduced to Mr. Pickering I liked him. Somehow he reminded me of Mr. John. The elderly gentleman was impressed by my ability to hold my own and I provided all the proper answers for his numerous questions. Halfway through the interview he chuckled and confessed, "When your father contacted me I was dubious about you. A contemporary and fresh from college. Also rumor had it that you are an extremely attractive girl, but now I am glad that I agreed to meet you!"

After chatting with me for an hour or so I scored brilliantly. Although amateurish in some of my business senses, Mr. Pickering thought I definitely had potential. He was more than pleased to offer the position to me. As a bonus he suggested that I should start immediately in order that his assistant could train me for a week before she left.

Exposed to the business side of Hong Kong I was intrigued and impressed. Soon I was very much involved with my new career and I encountered new friends. Every morning, diligently I left home with Father and reported for work. Forever punctual and always primly dressed I learned intelligently—from using the copying machine to taking statements from clients—nothing was too tedious or too difficult for me. My dazzling looks, rich family background and a graduate from London intimidated the other girls working in the same office. But presently my warm personality won them over. Although the youngest and most inexperienced among all the other secretaries, I was treated as their equal and soon fit into my new environment. I was happy and contented. I absolutely loved my job and adored my new identity. I declined all unnecessary dates and collapsing into my bed every night feeling absolutely exhausted gave me a sense of great satisfaction. I devoted all my energy to my work and concentrated on learning new skills. My dedication was more than admirable—meeting deadlines, working late, never uttering a complaint when documents had to be retyped. Mr. Pickering never regretted his decision in hiring me. I proved to be a gem and an added treasure to his staff.

One evening I let myself into the flat after a demanding day in the office. I was surprised to see the dining table beautifully decorated with Mother's best China. The fragrance of fresh flowers drifted into my nostrils. Sniffing the mouth-watering aurora of appetizing food, I invaded the kitchen. Ah Ying was busily cooking, evidently preparing a feast. I inquired, "Are we expecting guests for dinner?"

Absentmindedly, Ah Ying stirred a pot and responded, "Your brother has invited a lady friend for dinner!"

I nearly choked on the tea that I was drinking. I was flabbergasted. "You have got to be kidding! I must be working too hard. You mean Alastair is actually dating?"

Ah Ying shooed me out of the kitchen. She wanted to impress Alastair's lady friend. I was killing myself with curiosity. When I was walking toward my own room, Alastair came through the front door escorting a young lady. Tessie was demure and shy. I appreciated the young lady's charisma instantly.

Throughout the entire evening Alastair behaved impeccably—the perfect gentleman. My brother had met Tessa a few weeks earlier and immediately he fell for her. Since the initial meeting he had practically spent all his days with her. Apparently Tessa would be attending the same university as Alastair and he was thrilled.

Eventually Alastair returned to England with Tessa. One night after their departure Mother and I were alone in the flat. She voiced her concern, "Alastair is dating and Lynette will be married after the Chinese New Year! What about you?"

Biting from an apple I chuckled, "Mummy, I am really happy and content with my life now. I won't consider dating anyone for the sake of going out. It will be an added burden to my uncomplicated life. I am in love with my job!"

"How can you be in love with your job. It's an antisocial attitude—you have to go out and meet people."

I hugged Mother and gave her a peck on her cheek. "I have met enough people. I just don't fancy anyone in particular. I go out often enough on casual dates. There is absolutely nothing wrong with being on my own! If you are worried about grandchildren then Lynette should be obliging soon enough!" I laughed and disappeared into my room before Mother could utter another word.

Thirty-Six

I would be turning twenty-one soon and still be single. I wasn't even seriously involved with anyone. I had proved myself to be almost indispensable to Mr. Pickering. Lynette had gotten married the previous year and produced an adorable nephew for me. I was satisfied with the days just slowly drifting by...an occasional letter from Sui Fong would add trimmings to my day and a fleeting thought of Gavin would generate a slight smile on my face.

It was a Thursday morning and I was buried among heaps of paper on my desk. With a pencil stuck behind my ears and my long hair cascading down my back. I suddenly heard the telephone jingle. I fumbled for the ringing equipment that was hiding underneath a litter of files and documents. Static was audible on the line, and immediately I knew that it was a long distance call. My heart was beating frantically—I was nervous and curious. Sui Fong's welcoming voice rambled into my ear. Excitingly I leaped from my chair and howled into the receiver, "Sui Fong, it's heavenly to be able to hear your voice again—you have no idea how much I have missed you! I just love the sound of your voice!"

"How would you like to see my face?" Sui Fong's question was music to my ears.

I nearly dropped the phone. I screamed with exhilaration, "What do you mean?"

Sui Fong yelled her reply, "Cedric has passed his finals—he is now a qualified solicitor. We plan to return to Hong Kong in a few weeks' time and Uncle Edwin has offered him a position in his firm. I just can't believe that I will be seeing you soon!"

I was speechless and tears streamed down my emotional face. I wiped the tears with the back of my hand. I was laughing and crying spontaneously. Eventually I found my voice and exclaimed, "Sui Fong, after all these years we are going to be together again—it has been too long! I am so, so happy. I just can't wait to see you and Cedric again."

When I returned the receiver onto its cradle, my eyes were sparkling with tears. Slowly, I gazed out of the window but the panoramic view was lost to me. Instead I saw myself sitting in the kitchen…those days were lost to me so long ago…nursing hot chocolates and chatting with Sui Fong and Gavin. Almost instantly I returned to the present. Distinctly I could feel someone was watching me. Curiously I scanned the room and saw a familiar figure disappearing into the boardroom with Mr. Pickering. I asked my colleagues, "Who has just gone into a meeting with my boss?"

Sylvia hugged her shoulders dramatically and replied, "The most gorgeous man alive!"

Helen, the receptionist volunteered, "She is talking about Marcus from Jeffrey Kwan's firm. Have you ever seen him? I would consider him to be the best looking lawyer around town! Too bad he is married, but he is rumored to be a womanizer. We are not his type—his ladies are all married and ultimately glamorous!" she whispered and rolled her eyes toward the ceiling.

The name rang a bell for me but I couldn't imagine where I had heard it before. I shrugged my shoulders. I was still excited with Sui Fong's news. I couldn't be bothered with another lawyer. I saw enough of them every day.

"Melanie—you can't be alive—you mean you have never seen Marcus' gorgeous face? Wait till he looks at you—you will faint!" Another secretary drooled.

I smiled and waved my hands in the air then I pushed my hair off my face. "You are all exaggerating. He can't be that good looking. I never forget a handsome face."

"I am not surprised that Melanie hasn't had the opportunity to meet him," Sylvia interrupted. "On the few occasions that he has been around this office she had been away from her desk."

Shaking my head, I reverted my concentration to the mountain of paper work waiting for my undivided attention until the phone rang again. Once again my work was disrupted. I sighed and held the phone with my shoulder and continued to scribble on the pad. "Your mother is coming to town for lunch, so why don't you join us? We have invited your boss and a few other lawyers."

"No thanks, Daddy, I really have too much work to do."

Mr. Pickering appeared and clicked his tongue. "I insist that you join us for lunch! You can't work continuously without a break—a diversion will do you a whole world of good." He snatched the phone off my shoulder and barked into the receiver, "Make the reservation! Your daughter and I will be in the restaurant shortly even if I have to drag her by her hair."

I began to stack the files on my desk and teased, "Mr. Pickering. What violence—where are all your charming manners?" The other girls giggled.

"Come on, young lady, grab your handbag or whatever you young girls carry with you these days. I will see you outside the office in a few minutes. I am just going to the washroom." Mr. Pickering disappeared through the door.

I always kick my shoes off when I was working from my desk. I searched for my shoes without success. Frantically I bent my body hoping that I could find the shoes. A pair of brilliantly shined Gucci shoes materialized in front of me—I looked up and my shoes dangled from a pair of masculine hands. I gazed into a face that nearly choked me. I swallowed hard a few times and a deep voice whispered softly, "Cinderella searching for her glass slippers again. Every time we meet you seem to be searching for your shoes."

I smacked my forehead, of course! Marcus, the notorious Marcus—no wonder the name rang a bell. So many years ago I had waltzed in the arms of this gorgeous charming man. For an instant I could only stare. His smiling eyes told me that he also remembered that one dance that we had shared so many moons ago. I was no longer the shy and beautiful bridesmaid. I had matured into a stunning young lady. Marcus returned my gaze boldly and softly he remarked, "After our brief encounter I have often wondered what had happened to that young enchantress that captured my attention. On a few occasions your exquisite image has invaded my dreams."

I blushed and fidgeted with the pencil that was clutched tightly in my fingers, then Marcus continued, "So you are the assistant that Anthony Pickering has been raving about. When did you return to Hong Kong? I thought this was supposed to be a small town so how come we haven't bumped into each other until now?" He perched on the edge of my desk and waited for me to put on my shoes.

My eyes twinkled and I bestowed him with one of my famous bewitching smiles. Flirtingly I replied, "It was obvious that we were not destined to meet again until now."

"Now that fate has thrown us together, I don't think that I could let you disappear from my life again," Marcus countered flirtatiously.

When I was ready to leave he escorted me out of the office while the other girls watched enviously.

Thirty-Seven

The interminable yearning for the past came to an abrupt end for me. My future was no longer blurred. I began to blossom. I came to the conclusion that happiness did exist after all. Since Marcus reappeared into my life his presence penetrated my inner soul. Melancholy feelings no longer accompanied me and the void in my life was filled. Spontaneously our attraction for each other sparkled. It was imperative for us to be together whenever possible. Shirking rumors and criticisms, we searched for and discovered happiness. Despondency faded. Engulfed with utter bliss that resulted from our affair, my life was once again echoed with gaiety and songs—my love for Marcus shifted gears and exhilarated within a few short weeks.

My parents panicked. "Wei Ling, I have been contemplating having a quiet word with Marcus! I don't consider him to be an appropriate suitor for Melanie—do you?" Father's whisper drifted into my room through the open windows.

Mother softly replied, "I am against discussing the matter with Marcus. Melanie would consider it an intrusion on our part, and she will resent it. I don't think a discussion with Marcus would help matters. Melanie has to believe that his affection for her is an illusion. It will be more effective if we can convince Sui Fong to talk to her. The two girls have always shared a certain kind of intimacy. Melanie exhibits unflagging devotions for Marcus and our interference would ultimately annoy her. She has always been stubborn and she possesses exceptionally strong will-power and she will fight for her own beliefs. Let's ask Sui Fong to cooperate and find out what are Melanie's plans for the future. Don't rock the boat until it's absolutely necessary!"

I was expecting Sui Fong to contact me so when she visited my office I was not surprised but delighted to see her. "I will be off in fifteen minutes. Can you wait for me or have you made other plans with Cedric?" I inquired.

"What have you in mind for us? I can do with an evening without the guys. Just for old times sake let's do something enjoyable," Sui Fong suggested and sat on my chair. She waited patiently for me to clear my cluttered desk.

The phone rang. Smiling at Sui Fong, I picked up the receiver. When I heard Marcus' voice I blushed and whispered into the phone. "Sui Fong is waiting for me. We are planning to spend the evening together. Why don't I call you tomorrow and we can arrange to meet for lunch."

"That must be Marcus! Are you sure that you would rather spend the evening with me and not him?" Sui Fong teased and I dragged her off the chair and marched her out of the office.

I backed the car out of the parking lot and drove toward the outskirts of town. Finally I found the quiet restaurant where I often ate with Marcus. I introduced the owner to Sui Fong and we were escorted to an alcove where we were able to enjoy a delicious meal in privacy. Scrutinizing the intimate atmosphere of the surroundings Sui Fong remarked, "What a quaint little place! I gather you like coming to this restaurant—all the waiters seem to know you."

"One of our favorites...often Marcus and I eat here. He is after all a married man; therefore, it would be better if we were more discreet." I replied and stirred my cup of coffee while waiting for Sui Fong to make a comment.

She immediately pounced on the opportunity. "Are you really happy with Marcus?"

I gazed into Sui Fong's eyes with honest intensity. "I am in ecstasy whenever I am with him. When we are apart moments of uncertainty do surface because what we share between us can never last and our relationship is a flickering flame that would ultimately diminish. I don't fantasize any future with Marcus—let's just say that I am prepared for the consequences and I am just grateful for the stolen moments."

Sui Fong squinted at me dubiously, "Melanie, you are so young! Why waste your youth on a married man especially when he is so many years your senior?"

I shrugged. "Fate put us together so I am just grabbing the opportunity for some happiness. If hindsight is something that we can prevent then I would not have attended Ardelia's wedding. When I met Marcus for the first time, and when I was dancing with him, I had a premonition of some sort...I wouldn't say disaster...but somehow I knew that our paths would intertwine again."

In the flickering light Sui Fong sighed caringly. "I am not surprised that Marcus is attracted to you but what do you see in him? I hope it is not just his looks—I am aware of his sophistication and his ability to charm you off your feet!"

I shook my head. "I have persuaded myself umpteenth times that it's wrong for me to be involved with him but each time I see him or hear his voice I just can't seem to resist him. At first I did exert myself to ignore his advances but my heart somehow always ruled my head." I paused and took a sip of my cold coffee. "To hell with resistance—I will live for today! I realize that my parents would be upset. They would loath the relationship. After all Hong Kong is too small a town for such a scandalous affair. Even I sometimes flinch at my own behavior but I hope that they are understanding enough to sympathize with my feelings. I have no intention of destroying Marcus' marriage. I am not his first mistress and I will not be his last!" I held my chin and tapped my cheek with my fingers pensively.

Sui Fong anxiously grabbed my hand and interrupted, "Melanie, this is not a liberated town! This so-called prim and proper society that we live in will consider your association with him despicable—they will not take a nonchalant view. If my guess work is accurate they are already condemning you. Marcus' other lady friends are married women who are out looking for a fling—their affairs are harmless but you are different. You do represent a threat to the stability of his marriage."

My annoyance was increasing. Brusquely, I intervened, "Our so-called society and their attitudes nauseate me. I wish I was living in England again! No one would interfere with my affairs—they wouldn't even care. We live in a town of snooty people—they love to interfere with other people's lives. Hong Kong is just a big village, everyone has their nose in everyone's affair!"

In an agitated tone of voice Sui Fong interjected, "We can't change this town. They are gloating at you and your reputation is going down the drain. You will not be treated cordially again! This could be an irrevocable situation and you will not be accepted into society again. You cannot expect your parents or anyone close to you not to be perturbed."

I spat out my next words with distaste. "One would think that I am involved with some fraudulent activities—Marcus is far from being devious! He has not shown any underhandedness—all the cards were laid on the table from day one." With unsteady hands I extracted a tissue from my purse and dabbed the corners of my eyes.

I was glad that the waiters were serving other diners and they in turn were involved with their own chatter. Sui Fong concluded with resignation, "Melanie, I am concerned with your happiness! You can always depend on my support wholeheartedly. It's unfortunate that the timing is bad—the wrong time and the wrong place—fate would be kinder if you had met Marcus before he was married."

I was too intelligent to bury my head in the sand. I recognized the fact that my affiliation with Marcus was fatal. I was confused but I needed Marcus and craved for his attention. I was brave when I was discussing the issue with Sui Fong but basically I was scared—really scared for my future.

It was not too much of a bombshell for me when Ardelia contacted me and invited me for lunch. I was surprised that my parents had not voiced their opinions. Obviously they wanted my cousin to talk to me. Perhaps a confrontation with them should be avoided. When the dirty plates were cleared from the table Ardelia did not mince her next words. "I have no intention of beating around the bush. I somehow feel responsible for your relationship with Marcus. I am disgusted with your decision to get involved and horrified by your action. Both parents would be bereft. I can understand your feelings but I am astounded with Marcus' conduct—he should know better!"

I looked at my cousin remorsefully and rummaging through my clustered mind I tried to justify my actions but I just couldn't find the proper words to express my feelings.

"You are a very intelligent child so why should you subject yourself to criticisms? The damage to your reputation will be astronomical. Will you be able to survive such a scandalous affair? Will you be able to endure the humiliation? Carmine will be sympathized whereas you will be condemned. Is it all worth it?"

I blinked back my tears and stuttered, "I really appreciate what you are saying but I need time. I am very confused and lost at the moment."

Ardelia took hold of my shaking hand and remarked, "I curse the day that Marcus was introduced to you. I don't want to put pressure on you.

Sleep on what I have just said and if you feel that I can be of further help don't hesitate to call me."

On my way home Ardelia's words swam in my mind. Instead of going home I found myself driving toward Shek-O beach. I needed solitude. Sitting on the soft sand, I deliberated with myself. One part of me realized that my behavior was absurd and I cringed at my own actions. I was not blind to all the hardship that would confront me if I should pursue the relationship. Then I reminded myself that I was not expecting too much from the affair. I just wanted to be with Marcus. What would I do if Marcus should decide to leave his wife? Could I build my own happiness on other people's sorrow? Eventually Carmine would force a decision from Marcus—a casual fling most women could accept but to tolerate a serious affair would be an insult to Carmine. I had her pride to consider, I would not blame her if she eventually gave Marcus an ultimatum then what would his reaction be? Society would look upon Marcus as a heartless monster and what about his young son? Could I deprive this young boy of a father? But then I was aware that Marcus wasn't happy at home. Was it so wrong for us to fight for our happiness? No one would condemn our affair if Marcus wasn't married but he had taken his marriage vows and so for better or for worse he was married to Carmine and he had made a life time commitment. I would have to leave him because I had no other choice.

The following morning I was asked to go into Mr. Pickering's room when I returned to work. "Melanie, please, take a seat and let's have a chat." I was expecting another confrontation. Why couldn't everyone leave me alone? I took the chair and with downcast eyes I faced my boss across his desk.

"You have always proved to be smart. I fail to understand why you choose to put yourself in such a foolish predicament? There are many presentable young men striving for your attention—why Marcus? Are you going to destroy your own future? Hong Kong is too small a town for such a scandalous performance!" Anxiety displayed on my boss's face. Haltingly he continued. "I did not want to interfere with your private life but I did promise your parents to talk to you. Your mother herself called me and I just couldn't refuse to help her. I do have a daughter your age! What would my reaction be if I found her in the same predicament as you? I guess I would turn to my friends for assistance."

My eyes were moistened with tears. Aware that my appearance was awful even though I had been extremely particular with my attire and make-up so that I could hide my haggard face. I was exhausted and I had not been sleeping properly lately. I used to be so lively but my affair with Marcus had taken its toil on me. Patting my hands Mr. Pickering offered his sympathy, "Melanie I want you to think about your future—is Marcus worth all this pain?"

I didn't have the right answer for him instead I said, "Thank you for your kindness. I know that I don't deserve such consideration…" Stuttering, I was lost for words again. I found that I had not been able to concentrate. My mind was forever in turmoil. I tried to continue but I couldn't find the proper words so I looked down on the pair of hands that were folded on my lap.

Mr. Pickering's next words gave me a chill and shocked me. "As you know we are a very respectable firm of lawyers and we cannot tolerate scandalous behavior from any of our staff. This is not a television production of a soap opera. We are living in a real world and we have our code of honor and ethics to maintain. Where is your integrity? How can you expect us or your parents to tolerate and accept your indiscretion?"

I could no longer maintain my composure and I sobbed while I covered my face with my trembling hands. Mr. Pickering poured me a glass of water from the water jug on his desk and I accepted gratefully. I clung to the glass for dear life. In between sobs I muttered, "I didn't mean to hurt anyone—definitely not my parents or Marcus." Suddenly my sorrow was converted to anger. I was angry with fate and I was angry with Cupid for missing the target again! Why was it that each time Cupid decided to shoot his arrow it always aimed at the wrong fellow? I was forever falling for the wrong guy so what was wrong with my judgment? Feeling frustrated I yearned for his compassion, "Please do not threaten me with my job because you know that I enjoy working for you and I hope that you are aware that my work means almost everything to me. Please don't make me choose between Marcus and my job," I pleaded.

Mr. Pickering put his arms around my shoulder and removed the hair from my face. At the same time he gave me a tissue to dry my tears. "Melanie, please don't think that I am giving you an ultimatum. I just don't want to see you getting hurt because you deserve better from life! Don't throw your future away for a moment of lust."

I was no longer able to take any more criticisms. I leaped from the chair and stubbornly said, "I will prepare my letter of resignation and have it ready on your desk this afternoon. I will stay on until I have trained my successor."

Mr. Pickering waved his hand in the air and suggested, "Do calm down! It's not as drastic as you imagine! Somehow we will find a way to improve the situation."

I answered defiantly, "In order to correct the situation, I will have to leave Marcus. For the time being, I rather die then to live without him. I know that you may think that I am being rebellious and you probably believe that our relationship will not last but you have misunderstood my intentions and emotions. I do not want to break up Marcus' family. I don't want to take him away from his wife and I have no intention of depriving his son of a father. I certainly do not intend to cause a rift between his parents and him. I just want to be with him. I am not looking for status—my only wish is to be able to enjoy our relationship until it's time for him to go, and when the time comes I won't have any regrets!"

Mr. Pickering exploded, "You may not mind sharing Marcus, but what about his wife? How do you think she feels? What about your reputation? What about all the whispers and sneers?"

I screamed my reply. "How much is a pound of love worth? How can I measure love? I am not even making a sacrifice! Can't you understand? I do not expect eternity and I am not expecting undying love from Marcus. Please try to understand. As for the gossip and scorn, I will be immune to them eventually."

My boss pleaded with me, "This town is cruel. Do you have enough courage to face its brutality and its rejection?" After a moment of hesitation he suggested, "You have not taken a holiday since you started working for me so why don't you go away for a week? Leave Hong Kong—go somewhere peaceful—find a place where the sun is constantly shining and when you return you may find that your opinion has altered."

I looked out of the window and suddenly I missed the house in Highgate and the garden. I missed the peaceful life when I was living in England. Why did I have to grow up and fall in love? What happened to my happy childhood and my carefree personality? I smiled, "Your offer is very tempting—I think I will take you up on it. Your partner is on leave and Sylvia was complaining that she didn't have enough work to occupy her time. She can assist you while I am away."

I got up from my chair and straightened my crumpled skirt. I kissed Mr. Pickering on the cheek and whispered, "Thank you. I do appreciate your kindness." When I returned to my desk I took my cosmetic bag from my purse and made my way to the washroom. My reflection in the mirror shocked me. When did those bags appear underneath my eyes? My suntanned complexion was ashen. My hair had lost its shine and there were no longer sparkles in my eyes. I decided that I could do with a holiday.

When I returned to my desk, I found two messages from Marcus. I was too upset to talk to him as my nerves were stretched. I took a deep breath and motioned Sylvia to join me and I was engrossed with my work for the next couple of hours. I had always been intrigued by Bali. I was told that the Kuter Beach Sunset was fabulous so I decided to give myself a treat. I bought my plane ticket and I arranged for my accommodation. When I was leaving the building, I realized that I had not returned Marcus' calls but it was almost seven in the evening. He would have left for home and I had promised myself that I would never call him at home. Slowly I walked to the car-park with the intention to collect my car.

As expected there was a crowd of people waiting to pay for their parking tickets so I joined the waiting line. Someone tapped me on the shoulder and I turned. Marcus' wife Carmine stood behind me with a menacing smile on her face. "Now isn't that the absolutely gorgeous Melanie?" She hissed with sarcasm.

I could not really blame her for her hostility. Casually I nodded my head and smiled briefly.

"Too ashamed to talk to me?" Carmine challenged in her highpitched voice.

I saw the curious glances from the passersby so I decided that I had better not give Carmine an opportunity to create a scene. I ignored her sarcastic remark and decided that I would go for a walk instead of collecting my car. I could do with some fresh air because I felt suffocated by Carmine's presence. She followed me so I slowed my steps to be polite. When we were no longer within earshot of the waiting crowd, I looked at her with a frown.

"So how does it feel to be a toy? Marcus' latest play-thing?" Carmine's eyes blazed with hatred.

I ignored her again and proceeded. She wasn't discouraged by my silence, so she continued. "I suppose dumb blondes have always appealed to him but what about your bedside manners—do you satisfy him? He is accustomed to one particular type of female and I would call them whores!"

It was late and I had had a long and demanding day. I was upset with Carmine's outburst but I controlled my temper. I gave her a disgusted look and resumed my halted steps.

She followed and continued, "My husband has bedded countless mistresses. He destroyed their reputations and when he was through with them he discarded them like rag dolls but he always returned to me. He will always belong to me—not you or anyone can take him away from me. You just satisfy his sexual appetite!"

I lost control of my increasing annoyance and I seethed, "I have always considered you to be a lady but obviously I have misjudged you terribly." With a swing of my shoulder I crossed the road but I could feel Carmine's eyes burning into my back. Suddenly my body was chilled to the bones. I felt a distinct sensation that someone had just walked over my grave and I shivered. I asked myself desperately. Would I be able to wipe away this hatred that Marcus' wife so blatantly displayed? When I eventually returned home, I found the quietness in the house most soothing. I refused the offer of food from Ah Ying and collapsed on my bed with a beastly headache. I slowly closed my eyes and I dozed off to sleep.

Someone was shaking my tired body and lazily I opened my eyes. I saw my parents standing by my bedside and Mother was gently shaking me. Father said, "I hear that you have booked yourself a nice holiday in Bali. I wish I was going with you! You will love it! The rest will do you a world of good."

I was still half asleep and I mumbled, "I won't be leaving until tomorrow night but don't bother taking me to the airport. I will ask Sui Fong to give me a ride."

"Why don't you undress before you fall asleep again? You look absolutely exhausted." Mother kissed me good night and they both left my room and closed the door gently. My parents had been patient with me but when would their patience run out? When my atrocious behavior exhausted their patience how severe would the storm be? I shuddered with the thought.

Thirty-Eight

The next day when I was alone in my flat I called Marcus in his office and suggested that he should meet me for lunch in the Peak Cafe. I liked the serene atmosphere of the open-air cafe on the Peak. The restaurant was usually quiet. I wanted to talk to Marcus privately. Around noon time Marcus found me occupying a corner table which faced the south side of the ocean. I was deep in thought and didn't see him until he had almost reached the table. Marcus took the seat next to mine and I averted my face to smile at him adorably. I found myself drowning in his smoky dark eyes, so taking his hand and kissing his fingers I whispered softly, "Tonight I am going away for a holiday. I want some time to myself so that I can do some serious thinking."

An astounded Marcus watched me with a frown. "When did you decide to do that?"

"Mr. Pickering suggested that I should go away for a few days." With downcast eyes I muttered my reply.

After a moment of hesitation Marcus suggested with a twinkle in his eyes, "Why don't we go away together?"

"No, Marcus, I am going on my own. I need solitude and I need time to think. I have to sort out my future!" I blurted my reply.

The twinkle disappeared from his eyes and they were replaced by puzzlement. "Who has been talking to you?" Marcus demanded urgently, "Tell me—who has been giving you a tough time?"

When my reply was not forthcoming he took my face in his hands and kissed me gently on my lips, "Darling, please tell me—we have to communicate—don't shut me out from your world." He pleaded and kissed me again.

When I did not respond to his kisses, he shook my shoulders. I gazed into the open sea and lied in a soft whisper, "No one in particular has been talking to me. I do not want to be the cause of a tragedy. I just want to give you happiness. You have provided me with the happiest few months of my life and I will always treasure these moments."

Marcus clutched my hand and exclaimed, "Are these your parting words? Are you saying good-bye to me? Are you going to destroy the passions and devotions that we have shared? Am I hearing right?"

"No, Marcus, I couldn't leave you even if a hundred people were pulling me away from you. I just need some time to think and so do you."

"But there is such a final note to your words," Marcus insisted.

"Even love needs a holiday so why don't we give each other a breathing space? I will only be away for a week."

Marcus searched my face, "Are you not going to tell me where you are going? Let me take you to the airport tonight."

"Marcus, I don't want you to look for me. When I am away, spend more time with your family because I have been very selfish. I have taken too much of your time." I touched his face gently. My slight touch was like a butterfly fluttering on his skin. He caught my hand and kissed the palm. I felt a shiver short through my body and I wanted him in my arms. I yearned to hold him close to my heart forever. The thought of not being able to see him for a week was devastating for me. I had to find the strength to get away from him.

Dejectedly Marcus said, "If you feel that you need a break then I can't stop you…" After a few minutes of silence he sighed and continued, "I don't want to hurt you. I admit that in the beginning of our affair it was infatuation that I felt for you but this fascination soon veered to love. Constantly, I want to shower you with kisses. I want to reach for the moon and present it to you on a silver platter. If it is within my power I will give you the world. Nothing is good enough for you."

His words almost choked me. Before I could change my mind about the impending trip I signaled for the bill. While waiting for it I looked into the calmness of the ocean, but my feelings were far from calm. My emotions were in turmoil. I rose quickly from my chair and ran for my car. Marcus hurriedly left some money on the table and bolted after me.

Matching my quick even strides he whispered, "I can feel that you are drifting away from me. I have a premonition that I am losing you and I just can't bear the thought!"

Then I heard myself saying, "Adios my love, but I will return!" Without a backward glance I jumped into my car and sped away.

When I returned home I instructed the maids, "I will not be taking calls this afternoon except from Miss Sui Fong. Please bring me my suitcase because I should be packing if I don't want to miss my plane. Please also tell my parents not to tell anyone where I am going and I will call them from the hotel."

Shortly I found myself in Sui Fong's car and we were speeding toward the airport. She found me awfully quiet but she was aware of the reason. I had to escape in order to make a decision. We drove in silence until she pulled her car into the parking lot. After I checked my luggage through and I had my boarding card clutched in my hands, Sui Fong suggested a drink before I boarded the plane.

I said, "Sure but first I have something important to do!"

Sui Fong thought I had wanted to call Marcus but to her astonishment I walked past the phone booths and moved toward the book store. I winked at my friend and said, "I have to collect my best friends!"

"I don't know what you are talking about—I thought you are going on your own!" Sui Fong demanded.

I disappeared into the book store. When I reappeared, I had filled my overnight bag with four novels. Pointing toward the books I whispered, "These friends!"

Sui Fong laughed and I pointed toward my heavy bag and continued cheekily, "These books are my best friends. They are even better than you! They keep me company when I am lonely—they never desert me, and they never answer back!"

When we were in the airport lounge and after we had ordered our drinks, I took Sui Fong into my confidence. "Please don't tell Cedric where I am going because my intention is not for Marcus to contact me. I need time to be on my own. You do understand—don't you?"

Sui Fong put her fingers to her lips then crossed her arms on her chest and promised, "My lips are sealed. Your secret is safe with me. I agree that you do need time to yourself. But promise me you will try to come up with a positive decision. Whatever decision you make you can count on my support. One word of advice—I know you have always believed that we should fight for our happiness and the things that we want. But sometimes, some things should be best forshaken. You can't always reach for the stars. Whatever you choose to believe I want you to remember that you deserve a bright future so don't throw it away!" Sui Fong kissed me and left me at the departure gate.

A few hours later I arrived in Bali absolutely exhausted. I felt that all my energy had been drained from my body. I just wanted a bed. I hadn't realized that changing flights at Jakarta Airport would be such an annoying experience. The airport staff was far from efficient and my connecting flight was delayed. I collapsed into the car that was waiting for me at the airport, and I was glad that I was finally en route to the hotel. It was late at night and I couldn't see much from the moving car. The streets were dimly lit and all I could see were trees—plenty of green! Although, I was used to the heat in Hong Kong, nevertheless, I was grateful for the air conditioning in the car. When I arrived at the hotel I expected to see a highrise so it was to my amazement when I saw thatched huts scattered on an enormous ground. I was escorted into the main building which accommodated the reception lobby and what seemed to be a lounge. There were a few exits leading into the garden. I was curious but there would be enough time to explore the lovely place the next day.

After I had registered at the front desk I was led into the open garden through one of the exits and I found myself walking down a garden path with outdoor lights hanging from the palm trees. The twinkling lights glistened like stars in the sky. The door to my room was opened by a young Indonesian girl who had beautiful long black hair cascading down her back. Her body was wrapped in a colorful Batik sarong and she was bare-footed. With broken English she introduced herself in a shy voice. Labor being so cheap in Indonesia each room was provided with the luxury of a maid's service.

Although the huts looked primitive from the outside, the decoration in the room was modern and comfortable. A big bed standing on a raised platform was centered in the room. On one corner of the room there were colorful batik cushions scattered on the floor. Sitting on the low coffee table was a basket of mouth-watering fresh fruits of different varieties. A writing desk stood on the other corner and on the desk were brochures introducing the guests to all the facilities that the hotel provided. I decided that I would look into these pamphlets next morning. I needed a bath so I searched for the bathroom. There was a door leading to another room and when I walked into the adjourning room I felt that I had gone back in time. The room was roofless with an enormous bathtub standing in the middle of the room. It was not an ordinary bathtub but a modern jacuzzi. I could relax in the tub at night and watch the cloudless sky filled with glistening stars. In the day I could soak up the sun while relaxing in the tub. It was fabulous! The fragrance from the flowers in the garden drifted into the room with the breeze. I started to run water into this gigantic tub and while waiting for it to be filled I put a call through to my parents informing them of my safe arrival. After I had unpacked my few belongings, I drowned my tired body into the enormous tub of water scented with bath oil. Soaking my exhausted body I felt my tensed muscles began to relax and I gazed up to the sky. It was such a peaceful evening. I closed my eyes and allowed my mind to wander. This was a perfect hideaway haven for honeymoon couples. I never knew that paradise like this existed in our modern world. I would make the most of my holiday even though I had to enjoy this heavenly environment alone.

The following morning I was awakened by the chirping of the birds and the sound of waves lapping onto the shore. I didn't want to open my eyes but I was hungry so I dragged myself out of bed. I put on a pair of shorts and a halter neck T-shirt, then I went in search of the dining room. In the bright daylight I saw that each hut had their own little front garden enclosed by a low fence. Scattered in the garden were lounge chairs and a small table. I couldn't wait to fill my empty stomach so that I could start reading my books. I wanted to pamper myself. I walked through the enormous garden where couples were slowly strolling to and fro. This motion brought on an uneasy feeling of loneliness. I should have been with my loved one and not on my own—I began to feel sorry for myself. I wished that Marcus was with me.

I found one of the few dining rooms which was a beautiful outdoor restaurant. The guests were enjoying their breakfast leisurely, basking in the warm sun. Breakfast consisted of almost every kind of tropical fruits and juices. There was also a terrific variety of cooked food. I looked at the food and decided to attack the fruits. My plate was piled high with pineapples, mangoes, oranges, mandarins, and watermelon. I knew I was greedy but why not? I was after all on vacation. When I finished my third cup of coffee, I began to explore this wonderland. There was a lounge where one could relax in the evening and enjoy a quiet drink. I wasn't interested with the indoor facilities. I found an enormous swimming pool and it was gradually filled with hotel guests. Next to the big pool was a smaller and shallower pool for the children and infants. By the pool side lounge chairs scattered. There was also an outdoor bar that provided beverages for the guests all day long. I walked past the pool and headed toward the beach. The stretch of golden sand was endless—there were miles and miles of soft sand. Couples were lying on the sand sunbathing and I saw men and women lying on the beach spoiling themselves with relaxing massages performed by young Indonesian girls. Suntan lotion was rubbed sparingly onto the already tanned skin. Although I was enjoying the exquisite scenery, the sight of happy clinging couples tortured my lonely heart. I returned to the solace of my own garden and picked up one of my many books. The printed words were swimming on the pages and my mind was unable to register the contents of the pages. Marcus' handsome face soon replaced the moving words—concentration eluded me! I groaned and closed my eyes. Reluctantly I left my book and changed into my swimming costume. Hopefully a dip in the ocean would wash away thoughts of Marcus. I ran all the way to the shore of the ocean and dived in. The cold water tingled my skin and presently I found myself swimming relaxingly. I was perfectly contented with floating near the shoreline. When I emerged from the water a young Indonesian girl approached me and offered the service of a massage. Lying on the soft sand, I was enjoying the pair of soft hands gently rubbing the coconut oil on my skin. Eventually I dozed off. In my dreams, Marcus was laughing—he was smiling and gazing into my eyes then he gently kissed me. My dreams were interrupted when the young girl turned my golden body and I was lying on my stomach. I cringed at the bright sunlight but I refused to close my eyes again. The vision of Marcus was not allowed to take away the tranquillity that surrounded me. Finally I decided to abandon the beach and wandered aimlessly into the reception area. I was feeling restless. I needed something to divert my attention from Marcus. Maybe a local tour of the city would do the trick but I found nothing that took my fancy.

I was fitful and agitated with myself. I returned to my room and lounged on one of the reclining chairs. Sooner or later I had to think! After all that was the main purpose for this trip. I had a major decision to make. It was pointless to evade the issue. I found myself at a crossroads of my life. Which road should I take? The choosing was extremely soul searching but when a decision was made then nothing could hinder my decision to finish my journey. I told myself mournfully that for moral reasons I should leave Marcus, but I just could not resist the urge to be with him. Were our feelings for each other just lust and passion as everyone had suggested or were there deeper feelings involved? Was I really in love with Marcus or was I infatuated by him? He represented the untouchable—the forbidden fruits and that increased my obsession. Did our relationship lack the essential ingredients of true love? I was mortified by my own apprehension. Tears started to blur my eyes. Self-pity was soul damaging and I felt confused and began to panic. Would I be able to restrain myself and did I possess enough will-power to resist Marcus? I was quite positive that what we felt for each other was not lust.

It was an intense feeling we felt and I was willing to make any kind of sacrifice for him. I couldn't endure the thought of losing him or not sharing our dreams and planning for our tomorrow. But did we really have a tomorrow? Would our love be strong enough to conquer all the adversity directed toward us—could we fight the world together and would our frowned-upon relationship be ultimately accepted by society? I couldn't find the answers to my questions. Lost in my dilemma I had lost all sense of time.

I had heard so much praise for the Kutor Sunset and I wanted to watch the spectacular sight. I left my hut and slowly strolled toward the beach. The sun was setting and a warm orange glow covered the almost deserted beach. Walking along the shore, I saw a man walking with a stick in his hand. Hundreds and hundreds of what seemed to be ducks or geese followed him. If only I could paint, I would have captured the enchanting scene on paper. I sat on the sand by the shore and thoughtfully I wrote Marcus' name on the sifting sand. Each time I wrote his name the waves would wash it away. Would our affair be ultimately washed away? Did the pressure from our families represent the ceaseless waves? No force on earth could stop the waves from rushing toward the shore and finally demolishing all creations on the moving sand. I started to build a sand castle. It had been a life time since I had built another sand castle on another beach. When I had finished the task, helplessly I watched as the waves washed the castle away. The waves were like a knife carving my heart a piece at a time and it was a dreadful feeling. I did not know how long I sat on the sand but suddenly the beach was deserted and the sky was getting dark.

I returned to my room and changed into one of my summery dresses and slowly walked toward the restaurant. To my astonishment there was hardly anyone dining. I glanced at my watch briefly and with a quizzical expression I asked the waiter, "Don't you serve dinner here and where is everyone—do most of the guests eat in their rooms?" It was nice to hear my own voice after a day of silence.

"There is another restaurant and a table has been reserved for you." The polite and smiling waiter pointed toward a side exit and gestured to me to follow the sign. When I was approaching the open-air restaurant I could hear soft guitar music then a concrete dance floor with a stone wall behind it came into my vision. Three guitarists were performing on the stage in front of the stone wall. Tables with candles flickering surrounded the dance floor and stars twinkled in the sky while clinging couples were dancing to the music. I loved the romantic atmosphere and a slight breeze somehow lifted a bit of my depression. I had always loved spicy food;

therefore, I decided to concentrate on the tasty Indonesian cuisine that was served to me. I was dreading the idea of returning to my lonely room, so I decided to order another cup of coffee and lingered in the restaurant drowning my sorrow in the music. When the musicians were performing their final song, I took leave. Another five days and I would have to leave this place of Eden. I still had five glorious but lonely days to determine my future. With a heavy heart I sauntered back to my room through the garden. I saw flowers blooming by the path, so I picked one and stuck it behind my ears—anything to cheer myself. After spending one day in the sun my body began to tan and there was a slight glow on my face. I went into my room and took my dress off, then I wrapped my slim body with one of the natives sarongs that I had bought for myself earlier. It was too early for bed so I went into my secluded little garden. With the soft light shining behind me from the bedroom, I scanned the tropical garden. I thought I saw a dark shadow watching me from underneath a palm tree. I was a bit nervous but then my common sense took over. The security in the holiday resort should be pretty good and I shook away the fear. I lay on one of the lounge chairs and started to attack my book again. I must have fallen asleep and I must have been dreaming because I could feel soft lips kissing me and a hand was fondling my hair. This was ludicrous I thought to myself. I slowly opened my eyes. How could I be dreaming with my eyes open? Marcus was sitting bedside me, removing a piece of hair from my face. I pinched myself to make certain that I wasn't dreaming—was it possible to miss someone with such intensity? I closed my eyes and then slowly I opened them again. Marcus was still sitting there and smiling. Abruptly I leaped from the reclining chair and was instantly on my feet. Sighing I hugged him. With my two arms still circling his neck I asked, "What are you doing here? How did you find me?"

Before I could obtain an answer I found myself in Marcus' arms and immediately our bodies were entwined. My soul soared to heaven over and over again...

A few hours later we were soaking in the tub together and with my hair still wet I rested my head on Marcus' shoulder and gazing up to the sky I whispered, "Someone up there obviously likes me..."

Turning my face toward Marcus I kissed him gently and asked again, "How did you find me?"

With a slight grin on his face he replied, "All it took was a bit of detective work and one phone call—not forgetting my charming manners. There was definitely a conspiracy because no one would part with the information of your whereabouts and I wanted desperately to locate you. Suddenly it occurred to me that Anthony Pickering and my firm use the same travel agency. I took a shot in the dark by calling the agent and said your boss had once recommended an enchanting holiday resort to me, and it was a quiet place with the sun and the sea not forgetting the palm trees. She suggested Kutor Beach in Bali and she gave me the name of this hotel. She then went on to tell me that Mr. Pickering's assistant, meaning you, left the night before for this paradise. I thanked her and sent her a box of chocolate, in appreciation for her kindness. I then called this hotel and asked if you were a registered guest. With their confirmation I booked the next available flight. I told the office and Carmine that I had to leave town immediately for an important meeting. Her reaction was not exactly supportive as you can imagine but I don't think she knew that you were away."

I smiled sweetly and teased, "So you are really a devil in disguise bribing young women for information."

When I opened my eyes the next morning my first view was Marcus' thick eye lashes as he still had his eyes closed. I could not take my eyes off his handsome face neither could I believe that I had spent the whole night sleeping in his arms. We had had our stolen moments and I was contented with those few precious hours. I had never expected more. With Marcus sleeping so close to me I wanted to relish those special moments of absolute bliss.

The sky looked brighter—the sun was shinier—the grass was greener. The other guests' happiness no longer bothered me. I was in high heaven and I wanted to share my happiness with the entire world. I no longer avoided loving couples but wanted to mingle among these happy people. I couldn't help but fall in love with Marcus again under the Bali sun and stars.

When we were enjoying a leisure breakfast Marcus was impressed with my appetite. "How can a small stomach contain so much fruit?" His eyes had a twinkle when he was teasing me.

We spent the morning swimming in the ocean—splashing water at one another playfully. We had found our long lost childhood again. The complexity of our situation and the people involved were far from our thoughts. I no longer had the lost look on my face and my laughter could be heard from miles away. We were drowning in our affection for each other. No power on earth could separate us. When we woke from our afternoon nap Marcus suggested that we take a stroll on the beach. The waves were lapping onto our feet and we wandered aimlessly along the shoreline. When we were tired Marcus sat on the sand while I lay by him.

Watching me intensely, he said, "I would like you to listen to a story...when I was very young I fell in love with my neighbor. She was my world and I wanted to spend the rest of my life with her. Then I was sent away to further my studies in England and we were separated." I was listening with intense curiosity while Marcus continued. "My neighbor promised her undying love for me when I went away. During the first two years while I was away I did not have eyes for other girls and just concentrated on my studies. I realized that the sooner I graduated the sooner I would return to her arms." There was a distant look on his face while he was looking back in time.

"Her letters began to dwindle and soon there was silence. I was mad with anxiety. Then a dear John letter arrived. She had met someone else and was married without previous warning. Can you imagine how I felt? My world felt apart. The shock was so immense that I wanted to kill myself. I blamed my parents for sending me away. I didn't know how I managed to get through Law School. Women became my toys. I wanted to hurt them—I liked to inflict mental pain on them—I wanted to witness their suffering especially if the unhappiness was instigated by me. I floated from bed to bed and I left a string of broken hearts behind me. I had no sympathy for the women that I took to bed. I directed all my hatred toward them then I met Carmine during my final year of Law school. She had just arrived from Italy and she possessed a certain helplessness that appealed to my male ego. I wanted to protect her because she was so petite and fragile. She was alone in a strange country and shortly after her arrival to London she moved into my flat. She cared and cooked for me and she was the perfect cure for my broken heart. I thought she was in love with me and I married her on the rebound. She was pregnant soon after the wedding. My parents were upset. They never expected me to marry a foreign girl. My mother had big plans for a large wedding if I were to marry a Chinese, but when they were told that Carmine was pregnant with their first grandchild all was forgiven. When I obtained my Law Degree we returned to Hong Kong."

Marcus took my hand and kissed my palm. "I am not proud of my behavior before my marriage to Carmine and I vowed that I would provide her with a life time of affection. I meant to fulfill my promise but when we returned to Hong Kong our life style started to change."

I held my breath and waited for him to continue. "Carmine took to Hong Kong life style like a fish to water and she loved it. She had never been exposed to such a glamorous way of life. To be able to afford elegant things abundantly soon took hold of her senses. Our son was left in the care of the nanny and she was no longer the attentive young wife. She was spending money like water, but I didn't begrudge her extravagance because she was a deprived child. But I wanted and needed her attention...we started to drift apart. We were involved with too many social functions and we could never spend a quiet evening at home. She had lost interest in our sex life. All she cared about was her appearances and her status. I am not making excuses for myself. I guess I was not exactly blameless for her changes. As a young lawyer I was very involved with my work and I guess I neglected her. Due to cooling of affection at home I started to have wandering eyes again. After my first affair I proposed a divorce because we were obviously not happy together. Carmine absolutely refused. She told me that she was willing to keep a closed eye to my infidelity provided I was discreet. I didn't know what I was looking for in life so I wandered from one lady's bed to another searching for compatibility and that was when I met you. At that time I had no idea that you would make such a great impact on me. I have to be honest—you were just one of my many lady friends and I was going to part with you after I had my share of fun. I was surprised with myself because you broke my golden rule. Before you came into my life I had never dated single women because I didn't want involvement. There were enough married ladies who were perfectly satisfied with a casual affair. Then you appeared and my life was turned upside down. What more can I say?"

I was touched by Marcus' honesty so I said, "I only wish that fate could have dealt the right cards. We are like two pieces of magnets stuck together, but we still have our responsibilities to our families. I can make any sacrifice for you and I do not want to be the cause of your destruction. I have to consider your career. You still have to maintain a certain standard of living in Hong Kong. To tell you the honest truth I am scared not for myself but for you!" My memory reverted back to the day I confronted Carmine and I shuddered at the thought.

Marcus turned me around and searched my face. "As long as you love me, your love will be worth all the sacrifices in the world. If I had not met you, another girl would have entered my life and I would in any case have left Carmine. It is only a matter of time that I would ask her for a divorce so you are not to be blamed. If our marriage was built on stronger pillars another party would not have been able to divert my attention."

He was stroking my hair tenderly and I whispered, "I don't have any demands from our relationship and I don't expect to be your wife. I just want to share one part of you. I am happy just to see you whenever I can." I paused, then picking up a loose pebble from the sand I threw it into the ripples of the sea. I sighed when it disappeared into the water and I continued, "I do not have the courage to say good-bye to you because I do not think that I can endure the emptiness. But I don't want to be the cause of your heartaches either. I am very confused and I can't think properly." All my tensions and anxiety were unleashed and I started to sob.

"Melanie this is not a disaster. We should be glad that we have at least found each other—better late than never! Now that I have found you I can't see my future without you."

I pleaded with him, "Why can't we just carry on with seeing each other and not make any plans for the future."

Marcus sighed deeply. "You are still very young and I don't want you to become my backstreet mistress. You deserve a lot more from life. The time will come when you will resent the fact that I do not have my freedom. When I have to go home to fulfill my duties as a husband you will take offense to my absence. What about children? Don't you want any children of your own? Their existence may not be important now but you will soon miss them. Other young men will enter your life and I will lose you. I do want a divorce because life is just too short for us to live half-measuredly. I want to wake up in the morning with you in my arms, and I want to be able to come home to you in the evenings. I want us to do things together and plan our future together." Marcus shook my shoulders and pleaded.

I looked deep into Marcus' eyes and repeated myself, "I do not expect anything from our relationship because I don't want to marry you. I just want to be around you. I will be happy to spend whatever time you can spare me. Let's not think about tomorrow. I don't want to destroy your marriage and least of all your career. I just want to love you and not harm you." I continued with anguish in my voice, "In any case Carmine would never set you free!"

Marcus insisted stubbornly, "I will leave her because even if I stay with her, she will only have my body and not my soul."

"Why don't we talk about this when we return to Hong Kong? Let's enjoy this holiday because we may never be able to enjoy another holiday such as this again." I dried the tears on my face with the back of my hand.

"Don't talk like this. Of course we will be able to spend many more holidays together because we have a lifetime ahead of us." Marcus took me in his arms and kissed me tenderly.

For the remaining of our happy holiday we savored each moment of bliss. After we woke up in the morning together we visited the temples and shopped in the local markets buying souvenirs for ourselves. Marcus even insisted that I should watch a cock-fight but I had to cover my eyes as it was just too gory for my taste. We danced to the music of the three guitarists and strolled aimlessly and leisurely along the beach. Too soon we were on the flight heading back to Hong Kong and I was once again reminded of Gavin's words, all good things had to end. I left Marcus in the airport and took a taxi home. When I arrived home, I was exhausted but happy. I greeted my parents and walked into my room, "Don't you want to tell us about your holiday?" Father asked me.

I yelled my reply from my room, "I am too tired now. I will tell you all about it over dinner tomorrow night."

I closed the door softly behind me. How could I share my holiday with them? How could I tell them that the past week was the happiest time of my life?

Thirty-Nine

When I arrived at the office the next day, Mr. Pickering beckoned me into his room. "You look smashing—the bronze tan is most attractive—you should go away more often. In the mean time welcome back and it's sure nice to have you around again!"

I spent the rest of the day attending to the heaps of paper work on my desk. When I had finally finished I was rubbing the tiredness off my shoulders and the phone jingled. Sui Fong's voice drifted into my ears, "How would you like to go for a drink after work? You can share your Bali with me then we can go home together because your parents have invited Cedric and me for dinner."

Half an hour later I was sitting in the Clipper Lounge of the Mandarin Hotel. Sui Fong ordered our drinks then she asked, "So how was the holiday? You obviously enjoyed it tremendously because I haven't seen this serene look on your face for a while. I do love your bronze tan—you look so attractive!"

She chatted away and suddenly she pointed to the entrance of the Lounge and exclaimed, "What a coincidence! Guess who just arrived?"

I turned my head and saw Cedric walking toward us with Marcus on tow.

"How can Cedric be so insensitive? I thought Marcus and Melanie are not supposed to be seen together in public" Sui Fong muttered to herself. The newcomers joined our table and she remarked, "Marcus, you are looking well but there is something different about you. I just can't put my fingers on the difference!" Sui Fong screwed her eyes and scrutinized Marcus' handsome features. She returned her gaze to my face and a thought dawned on her. She looked at Marcus and exclaimed, "It's the color of your skin that is so different—you look just as brown as…" Then she stopped and covered her mouth embarrassingly. Then she whispered, "You two went away together!"

I blushed and put my head down. Winking at Sui Fong, Cedric chaffed, "Can you keep your mouth shut and mind your own business?" Turning his attention to the people who had just come into the Lounge and without thinking he whispered to Marcus, "Your father is coming into the lounge—why don't you ask him to join us?"

Jeffrey Kwan saw his son and with a broad grin on his face he advanced toward our table but the smile on his face froze when he saw me. Abruptly he turned and moved toward another direction. Spontaneously Marcus left his chair and grabbed his father's arm, "Dad, why don't you join us?"

The older gentleman replied with distaste, "I would never be seen with that shameful woman!" He pointed an accusing finger at me.

Marcus' tanned complexion turned ashen and he was seething. I wanted to avoid a scene so I excused myself and left for the restroom. I could hear Cedric's soothing voice muttered, "You should not be too put off by your father's reaction—it may be a bit strong but you should have expected Melanie to be the culprit. Parents never blame their own son. If Melanie chooses to be with you then she will have to learn to live with these unnecessary and cruel humiliations. This is not going to be the last time that anyone is rude to her!"

Sui Fong followed me into the restroom. I was shaking and tears were streaming down my face. There was a greenish tint to my complexion underneath the tan. Sui Fong put her arms around my trembling shoulders and said encouragingly, "Take it easy—take a few deep breaths and you will feel better!"

I heard myself whisper, "Don't I deserve some happiness? Why do I always fall for the wrong guy? What is wrong with me?"

Sui Fong shook her head sympathetically and answered, "God is very fair. He has given you almost everything. You have looks, you have brains and you are gifted in so many ways. There is something about you that make you so different from us. God is making you wait for your happiness. Be patient and the time will come when you will have your fair share of joy. Rome was not built in a day!"

I patted my face with a tissue and dejectedly I insisted, "I think I will go home first."

My friend suggested kindly, "I'll tell you what we'll do—why don't I go home with you and Cedric can join us later. I am certain that Marcus can do with some comforting. I will let them know."

Sui Fong insisted on driving my car but I was determined that I could manage. We left town and headed for home in silence. We were deep in our own thoughts. After a while Sui Fong broke the silence, "I am scared for you. I have a feeling that you are heading for disaster. I know that you would have eventually left Marcus if his parents had pleaded with you. I am afraid it's too late now—the damage has been done—I could tell from the determined expression on your face that you will fight for Marcus."

When a comment was not forthcoming from me Sui Fong continued, "Once upon a time you would have fought for Theo if you had his support but he was too weak so wisely you decided to let him go. Today, Marcus is a different kettle of fish. He has a strong character and he is stubborn. In a way your personalities are very similar—therefore the strong attraction. I can tell the two of you will not be easily torn apart and I am afraid you are in for a rough ride!" She was tapping her fingers on the window irritably and concluded.

Around eleven that same evening I was asked to answer the phone. Both my parents looked at Sui Fong and Cedric with puzzled expressions. I was gone for a long time then I returned to the room and dropped a bombshell on my parents, "I am moving out! I am going to live with Marcus!"

Mother dropped the glass that she was holding and the crashing noise was the only sound that was heard. My sudden decision to leave home was a shock for my parents. Father regained his composure first and demanded, "Melanie, what are you saying? Do try and make some sense!"

I replied stubbornly, "I just told you...I want to move in with Marcus."

Mother was horrified with my intention and she shouted, "But how can you do that—he is married."

I regretted my outburst but I wanted to be with Marcus so I softly muttered, "He just left his wife and he is in a hotel—he needs me!"

"You can't go! I will not permit you to make a fool of yourself." Father was saying and Cedric attempted unsuccessfully to control his uncle.

"Melanie, sit down and explain to us what is happening! You can imagine that this is quite a shock for your parents." Sui Fong intervened reasonably.

Mother rudely interrupted, "We thought if we gave you enough time you would see sense, but obviously we were wrong! Don't be foolish—you don't know what you are doing!"

I whispered and pleaded, "I do know what I am doing…I am only fighting for my happiness! Marcus and I belong together so why should we be separated?"

Father moved toward me and said, "Repeatedly, I have refrained from interfering. You should be old enough to be responsible for your own action. I wasn't even going to stop your sordid affair with him. There are backstreet hotels that you can use. If you want to degrade yourself then do it with discretion. Don't exhibit your dirty laundry in public. Your behavior is disgusting. To think that your mum had spent so much money on your education and what has become of you?"

Father paused to catch his breath and then he continued without mincing his next words, "Have your fun then say good-bye! Nothing good would come out of this mess!"

"We will never give you our blessing." Mother was saying, "My daughter will never become someone's mistress. If you choose to follow Marcus, then you no longer have a home. If you leave this flat tonight you will never be allowed to return."

Sui Fong was horrified. She grabbed Mother's shaking hand and intervened, "Don't threaten the poor girl! Let's try and talk some sense into her. Screams and threats will not improve the situation." Releasing Mother's hand she moved closer to me and held my hand.

Mother glared at my tear stained face and implored, "Think! Melanie, use your head! There are too many fishes in the sea, and you are not a dumb girl. There are many eligible young men waiting for your attention. After all Marcus is thirteen years older than you and is married. You are only twenty-one. You are naive—Marcus doesn't love you—he does have a reputation. In fact he is notorious for his affairs. Forget him!"

I returned Mother's gaze and begged for her compassion and upstanding, "Mummy, please try to understand—I have tried to forget Marcus but I have failed, so I am leaving! Don't make me choose between him and my family. I love you and I don't want to break your hearts but I have to follow my destiny." I sniffed.

"You sentimental fool! What destiny? We make our own lives! Why can't you find a nice young man then marry and settle down—be like

Lynette!" Mother was losing her control again.

I replied defiantly, "I am not Lynette! We are two different people! Can't you see that I just want to be with Marcus?" I got up from my chair and moved toward my room.

"Stop right there!" Pointing toward the front door Father warned, "If you walk through that door tonight—I caution you—you are not going to return! Our daughter is dead."

"Uncle Edwin, don't force Melanie into a corner. Why don't we let her go now and we can discuss this matter again tomorrow? None of us are capable of making a sensible decision tonight. Let's sleep on the problem!" Cedric implored Father while Sui Fong forced Mother onto a chair.

I moved closer to Mother and knelt on the floor, "Please forgive me! I can't help my feelings for Marcus...." I was sobbing and shaking Mother's hand, "Let me go to him! Please?"

Mother lost all control of her emotions and she yelled with anger, "I was brought up from an old-fashioned Chinese family and well-brought Chinese girls don't behave like you do. Your actions are beyond my comprehension!" Mother shoved away my outstretched hand and continued with vehement indignation, "I can't tolerate your stupidity and I won't! Your performance is degrading and a disgrace to our family's name. You are not my daughter if you don't curb your insane behavior." She slapped me across the face. I fell and stumbled on the floor. I touched my face with disbelief I could not believe that Mother would hit me. Sui Fong immediately came to my rescue and supported my crumbled body. Shakily I clung on to Sui Fong's supporting hand and got up on my feet.

I staggered into my room and I heard Sui Fong's pleading voice beseeching my parents. "I sympathize with your shattered feelings and your disappointment in Melanie but please don't put too much pressure on her. Ultimately she will come to her senses!"

Shortly I came out of my room and sadly I walked toward my parents and gave them a bunch of keys and I whispered, "Here are the keys to the flat and to my car. I am not taking any of my belongings. I am only leaving with my pride. I am not ashamed of my behavior because I have nothing to hide. If ever you find it in your heart to forgive me then I will come home to visit you." I kissed my parents and walked toward the front door.

Sui Fong was crying and she was hanging onto me, "I beg you! Please don't make any hasty decisions! There is always room for discussion!"

Father bellowed in a loud voice, "Don't stop her! We have just buried our daughter!"

≥a ≥a ≥a

When I arrived at the hotel in Causeway Bay, I was blinded by tears and grief. I didn't know where I was going and it was with great confusion that I finally located Marcus' room. When he opened the door, I collapsed into his protective arms. He helped me onto the bed and stroked my hair lovingly. He said, "Oh baby! I am sorry! Please don't cry—you are breaking my heart. Tell me what happened!"

I could no longer control my tears and I lost my voice. I cried and my heart-breaking sobs were the only sound that was audible in the room. Marcus muttered to himself, "Do I have the right to inflict such intense suffering on you? Why should my love cause you so much grief?"

After a while my sobbing subsided and haltingly I repeated my parent's old-fashioned and stubborn reaction. He cupped his face with his hand and sighed, "I experienced more or less the same response from my parents. I don't want to burden you with my ordeal tonight because there will be enough time at a later date to tell you. But I can't forget my son's pleading voice when I left him. When I heard his small voice my decision was almost swayed. But I couldn't turn back because you mean too much to me. In time I hope Nathan will forgive me."

I could not remember where I was when I woke up the next morning. My memory of the previous night was a blur. Slowly the events from the previous evening rushed into my mind's eye. Fresh tears filled my eyes. This had to be a nightmare—it couldn't be happening—Marcus and I were in Bali. I had to be dreaming and it was a nightmare. I should be waking soon! Then Marcus came into my vision. He was dressed in his immaculate suit and was ready to return to work. I jumped out of bed and rushed into the bathroom. I had to work too! I could not afford to lose my job because I was homeless and I needed the money. Putting on the same outfit that I had on the previous evening I left the hotel with Marcus. With a heavy heart I reported to work. With no trace of a smile Mr. Pickering greeted me sternly and I knew instantly that my parents had contacted him. Shortly I was sitting in the chair and facing my boss across the table. "It is still not too late to go home...." I heard Mr. Pickering saying.

As if I were waking from a dream I suddenly realized that I no longer had a family. Tears streamed down my face.

"Melanie, go home! Soon all will be forgotten and forgiven." My boss pleaded with me.

"No! I am sorry—I can't go home now. I made my choice last night and I will stick with it. I don't have any regrets!"

To and fro Mr. Pickering started to pace the floor, "Listen to me, Melanie—Jeffrey will never forgive Marcus and after all he is employed by his father. Financially Jeffrey can make life very difficult for the both of you. Marcus was born with a silver spoon in his mouth. He has never been deprived of material things nor have you! The two of you will not be able to survive. You can't live on love—be reasonable!"

I lifted my head and challenged my boss, "We are blessed with a good education and we are young and healthy so why can't we make a living?"

My boss stopped his pacing and interrupted, "Grow up, Melanie, you are living in Hong Kong! Marcus cannot join another firm. He is Jeffrey's only son and he will have to take over from his father eventually. As for you, how much can you earn? With your meager salary you can't possibly support a family. In any case, if you do not return home, I will have no choice but to expect your letter of resignation."

I was horrified and I refused to believe what I was hearing. Did I have to choose between my job and Marcus as well as my family? I suddenly understood. Father managed to obtain the position for me; therefore, it was within his power to take it away from me. Lifting my shoulders proudly I stood and extended my trembling hand to Mr. Pickering, "I have enjoyed working for you and I do appreciate all that you have taught me. Also I am extremely fond of you and I am full of admiration for you, but I wish you didn't make me choose between Marcus and my job. You will have my resignation letter!" I stormed out of the room.

When I returned to the hotel room I found Marcus sitting on the chair and he was looking out of the widow obviously deep in thoughts. I walked up to him and encircled my arms around him. Tenderly I inquired, "How come you are home so early?"

I kissed him behind his ears and he turned. He pulled me into his arms and then whispered against my hair, "I have bad news for you."

Bravely I braced myself for more discouraging news and smiled bitterly, "So what's new? Within twenty-four hours I have lost my home, my family, and my job. But I have found you!"

Detecting the bitterness from my tone of voice Marcus asked, "Are you regretting your decision?" Marcus was worried.

I shook my head dejectedly and kissed him briefly. I sat on the floor and leaned my body against his strong legs and whispered, "As long as we are together we will survive."

After a pause Marcus hesitantly said, "This morning when I returned to my office I was informed that there has been some changes in our firm's policy. Partners of the firm will no longer be paid a monthly salary instead we will have a bonus every six months. In other words I will not have any income during the next six months."

Expecting fear and resentment from me, he was puzzled when he saws the unexpected broad grin on my face. "No salary for the next six months is no big deal because I, my love, have even lost my job!"

Marcus didn't look too surprised; nevertheless, he inquired, "You mean you were fired?"

I nodded my head, "No—I was requested diplomatically to resign—on my father's instruction. I suppose our parents think that we would surrender to their wishes if they should tighten the purse string." I shrugged my shoulders nonchalantly and kissed Marcus briefly on the lips.

He was puzzled, "Why are you so happy? I was expecting more tears!"

"As far as I am concerned the worst is over. The most difficult part was whenI had to make a decision but now that I know which path to take; it will be a lot easier. Indecision is a horrifying feeling. Don't you think that it's time that you told me what happened last night to make you leave home so suddenly?"

Marcus watched me pensively. "When I left the Mandarin I was disturbed with my father's unpleasantness. In spite of his temper he is normally a very sensible man. I suspected that someone must have poisoned his mind and I guessed it was Carmine. When I arrived home, I was confronted by an irritated and fretful wife. I had hardly ever seen her fret or lose control of her emotions and I was puzzled by her odd behavior. After all when I returned from Bali, she didn't even bother to find out where I had been for the past week."

I rudely interrupted, "Don't be too harsh on her! It is never easy when a woman knows that her husband is involved with another party!"

Marcus put his fingers on my lips to silent me, "I hate to criticize my own wife but she is an extremely calculating and shrewd lady. I was curious and I wanted to find out the reason for her dramatic performance. She challenged my obligation toward the family. I didn't want another argument so I ignored her. My silence irritated her and she threw a tantrum. My intentions were to calm her but she started to scream. '*I will never give you your freedom. You will never replace me with that bitch of a woman. She is nothing but a whore and your parents would never accept her as their daughter-in-law. You can dream on and she will remain as your backstreet mistress*'. I was not impressed by her performance and I guess I must have lost my cool. I told her to mind her words and because she had brought the subject up I demanded a divorce. I reminded her that we are only married in name and that it was time for us to pursue our own happiness. I suggested that we should be freed of each other."

I listened with clenched fists and was trying desperately to control my trembling body. Marcus took me in his arms and whispered, "Are you sure that you want me to continue? We can talk about it at a later day."

Shaking my head I gestured for him to continue, "Carmine was beginning to turn hysterical so calmly I suggested that she should rest and we would continue with our discussion when she had more control of herself. Ignoring my recommendation, she instructed the maid to bring Nathan into the room. When he joined us she wagged an accusing finger at me and said to our young son, '*Your lousy father wants to desert us and start another life with his backstreet mistress. You will be without a father and you have that bitch to thank*'. Nathan was obviously startled by her actions and information. He grabbed my hand and implored, 'Daddy, please, tell me that Mummy is wrong and she is exaggerating. I don't want to lose you'! I dried the tears on his face and my heart was breaking because I could sense his fear, as his insecurity was being threatened. But I decided to be honest with him so I said, 'Nathan you are not going to lose me. I still care for you but I am no longer in love with your mother. I would like to marry a nice lady and you will like her. I will be moving out and I am begging your mother for a divorce. You can come and spend all your weekends with us'. Carmine shrieked, '*Over my dead body—I will never let you see your son if you move out. I will let you rot in hell because you will miss him. Then you will hate your whore*'! I was disgusted with Carmine's outburst so I asked her to take a better grip of herself. I demanded that she control her foul language and told her that she was behaving like a market woman. I was fed up and I wanted Carmine out of my sight. I told the maid to take Nathan out of the house. After his departure, we resumed our bitter argument. Suddenly, an expensive vase was flying across the room. The maid must have been terrified with our violence so she contacted my father. When my father arrived, he tried to calm Carmine but she could not be controlled. Then my father turned on me, '*You had better change your mind about marrying this other girl. Our family will never acknowledge her existence. I know that Carmine has her faults but I am sure she will agree to alter her ways*'. I pleaded with him and insisted that Carmine would never revert to the same Carmine that I had met in England. Hong Kong's life style was a bad influence and contributed to the destruction of our marriage. I told him that I didn't want to exist—I wanted to live again. Then to my ultimate horror my father suggested, '*I sympathize with your anguish but I suggest you have your fun without involving your family—*

all men do it but don't get hooked. Fool around with the right sort of women. Our family cannot tolerate a divorce. It has never been heard of and it will break your mother's heart. Melanie's parents would not want their daughter to be condemned for breaking up your marriage and they won't forgive you. Take a holiday—go away for a couple of days and when you return you will see a different light. In the meantime let Melanie get on with her own life. Take a woman with you but after you have had your fun come home and buy Carmine a nice present and all will be forgiven'. I pleaded for his understanding—I wanted him to know that I love you and that I insisted on planning my future with you. I was unable to convince him and he gave me an ultimatum. '*If you do not terminate your association with Melanie then I will have no choice but to ask you to leave—this behavior is not healthy for Nathan*'. Then Carmine howled, '*Leave us! Go to her but I will never grant you a divorce. The two of you can stew in your own disgrace*'. And I left."

The room had turned dark so Marcus turned on the soft lights by the bed and took my clammy hands. My tears were dried but I was in a daze. Marcus nudged my shoulders and his gentle touch jolted me back to the present, "Marcus, I am sorry that I have caused you so much grief! What can I do to amend?"

With utter astonishment Marcus shook his head and pulled me into his arms. "Why are you apologizing? You haven't done anything wrong! You love me and you have provided me with the happiest days of my life. I am beginning to live again. In time all will be forgiven and forgotten because we will ride this wave together. I need you to stand by me and we will come through O.K.!" He kissed me long and hard on the lips and for a short while our anguish, pain and resentment were forgotten and we were locked in each other's embrace.

Later When we had ordered some dinner through room service Marcus resumed our discussion, "We have to search for an appropriate place to stay. We can't possibly stay in a hotel indefinitely. Also, we have to buy you some clothes. As you know my father will not be forthcoming with financial help so we will have to survive with what I have in the bank and it is not much."

As we were on the subject of money, I thought I would make a few things clear, so reaching over to Marcus I tousled his hair. "I am not here with you for monetary reasons I intend to start looking for another job tomorrow. We don't have to find elaborate lodgings. We need a place that is comfortable and big enough for just the two of us."

Marcus watched my face searchingly. "I don't want to see you deprived of anything. You are used to a good life and I want to be able to provide for you properly." He paused then he continued hesitantly, "You will not be able to find another job as a lawyer's assistant. Words would have gotten around town by now. Your father would make certain that unless you return home another lawyer will not employ you. In any case I would rather you didn't work for a while. I am sure there is plenty for you to learn in order to be an efficient housewife...you won't have the leisure of a maid."

Marcus was in for a big surprise, but I wasn't going to tell him that I knew all I had to know about housework. He would find out soon enough. I rather fancied the idea of not working for a while so I happily agreed.

Forty

The following day we decided that Marcus should call his office and inform them that he would be taking a few days off work. He was a partner of the firm so his decision was not challenged. After a quick breakfast we bought a newspaper and started flat hunting. We viewed one flat after another and soon we were disheartened. The available accommodations were either too expensive or they were old and dilapidated. We were about to call it a day when I suddenly saw a "For Let" sign across the street on the second floor of a commercial building. Excitedly I pointed toward the sign. Marcus shook his head, "That is a commercial building and we are in Wanchai—the red-light district—the sign is probably for an office space."

"Let's go and find out." My spirit soared and I dragged Marcus across the street with me. Somehow I had a premonition that we had found our future home. The caretaker informed us that although the building was for commercial use there were domestic flats on the higher floors and a studio apartment was available. Frowning the old caretaker scrutinized our smart attires. He was dubious about us wanting to live in such a small flat. Upon my insistence he let us view the available flat and I fell in love with it instantly. There was a spacious room and built-in wardrobe lined one side of the room. There was a small bathroom and a small kitchen attached to it. The room was very bright and the windows did not look into noisy Wanchai Road but into another building's backyard. The surroundings were clean so what more could we ask for? The price was also right. I searched Marcus' face and implored him for approval.

Skeptically, he looked around the room and asked, "Are you sure this is what you want? It looks awfully small—are you certain that it's adequate for our needs?"

I took another glance of the room and beamed, "There is a bathroom; a kitchen and there is carpet on the floor! What more could I wish for? Maybe a 4,000 sq. ft. mansion with a swimming pool and a garden?" I winked at him and teased.

Immediately we signed the rental agreement. Marcus gave cash to the caretaker for the rental deposit and wrote a check for the rent. Since I had left home, it was the first time that I was really exhilarated with excitement. Getting the keys off the smiling caretaker I insisted, "Now let's go and buy some furniture."

My choice of furniture intrigued Marcus. We bought a big mattress and four very big cushions. Then we purchased a small television. Among our other purchases were a low coffee table and two sets of pretty sheets and pillow cases. Grabbing two pillows and two warm blankets, we left the store. Marcus was accustomed to Carmine's extravagant taste so he was astonished with my simple choices. With our shopping we returned to our new home. Marcus left me in the flat while he collected his suitcase from the hotel. When he returned to our newly acquired home the mattress had been delivered and put on the floor on one side of the room. I had already fitted the sheets on our new bed. I put the coffee table on the other side of the room and scattered the four cushions round it. The television faced the bed and the room was transformed. Marcus was amazed with my achievements.

I suggested eating out because I had not had the opportunity or time to equip the kitchen. I took Marcus to a small restaurant and for very little money we enjoyed a really delicious meal. During dinner he couldn't resist asking me, "How do you find all these cheap and good restaurants?"

"I don't lead an elaborate life like you do! I do have many down to earth friends!" I winked at Marcus and blew him a kiss across the table.

After dinner I insisted that Marcus should accompany me while I attended to some more shopping. As he had never traveled on the trams I thought the experience would amuse him. To my utter surprise he actually enjoyed the ride. We arrived in North Point, my favorite shopping paradise. I always looked forward to seeing my hawker friends and bargaining with them. I knew exactly what I was looking for and knew which hawker I should buy the things from so in no time at all I had bought towels for our daily use. I needed something to wear so a few pairs of jeans and some large T-shirt were purchased. Then I selected kitchen utensils for the kitchen. On our way home I gave Marcus the change from the money that he had given me and he was amazed. He couldn't understand how I could have managed to buy so much with so little money. The money that he had given me would not have been enough for Carmine to pay for one of her magnificent outfits. He smiled at me and sighed, "At the rate you are going, the money that I have in the bank would see us through till my next bonus check with no difficulty at all." He squeezed my hands and my love for him blossomed.

When we returned home, I suggested that Marcus watch television. Humming softly to myself I unloaded his suitcase on the bed and gradually all his clothing was neatly folded and systematically put in the closet. Shortly and contentedly I unwrapped my shopping for the kitchen. Soon the bathtub was scrubbed clean and a hot bath was ready for Marcus. I could hear him whistling in the bathroom and I smiled. I promised myself that I would spoil him lavishly. When Marcus returned to the room, he was astonished to find a pot of hot tea and two cups waiting for him on the low table. I stuck my head out of the kitchen and asked, "Are you hungry? Do you want me to cook something for you to eat?"

Marcus found me in the small kitchen and putting his arms around my waist he kissed my neck, "I am hungry but not for food." He carried me from the kitchen and put me onto our new bed.

We began our lives together...when Marcus returned to work, he refused all invitations for social activities. Immediately after work he would return to me and our new home. After his first day at work when he came home he found me working hard in the kitchen. Our small flat was immaculate and there were fresh flowers arranged in a vase and displayed on the table. He changed his clothes and before long a well-prepared meal was laid out on the table waiting for him. He looked at the food and whistled. His eyes left the table and searched my face then he kissed me and whispered, "I love you and thank you for providing me with such a comfortable home with your loving hands—definitely not just a pretty face!"

During dinner I disappeared into the kitchen and reappeared with a can of cold beer. I remembered that he enjoyed a beer with his food.

I had bought myself a second-hand sewing machine and one day I was happily sewing new curtains when the phone rang. I glanced at my watch and decided that Marcus must be calling to say hello. I had no other calls because no one knew my number and no one bothered contacting me. I picked up the receiver and said, "I miss you!"

There was a slight pause and then a giggle, "I am sure that you don't or you would have contacted me instead of waiting for me to call you!" It was Sui Fong's voice.

I was delighted, "How did you get my number?"

"Cedric called Marcus and the number was forced out of him. By the way we have invited ourselves for dinner tonight. I have missed your cooking!"

Hurriedly I hung the curtain and left for the market to shop for food. I was excited because I had not seen Sui Fong since I had left home and I was so looking forward to seeing her and Cedric. I had really missed them and my family. Hopefully in time I would be able to see my parents again.

I could hear the front door open and close. Then Marcus was yelling into the kitchen, "You better come and greet your cousins. They think that I have been ill-treating you!"

I sprinted from the kitchen and I embraced and kissed my two cousins. Sui Fong scanned around curiously. She gaped and then she exclaimed, "I was aghast with the district that you are living in and I thought you were living in the dumps and among the gutters but what a cute place! I should have guessed with Melanie's abilities Marcus had to be living in comforts and no less." Then she hugged me again.

When Sui Fong was lounging on the cushions she couldn't control her excited chatter, "I was expecting to find you, Melanie, tired and low spirited but instead you have such a contented look on your face. Happiness is oozing out of you, and you are positively glowing. Your constant melancholy look has vanished!" Sui Fong tapped her forehead thoughtfully and continued. "From my recollection the last time that I had witnessed such joy on your face was when Gavin visited you unexpectedly…I guess those days belong to another life time but I am really delighted with the change in you. Marcus is obviously good for you."

After the delicious meal we were all sitting on the cushions and chatting over some hot tea, "Apart from wanting to see you I am also here on a mission." Cedric put a piece of orange in his mouth and muttered. I was waiting impatiently for him to continue, "Uncle Edwin and Auntie Wei Ling are worried about you."

I interrupted excitingly, "You mean they have changed their minds about us and they are willing to see me again? Have I been forgiven?"

Cedric frowned then shook his head, "No! I am afraid they have not accepted the situation but give them time they will. Melanie, after all they have their own traditions to abide by, but they wanted me to tell you that if you want to change your mind and return home, the door is opened for you—provided you are willing to leave Marcus."

Without removing my eyes from Marcus' face stubbornly and with determination I said, "I am aware that my parents are concerned for my well-being but as you can see I am very happy where I am." I waved my hand around the room and with a serene smile on my face I continued, "I have never been so contented before in my whole life and unless they can accept Marcus as their future son-in-law I will not be returning to them. In any case my home is here with Marcus." I paused and shook my head, "I just don't understand why they dislike the man I love so much. If they can bestow me with affection then why can't they extend the same courtesy to him?"

Cedric looked at Marcus with embarrassment then he attempted to explain. "They do not deny that Marcus is a decent guy but they stubbornly believe that he is taking advantage of your young age and vulnerability. Marcus is married and a few years older then you."

With a cool calmness that astonished both Sui Fong and Cedric I replied, "Please stress upon my parents that if they don't accept Marcus then I can't possibly consider a reunion. I had experienced a great trauma in life but I have found my peace now and I would hate to have it destroyed."

Sui Fong countered while looking at Marcus pleading for support with her eyes, "Why don't you just go home and humor them? You can still see Marcus on the side."

I was appalled with Sui Fong's suggestion so with dignity I replied indignantly, "How could you even make such an inhuman and cruel recommendation? Of all people Sui Fong you should know that I will never do something so stupid!"

"O.K. Melanie I am sorry. I shouldn't have suggested it! I don't even think that it's such a good idea—I don't why I even recommended it." Sui Fong kissed me on the cheeks then turning to Marcus she asked, "I am not prying but are you truly happy? After all you are not accustomed to this type of a life style...."

Marcus winked at me and with a broad grin on his face he replied, "You can say that again! Of course I am not used to this type of life style. I have never been spoiled so luxuriantly but I can quite easily get used to it! I am truly a lucky man!" He pulled me into his arms and tousled my hair tenderly.

A few months swiftly drifted by and Marcus and I were left to ourselves. I was content with this newfound peace. After a long and bitter battle with Carmine, Nathan was finally allowed to see his father, so every weekend Marcus would take Nathan out and spend an afternoon with him. Each time I would decline the invitation to join the father and son. I believed that it was not the right time to impose myself on Nathan...the appropriate occasion would arise...we had a life time ahead of us.

Forty-One

One night both Marcus and I were asleep when the jingling of the phone woke us. I was always nervous with late hour phone calls. I passed the receiver to Marcus and switched on the light by the bed and glanced at the clock. It was three in the morning. When Marcus was listening he began to frown and I was bothered by his anxious voice. I heard him asked apprehensively, "Which hospital is he in? When are they going to perform the operation? I will go to the hospital immediately. Mum, take hold of yourself and calm down. I will see you shortly!" Marcus replaced the receiver on the phone and was out of bed almost immediately. He stretched and said, "My father collapsed in the washroom earlier on in the evening. It's probably his heart. He is in Cannosa Hospital and under observation. They are waiting for a heart specialist's opinion. The other doctors reckon that he will need a by-pass operation. As expected, Mum is in a fit. She just can't handle crisis, especially not this type! I will go to the hospital immediately—will you be all right?"

I nodded then I pulled the dressing gown round my shoulders and made Marcus a cup of hot coffee and reminded him to call me from the hospital. After he left, sleep eluded me and I was tossing and turning. I realized that it was impossible for me to sleep again so I read a book and waited anxiously and impatiently for Marcus' call.

I must have dozed off. When the phone rang, I jumped nervously. I opened my eyes and the room was basked in sunlight. I looked at the time and it was ten in the morning. Marcus was on the line, "Did I wake you? I hope you managed to go back to sleep after I left."

I could hear Marcus' tensed voice so I asked, "How is your father?"

"The doctors will perform the operation tonight. He is in Intensive Care now. I have asked my mother to go home and rest. If the operation is successful he will be in the hospital for at least a month. His chance of survival is only 50%..." Marcus continued hesitantly, "Carmine is somewhere in Europe and she is not expected back for another month...no one seems to know where she is. Nathan has been staying with my parents. Look—why don't you bring a change of clean clothes for me and meet me in the hospital?"

"Are you sure you want me in the hospital at a delicate time like this? Wouldn't your mother be upset with my presence?" I was worried.

"To tell you the honest truth Mother is very fragile and she is unable to handle crisis on her own. She will need assistance and plenty of it. I think it's time that she meet you. Come along as soon as you can." Then he hung up without waiting for a reply.

I put a set of clean clothing in an overnight bag, then I checked my reflection in the mirror. My tan was almost gone but there was still a light brown tint to my skin. I had tied my hair in a pony tail and there was not a trace of cosmetic on my face. I looked younger than my twenty-one years. Squaring my shoulders and taking a deep breath to control my nerves I left for the hospital.

Like a turtoise the cab slowly crawled up Old Peak Road. When it finally dropped me outside the Cannosa Hospital I literally threw some money at the driver and sprinted through the entrance and dashed for the lift. I waited nervously for the descending elevator. Hospitals had never been one of my favorite places. When I emerged from the lift, I stood in the corridor not certain at all of my direction. A nurse stopped me and asked politely, "Are you looking for someone?"

Shyly I muttered, "Yes...Mr. Jeffrey Kwan..."

Came the polite reply, "Are you his close relative? This is Intensive Care Unit and the patients are not allowed visitors unless you are closely related to him."

I was desolate and wasn't sure what I was supposed to say or do when I saw Marcus emerging from one of the rooms and walking along the corridor. I sighed a breath of relief and waved at him. Marcus immediately joined us. "Nurse, this lady is my fianceé."

He took my hand and led me into his father's room. I was frightened and I halted on the threshold. I had never in my entire life seen so many tubes and machines attached to a human body. Marcus nudged me encouragingly and uttered under his breath, "They are monitoring his heart and when he is stronger they will operate."

Marcus held my hand and gingerly we moved toward the bed. Mr. Kwan was as pale as death. On his face was an oxygen mask and his eyes were shut tightly. I insisted that Marcus change into some clean clothes. He looked exhausted and there was a deep shadow round his chin—he needed a shave badly—his hair was disheveled. I pushed him toward the adjoining room and reassured him that I would sit with his father while he freshened up. I pulled a chair closer to the bed and kept a close eye on the sick man. I was not annoyed with Marcus' father although he had rejected me. I was praying for his speedy recovery. My eyes hardly left the monitors and without moving a muscle I waited. I didn't know how long I had sat there because my motionless body began to ache. Eventually Marcus returned to the room. He patted my shoulder and softly apologized, "I am sorry but I felt asleep in the next room. I must have been overcome with fatigue." He brushed his hair with his fingers.

I stood up and left the room with Marcus, "Don't worry about me! I will do whatever I can to help."

While we were talking in the corridor I saw a small framed elderly lady with white hair approached us. Marcus greeted her and gestured for me to join them. "Mum, I think it is time that you meet Melanie...this is my mother Violet Kwan."

Nervously, I extended my hand and Mrs. Kwan hesitated, "You are not what I have expected—you look so young!"

Marcus took my hand into his hand and remarked, "Melanie has been keeping watch over Dad while I slept."

Mrs. Kwan smiled at me and nodded her head approvingly, then she went into the room to see her husband and we followed. When she saw Mr. Kwan lying in bed, she started to sob. Automatically I put my arms around her fragile shoulders hoping to provide some comfort and support for her. It must have been my soothing and encouraging voice because she collapsed into my arms and wept. When her sobs finally subsided, I assisted her into the adjoining room where Marcus was waiting for us. I insisted that Mrs. Kwan make herself comfortable on the settee, then Marcus said, "As soon as Dad's heart is stronger they will perform the operation." Mrs. Kwan's obvious grief was inconsolable and her soft sobs started again.

"Don't worry, Mum, Dad will pull through. I have instructed the hospital to employ special nurses for Dad. There will be someone to keep an eye on him constantly." Marcus put his arms around his mother protectively.

Frowning and waving her small hand toward the other room Mrs. Kwan replied hesitantly, "He should really have family with him and nurses are not family! Now that Dad is in the hospital you must attend to the office and I am too old to sit with him continuously. Nathan is too young and I can never depend on Carmine...in any case, I don't even know where she is!"

At the mention of Carmine's name Mrs. Kwan looked at me embarrassingly. I was standing by the window and gazing out. Slowly I turned my head and looked deep into Mrs. Kwan's eyes. With a soft smile I offered, "If you don't think I am intruding, then I am more than pleased to sit with Mr. Kwan until Marcus gets off from work every day. I can rest for a few hours and take over the night-shift again. When you come in the morning, I can go home and rest. I will come back after lunch and you can return home."

Mrs. Kwan looked at Marcus searchingly and she dubiously replied, "It will be very tiring for you. We don't know when Jeffrey will be off the critical list."

I moved closer to Marcus' mother and reassured her soothingly, "Mrs. Kwan I am young and I am not working. Don't be concerned for me. It shouldn't be long before Mr. Kwan will be on his feet again."

The older lady was grateful for my offer and accepted. Continuously Marcus paced the floor and Mrs. Kwan sobbed while I tried to comfort her with encouraging and sympathetic whispers. We waited patiently and anxiously for the result of the operation.

After many hours of waiting the heart specialist finally came to see us, "The operation was very successful. Mr. Kwan is basically a very strong man. He will be in the hospital for at least a month, and with intensive care, he will soon recover. We have to make certain that there are no further complications."

We breathed again and gratefully we thanked the doctor. When Mr. Kwan was settled into his room again his wife left for home.

Toward midnight I insisted that Marcus go home to sleep. I promised to sit with his father. Marcus was not happy with the thought of leaving me alone in the hospital, but I told him that I had always wanted to learn to knit and it was the perfect opportunity for me. I showed him my knitting needles and reassured him that I would call immediately should there be any further problems.

During the night Mr. Kwan woke a few times. Vaguely he glanced toward the corner where I was sitting but he showed no signs of recognition.

On the third morning after the operation when Mrs. Kwan came to the hospital, I greeted her with a cheerful smile. She patted my hand and remarked, "All the nurses marveled at your strength and dedication. They told me you would only go home to change and then would return almost immediately. You are never away for more than two hours!"

I smiled at her reassuringly and walked to the adjoining room. I made myself comfortable on the settee and through the slightly ajar door I saw Mrs. Kwan helped her husband to a sitting position and fussed over him. Mr. Kwan looked around searchingly and with a puzzled look he asked, "I have noticed a young lady sitting in that corner every time I woke up during the night. Who is she? She must be a very dedicated nurse. I have seen her during the day when you or Marcus have not been around."

Mrs. Kwan patted her husband's hand then she whispered, "That is Melanie—Marcus' girl friend!"

Mr. Kwan showed signs of disapproval and resulted in a fit of coughing, "What is she doing here?"

Smiling broadly Mrs. Kwan answered, "You must be on the road to recovery because you are so inquisitive. Melanie has sat with you constantly since your operation. I don't know how she manages—she hardly rests—she only goes home to change and cook. Can you believe it? She even had time to cook soup for you every day. I don't care what everyone says about this girl—she does have an extremely kind heart; therefore, she can't be bad. As a matter of fact I have developed a liking to her!"

I held my breath while they were talking and I breathed again when Mr. Kwan nodded his head with a slight smile on his face. I was grateful for Mrs. Kwan's support. That night when the room was quiet I took my usual seat in the corner with my knitting needles clicking away. I started to say a silent prayer. Suddenly I noticed Mr. Kwan beckoning me so I left my chair and nervously stood by his bed. Softly Mr. Kwan inquired, "Are you cold? You are trembling?"

"No, no, I..." stuttering I was at a loss for words.

Mr. Kwan patted on the side of his bed and invited me to sit, "My wife told me that you have hardly left my bedside for a couple of days. I would like you to know that I do appreciate your kindness. I guess I have misjudged you. I owe you an apology."

"It's not necessary—it's my duty—I would have done the same for my parents. Even though I am not married to Marcus, I consider myself his wife; therefore, I like to think that you are my father-in-law," I replied bravely. We chatted for a while then Mr. Kwan drifted off to sleep holding my hand.

When Mrs. Kwan arrived at the hospital the next morning she was pleased to find me sitting on a chair by the bed and feeding Mr. Kwan a light breakfast. I was overjoyed that Marcus' father was recovering. Both he and his wife had accepted me, and I was treated as one of the family.

When I returned to the hospital, Mr. Kwan had been transferred from the Intensive Care Unit to the Recovery Ward. I found the room and walked in quietly. Immediately I saw a young boy sitting on Mr. Kwan's bed. When Marcus' father saw me he waved and said, "Isn't it time that you meet Nathan?"

A younger version of Marcus watched me suspiciously and intensely then his young face broke into a lovely, shy smile. I was overwhelmed with emotion and I cuddled the young boy and introduced myself. "I am Melanie...I hope that we are going to be great friends!"

Mr. Kwan patted the young boy's head and said, "Melanie will be marrying your Daddy soon and she will be your stepmother...you will find her to be an extremely loving and kind person. You will like her!"

I was in high heaven! I searched Mr. Kwan's face over Nathan's young head and he winked at me. Hugging the child closer to my heart, my eyes were filled with tears. I whispered, "Thank you for accepting me!" Still holding onto Nathan's hand I kissed Marcus' father's kind smiling face.

For the remaining days while Mr. Kwan was in the hospital, I was with him constantly. I read him the newspaper and we watched television together. I fed him his food and reminded him to take his medication. All the hospital staff was amazed with my performance and marveled at my utter devotion to the patient. When Mrs. Kwan visited her husband, accompanied by Nathan, I would take the young boy out to the garden and we would share an ice cream together. I told him stories and we laughed at my jokes. Marcus was thrilled!

One afternoon when I returned to the room with Nathan giggling behind me, to my greatest surprise I found my parents visiting with Mr. Kwan. Without any hesitation I rushed into my mother's arms and started to weep, "Oh Mummy I have missed you and Dad!" I made every effort to control my emotions.

Father smiled and closed his arms around my shoulders and said, "Now that Jeffrey and Violet have accepted you into their family I guess your mum and I should not reject Marcus. You have our blessings if you want to marry him."

Wiping my tears with the back of my hand, I kissed Mother and then Father, "Thank you…you don't know how long I have waited for this day. My prayers have been answered!"

When Carmine returned to Hong Kong, she was furious with her parents-in-law. She refused to believe that they had adopted a different attitude toward me and accepted me as part of the family. Her own son, Nathan, was full of praise for me.

One evening when Marcus joined me in the hospital his Father stirred in his sleep and seeing us he motioned for us to sit by his bed, "Melanie I don't want you to waste your youth as Marcus' mistress because of the vengeance of another woman. Arrange for your wedding. I should be able to leave the hospital soon."

Marcus contested, "But I am not divorced and Carmine is very adamant with her refusal to give me back my freeman."

Mr. Kwan took Marcus' hand and put it in mine. "There is a price for everything! Your divorce will be finalized soon. I have made Carmine a proposal that she couldn't refuse. Cedric is taking care of all the legalities." He turned toward his son and continued, "You have wronged Carmine, but I can't deny you your happiness. I have grown to be extremely fond of Melanie—she is a decent girl and there is so much kindness in her. I don't want her to be contaminated by hatred. Through thick and think the two of you had better make the most of this opportunity." He smiled at me encouragingly and I hugged him so ferociously that I caused him a fit of coughing.

Mrs. Kwan arrived at the hospital to take Mr. Kwan home. I had left the hospital earlier to return to the Kwan's residence. I wanted to make certain that Mr. Kwan was made as comfortable as possible. He was still a weak man—his steps faltered and he hadn't quite regained his appetite. I was sitting in the living room waiting for their arrival. Suddenly the front door opened and Carmine came into the room. She halted her steps when she saw me. Her outfit was magnificent and she looked absolutely gorgeous, but her eyes burned with hatred. she screamed, "What the hell do you think you are doing in my parents-in-law's home? You are not welcome!" Rudely she yanked me out of my chair.

With a frightened expression on my face I pleaded with her, "Please let go of my arm—you are hurting me!"

I was relieved when Mr. and Mrs. Kwan arrived. They were appalled and disgusted with Carmine's atrocious behavior. With a stern tone of voice Mr. Kwan reprimanded his daughter-in-law. "Melanie is our guest and this is our home. We don't appreciate you creating a scene. If you can't behave then I will have no choice but to ask you to leave."

Carmine glared at the couple then she crumpled a piece of document that she had in her hand and threw it at me. With a loud voice she hissed, "I hate you! I hate you! I will make sure that you will pay for this." Then she stormed out of the room without a backward glance.

I was shocked by Carmine's violence and my eyes blurred with tears. Mrs. Kwan patted my shoulders lovingly and comforted me. Haltingly, I said, "I am awfully sorry. Maybe I shouldn't have come. I can understand Carmine's animosity." I retrieved the crumpled document from the floor and smoothed it out. It was the "Decree Absolute" for Marcus' divorce. Drying the tears from my face, I handed the paper to Mr. Kwan.

After a quick glance he returned the document to me and warned, "They might be legally divorced but because of Nathan I am afraid we will never see the end of this woman." Shaking his head he waved at the front door and added, "By the way, don't you think you should call me Uncle Jeffrey instead of Mr. Kwan?"

Fresh tears of happiness streamed down my face and I nodded. I was exhilarated so I stuttered, "Uncle Jeffrey…and Auntie Violet…"

Forty-Two

For the next little while I was involved with a whirlwind of activities. Almost every day I traveled between my home in Wanchai to Uncle Jeffrey's home in the Peak. I would spend a morning or an afternoon with the elderly couple. When I wasn't visiting with them, I was busy preparing for the wedding. Our parents decided that we should move away from our present lodging and as our wedding present they purchased a beautiful flat for us in Kennedy Road that overlooked the Royal Hong Kong Jockey Club. I was grateful and excited. The decoration of our new home became my full time occupation. Repeatedly I emphasized that I didn't want an elaborate wedding. I insisted on a quiet dinner with just the families. I was in extreme ecstasy and contented that I was able to marry Marcus; therefore, I had no intention of creating too much of a fuss.

I was deeply involved with the interior designer and I didn't see Sui Fong walking through the front door and her sudden exclamation made me jump, "You do look prettier every day—how do you do it?" Fondly she hugged me and gave me a bunch of fresh cut roses.

I sniffed the fragrance from the flowers and teased my dear friend, "You are always contradicting yourself—one moment you like my brown skin, but now that I no longer have time for the sun, you are complimenting me on my fair complexion—make up your mind!" I tousled her hair affectionately.

Inviting Sui Fong into the kitchen I offered to make her a cup of instant coffee, "Join me for a cup of coffee—I have been on my feet almost all day and I am utterly exhausted. You are a welcome break for me." I put the kettle on.

Admiring the kitchen Sui Fong asked, "I don't want to be tactless but why have you installed an air-conditioner in the kitchen?"

I looked at the air-conditioner mounted on the window frame and giggled, "Marcus enjoys my cooking and he knows how much I sweat in the summer so it's a bribe on his part. He hopes that I won't stop attending to domestic affairs after we are married!"

Sui Fong poked her head into the living room and commented, "It must have cost a fortune to put a real fireplace in the flat. Is it the reason for the penthouse?"

I poured the boiling water into the mugs and stirred in teaspoonfuls of instant coffee. "I miss our fire place in England."

"Talking about fireplaces, I just thought of something. I wonder what Gavin and Raphael are up to these days?" Sui Fong poured milk into her coffee.

Echoes of my laughter rang through the kitchen and confidently I replied, "I am positive that if Gavin should know that I am getting married he would be happy for me!" Then I smiled to myself...the thought of Gavin never failed to churn up memories of my happy childhood.

Sui Fong sat on the chair while I perched on the edge of the kitchen table. She remarked, "Funny how one's attitude could change over night...so...how does it feel not to be an outcast any more? Do you know that you are the envy of town? You are now the sweetheart of our so-called society. Blessed with a handsome and adoring husband and a magnificent home everyone thinks that you are so fortunate. Uncle Jeffrey and Auntie Violet are extremely fond of you."

Kniting my eyebrows, I frowned, "Everything is happening too fast. I haven't really had time to ponder over the changes. I have climbed so high in too short a time—I just hope that if I have to fall I won't hurt myself too badly."

Sui Fong patted my shoulders and replied, "Don't be pessimistic—nothing can go wrong now! You deserve all the satisfaction generated from a happy marriage. You have struggled and suffered enough. Put the past behind."

Not wanting the workmen to hear our conversation so in a hushed voice I whispered, "I can't help feeling guilty about Nathan."

"You shouldn't persecute yourself! Marcus would have left Carmine sooner or later. It was only a matter of time because their marriage couldn't survive. Marcus is a revived person. In Cedric's opinion, for all the times that he has been associated with Marcus, he had never seen your husband so happy and alive—you are a good influence on him and you two together do make a bewitching couple!" Sui Fong always had a supportive and encouraging word for me.

I suggested that there should be no honeymoon for us after the wedding because Uncle Jeffrey had not fully recovered and he shouldn't be returning to work; therefore, Marcus was needed in the office. I decided that our honeymoon could wait.

After an elegant but quiet wedding I settled into my new role as Mrs. Marcus Kwan and I was living in eternal bliss. Marcus would not deprive me of anything. He was attentive and showered me with tender loving care.

One sunny weekend Marcus and I were invited to join our friends for a water skiing party. I declined because it had been a while since I had visited with my parents and I wasn't really interested in the spot. Marcus left to join our friends and I found myself back in my parents' home and chatting with them. I loved and enjoyed these peaceful lazy afternoons with my family. Even though I had returned from England so many years ago, I still relished moments spent with my parents. Alastair had married Tessa a few months earlier in England and returned to Hong Kong. It had become a habit for them to visit Mother and Father during the weekends. Lynette would join us with her child. I had become extremely fond of my parents' first grandchild.

The maid came into the living room and politely announced, "Mrs. Kwan you are wanted on the phone."

I excused myself and picked up the receiver, "This is Melanie Kwan...who is this?" I began to frown.

Came the impersonal reply, "This is the Cannosa Hospital! Are you Mrs. Marcus Kwan?"

My hands were shaking and they were clammy and saturated with cold sweat. I panicked, "Yes I am Mrs. Kwan." My thoughts went to my father-in-law immediately. I asked haltingly, "Is my father-in-law all right?"

After a slight pause the voice continued, "Your husband has just been admitted into the hospital. He was involved in an accident—can you come immediately?"

I was trembling with tension. "Is he hurt badly?"

"You will have to talk to the doctor," came the uninformative reply.

I was choking with tears when I informed my family. I had to leave for the hospital immediately as it was quite a drive from Stanley to Old Peak Road. Father decided that I shouldn't be driving so Alastair and Tessa volunteered to accompany me. When we arrived at the hospital I could hardly control my sobs because during the interminable journey I had imagined the worst. We located the Emergency Ward and found Marcus. I was so relieved to find him alive. I rushed to him and sniffed, "What happened?"

Marcus grinned sheepishly. I was more than glad that he had maintained a sense of humor therefore he couldn't be in too much pain, "Four of us decided to ski simultaneously and one of the other skis hit my thigh. I couldn't put any weight on my leg so here I am!"

"That was a silly and dangerous thing to do!" I chaffed and continued with a flutter, "I have to talk to your doctor so I will leave Tessa with you and Alastair can come with me." I pulled Alastair with me.

The doctor was waiting for us in his office. Extending my trembling hand I made the introduction, "I am Melanie Kwan the wife of your patient who was involved in the skiing accident and this is my brother Alastair Au-Yeung. Please tell us the extant my husband's injury!"

With a reassuring tone of voice the doctor patiently explained, "Mrs. Kwan as you are aware that four people that were involved in the accident were skiing at full speed. When the ski hit your husband, the impact on his knee was tremendous. His knee cap was crushed and a bone on his thigh was cracked. We have to operate on his leg immediately or he will encounter difficulty in walking in the future. If we do not mend the bones properly, he will definitely be walking with a limp...."

"Is it a dangerous operation? How long would it be before he is fully recovered?" A hundred questions were going through my mind and I didn't know which question was more important.

Alastair calmly intervened, "When are you going to operate on him?"

The doctor smiled encouragingly and replied, "Mr. Kwan has signed all the necessary papers and we are just waiting for the availability of the operation theater. It shouldn't be too long. After the operation I am afraid Mr. Kwan will be in the hospital for about ten days, but his leg will be in a cast for six months or so. Then he will have to learn to use his leg properly again. Mr. Kwan is a healthy young man and from what I have gathered he has a strong character so it shouldn't take him too long to recover completely. I would guess around eight to nine moths from now.

In the meantime he will be in pain and discomforts. Plenty of patience and tolerance on your part would be my best recommendation. But for now let's get the operation out of the way and we can attend to the details later."

We waited in the room that was reserved for Marcus. The operation took almost three hours so I took the opportunity to inform our parents and reassured them that Marcus was in the best of care. While we were waiting nervously, I started to pace the room and suddenly I felt a wave of nausea and I felt dizzy so I staggered to the nearest chair and collapsed into it. Alastair grabbed my shoulders and putting a hand on my forehead he inquired, "Melanie, are you O.K.? It's the after-effect of the shock—you have to take it easy—it's going to be a long and winding road to Marcus' recovery. Plenty of patience will be required from you so don't wear yourself out now. This is only the beginning."

I rested in the chair and weakly I squeezed Alastair's hand and smiled. "I feel nauseated and dizzy…it must be all the anxiety. I just need to rest for a while."

I moved into the hospital with Marcus and hardly left his side. Continuously I attempted to amuse him and hoped to keep his spirit up. Marcus was an outdoor type and being restrained to a hospital bed with his leg in a cast was driving him insane. He was constantly irritable and snapped at me often but I didn't show any signs of displeasure or annoyance. The nauseated feeling and dizziness persisted and I decided that I had better seek the doctor's advice. There was probably nothing wrong with me and I was just overly exhausted.

My mother-in-law arrived for her afternoon visit with Marcus and I said, "Mother, I have a bit of shopping to attend to—can I leave Marcus in your care for a little while?"

I kissed Marcus briefly on the forehead and all the while he complained, "I don't know how you can still shop! Don't you ever get tired of spending money?" Auntie Violet glared at his son and was about to speak when I silenced her by putting my fingers to my lips and winked.

I left Marcus' room and took the lift to the next floor. I located the doctor's office and walked through the slightly opened door. Informing the receptionist I said, "I am Melanie Kwan, and I have an appointment to see Doctor Wong."

The young nurse gestured for me to take a seat and sweetly replied, "Please take a seat. Doctor Wong will be with you shortly."

After a few minute's wait I was ushered into the doctor's room and he pointed to a chair. With a kind smile on his face he perched on the edge of his desk and said, "Your husband is recovering reasonably well but he must control his temper. He is getting to be very unpopular with the nurses."

Defending Marcus immediately I said, "It is difficult for him to be in a cast and confined to a wheelchair. I do apologize for his sharp tongue."

Doctor Wong patted my hand encouragingly and inquired, "Now what can I do for you? I understand the appointment is for yourself."

I watched the doctor's kind face and stuttered, "I have been feeling dizzy and nauseated…I am tired easily. I seem to need plenty of sleep."

Dr. Wong took my pulse and asked, "When was the last time you had your menstruation?"

I couldn't remember so I screwed my nose and tried to think. "Come to think of it—it has been a while—with Marcus in the hospital I just haven't thought about it."

Doctor Wong returned to his desk and scribbled on a pad, "I would like you to go for a urine test and some blood tests. Here's a prescription for some vitamins. Take plenty of rest and I will see you again when the test results are available. There is nothing to worry about. I think you have exhausted most of your energy." With a reassuring smile the doctor escorted me into the receptionist area and requested for a urine and some blood tests for me.

There was a slight knock on the door and Doctor Wong came into Marcus' room. Humorously he asked his patient, "So how are you feeling today?"

"Would you feel good if you are confined to a wheel chair?" Marcus barked at the doctor rudely.

The doctor clicked his tongue and chaffed, "Consider yourself a lucky man. You could have been in a wheel chair for life."

I was alarmed so I pleaded with the doctor, "Don't say such a horrible thing!"

Doctor Wong smiled at me and returned his attention to Marcus,. "You are going to learn to use the crutches today and when you are comfortable with them I will discharge you. When you return home you should try and lead a normal life. You are expected to return for your monthly check-ups. Your bones have mended nicely. Hopefully in three or four months' time your cast will be taken off!"

Marcus was disgusted with the information. The doctor sternly insisted, "You will have to learn to cope with your disability and not depend too much on your wife. She will be needing plenty of rest."

Turning to me, he extended his hand and said, "I have your test results with me and I want to congratulate you immediately!"

I was baffled "Congratulate me?"

"What is going on? Can someone put me in the picture?" Marcus was alarmed and demanded an explanation, "I didn't know that you were ill—what is wrong with you?"

Doctor Wong waved his hand and intervened, "There is nothing wrong with your wife! You are going to be happy parents soon. Mrs. Kwan you are going to be a mother!"

For a short while I couldn't comprehend what the doctor was saying. Suddenly I scooped Marcus into my arms and shrieked with joy, "Marcus did you hear that? I am pregnant! Aren't you pleased?"

Marcus watched my happy face and soon a broad grin appeared on his face. "I can't say that I am not pleased. This calls for a celebration!" His good humor returned and he extended his hand to the doctor and muttered his thanks. With twinkles in his eyes he teased, "We do make a great pair—a pregnant woman and a cripple!" Even Doctor Wong laughed.

Forty-Three

Released from the hospital Marcus appreciated and welcomed his freedom again. With the aid of the crutches he returned to work but I was experiencing an extremely difficult pregnancy. Most of the time I was vomiting—it was impossible for me to stomach any food. Soon I was losing weight rapidly and Doctor Wong was alarmed. When we returned to the hospital to have Marcus' cast taken off the doctor warned us, "If Melanie's vomiting persists, I may have to prescribe a month or two of complete bed-rest for her."

I was worried and upset by the information but Marcus replied irritably, "What difference does it make whether she stays in bed or not? In any case she can't accompany me to any social functions because she is never well! She can't even cook—the smell of cooking nauseates her!"

Doctor Wong was appalled with Marcus' outbursts and attempted to reason with him while I remained silent and watched them nervously. "Melanie can't control her nausea. If she does not have food in her stomach of course she would be tired. I have prescribed for her iron tablets, but she needs a normal diet especially when she is feeding for two...the last thing that Melanie needs is stress; therefore, you have to be patient. Try offering her sympathy for her discomforts instead of complaints—you mustn't burden her with guilt! I am hoping that you are able to demonstrate more love and affection. I truly believe that caring and attention are the best medicine for her." I was utterly grateful to Doctor Wong's support and I wanted to hug him.

I was woken up with a sharp pain in my stomach and I was gasping for air. I could feel a knife twisting in my stomach and I moaned. I reached over for Marcus and when he turned around and saw my agonized face with perspiration on my forehead he panicked. He wanted to help but he didn't know what to do so he called my mother and described my condition and she advised him to contact Doctor Wong immediately.

It seemed like eternity before the doctor finally arrived. He gave me an injection to relieve the pain and soon my condition stabled. "I am afraid Melanie will have a miscarriage if she is not provided with enough rest. I have to insist on a complete bed-rest for at least a month. If no further complications develop then hopefully she can enjoy a normal pregnancy…we will have to wait and observe."

To my utter horror and disappointment I was bedridden. My days were long but I managed to rest and soon my appetite returned. In the meantime instead of returning home directly from work Marcus with weak excuses was returning late more and more often. There were many meetings and he seemed to have endless dinners that he had to attend. I was left constantly on my own. Jeffrey visited me almost every day and he would spend an hour or two chatting with me. On one of these occasions he said, "Melanie, you seem to have lost your fighting spirit—do you want to share your thoughts with me?"

Unhappiness had became my regular companion and I appreciated my father-in-law's thoughtfulness so I confided in him. "I feel that I have failed Marcus—why can't I enjoy a normal pregnancy? I feel that we are drifting apart and we are losing the closeness like we used to share. He has closed his door to me." I began to sob.

Patting my shaking shoulders Jeffrey advised, "You must get rid of these foolish thoughts immediately—it's not healthy for you or the baby and it's not going to improve your condition. All pregnant women feel insecure and it's only natural for you to have the same reaction. When the baby is born and before you know it all these dejected feelings will go. Marcus has been kept busy in the office. The firm is growing and he has to shoulder more responsibilities. With me being away is not helping either. Have more patience, for I hate to see your tears!" Jeffrey's considerate and sympathetic words brought some comfort to me and I dozed off.

I must have fallen asleep for a few hours for when I opened my eyes again the room was dark. I could hear a murmur of voices drifting from the living room. Straining my ears I attempted to eavesdrop—I was curious. I could hear Jeffrey's voice, "Have you seen Melanie lately? She is getting better and the color is returning to her face." I wondered whom he was talking to?

Cedric's soft whisper interrupted, "But she is not happy."

There was a slight pause then came Jeffrey's reply, "I agree with you but then all women in Melanie's current frame of mind would feel a bit of unhappiness and insecurity."

Another stretch of silence then Cedric remarked, "I am glad that Marcus is now a senior partner of the firm—I am really pleased for him—he does work awfully hard and he is a capable lawyer." Cedric stopped then hesitantly he continued, "Lately I have been hearing some gossip and I don't like what I have heard. I don't want you to think that I am a shit-stirring old woman with a devious tongue, but I would hate it if Melanie should get to hear these rumors. Hong Kong is such a small town and people do talk...."

Silence...then Jeffrey asked, "What have you heard?"

I was wide awake and my ears were pricking. I didn't want their conversation to cease so I stayed motionless in bed. I heard Cedric's halting question, "Wasn't Marcus engaged to a young lady before he left for England to study and she broke off the engagement to marry someone else?"

I removed myself from the bed and pulled a chair toward the closed door. I sat on the chair and put my head against the door. Came Jeffrey's soft reply, "That was a long time ago—what does she have to do with Melanie's present condition?"

Cedric continued hesitantly, "The lady in question has divorced her husband and returned to Hong Kong. Marcus has been seen with her on a couple of occasions."

Then Jeffrey's soothing voice, "I wouldn't put too much to what other people say. They must have bumped into each other and decided to share a meal or two...just for old times' sake."

I was trembling—why was the room so cold? I put my shaking hands on my forehead and wiped away the cold sweat that saturated my body. I realized that it was wrong for me to eavesdrop but I couldn't resist myself. They were after all talking about Marcus and his previous lady friend.

Cedric sighed and persisted, "I hope you are right in your guessing. I wouldn't want Melanie to get hurt, especially not in her condition. She should not be overly distressed...."

Gingerly I tiptoed to the bed and pretended to be asleep when Jeffrey came into the room with Cedric. I didn't want them to know that I had overheard their conversation.

The following evening Jeffrey returned to our home after dinner and asked to see Marcus. I told him that his son had gone out for the evening but he insisted that he would wait for Marcus' return. It must have been the murmur of the television that woke me or were there people talking outside of my room? I got out of bed and intended to investigate when Jeffrey's irritated tone of voice stopped me. "How is Melanie?" His voice was dripping with sarcasm.

Marcus' prompt reply, "Why do you ask? You see her every day—don't you?"

Jeffrey fired his next question at Marcus, "Don't you care how she feels or have you been too involved with seeing someone else?"

Marcus demanded indignantly, "What are you talking about?" He continued sarcastically, "So, I see...you have been in tune with the local gossip."

"I did hear a few things but I hope that they are only rumors like you have just suggested. You are a very lucky man—Melanie is a fabulous girl. It is going to be difficult to replace her." Vaguely I could hear Jeffrey attempting to reason with Marcus.

Then came Marcus' curt reply, "Dad, I am old enough to know what I am doing—I have no intention of replacing Melanie!"

Collapsing on the bed, I forced my fist into my mouth to prevent myself from screaming. Jeffrey sighed, "I hope you won't provide Melanie with a reason to leave you...if she decides to then no richness on earth can detain her...." I covered my ears with my trembling hands—I no longer wished to listen to the remaining of their conversation—it was just too painful for me....

I was dozing when the ringing phone woke me, "Melanie, this is your friend Carmine.... I hear that you are pregnant and resting at home. I thought I should call to extend my congratulation!"

I was astounded to hear Carmine's voice—we had no contact with each other since the divorce. I was baffled and suspicious of her sudden kindness but to be rude was not my nature so with a polite tone of voice I replied, "Thank you for being so thoughtful. I do appreciate your call!"

Carmine continued with sweetness oozing from her voice, "Did you know that Marcus' ex-girlfriend is back in town after divorcing her rich husband? Your husband has been seen with her on a couple of occasions."

I could detect the malice on Carmine's honeyed voice, "Yes I know—Marcus did mention that she has returned. Thank you for your concern." Not providing a chance for Carmine to speak again I replaced the receiver on the phone. Mutely I looked at the silent phone. Although, I had eavesdropped on Jeffrey and Cedric's conversation, nevertheless, I was distressed. I had lied to Carmine when I told her that Marcus had discussed his ex-girlfriend with me. My thoughts were disturbed and I was in turmoil.

Later Sui Fong visited and she breezed into my room cheerfully with a big bunch of flowers and a box of chocolate, "I have come to spoil you, and how is the Sleeping Beauty? I hope you are feeling better." She slumped onto the chair by my bed. Searching my face Sui Fong remarked, "You are certainly making progress.... I see you are finally putting on some weight!" When I didn't respond she frowned and inquired, "Is something bothering you? Are you feeling poorly again—do you want me to call Doctor Wong?" While waiting for me to answer she opened the box of chocolate. She put one sweet in her mouth and then gave me the box.

I put the untouched chocolates on the table and whispered in my little girl's voice, "Sui Fong, are you still my friend?"

Sui Fong stopped chewing then she exclaimed, "What nonsense are you talking about? That was a dumb question—don't crowd your mind with unwarranted ideas! Why don't you read instead of think?"

"I have done too much reading—I have watched enough television and I am sick and tired of knitting. I hope that I can lead a normal life again. Marcus is perfectly fed up and disgusted with my present sickly condition." I waved my hands in the air dejectedly and I was feeling positively rejected.

Sui Fong patted my hands soothingly, "You obviously need the rest otherwise Doctor Wong wouldn't have insisted—he should know best." Then she lightly patted my growing stomach tenderly.

Searching my friend's face I inquired, "Is there something that you should be telling me—don't you want to share the latest gossip with me?"

My unexpected question caught Sui Fong by surprise. She remained silent, obviously debating with herself. Finally with a determined look on her face she stammered, "I was introduced to Marcus' ex-girlfriend at a dinner the other night. If you want my honest opinion I don't think she is attractive!"

An uneasiness began to engulf me. "Don't be nasty! Why was she invited? Marcus didn't tell me..."

Shrugging her shoulders Sui Fong muttered, "Marcus told us that they had accidentally bumped into each other a few weeks ago...apparently she has been away for a few years. I guess Marcus was in a hospitable mood so he brought her along to the dinner."

I mumbled softly to myself, "So...she is not lying."

"Who is not lying?" Sui Fong demanded an explanation.

I pulled myself onto a sitting position and hugging my knees I whispered, "Carmine called this morning and told me that she saw Marcus with this lady."

Angrily Sui Fong screamed, "What a bitch! So what if Marcus was seen with his ex-girlfriend? They are just casual acquaintances. I would ignore Carmine's malicious tongue. She just want to hurt your feelings. I know it hasn't been easy for you but you must trust Marcus. The two of you have been through enough. It's not every day that you can experience another relationship equivalent to yours. Have more faith in yourself and your marriage!" Sui Fong cupped my face in her warm hands.

I was beginning to feel cold so I pulled the blanket to cover my trembling shoulders "I hope you are right? Sui Fong, I couldn't bear the thought of losing Marcus."

Sui Fong took my hand and chaffed, "What a morbid thought!"

I wish I had one half of her confidence.

A few more weeks crawled by and finally I was able to leave the confinement of my detested bed. I looked much healthier and my enlarging stomach was beginning to show. I was almost six-months pregnant. As the due date drew nearer enthusiasm and excitement replaced my suspicions and anxiety. I persistently occupied myself with the decoration of the nursery. I had wanted a little daughter for Marcus and a sister for Nathan. Cheerfully humming to myself I was folding the baby outfits when the phone rang, "What time are you going to Anthony Pickering's party?" Sui Fong's cheerful voice echoed over the phone.

I was baffled so I asked, "What party? I wasn't aware that I was invited to any party tonight!"

After a slight pause Sui Fong replied, "Didn't Marcus tell you? He must have forgotten! Your ex-boss is fifty today and there is a dinner and dance to celebrate. I tell you what—why don't you call Marcus and tell him that I will collect you. This arrangement will save him a trip home and he can go with Cedric straight from work."

I hesitated, "I just called and his secretary told me that he is not expected back in the office this afternoon. I will leave a message for him—he usually calls the office for messages."

I was excited about that evening's event. It had been a while since I had been out socializing. I would very much enjoy an evening out and what a surprise it would be for Marcus! Evidently he was not aware that I was able to resume my normal activities; therefore, he did not inform me of the party. I took special care with my appearances. With a slight touch of cosmetic applied to my face and wearing an elegant loose dress I was ready and waiting for Sui Fong.

Both Mr. Pickering and his wife were delighted that I was up and about again. Happy to be surrounded by friends, music, and laughter I was having a fabulous time. Just before dinner was served, to my utter disappointment, Cedric arrived alone—apparently, he was unable to contact Marcus during the day.

"Too bad your parents are unable to join us—I hear they are on holiday!" Mr. Pickering was chatting with me, "And Violet doesn't think that Jeffrey should come. When you see them next tell them that we miss their company."

I nodded my head absentmindedly. Anxiously, I kept an eye on the door. I was hoping to surprise Marcus. Suddenly my eyes sparkled when I saw him arriving. Excitedly I left my seat and rushed to him then my steps faltered. A woman came into my vision and she was holding Marcus' hand possessively while he was whispering in her ears. When the newly arrived couple came into the room, the chatter ceased and was replaced with a quiet hush in the room—everyone was embarrassed. No one expected Marcus to come with another woman. Sui Fong moved closer to me and hissed, "That is the ex-girlfriend!"

With a forced smile on my face I resumed my steps bravely. I knew that everyone was waiting and watching for my reaction. Squaring my shoulders and sucking in a couple of deep breaths I moved toward my husband and kissed him gently on the cheek. Marcus was astounded with my unexpected appearance. Stuttering he made the introduction, "Melanie...I didn't expect to see you...meet my out-of-town friend, Beth, and this is my wife Melanie."

Graciously I greeted Beth then I returned to my chair with wobbling knees. I insisted that Beth should join my table and I began to introduce her to all my friends. It was important to me that nothing was amiss—I had to be a perfect actress!

After dinner, when I was emerging from the restrooms with Sui Fong, she suddenly stopped me. Mr. Pickering was talking to Marcus and he was annoyed. "I am amazed with your insensitivity toward your wife—how could you bring your lady friend to this function? Do you ever consider Melanie's feelings—have you no compassion at all for her condition? I admire her strength and her dignity. She saved the embarrassing situation with her accommodating nature. Please show some signs of respects for her feelings. Your atrocious and selfish behavior was not an easy pill for her to swallow, especially in public."

Marcus stammered a reply, "I didn't know Melanie would be able to attend or I wouldn't have brought Beth along."

Mr. Pickering challenged Marcus unmercifully, "Do you honestly think that the other guests would not talk? What about Cedric and Sui Fong?"

I was shaking and my body was swaying. I thought I would faint. Sui Fong grabbed a chair and pushed me into it. Rigidly she stood beside me and held my cold clammy hands.

Came Marcus' reply, "Sui Fong and Cedric don't gossip—they have seen me a few times with Beth and they haven't told Melanie!"

"Why are you so sure that they haven't told Melanie? Your wife might just be smart enough not to confront you—don't take her for granted!" Mr. Pickering warned with a stern voice.

I sat motionless on the chair and mastering super determination and courage I held back my tears. I closed my eyes and then I shook my head hoping to erase the conversation that I had just overheard. My pride was hurt, but I didn't want sympathy. In any case Beth and Marcus might just be casual friends. If anyone should understand a platonic relationship, I was the one—didn't Gavin and I share such a relationship? To create a scene was uncalled for. I told myself that I was overly suspicious and I must put a grip on myself. I took a couple of deep breaths and with Sui Fong's supportive hand around my shoulders we returned to our table.

I sat and watched the other guests dance. Doctor Wong did impress upon me that I must not be over strenuous. I had no desire or intention of spending the remaining of my pregnancy confined to my bed. I blinked back threatening tears when Marcus was dancing with Beth. I decided that it was for the best if I didn't confront him. We were experiencing a rough patch in our marriage. I believed that every married couple had their up's and down's. After the birth of the baby Marcus would be sensible again. In the meantime I would have to bite my tongue and endure the misery in silence.

During one of Jeffrey's visits with me he expressed his concerns. "I am disgusted with Marcus' behavior at Anthony's birthday party. I am extremely proud of you. Your performance was admirable. I don't suppose too many women under the same circumstances could have handled themselves the way you did. You are a true lady."

Hesitantly I replied, "I was amazed with my own reactions, but I do understand that some men just can't cope with pregnant wives. Hopefully, Marcus is one of them. I don't believe in scenes. Anyway it's not long before the baby is born. I am sure that things will turn out right in the end. Don't worry, Dad, surely a marriage should be able to survive some waves." I smiled and patted Jeffrey's hand reassuringly.

He searched my face. "I can understand your feelings but don't allow the situation to get out of hand. You don't have to lose your cool but be firm and remind that son of mine that he has a responsibility toward you and the baby."

I hugged Jeffrey's frail body. I was grateful for his support, "I am certain that this is just a casual fling on Marcus' part. I am not saying that his actions don't hurt but better days await us after the birth of the baby...I know!" I crossed my fingers and I was desperate to convince myself. I was too confused to be able to think properly.

Sui Fong visited again. When I was making coffee for us she casually inquired, "How is Marcus these days—still going out a lot?"

I stirred the cup of coffee in front of me and sighed, "Yes...but I don't ask where he goes or with whom. I don't see the point. If he wants to tell me then he will. If I demand an answer from him I would only encourage him to lie and I can't tolerate dishonesty—I'd rather not know!"

Sui Fong started to pace the room then she stopped and exclaimed, "I just don't understand you—how can you handle the situation with such calmness? I would have wailed and screamed at Anthony's party. You treated that woman so cordially—I would have strangled her alive and scratched her eyes out—your reasoning and actions are beyond me!"

Returning to the settee, I gestured for Sui Fong to sit with me. Taking her hands, I put them on my growing stomach, "Sui Fong, this is a marriage that we are discussing. It's not a toy that we can discard any time that we choose. There is such a thing as give and take."

Sui Fong's snappy reply, "Seems to me Marcus is always taking and never giving."

Immediately and automatically I jumped to Marcus' defense, "Don't judge him too harshly—we all go astray at one time or another—it's called ego boosting. If I confront him then I will only push him to Beth, but if I maintain my cool I am sure that I will be able to ride this wave to the end."

Patting my hands Sui Fong whispered, "I just hope that you are correct in your judgment."

I stared out of the window and sighed, "I have to be right! I have no other choice but to believe that I am right. I can't bear the thought of losing Marcus. It will kill me! When I was younger I could insist on all or nothing but now I have to consider the baby." I smiled at my friend bravely with a silent prayer in my heart.

Forty-Four

The baby was due in two weeks. My stomach had grown enormous and I couldn't believe my own reflection in the mirror. I could no longer drive, so Jeffrey's chauffeur was at my constant disposal. Jeffrey and Violet accompanied me to wherever I had to shop for the baby—Mother visited every day and my home was Sui Fong's second home. Marcus was hardly around, but I chose not to voice any complaint. I was grateful for whatever time he was willing to spare me.

One night, on one of the rare occasions that Marcus would join his parents and myself for dinner, he remarked casually, "By the way I have to leave town for a business trip next week and I will be gone for a couple of weeks."

I refused to believe what I had heard. I beseeched Marcus with an astonished look, "Have you forgotten that the baby will be born in a week or two's time? Is this trip positively necessary? Doctor Wong doesn't seem to think that I should be on my own."

"You have enough servants around you, so what are you whining about?" Marcus snapped in exasperation.

"Have you lost your mind?" Jeffrey barked at his son annoyingly, "What business trip could be more important than your child's birth?

Melanie needs a husband not servants!"

Marcus realized that he had gone out of line. Immediately he kissed me and patted my stomach affectionately, "This trip is very important to me—I am sure that you wouldn't want me to miss this important opportunity. If I am successful I will become the legal advisor for an International Organization that is opening a branch office in the Far East. I will leave you with a forwarding telephone number so you can call me. When the baby is born, I will come back immediately."

He searched my face appealingly, so with tear-filling eyes reluctantly I stammered, "Of course, you must go. Your career should always come first. There will be plenty of time in the future for you to spend with the baby when you return."

Jeffrey was about to object so I intervened, "Dad I will be in good hands."

When the baby girl was born I had my family and friends with me, but I was without a husband and I needed him desperately. He was supposed to be in New York. Nathan wanted to name the baby Jackie so I decided that during Marcus' absence I would agree to let him choose his sister's name. Jackie was an adorable baby and she was beautiful. She was like a miniature doll and her grandparents just loved her. Frantic calls were made to Marcus but he was not in the office with his clients nor could he be located in the hotel. Numerous messages were left for him advising him of the arrival of his baby daughter. I waited impatiently and anxiously for his call but there was absolute silence. I was frantic and began to panic—did Marcus meet with an accident? Why wasn't he returning my urgent calls? Where was Marcus? With tears washing my face persistently I waited for Marcus. No calls—no flowers—no card. Marcus had simply vanished.

The third day I had an unexpected visitor in the hospital. Carmine walked into the room with an insidious expression. Sui Fong wanted the visitor to leave. She didn't think that I should tolerate the unwelcome intruder but not wanting to be rude I offered her a chair. After a few minutes of casual chatting Carmine dropped a bombshell, "Did you know that Marcus was seen in Hawaii with Beth? A friend of mine saw them leaving Hawaii and returning to the States. As a matter of fact they left last night."

Sui Fong was seething and hatred was burning in her eyes. She clenched her fists but I smiled and replied sweetly, "I know...Marcus had a few meetings in Hawaii—he must have bumped into Beth."

Carmine was disappointed, obviously she was expecting a display of hysterics, instead she found me calm and collected so she left.

I was far from being composed—I was shaking—I was in shock. I wished that I could cry but tears wouldn't come. I lost my focus and the room began to spin. I was in pain gasping for air then blackness engulfed me.

I could hear muffled voices then someone lifted my hand and I felt the prick of a needle on my arm. Almost immediately I was able to sleep but I dreamed of Marcus kissing Beth and they were hugging each other and laughing. They were dancing and it was just too much for me to bear and I heard myself screaming for them to stop.

Someone was gently shaking my shoulders and a warm towel was wiping my sweat drenched face.

When I slowly returned to consciousness I opened my eyes and I was grateful that I found myself sleeping in the hospital bed. Jeffrey was pacing the room with his hands behind his back and Sui Fong was sitting by the bed wiping my forehead and gently patting my hand.

Jeffrey stopped his pacing and hissed with anger, "What an unfortunate thing to have happened. I will never forgive Carmine. Her action was atrocious, calculating and treacherous!"

I blew my nose into a tissue and sniffed, "Please don't condemn her—I am glad that she told me. At least she has forced me to accept the truth. I guess I have not been honest with myself so now I have to face the consequences. If we don't hear from Marcus in a couple of days do you mind if I leave you with Jackie? I want to make a trip to New York. I have to beg Marcus to come back. I have to do it for Jackie. She shouldn't be without a father—I owe my daughter this much." I could no longer control my heart-breaking sobs.

That night a call came from Marcus, "Oh Melanie, I am sorry...can you ever forgive me? I went away on a fishing trip with my clients and the office was unable to pass on your messages to me. I must have caused you so much anxiety. I will never forgive myself!"

Why are you lying to me? I wanted to ask him but instead I said, "Both the baby and I are doing fine. We just miss you terribly! I have been imagining the worst! When are you returning to us?" I pleaded with him.

"Soon. I will be coming home soon. As soon as I have finalized my business here, I will be home."

"Would you like me to join you in New York? Your parents can take care of Jackie for a while," I offered in a small voice.

Marcus hesitated, "Your suggestion may not be such a good idea. When I attend meetings you will be left on your own in the hotel and I don't think that it would be advisable for you to travel so soon after the birth. Why don't you take this opportunity to recuperate? I will be home before you know it!"

I could detect a genuine concern from Marcus' voice and he sounded excited with the arrival of Jackie. I was glad that I had decided not to confront him. Hopefully, before long, the nightmare would be behind me. After all Marcus and I had been through some pretty rough times together. He couldn't throw our feelings and devotions for each other overboard without a second thought.

The following day a dozen balloons, half a dozen bouquet of flowers, two boxes of chocolates, and a cable arrived in the hospital for me from Marcus. A big cuddly teddy bear arrived for Jackie from her father. I read the cable with tears streaming down my face, 'I love you, stop, will be home shortly, stop, wait for me'. I clutched the cable in my hands and fell asleep with a contented smile on my face. I wanted to believe that all was well again.

By the time Marcus arrived home I had been home with the baby for two weeks. During these two weeks Jeffrey and Violet were with me constantly, or Mother and Father would visit. My home was full of people. Lynette would come with her son. She fussed and taught me how to feed and bathe the baby. Sui Fong and Cedric dropped by with Alastair and Tessa. If only Marcus was at home with me then my happiness would be complete.

On the day of Marcus' arrival I dressed Jackie in a cute pink outfit and wrapped her with a warm blanket. I paid extra special attention to my own appearance. I cuddled the baby to me and anxiously waited for Marcus in the airport. Before he came through the arrival gate I thought I saw Beth leaving the airport hastily. I rubbed my eyes and shook my head and decided that my imagination was playing a cruel trick on me, then Marcus walked toward me. He was smiling and I rushed into his open arms—my ordeal was over! Gently I put Jackie into his arms and the baby wailed, "You have been away for much too long...you are a stranger to Jackie!" I teased my husband lovingly and our small family left for home.

My days were full and I had recovered completely. If I wasn't busy attending to the baby's needs then I was occupied in the kitchen. Although there was a new addition to the home I made certain that Marcus was never neglected. Methodically and systematically I planned my days. Jackie was not allowed to interfere with our social life. With the assistance of a nurse our young daughter was blooming.

Although my thoughts and beliefs were westernized I wanted to keep our parents happy, so I maintained the Chinese tradition of celebrating our baby's one month birthday. Dozens and dozens of hard-boiled eggs with their shells were soaked in red tinted water. These red colored eggs and a pound of roasted pork were delivered to each of our many relatives. In return they gave little red packets to Jackie—these packets contained either money or small pieces of jewelry. Our parents insisted we should have an elaborate dinner reception in a restaurant to celebrate this special occasion, but I decided that I would rather invite the family home. After dinner Marcus was wanted on the phone and after he had hung up he looked anxious and almost angry. Without a word he left us. When the guests left, he still had not returned—I was baffled and worried. I was seeing our relatives into their cars when I noticed that Marcus' car was parked in the parking lot so I asked Jeffrey's chauffeur, "Did you see Mr. Kwan Junior leave earlier on in the evening?"

Hesitantly the young man looked at Jeffrey and Violet and reluctantly muttered a reply, "Yes, he asked me to drive him to…"

"Where did you take him?" Jeffrey was annoyed and the chauffeur turned to me with pleading eyes then he blurted, "I took him to Ms. Beth's residence."

Jeffrey couldn't control his anger and roared, "How do you know where that woman lives?"

The young man stuttered, "I have taken him to her home on a couple of occasions." I patted his shoulders reassuringly and asked, "You mean since his return from the States?" The chauffeur mutely nodded his head.

I felt faint and I had to steady my trembling body by holding on to the car door. I could not trust my own ears—my world was once again shattered. I had to be alone so I insisted that my parents-in-law go home. Dejectedly I stood on the threshold of the front door and scanned the empty flat. Such an elegant home—did it not have any meaning at all for Marcus? I trusted him and I was willing to forgive him. We had moved mountains to be together but what happened to our devotions for each other? What did I do that was so wrong? Mechanically I checked on Jackie and went into our bedroom. I stumbled onto our bed and beating the pillows with my clenched fists I moaned. I wanted to wait for Marcus but I knew I shouldn't. I should talk to him with a cool head. I needed to sleep but sleep escaped me. I sat on the bed and searched for a bottle of pills that were put in the drawer of the bedside table. Doctor Wong had prescribed these sleeping pills for me in case I needed them. When I found the bottle, with trembling hands, I swallowed two pills and fresh tears covered my face. Soon I fell into a deep slumber. The bright sunshine and the muffled voices of the maids woke me. I reached out for

Marcus but his side of the bed was empty. To my absolute disgust and horror he did not come home to sleep. I was hoping that I had a nightmare and when I woke Marcus would be sleeping next to me but I was mistaken. I staggered into the bathroom and was shocked with my own reflection in the mirror. I groaned and muttered to myself, *'No wonder your husband left you for another! Your face is swollen from crying— there are black smudges underneath your eyes. Your hair is disheveled— you are forcing your husband into some else's arms.'* I had a quick shower and I was beautifully groomed again.

I tended to Jackie's needs then asked the nurse to take her for a walk. I went to visit Jeffrey and Violet. "I have a favor to ask of you," I said to my parents-in-law.

Jeffrey asked anxiously, "Melanie, are you all right? I am so ashamed of Marcus—what can I say or what can I do to help?"

Sitting on the settee and nervously twisting the handkerchief that I was clutching in my hands, I muttered, "I'd rather you didn't say anything to Marcus or my parents. I don't want him to be aware that I know he has been seeing Beth. A confrontation will be fatal—he will leave me! I don't want history to repeat itself. If Carmine had not confronted him he wouldn't have left her. If I give him enough time and freedom, he will come back to me. I know that he still loves me. I have to be patient," I pleaded.

Waving his hands Jeffrey interrupted, "And in the meantime can you bear the pain and anguish of sharing him with someone else? Will you wait for him to return at night? Are you sure that you can manage?"

I swallowed my tears and pride and whispered, "I don't have a choice—I have to try—I have to give our marriage a chance—I just can't let go. If I am convinced that I have given us every possible chance and I still cannot save the marriage then I will leave with no regrets."

"But Marcus' behavior is atrocious and cruel. To have to endure the misery of sharing your husband is inhuman—don't inflict such pain on yourself—I don't want your faith in human relationship destroyed. There are decent people around." Violet voiced her opinion.

"Please, promise me...give me an opportunity to salvage my marriage."

The days were long but the nights were even longer. I was lonely and I was desperate for help. I restrained myself from complaining. I prayed that with my patience Marcus would return to me. I tried to lead a normal life and pretended that nothing was amiss. My existence was a constant charade and pretense.

It was my birthday. I had prepared a special meal for Marcus hoping that he would come home for dinner. To my utter disappointment he did not return home and ignored my numerous phone calls. I was desperate for company so I invited Sui Fong out for dinner. We decided to celebrate my birthday with a bottle of wine. Sui Fong searched my haggard face, "I don't know where you find the courage. I must say, looks can be so deceiving—you look so fragile and yet your will power is as strong as steel. Are you never going to confront Marcus?"

I smiled bitterly. "I don't want to put any pressure on him. I am hoping that Beth is content with just being Marcus' mistress. I don't want to be the one to give him the ultimatum."

Sui Fong took my hand and interrupted, "Marcus can't be so hopelessly naive to believe that he can keep the cake and eat it as well. There is only that much that you can take—I hope he is not going to take you for granted. I know you so well. When you decide that you have had enough you will go and nothing that Marcus or anyone can do to detain you."

I whispered, "I hope that day will never come."

Sui Fong and I parted company and I returned to a lonely home. Jackie was asleep so I went into my bed room. Lately insomnia became my partner and the sleeping pills were my salvation. I took two pills and lay in bed. I closed my eyes but sleep evaded me. The pills did not have any effect on my troubled mind and I was unable to find peace. Vaguely I remembered pouring some more pills into my palms and throwing them into my mouth. The taste was bitter. I still couldn't sleep. I wanted some fresh air so I decided to go for a drive. I grabbed my keys from the table. I remembered kissing Jackie and rushing out of the door. I backed the car out of the parking lot and drove the car onto the main road. Pressing my foot on the accelerator, I headed toward Shek-O Beach. I wanted to visit the beach that Gavin and I used to go to. I needed some sweet memory from my childhood to remind myself that life was still worth living. Tears started to blind my focus. The numerous sleeping pills were beginning to have an effect on me. I was losing concentration...suddenly, there was a blinding light in front of me—I heard a loud crush and the darkness welcomed me.

Consciousness returned to me but my whole body ached. My head was aching and the pain was almost unbearable. Vaguely I heard Mother's voice, "She should never have been allowed to mix sleeping pills with alcohol. She was lucky that she didn't kill herself or the other driver. She must have lost control completely! Why else would she have driven into the other car head on? She obviously didn't realize that she was driving on the wrong side of the road."

Sui Fong was sobbing. "I shouldn't have left her last night! I am to be blamed. She should not have been left on her own. I honestly thought Marcus would be home when I left her. Has anyone contacted him?"

Came Cedric's voice, "Uncle Jeffrey had sent the chauffeur to Beth's home. He did not go home to sleep last night, the bastard!"

I cringed—I didn't want to open my eyes. I wanted to sleep again because only in my sleep would I find peace. The door to the room was pushed opened and Marcus rushed in, "How is she? Melanie, are you all right?" He took my hand.

"Where were you last night when she needed you most?" Mother was crying and demanded an explanation. "She could have been killed!"

Sui Fong intervened, "Auntie Wei Ling, now is not the proper time for a confrontation."

Jeffrey softly whispered dejectedly, "Look at your wife…she is lying in a hospital bed—deathly pale and hardly breathing. Her head is bandaged and there are cuts and bruises all over her body—what do you have to say for yourself?"

Marcus cried, "Melanie, my love, please forgive me—give me another chance—I will not cheat on you again—I am still your husband."

Hearing Marcus' voice my eyes fluttered and I whispered, "Just stay with me—please—don't leave me!" My eyes closed again.

During my remaining days in the hospital Marcus stayed by my bedside faithfully. He promised me that he would never hurt me again. He had almost lost me and had no intention of risking my life. When I was released from the hospital, I was assisted onto my own bed. It felt strange for me to be in my own room again. When I saw the bottle of sleeping pills on the bedside table I shuddered and my eyes started to mist with tears. How could I be so foolish? If I had been killed, Jackie would be without a mother! How could I do it to my only child? Jackie was only a year old and she deserved more from life. My eyes were getting heavy and I dozed off.

The phone was jingling I wanted to answer but I was too exhausted.

The ringing persisted so mustering all my strength I picked up the receiver then I heard Marcus's voice, "I thought I told you not to call me at home! Melanie just returned from the hospital. Don't you have any decency?"

A woman's voice drifted into my ears, "But I have missed you terribly! When are you coming to see me? I haven't seen you since Melanie was admitted into the hospital…."

There was a slight pause then Marcus' voice, "I have promised

Melanie that I wouldn't see you anymore...."

I heard the vehement reply, "How would you like me to stage my own suicide? Will you then return to me?"

"Don't jump to the wrong conclusion. Melanie did not try to take her own life." I heard Marcus' defensive tone of voice.

Beth warned. "Marcus, as much as I love you I will not wait forever."

Marcus' imploring voice was burning my ears, "Why can't you be content just being with me? Why do you want me to choose between you and Melanie? I can't give up Melanie—she has been too good to me, but I want you as well."

Suddenly something inside me snapped. Calmly I left the receiver on the bed and slowly walked into the living room. Marcus was still talking on the phone. It had taken me one whole year to accept my fate and finally I came to a final conclusion. If Marcus returned to me he would always miss Beth as she represented the forbidden fruit. If I left Marcus then maybe he would cherish my memory. I was desperate for his affection but I didn't want him on those terms. When I walked toward Marcus and he saw the anguished and determined look on my face, I wondered if he knew that he had lost me forever, "Marcus, it's over—it's too late. I am returning your freedom to you—you can go to Beth! I am too exhausted to fight!"

Marcus pleaded with me, "Melanie, can't we talk? Will you not give me another chance? Even if it's for the sake of Jackie?" He searched my face for compassion.

"I'd rather divorce you now because Jackie is still too young to understand—I don't want her to hate you. If we carry on like this we will still be divorced a few years down the road. By then it will be too awful for Jackie because she would have grown too fond of you. You have been extremely fortunate that Nathan does not resent me, but I cannot guarantee Jackie's reaction. We have come to the end of the road—let us part as friends. Don't rob me of my pride."

I did not sleep in the room that I had shared with Marcus again. The pain was too deep. Instead I moved into the guest room.

Forty-Five

I was overcome by a wave of sadness when I stood in the reception room of Anthony Pickering's office. How many years ago did I work at one of those secretarial desks? I could still visualize my head buried in heaps of paperwork. Mr. Pickering came out from his office and beckoned me to join him. When the door was closed, I rushed into his protective arms. Was it possible that I was in his office in the capacity of a client? Who was going to take my divorce statement? I sat on the chair and gazed into the far distance. I heard myself muttereing, "Anthony, I have made a mess of my life—please sort it out for me—I want a simple divorce—no fuss and no complications. Marcus can decide what would be fair for Jackie and myself. I believe that Marcus is moving out at the end of the week but he can see his daughter whenever it is convenient for him."

"I don't suppose it would do much good if I ask you to reconsider?" Mr. Pickering tapped the pen on his palm and searched my face. "I know it has been awful for you and Marcus does not deserve any sympathy but what about your own happiness?"

I blinked back the tears and swallowed hard. "I am thinking of my own happiness! I am still young and I want to live again. I have to be on my own in order that I can find peace. It would be difficult and impossible to proceed with my own life when I can't get Marcus out of my system. In time I should be able to love again. I know that I will never forget him, but I can learn to forgive. I can't do more than what I have done already. I don't know how I have failed Marcus." After a slight pause I continued. "I guess I was born to be a loser. I don't want to be a failure and I definitely don't need fingers pointing at me. I can just see the sneer directed at me but I can't live for others. I am myself and I have to find myself again."

Finally it was agreed that Mr. Pickering would attend to all the legal details. Then I found myself in Jeffrey's office. With dry eyes I told Jeffrey of my decision for a divorce. My father-in-law paced the floor and sighed, "I can't honestly say that I didn't expect this outcome, but I just wished that you had agreed to us talking to Marcus."

"He is a grown man and he makes his own decision. We can't influence him in anyway. He has to be responsible for his own actions. It is pointless for me to have the man if I can't have his love and devotion. I have tried to survive with half-measured love, but I can't do it. I love Marcus too much to share him—it has to be all or nothing."

Nodding his head in agreement Jeffrey asked, "Do you have any plans for the future?"

I thought for a while and replied hesitantly, "I would like to get away for a while."

Jeffrey sat on the edge of his desk with his legs dangling he suggested, "Why don't you take a short holiday? Violet and I will take care of Jackie. When you come back, you may feel differently."

I looked deep into Jeffrey's kind face and responded with honesty, "I don't intend to go away for a holiday. I would like to return to England with Jackie. I want to pick up the pieces of my shattered life and start anew. I believe I will stand a better chance in England—Hong Kong brings back too many bitter memories."

Jeffrey resumed his pacing and after a long pause he sighed, "You know that we will miss you and Jackie desperately, but I agree with you. Try and start a new life. You don't have to worry about money. I will make certain that you are well provided for...."

Gratefully I smiled at Jeffrey and insisted, "I appreciate your offer but I want to make it on my own—send me whatever you think it's reasonable to maintain Jackie and I will take care of myself. I have a pair of hands and a good education; therefore, I shouldn't starve!"

I was talking to my parents and my mother attempted to reason with me, "What are you going to do in England? How can you make a living and look after Jackie? It would be too difficult!"

"Mum, if there is a world then there is a way." I stood by the window and sighed.

Father interrupted, "You and Jackie are very welcome to come back to live with us."

I returned my gaze to my father and smiled, "Thank you for the offer but I have to be on my own. I have to prove to myself that I am not a failure."

Mother intervened with indignation, "Melanie, you have not failed! If anything Marcus has failed you."

I took Mother's hand and kissed it gently. "Don't say that, Mum, Marcus has not failed me. Let's just say that we have come to the end of the road. His affection for me has deteriorated and I am disappointed but in time I will only remember the good times." With a bitter smile I continued, "We did have some pretty good times together!"

Father interrupted, "If you have made up your mind then we aren't going to interfere. Why don't you contact Peter? He is married now and I am sure he will keep an eye on you. If ever you find that life is too tough you know that you always have a home in Hong Kong."

It was awfully lonely and depressing for me to remain in the flat with Jackie. I was in tears persistently. How much more tears did I have to shed I asked myself constantly. In the afternoons I would wander around town aimlessly, sometimes I would have Jackie with me. On one of these afternoons, I was window shopping with Jackie and from the reflection in the shop window, I noticed a familiar figure watching me. I slowly turned around and standing in front of me was Raphael and with him was a young lady. He asked hesitantly, "You are Melanie, aren't you?"

I was overjoyed to see him. Grabbing his arm I shrieked, "Raphael, what are you doing here? You should be in Canada!"

"I have brought my family to Hong Kong for a holiday. Meet my wife Gloria." Pushing his wife forward he lifted the young boy off his shoulder, "And this is my son, Malcom!" Turning toward Jackie, who was clinging shyly to my hand and watching us with her beautiful big round eyes. "This must be your daughter. She is a replica of you—we heard that you are married."

I smiled and cajoled my young daughter. "Jackie say hello to Uncle Raphael and his wife Auntie Gloria. Also, shake hands with this gorgeous looking young boy, Malcom." Smiling shyly, Jackie put her small hand in Malcom's hand. "Have you seen Cedric and Sui Fong? I don't think they know that you are in town!"

"No, I haven't had time to contact anyone! Why don't you arrange a get-together dinner with your family? Here's my number." He scribbled a number on a scrap of paper and gave it to me.

Immediately I returned home with Jackie and called Sui Fong. I told her that I had something important to discuss with her and invited her for coffee. She suggested meeting me in the Clipper Lounge but I declined. I was in fear of walking into Marcus and Beth. Since he had moved out to live with Beth, I hadn't seen them and I didn't want to. When Sui Fong arrived, excitedly I blurted, "Guess who I bumped into in town earlier on?"

Sui Fong screwed her noise and guessed, "Don't tell me—Marcus!"

My face dropped immediately, "No! Raphael is in town with his family. I was introduced to his wife and son. He wants to have a reunion dinner. Will you make the necessary arrangements and choose the restaurant?"

Sui Fong shook her head cheekily, "Why me? You have always been an expert with organizing these sort of things."

Sadly I responded dejectedly, "I have lost my magic touch! Everything I touch seems to turn sour on me these days."

Sui Fong reprimanded, "What an appalling attitude."

I took Sui Fong's hand and implored, "When you are making the arrangement for the dinner, please, ask my family not to let Raphael know that I will be leaving town and that I am divorcing Marcus."

Sui Fong was baffled by my request, "Why the big secret?"

With determination I replied stubbornly, "If Raphael knows, then Gavin would know. I rather he didn't know." Sui Fong opened her mouth to object but I stopped her. "Please listen to me—please—I have my reasons. I only have my pride left."

Arriving in the restaurant where I was to meet Raphael, I was magnificently dressed. There was a sedate smile on my face but the sparkle had disappeared from my once smiling eyes. I had not aged in appearance, instead I looked more elegant with my maturity but mentally I had aged immensely. Everyone was excited about seeing Raphael and in the midst of the chatter and laughter our out of town guest inquired about my husband. There was an embarrassing silence and all eyes turned toward me expectantly.

Proudly I lifted my shoulders and lied. "He is out of own on a business trip."

During dinner Cedric asked, "How is Gavin?"

I cringed inwardly then came Raphael's reply, "He is well! As a matter of fact he is getting married next month. He did ask me to convey his regards if I should get a chance to see you. By the way, Melanie, he wanted me to wish you all the best." In a tiny voice I whispered my thanks.

I was in the restroom with Sui Fong and she confronted me bluntly, "I don't have the foggiest idea what goes on in that brain of yours! Why don't you want Gavin to know that you are returning to England?"

I grabbed Sui Fong's shoulders and hissed, "Did you not hear Raphael was saying that Gavin would be married next month? This should be the happiest time of his life! Why burden him with my misfortune? I belong to his yesterday! There are certain things that should be left unsaid. Believe me—Sui Fong—this is for the best."

When we were leaving the restaurant Raphael took me aside and whispered, "You are still very much in Gavin's thoughts. Do come and visit us—we would like to meet your husband."

I kissed Raphael gently on the cheek and bravely replied, "I will. I promise."

Raphael would have been horrified if he had known that shortly I would be starting a new life in England...alone with my young daughter, and divorced.

Forty-Six

Jackie stood on the chair and leaned against the dining table. She blew the four candles on her birthday cake while her three young friends cheered on. My daughter had grown to be an extremely pretty child and she loved the simple English way of life. She was put in a day nursery since our arrival in London; therefore, she was not in lack of friends.

I began my life as a working girl again. Mr. Pickering very kindly introduced me to a lawyer friend of his who had a small practice outside London, and I became his assistant. No longer a lady of leisure, my days were full and I had no time to miss the glamorous Hong Kong life style. Constantly kept occupied with my job; caring for Jackie and attending to the housework, I hardly had time to dwell in my past. I didn't allow myself to live with regrets. Jeffrey and Violet visited us once and so did my parents. They wanted us to return to Hong Kong but I declined. I was enjoying my simple and peaceful life in London. I had a terrific job; a beautiful daughter and my books became my companions. I was contented. Marcus had married Beth but I remained single. I had learned to exist independently without any further involvement. I did not need the complication of sharing my life with another person. Marcus was still very much in my thoughts.

One evening while I was preparing dinner for Jackie and myself the phone rang. Mother's voice echoed over the static, "Melanie, your father is in the hospital—he has suffered a mild stroke...."

I was worried and anxious, "Is he O.K.?"

Came Mother's reply, "He is recovering..." There was a pause and then I heard Mother's voice again, "Melanie, why don't you consider returning home? We do worry about you!"

It had been a while since I had last seen my parents so I suggested, "Mum, why don't I bring Jackie home for a visit. We can discuss the matter further."

Once again I found myself standing in the corridor of Cannosa Hospital searching for the Intensive Care Unit and did not see the doctor walking toward me. He stopped in front of me and our eyes met. I was certain that I had seen those eyes before, and I knew the face but I couldn't quite put a name to the smiling face. Seeing my puzzle expression the doctor asked, "Melanie, don't you remember me? I am Ray—we were neighbors when we were kids." Hoping to jolt my memory he continued, "I am Yvette's brother."

A smile appeared on my face immediately and I smacked my forehead, "Of course! Of course! How can I forget? How stupid of me! But how can you recognize me? We have lost contact for so many years."

"When your father was admitted into the hospital, I happened to be on duty that night. I recalled the name and wondered if it's the same Uncle Edwin that I knew...so I introduced myself. Your mother has put a photo of you and your daughter by his bedside. I must say your daughter has inherited your good looks!" Ray beamed at me, obviously he was happy to see me again.

"Thank you for the compliment but I think she looks more like her father. She is really a lovely girl and I am very proud of her."

Ray escorted me into Father's room. As soon as Father saw me he was overjoyed. I hugged him and kissed his forehead affectionately. I was happy to see that he was on the road to recovery. I pulled the chair closer to the bed and took his hand into mine. Father searched my face and said, "I am so happy that you are home. We have been concerned about you. You will make me an extremely happy man if you return from your life of exile. Surely, three years should be a long enough period for you to recuperate from your divorce. The wound should have healed by now."

I hugged Father again and I blinked back the tears. Hesitantly, Father continued, "Look kid, the daughter of a friend of mine started an employment agency. Then she decided to get married and moved to the States. My friend doesn't know a thing about employment agencies and yet he doesn't want to sell the agency. Apparently it is very successful. He heard of your return and would very much like you to run the operation for him. This would be a terrific opportunity for you. Why don't you consider his proposal?"

I thought for a while and said, "His proposal is definitely tempting and the position sounds challenging."

Father took my hand and stubbornly insisted, "Come home and live with us. Your mother is full of energy! Let her take care of Jackie. It would be good for Jackie to have a family around her again. Jeffrey and Violet would be pleased to have their granddaughter back in town."

The mention of my parents-in-law brought on a frown. Even though I had been divorced for more than three years I never lost my fondness for the elderly couple, "How are they?"

"They came to visit me and I guess you know that Marcus married Beth soon after your departure to England, but I hear that they are not too happy! Nathan is not too fond of Beth and she doesn't seem to get along with Jeffrey and Violet. Sometimes I sympathize with the poor girl...it's not an easy task to walk in your shadow. You had set very high standards for yourself and you were almost a perfectionist. After you left, Marcus with Beth, returned to your old home. They retained the same maids so it must be awfully difficult for her. I would hate to be in her shoes. She is constantly reminded of you."

I dabbed the tears from the corner of my eyes and sighed, "She wanted Marcus and she succeeded, so there should be no further complaints!"

Father shook his head and inquired, "Have you forgiven Marcus?"

I looked at Father and sadly I replied, "I have forgiven him but I don't think I can forget...it was a bitter pill to swallow."

Patting my hand Father wanted to know. "Don't you think about your own future? Don't you want to meet another young man and remarry?"

I gazed out of the window and whispered, "Once bitten twice shy! May be someday but not in the near future."

After much convincing and encouragement from the family I accepted the offer to operate the agency for my father's friend. I returned to Hong Kong with Jackie and moved in with my parents. I dedicated myself to my new responsibilities as the office manager of the employment agency. I was new to the trade so I had much to learn. Jackie was delighted with the attention that was bestowed on her from her grandparents. Marcus would collect her every weekend but each time I had made excuses not to be home. I still could not bring myself to see him.

I had made arrangements to meet Sui Fong and Cedric for a drink and she insisted on going to the Clipper Lounge. She didn't think that I should hide forever. I had a rough day in the office. I wanted to leave early so I tidied my desk and left for the hotel half an hour earlier than the arranged time. I picked up a magazine from the vendor on the street and made my way to the hotel. I was flipping through the pages of the magazine when I heard a familiar voice...a voice that had haunted me for so long. I removed my attention from the pages and the magazine slide off my hand. I bent to retrieve the magazine from the floor, simultaneously Marcus made the same movement and our faces collided. I felt a shock trembled through my body. Automatically I straightened myself and Marcus caught my hand. I yanked my hand away from his burning touch and with aloofness I acknowledged his presence.

Without my invitation Marcus sat on the chair next to mine and remarked, "It has been a long time..." Scrutinizing my appearance he chuckled, "So calm and collected—the perfect image of a successful career woman. I heard through the grapevine that you are doing extremely well. Do you mind if I buy you a drink?"

I shrugged my shoulders and replied nonchalantly, "If you insist."

When the drinks were ordered Marcus said, "I see your taste in drinks and perfume have not changed."

I chose to ignore his remark. When an answer was not forthcoming he continued, "I have missed you tremendously. Each time I went to collect Jackie I hoped to see you but you were never around. She reminds me so much of you!"

I lifted my shoulders and remained silent. I was trying desperately to control my mixed emotions. How could I still feel so much for this man? After all the hurt that he had inflicted on me and after all these years? Why couldn't life be kinder to me? Not discouraged by my silence Marcus blurted, "Return to me Melanie and let's try again!"

I couldn't believe what I had heard. I hissed my reply, "Are you going to divorce Beth and marry me again or do you want me to become your mistress?" Laughing bitterly I continued, "You can't afford to divorce Beth...it will be too expensive even for your standard! Nowadays divorced children are a dime a dozen. Jackie is no different from any child from a broken family, but it would be odd and embarrassing for her if I agree to become your mistress after our divorce. Even if I agree to give us another chance I can't subject her to this humiliation. Too much water has gone under the bridge and we can't rewrite history. I will make certain that you do not play a part in my future—I have my own identity and my self-respect!"

Marcus took my hand and pleaded, "I can understand your bitterness but I still love you and I know that you still have feelings for me! Why can't we try again?"

I crossed and recrossed my legs nervously. "When you started your involvement with Beth you should have considered the consequences. You took me too much for granted! I loved you so very much and your unfaithfulness almost killed me. It took a lot of courage for me to leave you. I refuse to be subjected to your rejection again. I have stopped dreaming the impossible dream. Let's just say that I have matured!"

Marcus pleaded, "I didn't know that you played such an important part in my life until you were gone...."

I interrupted impatiently, "You married Beth soon enough!"

Marcus countered, "I thought that I loved her."

I spat my next comment at him. "You don't know the meaning of that word. You want me now because you can't have me but if I return to you I would only be discarded again." I shook my head vehemently and continued. "Marcus you will never be happy because you don't know how to love. You only know how to possess." I was happy that I was provided with this opportunity to exorcise the shadows from my past.

"So...meeting secretly! Why don't the two of you find a more discreet place to meet? Do you have to wave your dirty linens in public? There are backstreet hotels." Beth shrieked with her high pitch tone.

Sui Fong arrived and heard Beth's outburst. She was aghast with Marcus' wife's behavior. She screwed her noise in distaste and took a seat. I had enough insults from Marcus' women so grabbing Sui Fong's hand I said sarcastically, "The air is beginning to stink—let's change tables!"

Without a backward glance I walked away. Cedric arrived and I could hear Sui Fong's angry complaint, "I hope the two of you will burn in hell! Haven't you caused the poor girl enough pain—why don't you leave her alone? As for you Beth, serves you right! You dug your own grave and now you can damn well lie in it!" Sui Fong put her arms around my shoulders and I haltered my steps.

Marcus turned to Cedric and sighed, "Sui Fong is right! Melanie has suffered enough." Then he warned Beth, "Don't give Melanie a hard time! She has taken enough from you, so be satisfied with your conquest."

"I refused to walk in her shadow any more!" Beth screeched.

Cedric looked at her with hatred in his eyes and jeered, "Don't compare yourself with Melanie—you are not good enough to be her shadow!"

When we reached the lobby of the hotel I was sobbing uncontrollably, "Are you O.K.?" Sui Fong put her arms around my trembling shoulders.

I wiped the tears with the back of my hand and I vowed, "I am fine! I apologize for my outburst but I have had enough! I am glad that I was able to have that confrontation with them. Now I can live again and I will. " Beaming I took a couple of deep breaths and lifted my slumped shoulders.

When I opened the front door I heard Mother's voice, "Melanie, is that you?"

I yelled my reply, "I have brought Sui Fong and Cedric home for dinner! I hope you don't mind."

Smiling Mother asked us to join her in the living room, "Not at all! You know your father always enjoys your company. By the way, Ray just called. Apparently his sister Yvette who has taken up residence in Vancouver is here on holiday. They are having a party for her tomorrow night and Ray would like you to join them. I accepted on your behalf!"

"O.K. Mum!" I kissed Mother affectionately on both cheeks and winked at Sui Fong, "Mum is worried that I don't have any dates!" I teased and hugged Mother's shoulders lovingly.

The following evening, looking my best, I arrived at Ray's home just before dinner was served. I was introduced to his charming wife. When I saw Yvette, we rushed into each other's arms. I was thrilled to see my childhood friend. Hand in hand we walked into the balcony and exchanged news. Smiling, my friend insisted, "Come and visit me in Vancouver—you will love it! It is the perfect city for you. I live on my own and there is plenty of room! I would like you to stay with me."

I took Yvette's hand and promised, "I will take you up on the invitation one day. There are people living in Vancouver that I would like to see again!"

We returned to the living room and sitting on the settee Yvette asked curiously, "You have friends living in Vancouver?"

Smiling I replied, "As a matter of fact you also know them. Do you remember the two brothers who used to visit us when we were neighbors?"

"Sure! Gavin and Raphael! I thought they were in England." Yvette stretched her legs and crossed her ankles.

"No! They emigrated to Vancouver many years ago," I Replied

Yvette thought for a while and exclaimed, "Come to think of it, I think you are right! A friend of mine is a close friend of the Fernados family. I thought I knew the name but I couldn't make the connection. My friend told me that one of them is divorced. In fact she wanted me to meet him. I wonder which one is divorced...Raphael or Gavin...?"

I was praying that it wasn't Gavin.

During dinner I sat next to one of Ray's colleagues. Terry was a doctor from England. He arrived in Hong Kong a few years ago with his wife. Their marriage did not survive the glamorous society of Hong Kong and they became victims of another divorce. The wife subsequently returned to England. Terry had a witty personality and a sense of humor. His jokes amused me and he managed to make everyone laugh throughout the entire evening.

It was time to thank our hosts and call it an evening because we all had to work the next day. Terry asked to see me again and why not? I agreed!

Forty-Seven

Terry had an amiable personality and he was a brilliant doctor. Absolutely dedicated to his work he was extremely popular with his patients. I was impressed by his abilities and we were compatible in many ways. There were evenings when I had to work late in the office and he would wait for me, hardly ever uttered any complaints. Patiently he would wait for me then invite me for dinner.

It was Saturday. We were visiting my parents and after dinner I asked Sui Fong to accompany me to Stanley Beach. I loved walking on the beach in the early evening when the sky was pink and the sun was a ball of fire fading into the horizon. I picked up some pebbles and threw them into the water. Sui Fong watched me for a while then she asked, "You have been seeing Terry quiet often—anything serious?"

I removed my gaze from the ocean and patted my hands to get rid of the sand. I sat on the sand and Sui Fong joined me. Hesitantly I replied, "Terry is a talented doctor and he seems to be kind. I suppose he would be a perfect candidate for a husband...but somehow...there is something about him that bothers me...he seems too good to be true. Anyway, ours is not what you may call a glittering affair. I don't feel any sparkle when I am with him. I guess I am overly sentimental, but something is definitely missing in our relationship."

Sui Fong crossed her legs and hugged her knees. Thoughtfully she remarked, "He seems to be fond of Jackie and he has become extremely popular with your family. Your parents like him!"

I nodded my head in agreement and smiled, "I know…if I should decide to remarry, my parents would think that he is a good choice and I can most certainly count on their blessings. But I still feel that I need more time."

Taking my hand Sui Fong brushed away the hair that covered half of my face. With sincerity she advised, "You have to seriously consider marriage again."

I was amused with her remark so teasingly I challenged, "Why is it so important for a woman to be married?" Abruptly I changed the subject and our topic of conversation was diverted.

Yvette was returning to Vancouver. Her short holiday turned out to be a six-month stay in Hong Kong. Before her departure I invited her for dinner. When the dirty plates were cleared away and we were waiting for our coffee I took her hand and insisted, "Yvette, we must keep in touch. I agree that I am not a good correspondent but I promise I will try to improve."

Squeezing my hand gently Yvette nodded her head and suggested, "You must come to visit me—you will love Vancouver!"

When the coffee was served, I added cream and sugar. Stirring the coffee I reminded my childhood friend, "When you return home you must try and contact Gavin or Raphael. They are extremely kind and warmhearted—especially Gavin. If you ever need a helping hand I am certain they will be obliging." After a slight pause I added, "After all, you hardly have any relatives in Vancouver."

Suddenly changing the subject Yvette inquired, "How are you getting along with Terry? Ray told me that you are seeing quite a bit of him!"

I shrugged my shoulders and played with the coffee spoon. "We do spent time together and I enjoy his company. He seems to be a nice man but somehow I feel that he is hiding something from me—some sort of a secretive past. He wouldn't discuss it with me. Each time I attempt to bring the subject up he would craftily divert my attention and change the subject."

Yvette thought for a while, then lifting her shoulders, she seemed to have come to a decision. "Don't let on that I have told you but Terry had a drinking problem. Apparently his wife couldn't handle his drinking habit and left."

I was appalled with the revelation. Immediately I asked, "How can he have a drinking problem if he is a doctor?" I was thoughtful, then I continued, "I thought all doctors are not supposed to drink; therefore, I was not surprised when he didn't drink anything alcoholic. I wasn't suspicious at all—I just took it for granted that he is a conscientious doctor. Doctors have to be alert constantly especially when they are on duty…you could have fooled me! Why didn't Ray tell me?"

Yvette drank her coffee then sighed, "I guess my brother is hoping that Terry's drinking problem is only a temporary setback. Obviously he is disciplining himself. I don't want to be a trouble-maker. I just thought that you should know." I was grateful that my friend chose to be honest with me.

Terry and I had been dating for two years and he had proposed marriage on a few occasions but I declined. I had hoped that he would be honest with me. I needed to discuss his drinking habit before I was able to make another commitment. During this time Terry showed no signs of being an alcoholic; therefore, I had no reason to confront him.

One evening during dinner Mother casually asked, "Melanie, you have been dating Terry for two years…don't you think you should seriously consider marriage?"

Father patted Mother's hand and interrupted, "Wei Ling, Melanie is a grown woman. She knows what she is doing. Don't put any pressure on her!"

Playing with the rice in the bowl with the chopsticks, hesitantly I whispered, "Dad, it's O.K.! We can certainly talk about my future but I will make the final decision. I don't think it's the proper time for Terry and myself to discuss marriage."

Mother was puzzled. "Are you concealing something from us? Two years is a long time—don't you feel enough for the doctor to consider a life-time commitment?"

I looked at my parents expectant faces and decided to be honest. "I admire his work—he is indeed a kind person and I can see a splendid future ahead of him but are these all the proper ingredients for a sound marriage? I feel that something is missing in our relationship." I paused. Deciding that perhaps it was the opportune time for me to voice my fear and suspicion I blurted, "Terry had a drinking problem."

Father frowned and voiced his opinion, "All doctors drink in Hong Kong—although they are not supposed to—they need the drinks to release their tension. We all drink and certainly a few drinks are harmless."

I looked at Father and exclaimed, "I know we all drink but what bothers me is that Terry doesn't drink at all."

"I fail to see your reasoning! If Terry doesn't drink, then why do you say that he has a drinking problem?"

Dejectedly and nervously I tapped my fingers on the table and replied, "I am saying that he did have a problem. He seems to have cured it but what if he should start again?"

The maid had cleared the table. Mother sat on the settee and started to peel an orange. Father was pacing the floor thoughtfully. After a moment of silence, he smiled encouragingly, "I don't see any reason for Terry to resume his bad habit. He is enjoying a successful career. If he hasn't touched an alcoholic drink in two years, chances are he won't do it again."

Father's words made sense. Maybe I was overly cautious and suspicious or was I trying to find a reason to justify my own action when I refused Terry's proposal repeatedly? I realized that it was the right time to settle down again. I was getting too old to chase rainbows. I needed stability and I should stop searching for undying love and devotion. I decided that I was better off to be loved than to love.

I was working late again. Terry collected me from the office and we agreed to have a quick meal before he took me home. The candle was flickering on the table and nervously Terry played with his glass of lime and soda. His eyes smiled and with hesitancy he murmured, "Melanie, I will be changing jobs next month. I have resigned from my current position and I will be joining a bigger practice. The hours will be longer but the work will be more demanding and challenging. Also my income will be increased immensely." He paused and waited for a reply.

I shrugged my shoulders then tenderly I patted his hand and responded encouragingly, "I will support your decision as long as you are going to be happy and content with the changes."

Terry took my hand and searched my face appealingly. Haltingly he said, "We have been together for more than two years now. Don't you think it's time we make our relationship official? I am extremely fond of Jackie and I believe the feeling is mutual."

I waited for Terry to continue. I wanted him to talk about his drinking habit but there was silence. I was disappointed. I prompted with my next question, "If we are to be married then we shouldn't have any secrets between us! Is there something that you would like to discuss with me?"

Nervously Terry looked away and softly he replied, "I guess sooner or later you would confront me. I gather you are aware that I had a drinking problem?"

Nodding my head I encouraged him to continue. "I used to be a bad drunk. After a few drinks I had a tendency to turn violent. I have therefore ceased drinking completely." He took my hand and assured me, "I have managed to curb my nasty habit. I don't see why I can't continue to do so! I promise you—I will not touch anything alcoholic again!"

I had no reason to doubt Terry. Although sometimes I had an awful feeling that I was more of a motherly figure to him than a wife, he needed my assurance and support constantly and I felt protective toward him. I wasn't certain whether it was a healthy sign but I decided to take a gamble again!

The wedding was just a family affair and only the relatives were invited. On the night of the wedding to my disappointment Terry broke his promise to me and became roaring drunk. I had no other choice but to let the matter ride. After all our wedding reception was a joyful occasion and I reckoned that he should be allowed to enjoy himself especially when he wasn't on duty.

After the wedding I plunged into another life style. Married to a doctor was extremely demanding. We would receive phone calls at all hours in the night—patients needed to talk or to see Terry. There were mornings when I found it awfully difficult to get up for work. I was constantly tired due to lack of sleep. Both Terry and I could feel the tension building between us. Thoughtfully Terry made a suggestion, "I am earning pretty good money now—I should become a junior partner soon—why don't you consider resigning from your job and becoming a full-time housewife?"

The thought was tempting, so I resigned. I believed that marriage was a give and take situation so I should be making some sacrifices. Contented with staying at home I savored the luxury of not having to get up in the mornings. But soon my days became long because Terry was working longer hours. There were days when he would not return home until late at night.

On a few occasions I asked Terry if it was absolutely necessary for him to work late he would say that he was in the hospital or had to visit a patient. One night, when I was reading in bed, the phone rang. It was the hospital and they were trying to locate Terry. I suggested that they should page him but I was informed that he wasn't answering his pager. I called the clinic and was told that the doctor had left around six that afternoon. I was puzzled—where was Terry? Then the front door bell rang shrilly and I opened the door. To my horror and disappointment Ray was helping Terry into our flat. Terry was incoherent as he staggered in. Embarrassingly Ray apologized, "I met him in the club and decided that it was dangerous for him to drive so I brought him home."

"Which club?" I was furious.

Ray explained, "Some doctors frequently patron a club in Wanchai. We often go there to discuss our cases and enjoy a few drinks."

Nervously I started to pace the floor, "When did Terry start to drink again?" I needed to know.

"I have seen him in the club a couple of times." Ray fidgeted on the settee.

Muttering I said, "He often came home late and when I asked him he would say that he was either in the hospital or with a patient, and I had no cause to doubt him. Most of the time I was asleep when he came in. When he is on night duty, he usually sleeps in the guest's bedroom so he won't disturb me. Anyway give me a hand to help him into bed and we will talk again tomorrow."

I tried to lift Terry's dead weight from the settee but he resisted. I tried again and Terry screamed obscene languages at me. I was horrified—I had never witnessed such disgusting behavior. I attempted to assist him again and impetuously he slapped me hard across the face and I stumbled. I was stunned and sat motionless on the floor—my face began to sting. Ray offered me a hand and unexpectedly I felt a sharp pain in my stomach. To my distinct revulsion and terror Terry had kicked me—he was behaving like an animal. My screams must have jolted Terry's senses. He got up on his feet and staggered into the guest bedroom. Ray helped me onto a seat and attended to my face.

The next morning a throbbing pain on my face woke me from my troubled sleep. I staggered into the bathroom and was paralyzed with my own reflection in the mirror. One side of my face was bruised and my eye was beginning to swell. I put an ice pack on my burning face and immediately put a call through to Terry, "Do you know what you did last night?"

Expecting an apology from him instead I received an abrupt and rude reply. "I am too busy to talk now—we will talk later!" He hung up.

When Terry returned home that night, he brought with him a big bunch of roses and a box of chocolates. Profusely he begged for my forgiveness and vowed that he would not touch another drop of alcohol. I hoped that his atrocious behavior was an isolated incident. I made excuses not to go out until the bruises had faded from my face. Jackie was curious so I told her that I had an accident.

A few weeks passed by. Terry was still returning home late and the hospital was searching for him frequently. I decided that it was time for me to confront him so one night I waited for him to return. It was almost midnight when I heard the front door opened. Terry staggered into the flat. I offered him a hand but he pushed me and losing my balance I fell. I attempted to stand when I felt a blow hit my face and I stumbled again. Without providing me with another chance to regain my balance Terry kicked me mercilessly. I was feeling dizzy and I was frantic. Fearing for my life I dashed into the bedroom and locked the door. That night sleep eluded me. My body and my face were in an awful lot of pain. What was happening to my life? I had to wake up from this nightmare.

The next morning I refused to leave my bedroom until Terry had left for the clinic. When I was alone, I nervously contacted Ray. I was grateful that he agreed to meet me in our home. When Ray was shown into my room, he was appalled with the blue and purple marks on my face. After examining my stomach he prescribed painkillers and a sedative. I was in shock. Bravely, I blinked back my tears and I implored Ray, "What has become of Terry—why has he started to drink again—what am I supposed to do?"

Seeing my pitiful face Ray told me the truth, "Terry is not coping with the increasing demand and pressures from working for a big practice. He is encountering all sorts of patients. Unfortunately your husband has developed a popularity among the professional girls."

I beseeched Ray and interrupted, "What do you mean by professional girls?"

Ray was embarrassed. Hesitantly he explained, "Women who cater to men's needs...."

"In other words call girls!" I was disgusted.

Nervously Ray crossed and recrossed his legs. He was too ashamed to look me in the eye and softly he replied, "These are high class call girls—hostesses who work in clubs. I have warned Terry not to get involved with these types of people but he is too weak to resist their charms and stupidly he has ignored me. I guess free women and free drinks can be very tempting."

While Ray and I were talking to my utter horror and surprise Mother walked into my bedroom. When she saw my battered face, she was furious. Fretfully she touched my face and demanded an explanation, "This has happened before hasn't it? A few weeks back you lied when you told me that you weren't well; therefore, you made excuses not to see me. You didn't want me to see the bruises." Mother looked at me searchingly. When I was a child, Mother had never raised a hand on me or any of her other children. Our family had never been subjected to violence and brutality. Mother was aghast with her discovery, "Your maid called me this morning. She was woken by your screams last night and she saw Terry hit and kick you. I am going to call your father and I think it's best that you and Jackie should return home with me immediately. You can't live with this animal!" Mother stormed out of the room and contacted Father.

While I was recuperating in my parents' home Sui Fong came to visit me. When she saw me, indignantly, she shrieked, "Melanie, you have to divorce Terry! He is no longer the same person that we used to know. Cedric had seen him a couple of times with some professional girls and they are encouraging him to drink. Cedric didn't want me to tell you but I guess I should have told you."

Engulfed by grief and confusion I muttered, "I trusted him—I never asked where he was or what he was doing! When the hospital could not locate him, I asked Ray repeatedly to cover for him. I was more than pleased and relieved when Ray joined Terry's practice—I never thought he would cheat on me."

Sui Fong pulled her chair closer to my bed. Taking my battered face into her hands she reasoned with me, "Ray can't cover for him indefinitely. You will never know when he has been drinking—it is just too dangerous to live with a man who is an alcoholic and who has a tendency to turn violent when he is drunk! If he is not careful he will lose his license. Leave him, Melanie, before it is too late! He will destroy you mentally if not kill you first. In any case you can't possibly subject Jackie to this animalistic behavior and it is not healthy for the child!" Sui Fong was shaking my shoulders dramatically.

That weekend Marcus came to collect Jackie from my parent's flat and he insisted on seeing me. When he saw my face he couldn't help but put his arms around me and I cried softly on his shoulder. Stroking my hair tenderly he whispered, "It was easier to compete with another woman—it is impossible to compete with a beer bottle!"

When he was confronted by Father, Terry admitted that his drinking habit was getting out of control but he reassured Dad that he would mend his ways. Later when Father was talking to Mother and me, he stubbornly insisted, "I know Terry will not change—he is too weak in character—regrettably we have all been fooled by him. I am certain that he is an alcoholic. No doubt he drinks during lunch; therefore, his hands shake. Since the unfortunate marriage he has gained so much weight—I don't think he is getting fat but he is bloated with his constant drinking. It is never an easy task to live with an alcoholic. Melanie should not be subjected to such violence."

When I recovered, I insisted that I should return home with Jackie. But Father was dubious with my persistence. "Melanie, you should seriously consider a separation. Unless Terry pulls himself together and stops his drinking you won't have a future with him. I don't want him to hurt you or Jackie."

"Dad, I appreciate your concern but I owe it to myself to have another go at the marriage. I can't afford another divorce. I have to consider my reputation and morally it is not healthy for Jackie. I only wish that the nasty side of Terry's character will not emerge when he is in the presence of Jackie." I shivered. Kissing my parents, I reassured them, "I will be extremely careful and please don't worry about me!" Against my parents' wishes and advice I returned home.

Instead of improving Terry's conduct deteriorated. He no longer crept into the guest room at night. Time and time again he would return home late at night blindly intoxicated and woke the entire household. Creating scene after scene, I was beginning to worry about Jackie's safety. There were too many nights when I had to lock myself in Jackie's room and comforted her.

Two weeks after I returned home Marcus invited me to join him for a cup of coffee. I was nervous—my hands were shaking uncontrollably—I was under too much stress. Searching my face Marcus was concerned, "Have you not been sleeping at night? You look exhausted!"

I attempted a feeble smile and swallowed hard, "I can only sleep with the help of a tranquilizer—my insomnia is getting from bad to worse!"

Marcus took my trembling hands and implored, "I gather it hadn't been easy for you! Look I have a suggestion. Beth will be going away for a six-month holiday. You know that Jackie and I are very close and she adores my parents! Why don't you let Jackie come and stay with us for a while and she can spend more time with my parents? This opportunity would give you a break. I asked her last week and she loved the idea of staying with me."

I bit my lip hard. I was confused and I was in turmoil. I was unable to make any sensible decision. Hesitantly I whimpered, "If she agrees and if your parents don't mind having her around then I think she should stay with you for a while. She is almost eight years old and before we know it she will be growing up and she will be independent. You should enjoy her company while you can." I paused then I added, "I would still want to see her when she is not attending school!"

Patting my hand reassuringly Marcus promised, "You can visit her every day!"

A happy Jackie moved into her father's home. Although I missed my daughter dreadfully, but for the time being, I didn't have to worry about her safety!

Forty-Eight

A letter arrived from Vancouver and it was from Yvette. When I excitedly opened the letter, a photograph fell from the envelope. Retrieving it from the floor, I was startled to see Gavin's handsome face smiling at me from the photo. He had not aged although his attractive face had matured. I started to sob, after seventeen years, he had returned from the past. Sitting on the floor and trembling, hurriedly I read the letter while tears spilt onto the pages.

Dearest Melanie,

Surprise! Surprise! How does it feel to see your childhood sweetheart's face after so many years? I believe it's almost more than seventeen years! I took the photo of Gavin when we were skiing last week—I thought you might like to keep it. When I returned from Hong Kong, I was invited to a friend's for dinner. Surprisingly Gavin was among the guests. We didn't recognize each other but when I was introduced to him immediately I remembered him. I asked if he could recall a girl by the name of Melanie and you should have seen the amazed look on his face—he must have been quite a fan of yours! I told him that I had seen you in Hong Kong just recently and throughout the entire

Return

evening he asked numerous questions about you. For your information, he is the divorced brother and not Raphael. Gavin is now living on his own and I believe is extremely successful with his career. He has been extremely kind, taking me out for dinner every now and then. Although I have a faint suspicion that he is prying for news about you!

    I was horrified when Ray wrote and told me about Terry's nasty behavior! How can you let him ill-treat you that way? I told Gavin and he seemed awfully upset by the news. I think he still cares a great deal for you. Enclosed is his phone number and address. I am certain that he will love to hear from you. Why don't you call him or drop a line? We would love to have you come for a holiday—just for old time's sake! Why don't you seriously consider giving yourself a breathing space? Will be in touch again!

Love, Yvette.

    I sat crossed leg with my hands holding my head. Reminiscing the past, I could remember the fabulous times that I had spent with Gavin. His tenderness, his caring, and his faithful devotion were never far from my thoughts. Why did he have to live on the other side of the world? If only I could reach out and touch him. I could still hear his voice and fleetingly I thought I could feel his lips crushing mine. It would be terrific if his tender touches could caress my face again. I closed my eyes tightly and biting my trembling lips I screwed the letter into a ball. I collapsed and cried. I couldn't afford to dwell in the past and regrets should not be allowed to invade my confused mind. Nevertheless, I cried for my lost friendship and I cried for my misfortunes or were the mishaps my own doing? If Gavin hadn't left for Canada so many moons ago would history be written differently? Would I have made the same mistakes or would my life be different? I asked myself repeatedly.

    That night I waited unsuccessfully till midnight for Terry to come home. I was angry and I was fretful. Suddenly I frantically searched in the waste paper basket for Yvette's crumbled letter. When I found it, I smoothed out the crushed pages and jotted down Gavin's phone number. I put the letter with the photo in my drawer. I waited for another hour for Terry. I started to pace the room and suddenly I stopped. The next moment with determination I put a long distance call through to Gavin. After a few rings he answered, "Hello...."

    I stared into the receiver as if I could see Gavin's face. Then shyly I asked cheekily, "Guess who...?"

    There was a slight pause and Gavin said hesitantly, "Say a few more words...."

I yelled into the receiver, "It's me! You silly billy!" I was laughing and crying spontaneously.

On the other side of the world I thought I could hear a sharp gasp and Gavin's excited voice came on the line again, "I have to be dreaming! It can't be you, kid! It has been such a long time."

I wasn't certain that Gavin could recognize my voice but when he said kid I returned to my golden days of my childhood. He did remember!

"How can you still recognize my voice?" I was curious.

A slight chuckle that sounded like music drifted into my ears, "I see you still ask too many questions—how can anyone forget that unique laugh! Your laugh has haunted me constantly!"

I was sniffing then Gavin teased, "Don't tell me you are still crying!" When I didn't reply he continued, "You are unhappy—Yvette told me! How are you, sweetheart?"

I was sobbing uncontrollably and I couldn't utter a word. Vaguely I heard Gavin said, "Hey! You are wasting a lot of money—long distance calls are expensive—you should be talking instead of crying. I am beginning to think that you don't want to talk to me!" After a slight hesitation, Gavin continued, "Give me your number then hang up. Take a few deep breaths and wash your face. I will call back in half an hour. In any case I need time to recover from the shock. I don't get lovely surprises like this every day! Maybe once in every seventeen years?"

I nodded my head. Foolishly I had forgotten that Gavin couldn't see me. I closed my eyes and I could feel his hand gently stroking my hair.

"What is your number?" Came Gavin's voice. Haltingly I repeated my number then I hung up. I sat on the settee motionless. After a long while I opened my eyes and I inhaled deeply a couple of times. I straightened my slumped shoulders and marched into the washroom to splash cold water on my face. I was smiling at my own reflection in the mirror. Then I started to laugh and I couldn't control my hysterical laughter until the phone rang. Gavin and I chatted for about half an hour! How long would it take to talk about seventeen long years? I promised Gavin that I would consider visiting Vancouver and I also promised to write! That night I fell into a deep slumber without the assistance of sleeping pills.

The following morning I was up very early and excitedly I dialed Sui Fong's number. When she heard my voice she demanded anxiously, "Has Terry hurt you again? Melanie, why are you calling me so early in the morning?"

"Sui Fong...." I said with exhilaration and there was a hint of laughter from my excited voice, "I have something to tell you...can you meet me for coffee immediately?"

I waited impatiently for Sui Fong to arrive. When I saw her approaching figure, I jumped from my chair and put my arms around her. Sui Fong released herself from my hug then she took my hand and watched my face searchingly, "What brought on this happiness? It's been a while since I have seen such radiance in your face. Please tell me what happened. You are killing me with your silence and I am dying of curiosity!"

I put my shaking hands on my thigh to steady them as I returned to my seat, then I inhaled deeply and blurted, "I spoke to Gavin on the phone last night!"

Sui Fong dropped her cup and spilt coffee all over the table, "What do you mean? You spoke to Gavin last night? Our Gavin?"

My eyes grew round and big. I exclaimed, "The same!" Then I shoved Gavin's photo and Yvette's letter into Sui Fong's hands.

When she had finished reading the letter her eyes were misty. Unshed tears were glittering in her dark eyes and she muttered, "Good old faithful Gavin. I had often wondered what would have happened if you had followed him to Canada. He had never failed you. Whenever you needed him, he had always been there for you. I am convinced that when you were divorcing Marcus and if you had contacted him he would have insisted that you go to Vancouver."

I gazed out of the window and sighed. Stubbornly I insisted, "He was getting married. It would have been unfair to burden him with my problems!"

Sui Fong was shaking my shoulders forcefully, "You have to go and visit him—you owe yourself that much!"

"I can't! Sui Fong, not now.... I have to give my marriage another chance! I can't afford another divorce—mentally or morally!" I whispered dejectedly.

Sui Fong shrieked, "What marriage? You don't owe the bastard Terry anything! If I had my way I would have him arrested a long time ago! You are just too soft and kind-hearted! How can you still feel sorry for him? Sometimes I feel like strangling him with my bare hands. I am sure you are aware that Cedric has refused to talk to him." Sui Fong continued disgustedly, "There is nothing worse than wife-battering—not once—not twice but how many times now? Do you want him to murder you before you are willing to let go? How often do I have to remind you? Your stubbornness will be your ultimate downfall! You just take my words!" Sui Fong angrily wagged her accusing finger at me and warned.

That night although I feigned sleep when Terry came into my room, nevertheless, I was yanked out of bed forcefully. Terry was yelling obscenity, "You God damn cheating bitch!" He pulled my hair and continued to screech, "You have been communicating with your childhood boyfriend—I will kill you!" Then he kicked me with such force that I was thrown across the room and my head hit the wall. He was waving Gavin's photo at my face, "When I came home tonight I found his photo that you have hidden in your dresser..." He tore the photo to shreds.

I tried to stop him and I screamed, "Control your temper and let me explain." Trying to regain my balance I tried to stand on my feet but Terry kicked me repeatedly showing no mercy. I covered myself but the blows and kicks were hitting me like falling rain beating against the window pane. I felt a sharp pain on my face and gratefully I passed out.

When I returned to consciousness the room was spinning and I was staring into unfamiliar surroundings. I heard Mother's soft sobs and Dad was angrily hissing, "I will have the bastard arrested! Melanie would have been killed if the maid had not called the neighbors for help. Terry is an animal—he should be locked up—he is unfit to be living in this world!"

Vaguely I could hear Cedric's steady voice, "Uncle Edwin, control yourself! We will deal with the bum later! Let's attend to Melanie's wounds first!"

Mother's soft agonized question, "What did Ray suggest?"

Came Cedric's whispered reply, "The bruises on her face and body will fade although she will be uncomfortable for a few weeks but the cut on her face is deep. The maid saw him threw a crystal ashtray at her—it only missed her eye by an inch—he could have blinded her. Ray is trying to contact the best plastic surgeon in town. He reckons that Melanie will need a few stitches on her face."

Mother was sobbing again, "This will mean that Melanie will be scarred for life."

"If a skillful surgeon stitches the cut then the scar will begin to fade in a few years time. There is always cosmetic to cover the damaged area on her face." I heard Cedric's assuring reply and I was engulfed with darkness again.

When I came round, my face was bandaged. The pain was numbed by medicine. I was dry-eyed and I couldn't cry—I was beyond tears. Sui Fong was sitting by my bed and gently patting my hand, "Ray gave me Yvette's number and I called her. Gavin phoned earlier and he was extremely worried about you and anxious over your safety! We have decided that when you are well enough to travel you are going to Vancouver for a visit." I was protesting with a wave of my hand. Sui Fong stubbornly insisted, "Don't argue! You will be staying with Yvette—you do need to get away. Uncle Jeffrey and Auntie Violet came to visit when you were asleep. They didn't bring Jackie instead they told your daughter that you have gone away for a holiday. Jackie took it with good spirit because she is absolutely pampered by her adoring grandparents and Marcus to say the least. You don't have to worry about her—just go and enjoy yourself. When you return we will then decide what we are going to do about Terry."

Cedric was pacing the room and he interrupted. "Uncle Edwin has contacted the police! We will decide whether we want to press charges against Terry at a later date. Knowing him, he will say that you provoked him. Anyway, we will make a decision after you return from your holiday. In the meantime try to recuperate. A few weeks in Vancouver will do you a world of good. No doubt Gavin will shower you with tender love and care, and it is exactly what you need!"

During the next few weeks I was tormented. The physical pain was slowly subsiding and the bruises were fading. The stitches were removed from my face and a slight scar was vividly visible. Terry's antagonistic conduct distressed me and I constantly screamed in the night. I would wake up trembling and drenched with cold sweat. The nightmare of Terry's violence haunted me persistently.

When I was released from the hospital I returned to my parent's home. Terry visited me a few times and he profusely apologized. He had no defense for his atrocious actions. He was agreeable to me taking a holiday but the discussion of a divorce was craftily ignored. He insisted that I would react differently when I returned from my pending trip. Terry had become a stranger to me. I was disillusioned and disappointed. I had to be honest with myself—I had never really loved him. I admired him for his talent and ability and I had respected him. Unfortunately he had taken the respect from me and I was left with no other feelings for him— I had completely lost faith in our relationship.

Sui Fong was coaxing me to finish my lunch. I pushed the plate of unfinished food away and murmured, "I wish I don't have this guilt feeling! Somehow I feel that I have failed in my marriage again! How could Terry change overnight? I feel I don't know him anymore...what did I do to make him change? Is it because he realized that I didn't love him?"

Sui Fong removed the food tray from my bed and replied vehemently, "You are not the guilty party but Terry—he should be ashamed of himself! You have this tendency to blame yourself. Terry has always been weak in character; therefore, he can't resist temptation. He is vulnerable and those so-called professional girls took advantage of his weakness. I don't think he has changed—it's just that this nasty side of him never surfaced and he had pulled the wool over your eyes."

I searched Sui Fong's face for assurance, "You must agree with me that when Terry is not influenced by alcohol he is a reliable doctor and he does have a kind heart."

Thoughtfully Sui Fong frowned and whispered, "If you are adamant with your belief that Terry is such a noble person then he is a very sick man. This is a perfect case of Dr. Jekyll and Mr. Hyde. If alcohol can effect him to such a point that he can lose all his perception and turn to violence then he definitely needs medical help and he should avoid alcohol like the devil himself. He is a doctor. I would have thought he should know better! There is no justification to his vindictiveness—how could he throw something as lethal as a piece of glass at you? Anyone with a bit of brain would know that the glass would cut your face!"

I interrupted. "He is persisting that he did not scar my face intentionally."

Sui Fong touched the scar on my face tenderly, "Of course he has to make an excuse to defend his own actions. I suppose he can always insist that you provoked him by having an affair with Gavin. I would like to remind him that Gavin is living on the other side of the world." Sui Fong grunted sarcastically and she was fuming with indignation, "Look! Don't ponder over this issue of guilt. You will be leaving for your holiday next week and you have lost enough weight—skin and bones! You don't want to alarm Gavin." The thought of Gavin brought a faint smile to my melancholy face.

When my bags were packed and I was ready to leave for the airport Marcus called and reassured me that Jackie was in the best of care.

I waved at my family and boarded the flight for Vancouver!

Forty-Nine

Feeling absolutely exhausted, mentally and physically, I was happy to be leaving Hong Kong for a while. Away from my nightmarish environment I was able to relax and I slept throughout the entire journey. When the plane finally touched ground at Vancouver International Airport, the sun was shinning brightly in the clear blue sky. The air was fresh and I inhaled deeply. I was beginning to feel alive again especially when I felt a flutter in my heart. Yvette had promised to collect me from the airport but engulfed with holiday spirits I took my time in collecting my luggage and I was the last passenger to walk through the arrival gate. Yvette was waving frantically when the familiar figure of Gavin came into my vision. I gasped when I saw his handsome face. His attractive eyes were smiling at me and the years that we were apart faded away…biting my lips to hold back threatened tears, I kissed Yvette on both cheeks then I turned to Gavin. Automatically I covered my face with my trembling hands because my vision blurred and tears spilt from my misty eyes. Gently Gavin removed my hands and touched the scar on my face. Tenderly he put his arms around my thin shoulders and sighed, "I am stunned by your appearance. You have lost so much weight and though you are all smiles when you came out I couldn't help but notice the deep hurt that is so apparent in your sad eyes." He crushed me into arms. After seventeen long years I couldn't believe that Gavin was holding me in his arms again and it was heavenly.

Yvette was chatting excitedly. "I couldn't afford to take time off but Gavin has two weeks holiday so when I go back to work he will keep you company." Turning to Gavin she suggested, "Why don't we take Melanie home first?"

During the short drive from the airport to Yvette's apartment I marveled at the trees and the immaculate manicured lawns. The city was sparkling clean and new. The houses were stylish and the roads were wide. "I have missed the gardens, the tress, and most of all the open space." Gavin winked at me knowingly.

Leisurely I unpacked and gave Yvette her presents then I threw a small packet at Gavin and he caught it effortlessly. Unwrapping the small box Gavin was delighted to find a key chain with a small gold tag attached to it. A few tiny words were engraved on the tag, "You have returned to me." Gavin picked up the key chain and put it to his lips. Looking at me he whispered, "I will treasure this forever!"

Suddenly my stomach grumbled—I had not eaten at all on the plane. As a matter of fact I had hardly eaten since I left the hospital a few weeks ago. "I am hungry." I blushed and laughed.

Gavin drove us to Stevenston Village in Richmond and found a small restaurant by the pier. I couldn't take my eyes off the calm blue sea. "I have ordered your favorite—fish and chips—but here we don't serve it wrapped in newspaper."

I returned my gaze from the sea and searched Gavin's face. I murmured, "You still remember..." My voice trailed off.

Patting my hand Gavin remarked, "How can I forget?" Then pointing to the few clouds that were floating aimlessly in the sky and with a twinkle in his eyes he teased me. "See those clouds in the sky—still want to be one?"

"Of course—more than ever!" I giggled.

Yvette looked at my face then at Gavin's. She was baffled with our exchanging remarks. Shrugging her shoulders and shaking her head she exclaimed, "I have decided that the two of you are mad—you are not making any sense."

After lunch Yvette had to return to work but before she jumped out of the car she said, "I have an important date tonight with a gorgeous man and I will not be coming home until late! You will have the entire apartment to yourselves." With a teasing smile she winked at Gavin conspiringly.

Gavin patted her hand and smiled. "Keep your naughty thoughts to yourself! My parents have invited Melanie for dinner and we will be spending the evening with them!"

When we were alone in the car Gavin asked tenderly, "Would you like to rest or would you refer to do some sight—seeing?" He kissed me gently on my lips.

I touched my lips and beamed. "I don't have too much time in Vancouver. When I return to Hong Kong I will have all the time in the world to sleep so let's go sight-seeing!"

We left Richmond and crossed the Oak Bridge then we headed for Downtown Vancouver. Gavin took me to Jericho Beach. I kicked off my shoes and ran until I was breathless. I loved the carefree feeling with the wind blowing on my face and my hair flying loosely in the air. We found a big piece of dried driftwood and sat on it. I let the sand sifted through my fingers. Gavin was content just watching me. I turned my face toward him and murmured wickedly and flirtatiously, "You know…you are devilishly tantalizing." I traced my fingers on his lips. Gavin was startled with my sudden action and he was stunned. Touching his face gently I whispered, "I know that I am married and I belong to another world but for the next two weeks let's just pretend that you are dating me and I am sixteen again!"

Aunt Pearl opened the door and I rushed into her welcoming arms. I exclaimed, "It's so nice to see you and your family again!"

She gently released herself from my arms and scrutinized my face. Defensively I averted my head so that the scar on my face was not visible. Aunt Pearl touched the scar briefly and whispered, "Don't be ashamed of your scar. Beauty is only skin deep and you are still the same Melanie. Gavin told me about your nasty experience…in time it will all be behind you."

"Welcome to Vancouver! So you have decided to visit us and it's about time, too!" Raphael gave me a bear hug.

A delicious home-cooked meal was served and I was exhilarated to see the Fernados family again. During the next couple of hours I provided them with all the latest gossips from home. Discreetly I covered my mouth when I yawned. Gavin took my hand and said to his mother, "Mum, Melanie is tired. I am going to take her home. She's had a long day, and she needs her beauty sleep."

Tenderly he lifted me onto my feet.

When we arrived home, Yvette had not returned from her date. Gavin suggested, "Go and have a shower. I will make you a hot drink and I will keep you company until you fall asleep."

Happily and contentedly I nodded. When I emerged from the shower I was rubbing my wet hair with the towel and a hot chocolate was put on the bedside table waiting for me. I searched for my over-night bag and took out a bottle of pills. I swallowed two with the hot drink. I retrieved a packet of cigarettes from my purse and lighting one I inhaled deeply. Sitting on the floor, I smiled lovingly at Gavin.

He joined me on the floor and frowned, "I didn't know you smoked or I would have offered you one of mine!"

I screwed my nose and replied, "I have been smoking for a while now. I find that smoking relaxes my tense nerves."

Taking the bottle of pills and reading the label on the bottle Gavin asked, "What is this that you are taking?"

I closed my eyes and sighed, "Sleeping pills! I have depended on these pills for many years now. They have been a great help to me."

Gavin took my hands and gently kissed the finger tips. "That accounts for your shaking hands! You should quit this habit—the pills are not good for you."

I was beginning to feel drowsy. I snuggled into my bed and whispered, "I have tried to kick the habit but I guess I just don't have the determination or the will-power, but one day when I find my peace of mind again then I will flush the pills down the toilet."

Gavin sat on the bed and put his arms around me, "Sweetheart, I guess it hasn't been easy for you. My heart is broken by all your misfortunes. Why didn't you confide in me? I would have helped…you know you can depend on me!"

I kissed the palm of his hand and I gazed into his dark eyes, "Gavin, my ever faithful guardian angle. I had to grow up and pay for my own mistakes! Just spare me two weeks of your time and I will be eternally grateful," I exaggerated.

Tenderly Gavin covered my shoulders with the thick blanket and said reassuringly, "I have a whole life-time for you!"

Taking his hand, I held it tightly, "If only you had said these words seventeen years ago…but it's still not too late because I still have thirteen days here with you!" I moved closer to Gavin and my tensed muscles began to relax. I was dozing off to sleep.

I heard a soft whisper, "Good night my love and welcome home!" I felt soft lips gently brushing my cheeks.

Vaguely I heard Yvette quietly preparing to leave for work but I was too exhausted to get up so I surrendered to my much required sleep again. I was dreaming that I was back in England and living in the house in

Highgate. The sweet perfume of roses was drifting into my nostrils and something soft was tickling my face. I felt soft lips brushing my hair and I didn't want to open my eyes because I didn't want my dream to fade away. Gentle hands were shaking my shoulders. "Wake up, Sleeping Beauty. Do you intend to sleep your holiday away?"

I quickly opened my eyes and Gavin was tickling my face with the petals of a white rose. I pinched my arm and exclaimed, "I am not dreaming!" I put my arms around him and buried my face in his shoulder.

I had been in Vancouver for three days and Gavin had introduced me to his world. I fell in love with it with no hesitation or reservation. That evening we were indulging ourselves in Japanese sushie, when Yvette suggested, "Gavin, why don't we go back to your house for coffee?" Turning to me she said, "Gavin has a lovely house. I don't suppose you have seen it or have you?"

Reluctantly Gavin hesitated, "I have lived on my own since my divorce and being a bachelor I am not too enthusiastic with domestic work. Melanie will be horrified with the mess."

I waved my hand and insisted that we should go to Gavin's house. I wanted to see where he lived.

When we arrived, I was impressed with the lovely front garden. White roses were in full bloom and there were so many of them. Wistfully I wondered if these roses ever reminded Gavin of me? When he opened the front door, I experienced an odd sensation of déjà vu. I felt instantly that I knew the house and that I had been there before. Immediately I knew my way around and found the kitchen. When I put three mugs of coffee on the coffee table Yvette was intrigued, "Are you sure you have never visited this house? You seem to know where everything is! Is there something that I should know?" Squinting her eyes she watched us with suspicion.

I warmed my cold hands with the hot mug and teased, "Of course I have been here before...in my dreams!"

Curiously I toured the house and I just loved it. There was so much that I wanted or could do to it and if only I could live here.

"Melanie, stop day-dreaming and wipe that far away look off your face. I want to have a serious discussion with you." Yvette's loud demand jolted me back to attention. I took a sip of the hot coffee then I threw a cushion onto the floor and made myself comfortable.

"Are you going to divorce that beastly character when you return to Hong Kong?" Yvette asked indignantly.

I closed my eyes tightly and leaned on the settee. A sorrowful expression appeared on my face.

"The poor girl is on holiday! Is it necessary to mention this depressing topic?" Patting my shoulders, Gavin sat next to me and put his protective arms round my shoulders.

Yvette sat on the settee and curled her legs. She said to Gavin, "I don't want to spoil Melanie's holiday but she has to make a decision. She can't subject herself to brutal torture! Have you not noticed that she has gained weight since her arrival into town? I can even detect a glimpse of the happy and carefree Melanie we knew before all these nasty businesses of divorces and wife battering."

I smiled at my friends feebly and hesitated, "I don't want to think about divorce just yet…I still feel that I have somehow failed and I should try again! I guess I shouldn't have married Terry. I married him for all the wrong reasons and I think he knows and resents it."

Yvette opened her mouth to object but Gavin interrupted, "Yvette, I think there is some truth in what Melanie has just said! It is definitely damaging to a man's ego if he knows that his wife doesn't love him. I do agree that Terry's attitude is wrong—we are sophisticated people—he should have tried to improve his relationship with Melanie by showing her more affection and in time I am sure Melanie's feelings for him would improve. Who knows…respect and admiration might eventually change to love. But instead Terry has turned to drinks." Gavin paused and took my hand then he continued, "Melanie, it is not easy to share a life with you! You are basically a strong and stubborn girl with your own beliefs and standard. You are a perfectionist and it is awfully difficult to live up to your standards. You expect others to behave like you do and if they don't then you feel hurt but you refuse to discuss your feelings or voice your opinions. You will bear the entire catastrophe until you break down…to a point of no return!"

Nodding my head I sighed, "Gavin, you know me so well and you are entirely accurate with your judgment of my personality. I know my own faults but I just can't change. When I was married to Marcus, if I had swallowed my pride and begged him to give up Beth, I might have succeeded but it was an all or nothing situation—I wasn't content with the physical presence of the person. I wanted and needed his love and attention! Now with Terry, I can't bring myself to point out his weakness. I guess I just don't care enough. I reckoned that he should be mature enough to discover his shortcomings." I sighed deeply and thought for a while before I continued, "I will have to work harder to overcome my stubbornness. Hopefully I will be able to find the essential ingredients to rebuild my damaged marriage…."

Yvette was aghast with my opinion and impatiently she waved her hand in the air and sneered, "I can't agree with you. You may be dead before you reach your goal. Next time 'round you may not be so fortunate as to get away with just a scar on your face!"

"I will try and I intend to salvage the marriage!" I insisted with determination.

Gavin started to pace the floor and thoughtfully he addressed me. "Melanie I agree with you. After all you did marry Terry for better or for worse. Give it your last shot but if things don't work out and you find that you cannot survive in Hong Kong after a second divorce then immigrate to Vancouver. Bring your daughter with you and start a new life for yourselves. We are here to lend a helping hand."

"Thank you for the offer—I know that I can always depend on you—you are always exceedingly thoughtful." I wanted to control my tears because I didn't want Gavin to see me cry. I jumped on my feet and excused myself. I went searching for the washroom. Somehow I found myself wandering into Gavin's bedroom. The bed was not made but it looked invitingly comfortable. Suddenly I felt drained of all emotions and energy. Without any hesitation I crawled into his bed and closed my eyes.

Vaguely I heard Yvette's voice. "I have found her...she is asleep in your bed, but we had better wake her because I have to work tomorrow and I can't afford too many late nights."

Gavin whispered, "She must be tired! Why don't I take you home and we will let her sleep here tonight. I will sleep in the guest bedroom." Gavin turned off the light in his room and closed the door gently.

For the remaining days of my holiday I lived my life to the fullest. I went sight-seeing with Gavin and together we browsed around the big department stores, Woodward's and Eaton's, and we shopped to my heart's content. I treasured all the attention that Gavin bestowed on me and I relished his tenderness and thoughtfulness. I wanted the memories to be engraved in my mind when it was time for me to return home.

Tearfully I thanked Yvette for her hospitality and I promised to write. I said good-bye to Aunt Pearl and her family then reluctantly Gavin took me to the airport. We were having a cup of coffee before I boarded the plane and Gavin said, "I have to collect something from the car—don't leave until I come back."

Gavin returned with a big parcel wrapped with pretty paper. Putting the present in my hand he said, "This is for you—open it!"

I was thrilled. Impatiently I ripped the wrapping paper and sitting in a box was a gorgeous looking cuddly toy lion. The soft fur tickled my skin when I caressed the soft body. Smiling Gavin insisted, "I want you to keep this lion by your side constantly and you will never be alone again. I will always be with you in spirit and in thoughts. I want you to touch the lion whenever you feel sad or depressed and need a friend because it will represent me—I will not be far away." He took my face in his hands and kissed me deeply while whispering against my hair, "I guess I am seventeen years too late but Melanie I do love you and I guess I always have. If things get too rough, then come home to me."

I clutched the soft lion and returned Gavin's kisses. Clinging to him I wished that I could forget Hong Kong and with the snap of my fingers I could erase the past.

Fifty

My nightmarish life style began again. When I arrived in Hong Kong instead of going to live with my parents, I decided to return home to Terry with the hope to salvage my shattered marriage. My parents were aghast and horrified with my decisions and attempted to dissuade me but I was adamant. Jackie loved living with Marcus and her grandparents. She refused to return home with me. I didn't really blame her and decided not to challenge her decision. After all she was Marcus' child as well. If she was happy with her father then I was glad for her. I called Marcus, "I am delighted that Jackie is happy with you. When Beth returns and if she creates a fuss then Jackie can return to me—the door is always open to her!"

There was a slight pause then Marcus' soft whisper echoed over the phone, "Why did I ever let you out of my life? I hope I don't have to regret my decision for the rest of my life."

At first Terry was delighted that I had returned and for a short period of time he curbed his drinking habit and life was barely bearable. After a while he mistook my loyalty for lack of courage and reverted to his alcoholism and womanizing. Dejectedly I took each day as it came and I lost interests in almost everything. When loneliness engulfed me I would sit and watch the soft lion for hours. I stayed out of Terry's way in order that he was not provided with an opportunity or an excuse to use violence on me. I wasn't happy and I wasn't hurt or upset. I was beginning to feel numb to all emotions and my life was a complete void.

Sui Fong and Cedric constantly invited me for dinner and during one of these occasions Sui Fong reprimanded me, "Melanie where is your fighting spirit? How can you live the way you do? You are not living but simply existing." She was appalled with my attitude and my acceptance to life. She continued, "Don't you want a better life? You are not even forty years old and yet you are behaving like an old crippled woman. Also, you should really cut down on your sleeping pills! What happened to your laughter?"

Smiling I teased half—jokingly, "I left everything behind in Vancouver—I neglected to pack my life and laughter."

Cedric took my hand and gazed into my sad eyes appealingly, "Take up Gavin's offer and go to Vancouver. You don't have to worry about Jackie, so give yourself a chance to rebuild your life!"

I shrugged my shoulders and shook my head dejectedly, "I lack the courage to start again. My future is a blank sheet of paper. I think I know why I have failed with both of my marriages. Unconsciously I have tired to replace Gavin therefore no other man could live up to my expectations. Gavin had pampered me and spoiled me rotten."

Sui Fong, sighing, interrupted. "Then go to him—there is nothing to detain you here. I have always felt that it was more than a platonic relationship between you and him. It is still not too late—you have been blessed with another chance!"

I gazed out of the window into the dark street. I whispered, "It is too late! How can I go to him with two broken marriages behind me? He has offered a helping hand but is it love? Does he still love me or is he feeling sorry for me? I cherish his memories, and memories they will remain because we won't have a tomorrow!"

Sui Fong waved her hand impatiently and intervened, "Are you going to be stubborn for the rest of your life? I hope you won't regret your decision!"

Attempting a feeble smile I replied hesitantly, "I am paying for my mistakes now. Maybe in another life Gavin and I will have a chance to be together."

Due to my depressions Sui Fong and Cedric were anxious over me returning home alone. I seemed to have given up hope for any future happiness. When Cedric paid the bill, he insisted that they would escort me home. When we arrived the living room was quiet but all the lights were on. From the bedroom soft music and laughter drifted into the living room. I was baffled. I opened the bedroom door and said, "Sui Fong is here with Cedric...." The laughter ceased but there was no reply so I walked into the room.

Terry was in bed with another woman. When the stranger saw me she screamed and grabbed the sheet to cover her naked body. She dashed for the bathroom. Cedric heard the commotion and joined us. My cousin was stunned and horrified but there was absolutely no sign of remorse or embarrassment on Terry's face. I should have been angry and hurt but I felt numbed. I lifted my head and straightened my shoulders. Retrieving my purse from the table I requested that my cousins should take me back to my parents immediately and there I remained waiting for my pending divorce.

I was wanted on the phone. Cedric's voice drifted into my ears, "Don't stay at home and sulk. Make yourself pretty and we'll have a drink at the Clipper's Lounge. We are waiting for you!" Without giving me a chance to respond he hung up.

Staying at home constantly was depressing, so I changed and drove to the Mandarin Hotel. Standing on the threshold of the Lounge, I scanned the room searching for Sui Fong. When she saw me she waved and I saw a familiar figure sitting at the same table. I was intrigued and when I approached their table, Gavin turned around and gazed into my eyes with a twinkle in his eyes. I dropped my handbag and gasped. Amazement and happiness displayed on my face instantly. I stood motionless and just stared.

Gavin stood up and pulled a chair for me, "Are you going to sit down or do I have to drag you by your hair?"

Immediately I regained my composure and rushed into Gavin's welcoming embrace, "How come you are here in Hong Kong? When did you arrive?"

Gavin kissed me deeply and chuckling he teased, "Why is it each time we meet, you have to bombard me with so many questions?"

When my drink was ordered I turned to Gavin and puzzlement returned to my face. He took my hand and explained, "I flew in from Vancouver an hour ago. I wanted to surprise you! When I heard about your divorce I wanted to come immediately but I couldn't take leave. Now that I have to look after you, I can't afford to lose my job. You are an expensive lady—you break me financially whenever we are together!" We all laughed at his sense of humor. My laughter was a strange sound to my ears.

Cheekily Sui Fong wrinkled her nose and confessed, "After you left Terry and agreed to a divorce we thought it was a terrific idea to share the good news with Gavin. As expected he wanted to come as soon as he could. We decided that it was best to keep you in the dark until his actual arrival—we didn't think you should have any more sleepless nights!"

I waved a finger at Sui Fong accusingly and complained, "So there has been a conspiracy! How do you know that I wanted to see Gavin?"

Sui Fong winked at Gavin, then smiling she mocked, "Obviously your little sweetheart doesn't fancy your company. Let's make other arrangements—I have plenty of single women who would love to entertain an attractive man like you."

I grabbed Sui Fong's hand and shrieked, "You can settle the bill then disappear and forget about your young women because Gavin is staying here with me!"

Feigning annoyance Sui Fong grumbled, "You ungrateful creature! It's that all the gratitude I deserve—paying for the bill?"

Roaring with laughter fondly I kissed Sui Fong's cheeks. I took some dollar bills from my purse and gave them to the waiter. Smiling brilliantly I added, "There should be enough for my cousins to order a piece of cheese cake."

Happily we headed toward the parking lot. I clung onto Gavin possessively. When we arrived home, I was surprised to find Alastiar and Lynette with their families waiting for us. My parents had invited them for dinner to meet Gavin and they were delighted to see him.

Alastair punched Gavin on the shoulder playfully and said, "How long has it been since you have visited Hong Kong? You must be a stranger to your own hometown!" Beckoning to his wife he introduced, "Tessa come and meet our long lost friend Gavin. Our friendship has gone back to a quarter of a century. We shared some pretty good times together—didn't we?"

Tessa smiled and extended her hand to Gavin, "Although I have never met you I feel as though I know you. Your name has popped up every so often!"

Lynette grabbed Gavin's hand and introduced him to her husband. When we were catching up with all the latest gossips Jackie and Lynette's son rushed out from a room chasing each other. Lynette caught Jackie's small hand and said, "Calm down! You two monkeys! Come and meet Uncle Gavin!"

My daughter scrutinized Gavin with her big brown eyes then she whispered shyly, "You must be my Mummy's friend from Vancouver. Can I come and visit you with Mummy?"

Gavin was genuinely astonished with Jackie's out-going personality. He scooped her small body into his arms and said, "You must be Jackie! You are more beautiful than I have imagined. Of course you must come and visit me. I don't have too many toys to entertain you but I have a big garden that you can roam around in all day!"

Blushing Jackie buried her head in Gavin's shoulder and replied in a small voice, "I have heard all about your garden and your lovely house—Mummy told me!"

Lynette introduced her son to Gavin and the children rushed out of the living room and disappeared.

"Gavin now that you have met all the additions to the family come and have a drink before dinner." Father offered.

Mother came out from the kitchen and embraced Gavin, "It has been too long—you must visit us more often!" Then she kissed him and inquired, "So, how are your parents?"

Gavin chuckled, "Mum still complains and Dad still listens."

"Gavin, make yourself at home! You are not a stranger but part of the family. I have to give Ah Ying a hand to finish preparing dinner."

I stopped Mother and offered, "Why don't you relax and I will help."

Mother was about to object when Father interrupted, "Give Melanie an opportunity to make herself useful again! She has lost interests in almost everything!" Father gave Mother a drink and offered her a seat.

Gavin followed me into the kitchen. When Ah Ying saw us she dropped the stirring spoon in the sink and wiping her wet hands on her apron she beamed excitedly, "I am glad to see you. Our missy here can do with some cheering up. Hopefully she will eat properly again."

After dinner, lounging in a chair and stretching his long legs Cedric said to me, "Didn't you have any suspicion that Gavin was arriving? Did it not bother you that he did not contact you when you left Terry?"

Contentedly I sat on the floor and leaned my head on Gavin's legs. "I hadn't spoken with Gavin since I left Vancouver. My sixth sense told me that you guys were cooking something because Sui Fong has been behaving mysteriously. I have often wondered why she didn't insist that I contact Gavin—she didn't even ask!"

"By the way, Gavin where are you staying?" Mother inquired.

"With us—I hope!" Sui Fong interrupted.

Father said, "You are very welcome to stay with us. We do have plenty of spare rooms now that Alastair and Lynette have their own homes...."

Politely Gavin declined the invitation, "Thank you for the offer but staying with Sui Fong and Cedric would be more appropriate. I expect Melanie to be my tourist guide! After all I was her chauffeur while she was visiting Vancouver. It's time she repays my kindness." He winked at me and teasingly he asked, "Melanie, are you a good driver?"

I smacked his legs and replied indignantly, "I will try not to kill you!" I looked my watch and jumping to my feet I exclaimed, "Jackie, it's time to say good-night to Grandpa and Grandma. I have to take you home!"

Jackie came into the room and waving her small hands she objected, "Do I have to leave so soon—it's still early. Auntie Lynette is still here!"

"We have to be going!" Lynette said.

I collected my keys and grabbed Jackie's small hand. I said to Gavin, "If you are not too tired perhaps you may like to come along for the drive. I will take you back to Cedric's."

Sui Fong threw Gavin a key and winked at him, "This is the key to the front door and you don't have a curfew!"

On the way to Marcus' flat, Jackie chatted continuously. Excitedly she pointed at her school then she told Gavin where she went for her painting lessons. Happily she introduced Gavin to her Hong Kong. When we arrived at our destination she jumped out of the car then she sprinted back to us and demanded, "Don't forget to take me and Mummy to Vancouver!" Then she kissed Gavin on the cheek and ran toward the front door. Frantically waving her small hand and blowing kisses she disappeared with the maid that was waiting for her.

When we were alone in the car Gavin patted my hand and said, "You have a lovely daughter!"

I replied while backing the car out of the driveway, "Jackie is the only good thing that has resulted from my disastrous marriage to her father!" Changing the subject I inquired, "Do you want to go back to Sui Fong's or would you like to go somewhere else?"

"Are you tired? Would you like to go home?" Came Gavin's thoughtful reply.

I chuckled and tapped my fingers on the steering wheel, "Are you out of your mind? Do you visit me every day? Do I get to see you all the time? It is imperative that I don't let you out of my sight during your stay in Hong Kong! I may lose you to other young women!" I flirted with him.

"Melanie, do you mind driving to Shek O Beach—I do so want to visit the beach with you again!" I nodded my head happily. We drove in silence until we reached our destination. It was heavenly to be walking along the moonlit silvery shore of the beach with Gavin. He put his arms around me and sitting on the sand I leaned on his shoulder, "What are your plans for the future?" looking into the ocean Gavin asked softly.

Hesitantly I whispered a soft reply, "I suppose I will wait for the divorce to finalize. It shouldn't take more than a few weeks. Then I will look for a job and hopefully I can learn to live again like a normal person.

I often feel that I have gone 'round one circle with my life and my only achievement is Jackie." I sighed.

I could feel Gavin's breath on my skin. In the dark his face was hardly visible. "How would you like to rebuild your life in Vancouver? Jackie is happy with Marcus. In a few years time she will have to leave Hong Kong to further her studies abroad but if you are living in Vancouver she can continue her studies in Canada."

I thought for a while and hugging my knees I murmured, "The idea is definitely tempting but I hardly know a soul in Vancouver! I don't know if I have the courage to start anew in a foreign country."

Gavin held me close and I buried my face in his shoulder, "There is always me!" He reassured me with tenderness.

"I can't depend on you forever! You have your own life to consider and I don't want to be a hindrance to you!" I purred against his hair.

Taking my hand and kissing my fingers gently Gavin tenderly asked, "Has it ever occur to you that I don't consider you as an obstacle in my life? I happen to enjoy taking care of you! After all I did spend my younger days doing just that!"

Snuggling closer to Gavin I twirled his hair playfully and replied teasingly, "What about your other girl friends? Would they mind?"

Gavin took my face with his hands and kissed me deeply. "You are over-reacting again! Why don't you let me be the judge to that?"

Smiling smugly I promised, "I will give you my decision before you leave. But for now do you want to count the stars with me?"

Gavin took me into his arms again and kissed me until I was breathless. Life was unpredictable—the last time we had sat on this beach we were saying good-bye to each other…so many years later we were making plans for the future.

Gavin and I had spent the day sightseeing then we returned home for dinner at my parents. I wanted to experiment on a new recipe. Ah Ying was delighted that I had renewed my interests in cooking. Softly, the chatters from the living room drifted into the kitchen, "Aunt Wei Ling, I have made a suggestion to Melanie and I think you should hear about it." Gavin's soft voice was hardly audible.

"You have asked her to marry you!" Came Sui Fong's excited screech.

Gavin replied, "No, Sui Fong, now is not the right time to discuss marriage with Melanie. I have asked her to consider living in Vancouver for a while. I can assist her in finding a job and I think she should embark on a career as soon as possible. A change of environment will do her a world of good!"

I stopped chopping the onions and pushed the chopping board to Ah Ying. I strained my ears and eavesdropped.

"I am of the same opinion because her marriages have utterly ruined her," Mother said. "When she divorced Marcus her world fell to pieces because the red carpet was pulled from under her feet. It took her a few years to regain her confidence. Then the humiliation caused by Terry's atrocious and brutal behavior did more damages to her soul. The physical pain was excruciating for her and mentally she was tormented. I am surprise that she has maintained her sanity."

Sui Fong's softly said, "I think Melanie is very brave—I would have killed myself!"

"I am certain that the thought has crossed Melanie's mind a few times," Mother said. "Both Edwin and I were worried. Look at her appearance now—she looks under-nourished but since your arrival into town I have noticed a bit of color slowly creeping back onto her face. Gavin you are a good influence on her. If any one can help her to erase the pain you are the one!"

"What she lacks is courage and encouragement," Gavin said.

"I will convince her. I will miss her terribly when she is gone but Cedric and I can visit her." Sui Fong volunteered.

"If it is agreeable with you, Melanie can stay with me until she has found a job. She will probably need plenty of time to adjust to her new life and regain her confidence before she is able to face the business world again. But I know she can do it! She has many hidden talents and she should not deny herself the opportunity to discover them!"

I smiled to myself…Gavin had indeed returned to me. He was making plans for my future.

Fifty-One

After spending two glorious weeks in Hong Kong, regrettably, Gavin's return to Vancouver was unavoidable. He had hoped that I would agree to return home with him but I was indecisive. He did not want to put unnecessary pressure on me, so we said good-bye with a promise from me that I would seriously consider his offer.

The pending divorce finally came through and I was a free woman again. I missed Gavin tremendously. I cherished his memories and I scorned at my own weakness. Soon I lost interest and concentration in my books—reading could no longer fulfill my empty days. I needed more substance from life. I began to live for Gavin's letters and long distance calls and when they came my heart would flutter with excitement and anticipation. I realized that I was fortunate to be blessed with a second chance. I had lost Gavin but miraculously he had returned to me—could I let him go again? I began to toy with the idea of emigrating to Vancouver. When my parents approached the subject again, I finally agreed to give myself another chance. Marcus was happy for me and I took Jackie to the park for an ice cream and informed her of my decision.

"I have decided to move to Vancouver and you are welcome to join me whenever you are ready. In the meantime I will try to reestablish myself and periodically I will come back to Hong Kong to visit you!"

Jackie was happy with my decision.

I took my daughter's small hand into mine and softly asked, "How are you getting along with your stepmother?"

Kicking the lose sand and screwing her tiny nose, Jackie replied in a small voice, "Nathan and I don't like her but then she is always traveling. She doesn't really bother me. But should she stop her travels then I will come and live with you!" She cuddled me with her small arms and kissed me.

I would miss Jackie terribly but hopefully one day my daughter would decide to join me in Vancouver. There was no prediction to life and I kept my fingers crossed. After two divorces and two broken homes I was left with very little personal belongings so with two suitcases I arrived in Vancouver and hoped to begin a new life again.

I had been in Vancouver for almost two months and on a Friday evening after dinner Gavin suggested, "Melanie you must terminate your dependence on sleeping pills. They are not healthy for you and your hands are shaking badly!"

Nervously I fluffed the cushions that I was cuddling and hesitantly I stammered, "I am too afraid of the long nights. I still suffer from nightmares."

"You must combat your fear. I never leave you at night—I am only sleeping in the next room." Gavin was pacing the room then he stopped and insisted, "It is a holiday on Monday so I have three days off work. Why don't you try to sleep tonight without your pills? Flush all your pills in the toilet and I will keep you company if you cannot sleep!"

Just the thought of not taking my pills caused a shiver down my spine and I hesitated. After thinking for a while I shrugged my shoulders and jumped up on my feet. With strong determinations I emptied all my pills into the toilet bowl. When I joined Gavin in the family room he said, "It is still early.... I would like you to take a drive with me." Gavin collected his car keys and put a wrap round my shoulders.

When I was in the car curiously I asked, "Where are we going? I thought you wanted me to sleep so why are we going out?"

Gavin put his fingers on my lips to silent me.

"Stop acting so mysteriously!" I exclaimed.

We drove in silence and shortly the car was parked on the driveway of the Fernados' residence where the lights shone through the windows onto the darkened street. "My parents must still be playing Mah Jong." Gavin muttered to himself and opened the front door with his key. Standing on the threshold of the door Gavin yelled, "Mum I have come to collect something from the store room. Don't let us interrupt your game because we are not staying!"

Struggling with two big boxes, Gavin beckoned me to help. We moved the boxes into the car and I was killing myself with curiosity. When we reached home Gavin took the boxes into my room and said, "Why don't you make us each a hot drink then bring the drinks in here!"

Leaning on the bedroom door with my hands on my hips I demanded indignantly, "What are you trying to do?"

Gavin gently pushed me out of the room and pleaded, "For once just do as you are told! Don't argue! I am dying for a hot drink—let's have hot chocolate."

Since I arrived in Vancouver Gavin insisted that I should stay with him. I had resumed the role of a housewife and took care of all the domestic work. The kettle was filled with water and was soon boiling. I put two mugs on the kitchen counter and I scooped spoonfuls of hot chocolate powder into the mugs and waited for the kettle to boil. Suddenly and unexpectedly Elvis Presley's husky voice drifted into the kitchen and he was singing *Blue Hawaii*. Instead of pouring the water into the mugs the water was dripping onto the counter. Excitedly I dropped the kettle with a clang and rushed into my room. Sitting on the floor by my bed was the record player that belonged to me when I was living in England. Scattered around the player were records—dozens and dozens of records—I knelt on the floor and picked up the records with trembling hands...tenderly, I caressed them. Tears started to spill from my face onto the much treasured records.

Gavin's soft whisper brought me back to the present, "My welcome home present to you." Kneeling beside me he took me into his arms and kissed me tenderly. Then he promised, "Tonight and many more nights to come we will listen to these records and I will stay with you until you sleep."

That night I hardly closed my eyes but I was no longer frightened of the darkness. We listened to the records and reminisced the past. When the sun shone into my room the next morning Gavin insisted that we have a light breakfast and drive to the beach. Running and playing on the beach, we whiled the morning away. After lunch we returned to Richmond and spent a few hours shopping in Lansdowne Mall. Gavin patiently selected new outfits for me. I was like a small child on a Christmas morning. Happily I skipped from shop to shop with excitement. Before we returned home, we shopped for food. I was exhausted and I wanted to lie down on my bed but Gavin insisted that I should cook dinner because he was starving. Helping me and chatting with me, we prepared the food. When the dirty plates were washed and put away I filled the bathtub with hot water. I added scented bath oil into the water and soon my body was soaking in the tub. The music of my favorite records drifted into the bathroom and I found myself slowly closing my eyes. A loud knock on the bathroom door startled me and Gavin yelled, "Don't fall asleep in there or you will drown yourself."

After drying myself with a large soft and warm fluffy towel I returned to my room and crawled into bed. But as soon as my head hit the pillow I was wide awake again. Gavin disappeared from the room and returned with a deck of playing cards. I jumped out of bed and sat on the floor and we began to play the games that Gavin had taught me so very long ago. Shortly the cards fell from my hands and I was dozing off to sleep. Gavin immediately tucked me into bed and he sat on the floor by my bed. It was morning again. I had slept through the night without a stir. Gavin tried to yank me out of bed, "I have arranged for us to play Mah Jong with my parents! It is going to be an all day session so get changed and wear one of your new dresses. We should be on our way shortly."

I rubbed my eyes and slumped on the bed. I complained. "I am too tired to play—I can't concentrate!"

"You can! I thought the word *can't* didn't exist in your vocabulary!"

It was after midnight when we returned home. When Elvis sang the last note of *Blue Hawaii*, I was asleep. Sleeping pills was no longer a necessity and I was rid of the habit. Gavin returned to work on Tuesday. I had plenty of free time on my hands so I decided to tidy his wardrobe. That evening when he returned home he was impressed with the transformation. He selected a few shirts and said, "I won't be wearing these colorful shirts anymore. Let's give them away!"

When I was folding the discarded shirts I toyed with an idea, "Do you mind if I keep these shirts?"

Gavin was puzzled and he asked, "What are you going to do with them?"

Grinning mischievously and mysteriously I replied, "You will see...."

When Gavin returned from work the next day he discovered that I had cut his shirts into small pieces and I was busily sewing. Gavin was baffled. Smiling I explained, "I want to make two patch-work covers for the cushions with your old shirts!"

The making of the patch-work covers was awfully time consuming and tedious. Stubbornly I sewed continuously and tirelessly. Eventually when the mission was accomplished Gavin was indeed impressed and my hands no longer shook.

Gavin was reading a pamphlet and he asked, "How would you like to take a course in computer skills? I have noticed that your mind no longer wanders when you are concentrating. Also I think it's a brilliant idea that you should take some driving lessons and learn to drive on the other side of the road. When you have acquired a driving license, we can look into purchasing a small car for you...you can start job hunting!"

Six months later I started a career as an Office Administrator. I was happy to be working again, Between my demanding job and domestic work my days were full. I could no longer envision myself living without Gavin, my work or Vancouver. With Gavin's assistance I had picked up the pieces of my shattered life—a new and confident Melanie was born.

I was attending to the cooking one night and the phone rang. I picked up the receiver and I was surprised to hear Marcus' voice. "Is Jackie O.K.?" I demanded anxiously.

"She is fine! There is no need to panic. I just wanted to discuss something with you." Marcus' voice echoed into the receiver. I waited impatiently for him to continue. I didn't like the suspense. "Beth has decided to settle down in Hong Kong again. I am afraid she hasn't been getting along with Nathan and Jackie. Carmine has agreed to send Nathan to a boarding school in England. What do you say if I suggest that Jackie live with you in Vancouver?"

I nearly dropped the receiver—I was astounded but excited, "Are you positive with your decision? How does Jackie feel about the idea?"

Marcus sighed deeply and replied, "Ever since your departure she has missed you awfully. She just couldn't help but talk about you constantly and this adds to Beth's irritation. I don't want to lose Jackie but for her own happiness she should be with you."

When Gavin came home he found me in the kitchen but I was extremely quiet. He gave me a peck on the cheek and inquired, "A penny for your thoughts." Ruffling my hair, he waited for my answer.

Drying my hand with the apron hesitantly I whispered, "I have really enjoyed staying here with you and I appreciate your concern and anxiety over me but I think that it's time I have my own place."

Gavin was startled. He put his arm around my shoulder and asked anxiously, "Are you unhappy living with me? Have I done something wrong?"

I repeated my conversation with Marcus. Gavin smiled and walked toward his room. "We will talk further after dinner."

After a quiet meal and when Gavin was relaxing with a drink in his hand, he suggested, "Melanie stop pacing the room. Do sit down and stop fidgeting. You are making me very nervous."

Immediately I ceased the pacing and sat on one of the patch-work cushions, while cuddling the other.

"How long have we known each other?" Gavin asked.

Frowning I counted my fingers and replied, "I would say over twenty-five years…"

Gavin continued, "How long have we lived together?"

I shrugged my shoulders and replied, "Going on almost two years…."

Gavin sighed then he sat next to me and took my hand, "Twenty-five years is an extremely long time and I am afraid that during this lengthy period of time I have grown too accustomed to your face. I don't think that I can live without you and I hope that the feeling is mutual."

I nodded my head and without providing me with a chance to reply he continued, "How about redecorating your room to Jackie's liking and we share the same bedroom legally?"

I screwed my nose and kissed the tip of Gavin's nose, "Funny way of proposing marriage."

Gavin embraced me and whispered against my hair, "Not funny but original!"

I removed my body from his embrace and searched Gavin's face, "I don't want you to marry me because you feel sorry or responsible for me."

Taking my hand Gavin kissed the palm and replied truthfully, "I admit when you first arrived I did feel some sympathy for you. Since then you have courageously rebuilt your life and gained confidence again—you are a complete person now. You don't need my sympathy anymore. You are capable of holding a challenging and demanding position. You have proved to be a competent housewife again. You no longer require my help. I therefore think now is the appropriate time for us to discuss marriage. Unless you think that I am not good enough to be Jackie's stepfather."

"But, but…." I was lost for words and then I stuttered, "Do you honestly think I am ready for marriage again? I am scared."

Gavin searched my face and said, "We have practically been cohabiting as husband and wife. We just have not shared the same bed! How would you like to start now?" Lifting me from the cushions, he carried me into his room.

I took a week off work and left for Hong Kong. While I was away, Gavin took on the responsibility of decorating Jackie's new bedroom. It was decided that when I returned to Vancouver with Jackie together we would prepare for our wedding.

I was having coffee with Sui Fong before my departure for Vancouver. She smiled and said, "You should have married Gavin twenty years ago—what a waste!"

I patted my friend's hand and gazed out of the window, "It was not meant to be. We had to live our own lives and make our own mistakes. If I had married him then we would have been divorced by now."

Stirring the coffee Sui Fong nodded her head and replied, "I guess you are right…you needed time to mature."

With a contented look on my face I whispered, "Not ever in my wildest dream did I ever imagine that Gavin would return to me."